THE LOST VALOR OF LOVE

THE LOST VALOR OF LOVE

E A CARTER

For Marcelle

My constant friend in a fleeting world

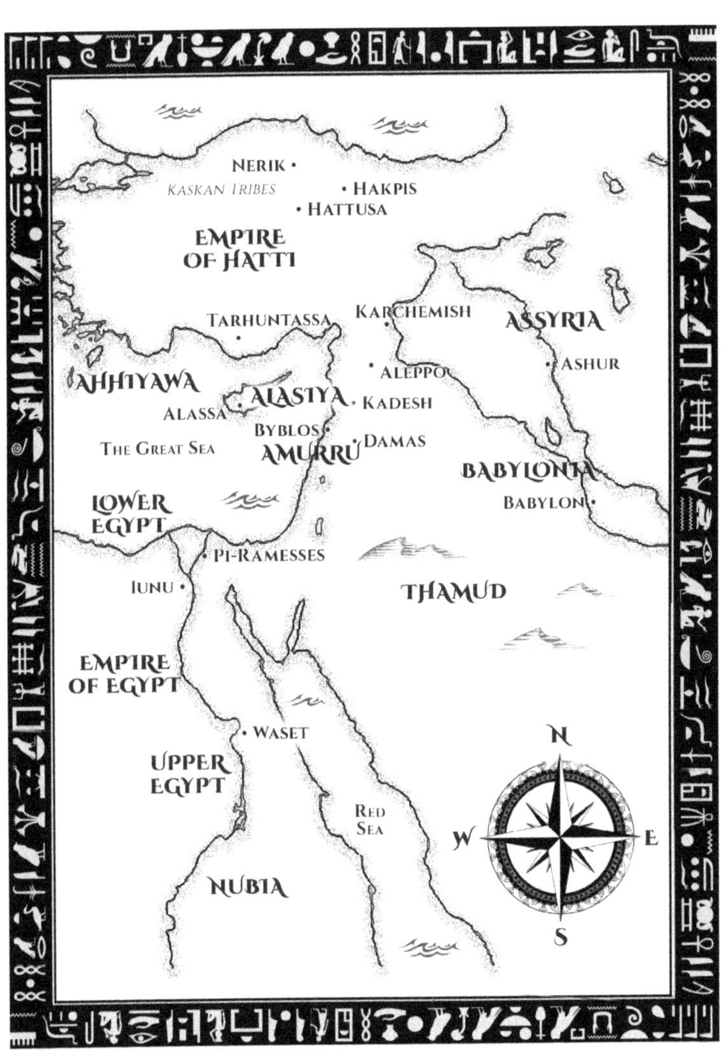

NERIK •
Kaskan Tribes
• HAKPIS
• HATTUSA
EMPIRE OF HATTI
TARHUNTASSA
KARCHEMISH
ASSYRIA
AHHIYAWA
ALASIYA
• ALEPPO
• ASHUR
ALASSA
KADESH
BYBLOS •
The Great Sea
AMURRU
• DAMAS
BABYLONIA
LOWER EGYPT
BABYLON •
• PI-RAMESSES
THAMUD
IUNU •
EMPIRE OF EGYPT
WASET •
UPPER EGYPT
RED SEA
NUBIA
N
W   E
S

PROLOGUE

PI-RAMESSES
Summer 1274 BCE

PROLOGUE

City of Pi-Ramesses, Summer.
Reign of Ramesses II, Year 6

In the sweltering heat of the Egyptian sun, the pharaoh's eyes are cold, like the icy, silent winters of Tarhuntassa. He sweeps his *khopesh*, slick with blood, high into the burning air, and heavy, dark gouts soar from his curved blade toward the pristine white pillars of the palace, where they land in a perfect arc, staining them the color of my love.

The taut muscles of his body, and his kilt are a canvas, splattered with the essence of the man who has sacrificed everything so I might live. Were it not my own love's life the ink for such art, Ramesses's work could almost be considered beautiful. Almost.

And when he comes to me tonight, will he think of this brutal battle as he is taking me, possessing me as his own? Will he speak of it, reminding me I was destined to be a queen, though not of Egypt, but of her enemy? Will he gloat about his triumph, not just over Egypt's commander, but over Urhi-Teshub, the Crown Prince of Hatti, to whom I once belonged? The one, who far too late I learned, loved me. Though not like this. Never like this.

The image of Ramesses entering me, his body still drenched with the blood of my love fills my mind. I swallow the bile rising in my throat, tasting metal, the scent of butchery heavy in the enclosed space. I am able to see my bleak future. Once he has taken his fill of me, I will be sent away, like all the others, condemned to the corridors of his harem, to live in the shadows, forgotten, alone and unloved, with only this, my meager store of memories to comfort me.

My love fights on, for love, for honor, for us; his powerful body torn apart by the one who believes himself a god. I try to see the man who cradled me against him only a few hours ago, his tenderness as he made love to me for the first and last time. His mouth on mine, our souls entwining. He is unrecognizable. I blink back the tears burning in my eyes, ashamed. I promised I would not cry. But my chest is aching, and my throat is raw, the agony of holding the pain inside, exquisite. With every blow he suffers, I flinch. He bleeds outward, and I, inward. Together, we are dying.

Powerless, just as I have always been, I watch them battle, my hands clenched into fists, my fingernails cutting into my palms. The one I love, despite knowing his fate, remains steadfast, valiant, and honorable against the relentless onslaught of the pharaoh, who must cheat to bring down Egypt's indomitable commander.

Beneath their sandaled feet, the pristine white sand turns red, drinking up the fluid of my love's life, thirsty in this accursed heat. Another savage assault and Ramesses's *khopesh* slices deep, carving into bone, becoming stuck. He staggers, struggling to free his blade. He heaves once, twice, grunting with the effort. It is a nightmare. With a sickening snap his sword bursts free and my love, reviving from shock, roars in agony.

My thoughts splinter. I imagine myself kneeling in the soaking black-dark sand, gathering up his life essence, drawing it into the material of my gown so I can return it to him, drop by precious drop.

My love rallies, but Ramesses plays foul once more. Overcome, my love falls to his knee. He looks at me, his chest heaving, his breathing ragged in the thick, claustrophobic air. I see his suffering, not just from his pain, but from knowing he will soon face his annihilation as the gods claim his debt, separating our souls for eternity.

I step onto the grounds, desperate to go to him, to ease his pain, the memory of our first encounter exploding into my thoughts; the long, cold night I spent tending his injuries, fighting his delirium, struggling to keep him alive. The night he tried to kill me. Our love, born in violence, dying in violence.

He calls to me, my name on his lips ragged and bloody. His final words tear me apart. I feel a forbidden tear slip free, hot against my face.

Furious, Ramesses roars and strikes him down, and the one who sacrificed everything to hold my heart in his hands for the briefest space in time falls to the ground, dying.

Numb, I watch Ramesses as he staggers, panting, staring battle-blind at his butchered commander. A bright gleam pierces my blurring vision. I shove away my tears. In the burning light, a fallen dagger, forgotten—like me—beckons.

I beg the gods for forgiveness, and run.

PART I

EMPIRE OF HATTI

Summer 1287 - Late Summer 1275 BCE

ONE

City of Kadesh, Summer.
Reign of Muwatallis, Year 8

Istara had never been in Baalat's sanctuary before. She decided she didn't like it. It had to be a mistake; her mother couldn't mean to leave her here alone with the golden statue of the goddess, shrouded in a suffocating haze of opium incense.

"Please," Istara said, tugging on her mother's hand, "I don't want to stay here. It's dark, and the smell makes my head hurt."

When her mother didn't respond, Istara tugged again, harder, but the Queen of Kadesh's gaze remained fixed on the image of the goddess. With a heavy sigh, her mother sank to her knees and whispered a prayer, for forgiveness.

Uneasy, Istara touched her mother's hand, bare of the usual glittering array of rings. "Ama?"

Her mother looked down at Istara's hand on hers. "I have abused my power as high priestess," she said, quiet. "For weeks now, I have been taking the goddess's food and giving it to you. I could not bear to see you starve."

Istara eyed the image of Baalat, fear slicing into her, deep. "But the punishment is—"

"I know." Her mother's fingers touched Istara's lips, silencing her. "I pray she understands, and will forgive me."

Istara thought of all the scraps her mother had given her over the weeks, almonds, and dried figs, once she had even surprised Istara with a little piece of honey crystal. That was a good day.

Now Istara imagined her mother stealing from the offering bowls at the goddess's feet. A terrible, awful crime. She looked at her mother's gaunt, worn face, her fragile beauty diminished by extreme hunger, and saw her desperation. Overcome, Istara hugged her, her hands brushing against her mother's shoulder blades, protruding, sharp.

"Oh Ama. I do not deserve you."

In her mother's quiet embrace, Istara closed her eyes and recalled the day when everything began. It was raining when the Egyptian army streamed out of Labwi Wood, driving their fancy horses and chariots over the pretty meadow outside the city walls. For two days, the soldiers worked to set up a vast city of tents; Istara was certain about that part because she had watched.

Her father sent couriers to Hatti's far-off capital, Tarhuntassa, to King Muwatallis. The gates slammed closed, and Istara learned a new hateful word. Siege. Weeks passed. Her lessons dwindled, then ended, the palace's quiet order turning to chaos.

Rooms were closed off, deemed unnecessary. Soon there was no fuel left to burn in the braziers, and Istara shivered in her bed as the stone walls sweated out the heavy rains of spring.

Her father changed, becoming angry, shouting, sometimes even breaking things. The food ran out. They braved hunger for two days, waiting for Muwatallis to come, her stomach cramping so much, she cried. The cats disappeared, even her favorite, the stable cat, Mada and her litter of kittens. The hunting dogs followed soon after. Then, one by one, the horses in the stables vanished, until even Istara's pony Kuma was gone, and the stables lay silent, the quiet, deafening.

The night Kuma disappeared, there was meat on Istara's platter for the first time in almost two weeks. Both her mother and father had come to her, to sit in silence while she ate, their eyes haunted. Despite her heartache, Istara could not disappoint them. She ate her beloved friend, trying not to think of the happy hours she had passed with her, each bite tainted with bitterness against the Egyptians. As soon as her parents left, she cried until she fell asleep, dreaming of Kuma being taken away, whinnying in fear, to be cut into pieces to feed the starving people. To feed her own mistress.

The next day, Istara slipped away to the rooftop garden of the palace, stripped bare of its vegetation and hurled rocks over the walls, calling the Egyptians every name she could think of. When she ran out, she created new ones.

Exhausted, she sagged, panting against the wall, glaring at their camp, filled with hate. From its edge, surrounded by soldiers, one young man emerged, dressed in gleaming armor. He stopped and looked up. Right at her.

Indignant, she rose and returned his gaze, focusing all her unhappiness on him. Her fingers shaking, she prised a large rock loose from the wall and heaved it over the side, screaming out the worst insult she knew. *Dirty bottom eater.*

The rock tumbled, useless, straight down into the olive grove beneath the city's walls. Humiliated, she looked back at him, waiting for him to mock her. Instead, he lifted his hand, inviting her to join them. One of his men pulled his ration bag from his belt and held it up, a heartbeat later, the others joined in, holding theirs up, silent.

Shamed, she backed away so she could no longer see them. On the long walk back to her apartment she experienced confusion, no longer certain who to blame for Kuma's death. She decided she would think about it when she was older and wiser, when she had had more lessons. Until then, she had learned nothing was as simple as it seemed.

Istara looked around, afraid. Now, after three months of hunger and waiting, she was going to be locked in here, in Baalat's dark, oppressive sanctuary. Istara felt her mother's thin fingers wrap around her arms, her grip so faint, it felt like a whisper.

"I cannot remain with you much longer," she said. "By your father's command, you must stay here until I come for you. We have lost. King Muwatallis has not come. Today your father will open the gates and kneel before the Pharaoh of Egypt."

"But I heard you say if he kneels to Egypt," Istara said, pulling back, anxious, "the King of Hatti will punish us all."

Her mother looked away, blinking hard. She took Istara's hand and led her back to the sanctuary's thick cedarwood doors. "You have suffered much these past months, and without one word of complaint," she murmured, changing the subject. "I am proud of you. But today, you must face one last challenge and wait here, alone, until my return. You must trust your father's judgment. He only thinks to protect you."

Istara clung to her mother's hand, her small store of courage fleeing. She had thought she was ready, but she wasn't; in the meager light of the single flame there were too many shadows lurking, sinuous, at the edge of her vision.

"Promise you will come back to me," she whispered.

"I promise." Her mother brushed the hair from Istara's forehead and smiled, though it didn't reach her eyes. "You are safe here in the goddess's sanctuary. Stay close to her, and she will protect you. Soon this will be over, and we will be happy again."

She prised Istara's fingers free and went outside. Istara made to follow her, but her mother shook her head, a warning flaring, sharp, in her eyes. She gestured to the guards to push the doors closed. They came to with a low boom. Istara jumped. She didn't like that sound. A scraping noise followed as the guards settled the beam into place, locking her inside. She pressed her ear against the thick door. She couldn't hear anything. She tried to be brave, but her heart pounded so hard it hurt.

Her back pressed against the door, she peered into the dim, smoky space, its pillared edges lost in deep shadow. She counted to three before darting through the darkness to the little pool of light at the base of the statue. Huddling against the cold stone platform, she wrapped her arms around her knees and waited, hoping with all her heart the lamp wouldn't run out of oil before her mother returned.

❋ ❋ ❋

Ramesses, Crown Prince of Egypt, eyed the barred doors to the sanctuary of Kadesh's goddess, uneasy. It was a crime, what he was about to do. His father had commanded him to take the temple's gold, the only price Kadesh would be forced to pay for standing against Pharaoh Seti. But instead of keeping their gold in a temple storeroom, like sensible people, the Kadeshites had secreted their wealth into the sanctuary of their deity. Ramesses cursed, certain his sacrilege would return to haunt him one day.

He breathed a prayer to Horus for protection and lifted the carved beam away. With a soft groan, the doors opened. A thick haze of opium incense surrounded him, making his eyes water. Cautious, he stepped over the threshold and breached the sacred residence of the goddess. Nothing happened. He felt foolish. Of course he would not be struck down. These provincial gods were not powerful. Not like Egypt's gods.

No more than twenty paces distant, the goddess stood alone, with enough gold and gems piled around her to cover the costs of their entire campaign. He hesitated, even with the doors open, the pillared edges to either side remained cloaked in shadow. His hand moved to the hilt of his dagger. He could hear someone breathing, ragged. He called out to his second-in-command.

"Captain Sethi. Torches."

They found a child, similar to the one he had seen throwing rocks from the palace roof a week ago. No more than seven or eight years old, she wore a shabby temple robe over her bare-footed, emaciated body. Under the effect of the opium, she stood, quiet, her eyes sliding, unseeing over his men. In Sethi's gentle grip, she staggered, struggling to stay on her feet. His captain cleared his throat.

"Should we bring her with us?"

"No," Ramesses answered, terse. "They closed her in here, drugging her with the opium for a reason. My father asked me to bring him the goddess's gold, nothing more. For all we know, the child is intended for sacrifice."

Sethi's eyes darkened at the suggestion. His grip tightened on her shoulders, protective. "My lord, we cannot leave her to die," he said as he glanced down at her, his expression softening. "She is just a little girl."

"She stays," Ramesses said, gesturing toward the pillared shadows, impatient. "Put her back where you found her."

Sethi hesitated. Irritated, Ramesses grabbed the waif's arm. "It is my command." He pulled the girl to him. "Release her."

Taller, older, and stronger by far, his captain resisted for as long as he dared. "My lord," Sethi murmured, "I beg you. Be merciful."

Ramesses considered the girl, reviving in the freshening air. She was a pretty thing, beautiful even, for a child. Her black hair, tumbling in thick waves down to her shoulders framed her heart-shaped face. A worthy sacrifice to a god. She gazed up at them, calm. Her dark eyes, framed by thick lashes, moved from him to Sethi; back and forth, examining them, her mouth shaping itself into a little, round 'o'. She pointed at Sethi's *khopesh*, saying something incomprehensible, her small voice sweet and inquisitive.

He caught Sethi watching him, waiting.

"To Ammit with your bleeding heart," Ramesses scoffed. "Why must you save every stray you find? Are you a warrior or a priest?"

"Can a man not strive to have the qualities of both?" Sethi asked.

"Bring her, then," Ramesses sighed, relenting. "If your grasp of Akkadian is sufficient, you may deliver her to their high priestess, forbidding her against the crime of human sacrifice. Be grateful I am in a generous mood today."

He left the sanctuary and inspected the heaped baskets, ready to be taken to his father. The pharaoh would be pleased. Ramesses began to say something to Sethi, before realizing he was alone. He turned. Still within the sanctuary, Sethi knelt before the girl. He offered her a fig from his ration pouch. She took it and devoured it in one bite, like a heathen. Her eyes drifted back to his pouch, looking for more.

Smiling, Sethi found another fig, then offered his biscuit, watching, delighted, as she gobbled up his evening meal, piece by piece; the Crown Prince of Egypt's second-in-command, willing to go hungry so a child of no consequence would not.

Putting his back to them, Ramesses suppressed a familiar ripple of envy toward the man who had come out of nowhere, rising to prominence from the gutters of Pi-Ramesses. Of no blood, and without family, Sethi had made a name for himself as a street fighter, whom none could defeat. The pharaoh had tested Sethi against his commanders. Not one of them had been able to take him down. Not even with weapons against Sethi's bare hands.

Sethi accepted the pharaoh's offer of a career in the military. One success followed another, his daring strategies during his first campaign earning him promotions and wealth.

At first, Ramesses had resented Sethi, but as time passed, he found himself growing to like him. Charismatic, honorable and clear-headed, Sethi was by far the best soldier Ramesses had ever fought alongside. And, wherever Sethi went, there was never a shortage of willing women. Together with Ahmen, Ramesses's oldest friend, they frequented the whorehouses, breaking hearts in every city. It was a good life.

Still, it was at times like this Ramesses couldn't escape the feeling of his own lack. Maybe it was because Sethi was three years older than him. He did have more experience. He was better in combat; there was no doubt. But Ramesses wasn't sure that was it. He caught

Sethi brushing the hair away from the little girl's eyes, affectionate. Ramesses suppressed his annoyance. They had work to do. He called Sethi to him, impatient.

His captain approached, the girl at his heels, trusting as a lamb. Ramesses endured a fresh stab of envy. With almost no effort, Sethi drew people to him, like moths to a flame. Ramesses wanted that kind of power. He was Crown Prince of Egypt. Sethi was no one. He glared at Sethi as his captain set the little girl on a ledge at the base of a pillar, before joining the others to help load the goddess's gold onto waiting carts.

Bored, Ramesses looked at the little girl and offered her a smile. She ignored him, edging to one side to look around him, her eyes following Sethi as he worked. Ramesses reached into his pouch and held out a fig, gesturing for her to come and take it. Wary, she slid off her perch and reached out, cautious. He pulled his hand back. She looked up at him, confused. He smiled at her. A faint smile ghosted her lips as she smiled back at him, uncertain.

He caught Sethi watching him, expressionless. Triumphant, he tossed the fig onto the ground. The girl scrambled after it with a little cry. He walked away, satisfied. No one was going to get the better of him, especially not a nobody like Sethi.

✳   ✳   ✳

Alone in the rooftop garden of the palace, Istara watched the last of the Egyptian army march into Labwi Wood. They left the meadow a hardened, dusty wasteland blackened by the scars of hundreds of fire pits. She had loved that meadow. Every summer it hummed with fat bees and butterflies kissing the riot of wildflowers. She used to go down and watch them. Now, it was ruined.

She thought of all the friends she had lost, her father's old dog, who was too old to hunt, but often came to sleep beside her bed, and Mada, with her beautiful litter of kittens. Who could kill kittens, and eat them? A tear slipped free as Istara thought of Kuma. She had loved her pony so much. And now all of them were dead, and for what?

For a dull stone stela to be put up in the palace square, forever claiming Kadesh as a vassal of Pharaoh Seti, Blessed of Re. It was just a rock. Why did they all have to go hungry and eat their friends, for a rock? None of it made sense. Whenever she brought it up, those around her changed the subject; even her Aunt Rhoha, who wasn't afraid of anything, or anyone.

One good thing happened, though. The Egyptians had left provisions, bags of grain, and corn—probably stolen, Istara had heard someone mutter—and they had been respectful, even if she couldn't understand anything they were saying. So, now, just like before they came, the smell of roasting meat and baking bread filled the palace kitchens, and from the farms, food poured into the city.

A week passed. A caravan of horse traders arrived. Istara's mother came to her, smiling, saying someone was waiting for her in the stables. Istara ran as fast as she could to the stable yard. There, in Kuma's empty stall, a new white pony whickered, her muzzle soft as down. Istara named her Saharu, and promised her no one would ever eat her so long as she lived. But this time, just in case, Istara decided not to love her pony quite as much.

Two more weeks passed, and summer reached its height. Apart from the desolation of the meadow, the memory of the Egyptian siege began to fade. Istara realized she was happy again, just as her mother promised they would be.

Four days later, as Istara dozed in the shade of an almond tree during the hottest part of a broiling afternoon, the sound of horns echoed across the walls of the city, just like the ones she had heard in the spring. She sat up, alarmed. Horns were bad. Already, gardeners, servants, and guards crowded along the terrace wall, shading their eyes against the glare of the sun, murmuring, fearful.

Her heart pounding, she pushed her way through, trying to see. The wind gusted, hot and dry, making the purple flags on the walls snap and buckle, sharp against the quiet air. The horns blasted again. She caught a glimpse of movement, far to the north, beyond the cedar wood.

Rising on her toes, she squinted into the distance, her hair billowing around her, catching in the wind. Impatient, she gathered it together and twisted it into a rope. There, a gleam. Her attention snapped back to the north. She searched the heat haze. Was that the faint pounding of drumbeats?

Her eyes burning, she waited, begrudging even the need to blink. The horizon shimmered, a liquid wall of silver, shifting, moving, deceiving. Something dark coalesced within the viscous surface. From its depths, four black horses, peacock plumes atop their bridles, stepped through as though arriving from the immortal realm. Behind them, standing proud in his chariot, the reins wrapped around his powerful arms, a man emerged with the bearing of a god, his golden armor gleaming white in the burning light. On his back he wore a sword, its massive hilt rising above his shoulder. The chariots of two more men appeared, one man almost the same age, the other much younger. And behind them, from out of the impossible wall of nothing, a host of thousands followed, lines upon lines of chariots, streaming onto the northern plain.

Muwatallis, the King of Hatti, had finally arrived.

TWO

Urhi-Teshub, Crown Prince of Hatti, pulled his horses to a halt and eyed the imposing stela set in the center of Kadesh's palace square proclaiming Pharaoh Seti's triumph over Hatti. His father, Muwatallis, stared, rigid and expressionless at the bombastic thing. Urhi-Teshub knew his father would not accept the loss of Kadesh, not after everything he had done to prepare for this battle, or everything he had had to leave behind unfinished in Tarhuntassa, Hatti's capital.

The date on the stela was more than a month old. Pharaoh Seti and his son Ramesses would be back in Pi-Ramesses by now, celebrating. Urhi-Teshub bit back a curse. He had been anticipating drenching his blade with Egyptian blood, to prove to his father his last year campaigning against the Kaskans with his uncle Hattusilis had been well spent. But now, after two months of preparation and one of hard marching, his sword would remain dry, just as it did two years ago when Pharaoh Seti claimed the city states of Amurru; his sudden, unexpected predations catching Hatti off guard.

But the pharaoh had been a fool to leave Kadesh undefended. For two years Hatti's king had seethed over his Amurrite losses to Egypt. And now, to find this? Urhi-Teshub shook his head, grim. Kadesh would pay.

His father's voice boomed across the square, where the city's assembled officials, nobles and royal family stood waiting, pale and trembling; their thin faces betraying the extent of their long wait for assistance.

"Tear it down," his father bellowed, putting his back to the offending stela. "Kadesh belongs to Hatti, regardless of Egypt's pathetic scribblings."

A gesture from Hattusilis, and orders went down the lines. Soldiers came forward bearing mason's tools. They surrounded the edifice, glistening like beetles, the thudding of their mallets loud in the still, oppressive heat of the square.

His father pulled the reins from his arms and left his chariot, watching as the men labored to break the stela apart until only a jagged lump remained. A thick haze of dust billowed out, making Urhi-Teshub's throat itch. His eyes watering, he suppressed a cough. The soldiers stepped back, panting, their bodies drenched in sweat.

His father made a wide circuit around the stump, stepping, disdainful, over its broken pieces. He stopped and looked over his men, his eyes glittering.

"Everything of value is to be taken." The King of Hatti's voice carried across the square, echoing over the soldiers and down into the city. "Every animal, every store of provisions, every bolt of material, every hoarded ingot of gold and silver. Spare only the image of the goddess herself. You will leave them nothing but the stones we stand upon. If anyone resists, put them to the sword, be it man, woman or child. By my command, you will show Kadesh no mercy."

The pleas began, quiet at first, soon escalating to desperate wails as the soldiers stripped the nobles of their gold, jewels, and embroidered tunics. Some of the women were left wearing nothing, their thin frames and slack skin exposed for all to see. Several of the soldiers laughed, mocking them. Urhi-Teshub shook his head, glaring at them, disgusted.

His father turned his attention to Amunira, Kadesh's king, and gestured for Urhi-Teshub to join him.

"Prince of Hatti," his father began as Urhi-Teshub navigated his way around the broken remains of Seti's stela, "how shall we punish our disloyal vassal? Think well, for one day you shall be Hatti's king, and the lessons you learn today will be of great value to you then."

Urhi-Teshub caught the vindictive glint in his father's eye; he would not do his father's dirty work for him.

"My lord king and father," he answered, choosing his words with care, "you have taken all Kadesh has left to be taken after having endured a long siege. There is nothing left to them now save their lives."

His father smiled, cold, as he pulled his daggers from their sheaths. "Shall we take their lives as well, my son?"

Urhi-Teshub looked at Amunira, stripped of his finery, waiting, stoic. Behind him, his queen, Azfara, stood wearing only a thin linen shift. A beautiful woman. Her gaze met his, pleading. He turned his attention back to Amunira, trying to gauge the man, his worth as a king. Amunira met his eyes, courageous, honorable, ready to die.

Urhi-Teshub recognized in him the many qualities lacking in his father. Here stood a good and noble king who had suffered much, who had been forced to make a terrible choice to protect his people. Urhi-Teshub would not sacrifice this man just to gain his father's approval. A thought crossed his mind.

"Is there not another way?" he asked, his eyes on Amunira. "To kill them would only give rise to a new nobility, perhaps ones chosen by Pharaoh Seti. We have the perfect opportunity to ensure King Amunira's continued obedience, despite his treachery of having allied himself to Egypt."

A soft hiss filled the quiet as his father slid one of his daggers back into its sheath. A creak of sun warmed leather followed as he rested his hand on the dagger's pommel. "I am listening."

A flicker of gratitude flared in Amunira's eyes. Urhi-Teshub ignored him. "Hostages," he said, gesturing along the line of nobles. "Just as Lord Hattusilis takes the Kaskan children from the conquered tribes, let us take these children with us to Tarhuntassa to educate under your command. Once they are grown, send them back to Kadesh to serve as your loyal administrators."

His father rubbed the pommel of the other dagger against his jaw, its fluted edge rasping against his stubble as he looked over the children among the nobles, unimpressed. His gaze moved to one of the young women standing near the queen, stopping to linger on the faint curves of her body. He nodded at her. Urhi-Teshub turned. A little girl, a pretty, dark-haired thing, peeked out from behind the woman's shift.

His father pointed his dagger at her. "The girl," he said, his voice taut. "Bring her to me."

With a cry, Azfara rushed over to the child and put her behind her, out of his sight. "Your Majesty," she pleaded, her face tight with fear, "I beg you, not her."

"Ah, the desperate look of a mother," his father smiled, slow. "So, I have flushed out Amunira's brat."

Before Azfara could answer, the young woman who had first hidden the child brushed past Azfara as though the queen were of no consequence.

"Your Highness, of what use is a child?" she asked, soft and enticing, bowing low. "Such a burden. Let me offer myself to you instead. I am Lady Rhoha, sister of King Amunira. Allow me to devote my life to your pleasure as your concubine."

Urhi-Teshub looked from his father to the woman, who could be no more than twenty. Even in her diminished state, there was no doubt the woman knew her beauty was astonishing. With a few weeks of feeding, her body would once more be ripe and full, ready to give great pleasure. Her thick, dark brown hair fell to her waist in rolling waves, unbound without its jewels. Dark and sultry, she would be a match for any of his father's most exotic concubines. She licked her lips, slow, seductive. Urhi-Teshub raised his brow. Was she trying to seduce his father *here*?

"I have concubines enough," his father grunted. "The girl, Urhi-Teshub."

Rhoha opened her shift, exposing the curve of her perfect breasts. She stepped toward his father, her eyes wide and trusting. "Then, instead of the child," she breathed, "take my life. To be killed by one's king—a god—there can be no greater end."

His father narrowed his eyes. "You dare try to divert me? You are no one, worthless. Beware I do not send both you and the child to the gods today." He shoved her aside, pointing once more at the girl. "I will not ask again. Bring me Amunira's child. She will be the price for Kadesh's crimes. My blade awaits."

Her eyes bright with tears, Azfara clung to the child, her knuckles whitening, shaking her head, defiant.

"Lord King of Hatti," Amunira cried out, his voice ringing across the square, "it was I who opened the gates. I knelt before Pharaoh Seti. If it is blood you seek, take mine. The child is innocent."

An ominous silence fell, in the midst of it, footsteps approached.

"Brother," Hattusilis murmured as he approached, his voice, as always, soothing, reasonable, "none doubt your judgment against Kadesh. But, if you kill the child, how could you hope to retain the loyalty of this kingdom? As soon as we leave, Kadesh will rally once more to Egypt."

"And?"

"Instead, let us expand on the prince's suggestion," Hattusilis continued. "Take this child, along with these others to Tarhuntassa, as hostages. So long as Kadesh remains loyal to you, Amunira's daughter will live."

A long silence stretched. Urhi-Teshub could hear the girl's shallow breathing, hidden behind her mother's shift. He hoped his father would see sense. He wanted no part in the murder of a little girl.

His father grunted. "You speak sense as usual, Brother, but my blade will taste blood this day. Who will stand in her place, since my son has convinced me to spare the king?"

"Take Queen Azfara," Hattusilis answered without even a heartbeat's hesitation. "Forbid Amunira on pain of his child's death, from taking another wife. Then you shall hold the only heir of Kadesh in your hands to be raised as you see fit. When she is of age, marry her to a man who is loyal to you, and through her he shall be king, guaranteeing Kadesh's continued loyalty to your throne."

His father scratched his chin with the dagger's pommel, his gaze on the queen. "The woman will have to suffice," he sniffed. "Urhi-Teshub, bring her to me."

Reluctant, Urhi-Teshub took hold of Azfara's arm. She shook him off and knelt beside her daughter.

"Istara, my love," she said, her voice shaking, "because the Egyptians came into Kadesh, Ama must go to the gods. Be a good child. Learn your lessons, and be faithful to Baalat. When I am gone, she will watch over you. Never forget I love you."

Urhi-Teshub sensed his father's impatience. He took hold of Azfara's arm once more. She rose, trembling in his grip. Confused, Istara looked from her mother to his father, who flexed his fingers on his dagger's hilt. Comprehension, then horror, filled her eyes. Urhi-Teshub couldn't bear it. He looked back at Hattusilis, desperate for his intervention. His uncle shot him a cold, warning look. He had to sacrifice the mother to save the child. Urhi-Teshub felt sick. It was enough to take everything in the city. There was no need for blood, either of children or of queens.

Istara fell to her knees, sobbing. Her little hands clung, desperate, to her mother's shift. "Ama, don't go. Ama stay . . . Ama . . ."

Azfara shuddered and shook her head, pulling against Urhi-Teshub, trying to free herself. All around him, noblewomen erupted into wails, begging for mercy. Lady Rhoha sank to her knees, prostrating herself, clutching his father's feet, kissing them, pleading with him to take her life instead. He kicked her aside, his face dark with anger, bellowing for someone to get rid of the girl.

Soldiers rushed forward. Urhi-Teshub pushed in front of them. They would not have her, not like this. They fell back. Sick with guilt, he let go of Azfara and took hold of Istara's shoulders. Screaming for her mother, she fought him, the material of Azfara's shift tearing free in her fingers. He tightened his grip, cursing, frustrated. She was strong, like a wild piglet. He pinned her between his legs, forcing her to hold still, holding her head in his hands, turned away, so she would not see what was to come.

Amunira took hold of Azfara. "Had I not allowed the Egyptians in," he spat, clutching his wife against him, protective, "you would have arrived today to a city of rotting corpses, of no use to Hatti. If it is blood payment you seek, take my life, as accorded by law. As is right!"

"Enough!" Urhi-Teshub's father bellowed, furious. "It matters not what you bleat at me. If you had had enough faith, the gods would have protected you."

He drove his dagger into Azfara's back, twisting the blade, vicious. Her eyes widened. She juddered, her legs giving out as he yanked the dagger free. Blood and gore splattered onto his chest. She cried out, a high, thin wail. Amunira scrabbled to hang on to her, even as she slid to the ground, already dead.

The child thrashed, crying out for her mother, frantic. Urhi-Teshub tightened his hold. He couldn't let her see. There was blood everywhere, pumping out of Azfara in massive gouts. Istara's teeth clamped onto his finger. She bit him, hard. He swore and shook himself free. No more. It was enough.

He picked her up and pressed her face against his chest. The place stank of hot blood and fear, reminding him of temple sacrifices. Men and women wailed, their cries escalating, spreading across the square, their horror washing over the city, filling the air with grief. Ignoring his father's shout to remain, Urhi-Teshub left, stumbling over the broken stela fragments in his haste to get Istara away.

His father shouted again, furious. Urhi-Teshub pressed on, determined, knowing he would pay dearly for his disobedience as he continued to stride past the soldiers in the square, past the market stalls and lanes and down through the city, Istara's small fists beating against his chest.

He did not stop until he came to the river outside the city's walls. Setting her down on the riverbank, he dipped his hands in the cool water and cleaned the dried blood from his finger. Cupping some water in his hands, he brought it up to her lips and offered her a drink.

She looked up at him, fearful, her face swollen and blotchy. She hiccupped. A tear, stuck to her eyelashes, slipped free. His heart ached for her. At times, he hated his father. What he had done today, out of vengeance for Amurru was unforgivable. For the hundredth time, Urhi-Teshub vowed to be a better king than his father. He would start by taking responsibility for this little waif on the march home, watching over her until she was safe in Tarhuntassa.

He waited, patient, as the water trickled out between his fingers. Istara licked her lips. She had to be thirsty. Heat radiated from the hard-packed earth, broiling hot. He lifted his hands closer and nodded at her, encouraging her. Her eyes never leaving his, she leaned forward, slow, and sipped, wary, a lamb before a wolf.

THREE

"Brace yourself," Urhi-Teshub warned just before one of his chariot's wheels dropped into a deep rut.

Istara tightened her grip on the box's edge, staggering as the box tilted at a steep angle. She felt Urhi-Teshub press his thigh against her back, steadying her.

"Soon we will be in Tarhuntassa," he said, as he shifted his weight and steered the horses around a boulder. "Once we arrive, you will be taken to the nursery along with the rest of the children from Kadesh."

"I know," Istara murmured, keeping her eyes open for more ruts.

Urhi-Teshub guided the horses along the rocky stretch, the lean muscles in his arms shifting and flexing as he called to them with encouraging words, low and reassuring. Once clear of the rough patch, he continued, "As soon as I am able, I will go to my stepmother, the queen and ask her to look out for you. She raised me after my mother died. She is a kind woman and will be good to you."

Istara knew he meant to offer comfort, but there could be no other mother for her than her own. And now she was gone, living in the immortal realm with Baalat. The first night they left Kadesh, Istara dreamed of her mother holding her, telling her stories and kissing the top of her head like she used to do. It felt real. But it wasn't.

As those first long iters passed under the horses' hooves, Istara had grieved for the loss of her parents, her home, and her new pony. Urhi-Teshub never said anything, but she knew from the way he looked at her it made him sad. Those evenings, he would give her extra rations at dinner and hold her up so she could brush his horses' manes. One night, not long after they left, he gave her a little carved horse he had made while she slept. She called it Kuma and kept it with her always. It helped to take the hurt away, a little.

Urhi-Teshub leaned back on the reins, slowing the horses. "Quick," he said, tilting his head toward the horizon, "before we descend into the valley, look to the west. There is Tarhuntassa."

She peered over the box's edge through the gap between the hills. In the distance, thick, towering walls circled a vast city atop an enormous plateau. At its furthest end, the walls of a smaller city rose. The royal enclave. She stared at it. The enclave was massive, bigger than the whole of Kadesh. A gleam within the royal citadel caught her eye. Curious, she looked up at Urhi-Teshub.

"What is the shining light?"

Without troubling to conceal his pride, he answered, "It is the pillar in the central court of the Temple of the Storm God, Teshub, for whom I am named." Urhi-Teshub smiled, a rare thing. "My father, who represents the sun, had it covered in panels of gold. When the sun's light strikes it, it is a beacon for all to see, to remind them they look upon the home of Hatti's king, The Sun."

She gazed at the shining pillar, transfixed, watching it sparkle and gleam as it caught the light. "It is like nothing I have ever seen," she whispered, filled with awe.

"Tarhuntassa is beautiful," Urhi-Teshub said, still smiling. "The royal gardens bloom with colorful flowers carried from Babylon, and the palace's floors are laid with marble, shipped from the island quarries of Ahhiyawa. Even on the hottest day, marble remains cool to the touch and is so smooth you can slide across a whole room without stopping. I expect you to try at least once."

Istara mouthed the strange, new word. *Marble.* Did he really mean it when he said she could slide across the floor? She peeked up and caught him watching her, indulgent. Embarrassed, she focussed her attention on the beam of light. They descended into another valley, and the vast city with its glittering pillar sank beneath the horizon as if its wonders had been nothing more than a figment of her imagination.

As they descended deeper into the valley, shadows closed over them, reigniting within Istara a familiar feeling of gloom. Soon she would live in an enormous place, alone, among thousands, with no one to care about her. King Muwatallis, or, rather, The Sun, drove in front of them in somber silence. From what she had overheard in the camp, missing the opportunity to confront the Egyptians had been a humiliating blow, one he never intended to let happen again.

She studied Hatti's king. He leaned back against his reins, slowing his horses for the descent down another steep slope, the powerful muscles in his back and shoulders rippling. She had managed to stay clear of him for most of the march, but there was one evening, halfway through as she ate her evening meal with Urhi-Teshub, Muwatallis had arrived, accompanied by four of his bodyguard, the intimidating, spear wielding, *Mesedi*.

That night, the King of Hatti had accepted a cup of wine from his son and seated himself upon a stool, his elbows on his knees. They spoke of mundane things like Hattusilis's lame horse, and Urhi-Teshub's next campaign in the north. Her appetite gone, she crept back from the fire, watching him, wary, waiting for him to turn on her.

He had never looked at her once. All she had seen was a father talking to his son. They talked long into the night. Despite her fear, sleepiness overcame her. She curled up, shivering, near the horses, too afraid to go back to the fire, dozing until the warmth of a thick blanket settled over her. She roused, expecting to see Urhi-Teshub's kind eyes, but instead found those of the man who killed her mother eyeing her, troubled. She turned her face to the ground, terror clawing at her. He was going to kill her now too, she was sure of it.

"Asuru, my love," the King of Hatti murmured, "I beg you, cease. I can feel your anger condemning me all the way from the immortal realm. I swear I will remedy this wrong. The child will not suffer for what I have done."

His words made no sense. Istara had held her breath, waiting for the hiss of his dagger leaving its sheath, instead, with a creak of leather, he was gone.

Urhi-Teshub carried her back to the fire and lay her head on his lap. He stroked her hair, his calloused fingers gentle and soothing, calming her. Warmed by the heat of the fire, she slept and dreamed of home, reliving the lost days when she had been safe and happy.

A horse whinnied, startling Istara. She blinked, returning to the present. She glanced again at Muwatallis. Once in Tarhuntassa, lost in the vast grounds of the royal citadel, she expected it would be easy to keep her distance from him. Perhaps if she was fortunate, she would never need to see him again.

She stole a look at Urhi-Teshub, her protector and at times maybe even her friend. Soon he would leave her among strangers. Her chest tightened, the thought of losing him suddenly unbearable.

"Will you come and visit me?" she blurted out.

"Whenever I am in Tarhuntassa, I will," he said, not taking his eyes off the road. "But I must return to my uncle's city of Hakpis where I live. Together with my uncle's armies, I have been campaigning to regain the lands lost to the Kaskans." His eyes darkened, and his jaw jutted out a little, betraying a stubborn streak Istara had come to recognize. "They are heathens and have desecrated the holy city of Nerik. I have sworn an oath to Teshub I will not rest until Nerik is his once more."

"How long will that take?" Istara asked.

"Years." Urhi-Teshub sighed. "It is an endless war; we have been fighting to reclaim Nerik ever since my great-grandfather, Suppiluliuma II was the king."

"Oh." Istara looked down at her feet, disappointment flooding her.

"If you like, I will write to you," he offered.

"I don't know how to read," she murmured, ashamed.

"A scribe could read my letters to you," he suggested

"No. I want to read them myself," she answered, determined, "and I want to be able to write too, so I can write you back."

"Then you shall learn to read and write," Urhi-Teshub said, decisive. "I will see to it. This much at least I am able to do." He pointed at a wide road, paved smooth with flagged stones rising up out of the valley floor. It snaked away between the hills into the distance. A pair of towering statues depicting a strange god flanked either side of it, just where the road began. "Finally," he said. "The royal road. At last."

It took most of the rest of the afternoon to cross the remaining iters to Tarhuntassa and to complete the long, winding climb uphill to its gates. Horns had been blaring from the city's walls for more than an hour, announcing the arrival of the king's army. Atop the final turn, Istara discovered a multitude waiting, cheering and crying out the king's name.

Movement along the ramparts caught Istara's eye. She gaped. *Chariots?*

"You might want to close your mouth," Urhi-Teshub chuckled, "else the flies will get in."

Istara pressed her lips together but kept watching, fascinated. Driving two abreast, the chariots' outer wheels almost touched the rampart's edge. A deafening blast of horns erupted. Urhi-Teshub nudged her with his knee and nodded at the gate. The vast wooden doors opened, splitting the metalwork sunburst covering its surface in two, its spikes, huge, sharp and forbidding, the sight of it both beautiful and terrifying.

Up they went into the city, along its winding streets toward the citadel walls, past temples, bazaars, residences, parks, squares, horse markets, stables, garrisons, and arenas. Wide-eyed, Istara clung to the top of the chariot gazing at the people thronging the streets and squares, filling every doorway, leaning out of windows, balconies and roof gardens. Flowers of every color and size drifted down from above, turning the floor of the chariot into a soft, scented carpet.

As they drew close to the royal citadel's gates, they passed an elegant villa, its terrace shaded by potted palms. Colorful hanging linens billowed around its edges, caught in the late summer breeze.

Young women, all of them breathtaking, called out to Urhi-Teshub, their sun-bronzed breasts draped in gold and gems.

He smiled up at them. Singling out the most beautiful one by name, he asked if she would join him at the feast. Her lips curved, seductive, as she threw him a rose, dark red, its petals soft. It landed in the chariot beside his feet. Istara picked it up and inhaled its rich, enticing scent. She held it up to him.

"The lady gave you this."

A look of pleasure crossed his face. "Save that one for me, little one. I will keep it with me when I go north."

She watched him, curious, as he smiled to himself. "Do you love that lady?"

"Love?" He raised a brow, considering. "No, but I do like her very much."

Istara looked back at the woman, who could be no more than twenty, watching Urhi-Teshub, her eyes filled with longing. Istara thought she looked kind.

"Do you think she could be my friend, while you are away?" she asked.

He burst out laughing. Her cheeks burning, Istara hunched into herself, understanding enough to know she had said something foolish.

"I would not advise it," he said, still chuckling. "She is not a lady, but a whore."

Surprised, Istara turned around and inspected the woman. "But she is so pretty and clean," she said, disbelieving him, thinking he must be teasing her. "I thought whores were dirty and ugly—at least that is what my nurse told me."

"Most are, it is true," Urhi-Teshub conceded. "But these women are courtesans, trained in the art of love and owned by no man. Courtesans are beautiful, skilled and very rich. The wealthy compete for their attention, sending gifts to entice them. Tonight will cost me much, but it will be worth it."

Istara looked at the rose in her hand and hoped she understood. "So the rose means she chose you?"

"It does." He smiled, his eyes unfocusing. "And tonight I shall be the envy of all men, for Adar is the most coveted of them all." Calling to his horses with a happy shout, he brought them to a trot, guiding them through the gate into the glittering splendor of the royal city, Istara's new home.

❊   ❊   ❊

Three long, lonely weeks had passed in the harem's nursery before Istara was summoned to the queen's residence. She looked around, wide-eyed, at the opulence of the Queen of Hatti's vast reception room. Cushioned divans and potted palms encircled huge, colorfully-painted pillars. High above, even the ceiling bore painted scenes of gardens and exotic birds. Istara wondered how they did it. She would have to ask Urhi-Teshub, he would know the answer. He knew a lot of things.

Around the room's edges, pink, blue, and purple-dyed linen hangings created little alcoves. Within them, Istara glimpsed beautiful women reclining, their heads and necks laden in jewels, watching her, whispering behind their feathered fans.

Beneath her feet, a gleaming floor of polished marble. It was the first time she had seen it. Urhi-Teshub was right; it was slippery. So much nicer than flagged stone. A little part of her longed to see how far she could slide across it.

On the dais, an empty chair gilt in gold waited, a thin blue cushion on its seat. Two of the queen's royal guard flanked it, standing still as statues, their leather armor embossed with gold. A door in the dais's paneled wall opened. The women in the room came to their feet, then sank to their knees, the whisper of their gowns soft against the marble.

Istara knelt, her heart pounding. She had no idea what to expect, nothing here could be compared to home. Her mother hadn't had her own reception room with divans and guards and a chair gilt in gold. Tarhuntassa was another world, exotic and strange, filled with complicated hierarchies and power, even in the harem's nursery.

A heavy rustle of material swept past. Istara peeked up. Tanu-Hepa, twice-crowned queen of the empire of Hatti, wore a draped gown of pure white, edged in gold thread. An intricate filigreed crown had been woven into her dark hair, and a fortune of gems and gold glittered on her throat, arms and fingers. She processed to her chair and waited as her attendants arranged her gown so she could sit. Another attendant came forward carrying a footstool, also gilt with gold. Istara stared as the attendant lifted the queen's feet onto it, even her sandals were made of gold.

Tanu-Hepa raised her hand, languid, and beckoned Istara forward. Trembling, Istara came to her feet and moved to the bottom step of the dais, feeling as though she were in the presence of a goddess.

"Welcome, Princess Istara of Kadesh, to the Court of the Sun," Tanu-Hepa said, her voice melodious and refined. "The crown prince has spoken to me of you, and the king has decreed you will live with me, here in my residence."

Istara gaped. She was going to live *here*? She thought she was going to have to live in that horrible, hateful nursery forever, where babies were always crying, and she had to share a pallet with two other children, who kicked her in their sleep.

At a nod from the queen, one of the noblewomen came forward, smiling, and held out her hand to Istara, to take her away. The noblewoman's gown and jewels far outranked anything Istara's mother had owned.

Shy, Istara shuffled backward and bumped into the guard who had brought her from the nursery. Soft ripples of amused laughter drifted through the room, but she didn't care. They could laugh as much as they wanted, all that mattered to Istara was she would never have to go back to the nursery again. She took the hand of the noblewoman, silently vowing never to forget what Urhi-Teshub had done for her. Ever.

Istara watched, fascinated, as Hatti's queen prepared a platter from two of the trays on the table and passed it to her steward. He placed it before Istara with a flourish.

Istara looked at the golden platter, piled with creamy morsels of roast calf glistening in its juices. A compote of apples and raisins, spiced with cinnamon and honey, sat at its side, waited to be mixed into the meat. Her mouth watered. She looked up and caught Tanu-Hepa's indulgent look.

"Eat," she said, nodding at Istara's platter, "before it gets cold, but do leave a little room for the sweet. We shall have my favorite, specially made for your arrival, honeyed almond cake."

Istara ate. The meat was so tender, it melted in her mouth. Not like the gristly bits of dried meat she had had to gnaw on at the nursery. She ate all of the compote. Cinnamon was her favorite, she usually only tasted that rare and expensive spice on her year day. She couldn't imagine the impossible luxury of having cinnamon every day. She wondered what honeyed almond cake would taste like. She hoped she would like it so she wouldn't have to disappoint the kind and gentle queen.

She didn't need to worry, though she wished she hadn't eaten all the compote. Now she would struggle to finish her cake. It was so perfect she could almost cry. Then she felt guilty. How could she enjoy her food—how could she enjoy anything—after what had happened to her mother? She put her cake down and pushed her platter away.

Tanu-Hepa set aside her wine. "Is something wrong with the cake?"

Istara looked down at her hands, sticky with honey. "No," she said, quiet. "The cake is very nice, but I feel bad eating it."

"Why?"

Istara shook her head. She didn't want to answer.

Tanu-Hepa lifted a clean napkin from the table and dipped it into a bowl of warmed rose water. She knelt beside Istara and ran the damp cloth over each of Istara's fingers, one by one, until all the honey was gone. Istara watched her, thinking of how her mother used to do the same. She pressed her lips together, suddenly missing her mother so much her throat ached. She wouldn't cry in front of the queen. She couldn't. Tanu-Hepa set the napkin aside.

"Urhi-Teshub has told me all," she said, brushing back a strand of Istara's hair, just like Ama used to do. "My heart aches for you, to have lost your mother while still so young."

Istara struggled to fight the flood of memories. The heat of the square. Her mother's high, thin cry as Muwatallis stabbed her. The sharp metallic scent of her blood. Her father's hollow, shocked voice, calling her mother's name over and over. She caught Tanu-Hepa gazing at her, the queen's gentle eyes glistening with tears.

Istara crumpled. She sobbed her mother's name, begging it to all be a bad dream. With a low cry, Tanu-Hepa pulled Istara into her lap and rocked her back and forth, holding her, murmuring nonsense words of reassurance into her hair, just like Ama used to do. Unable to do anything else, Istara clung to the Queen of Hatti and wept.

It was a long time before Istara felt calmer. She hiccupped and looked up at Tanu-Hepa, shy. Brushing her own tears away, the queen rose and held out her hand. Istara took it and followed Tanu-Hepa onto a balcony overlooking a torchlit garden. After a long while, the queen sighed.

"I will never be able to replace your mother," she said, "but if you give me the chance to care for you, I will try to make your life as comfortable as possible in Tarhuntassa. You have lost your mother, and I have lost a son. I think we could find comfort in each other's company."

Within the garden, pairs of women dressed in white floated little boats bearing flowers and burning lamps onto the waters of the pools, creating little islands of light. It was very beautiful, but it only made Istara feel worse. They didn't have lamp boats in Kadesh. Was nothing here going be familiar? She looked up at Tanu-Hepa.

"Who is Asuru?" she asked, suddenly needing to understand Muwatallis's vow to remedy his wrong, made the night he joined Urhi-Teshub by his campfire.

A look of anguish sliced across Tanu-Hepa's face. She closed her eyes and shook her head. Istara felt terrible. How could she know her question would hurt the queen?

Tanu-Hepa brushed a fresh tear from her eye and gave Istara a watery smile. "I can see you will keep me on my toes," she said, though not unkindly. "Asuru is Urhi-Teshub's birth mother. When he was born, there was a terrible winter storm. Prince Muwatallis was alone with Asuru when things went wrong. She died, and he had to cut her open to save Urhi-Teshub. Muwatallis has never been the same since then . . . Asuru was the love of his life."

Istara shook her head. Poor Urhi-Teshub, he lost his mother before he ever knew her. Somehow knowing he had lost his mother too made her feel less alone. Maybe that was why he had protected her. She thought of Muwatallis and wondered if he had agreed to Urhi-Teshub's request to move her out of the nursery to the queen's palace because of his promise to Asuru. Istara shook her head. It didn't matter. She still hated Hatti's king for what he had done. Nothing he did could ever make things better, not even living with the Queen of Hatti and having cinnamon every single day for the rest of her life.

❋   ❋   ❋

Alone in a pillared pavilion, its indigo-dyed linens drifting around her, Istara sat cross-legged upon a divan. Her tongue between her teeth, she concentrated on pressing her stylus against her wax tablet. Careful not to smudge her work, she turned her hand to complete the last stroke of one of the more difficult letters. A piercing cry startled her, sending her stylus slicing across the wax.

She looked up, irritated. A peacock processed along the crushed gravel path, his tail feathers dragging behind him, rustling against the pebbles. She looked back down at her tablet, despairing, all her effort for her tutor, ruined. Resigned, she lay the tablet in a patch of sunlight to let the wax soften, so she could smooth it over and begin again.

Leaning back against the thick cushions of the divan, she gazed up at the hangings moving in the soft spring breeze, watching how they filtered the sunlight. She stretched, thinking of the evening ahead. Today marked her year day, and Tanu-Hepa had promised her a treat at dinner. Istara wondered for the twentieth time what it would be. She hoped it would be honeyed almond cake, her favorite.

"You are hard to find."

Istara sat up, searching through the rippling hangings, her heart in her throat. It couldn't be. A young man stepped into view, just outside the pavilion.

With a cry, she lunged from the divan and barreled into his waiting arms.

"Urhi-Teshub!"

"Hello little one," he said, laughing as she danced around him with delight. "The queen tells me I have returned home just in time for someone's year day. So tell me, what year are we celebrating? You look about ten."

She giggled, pleased he thought she was older. "No. I'm only nine. But, I have almost mastered writing the whole alphabet. I could have shown you my work, but a peacock came by and ruined it."

"Did he now?"

She caught his mocking smile and laughed, realizing how silly she must have sounded. "He did. Look there he is, behaving as though he is innocent. Wait, I will prove it to you." Picking up her tablet, she smoothed it over and began the work of writing out her name, her tongue once more escaping her lips. "There, you see. Now I will write your name."

She handed him her tablet, proud of her work; she had done everything right. She waited. He nodded, impressed. "You learn fast. What about my letters, have you been able to read any of them yet?"

"Yes, all of them, I mastered reading before the winter solstice passed. Is it really true so much snow fell last winter it was as high as your chest?"

"It is," Urhi-Teshub frowned, "and I hope never to have to experience such a thing again."

Taking the tablet back from him, she hugged it to her chest, inspecting him. "You have grown taller," she said as she looked him over, "and your chest is bigger too. Is that a new sword?"

"Not very." He reached over his shoulder and pulled the sword free, holding it up with both hands, the muscles in his arms flexing. "I have had it for almost a year now," he said, showing off a little with it, slicing it through the air, "a powerful weapon. I have felled many a Kaskan with this blade."

"So you are winning," Istara smiled, her hopes igniting.

"We are making progress," he answered, wry, as he slid the sword back into its scabbard.

"How long will you stay?" she asked, hoping it would be more than a day or two.

"Uncle wished to return to make offerings to Teshub at the festival," Urhi-Teshub replied, crossing his arms over his chest, eyeing one of the courtesans processing along the path, "and to seek the omens before we push further north. Once the rituals are complete, we will depart."

"A week then, at least," Istara twirled, pleased. "Will you see Adar while you are here?"

"Who?" he asked, glancing at the peacock as it fanned out its tail feathers, their jeweled colors iridescent in the sunlight.

"Adar, the courtesan who gave you the red rose the day we arrived from Kadesh."

"What a memory you have!" he laughed, tousling her hair. "That was what? Almost two years ago, and still you think of it?"

"She was very pretty," Istara shrugged, "and you liked her. I just thought you would want to see her again."

"Little heart, I am a warrior, women come and go," Urhi-Teshub said, shaking his head, his gaze straying once more to the courtesan, who behaved as though she could not see him. "Adar is just one of many. In truth, I had forgotten about her. Now come, gather up your things. I have a present for you, carried back in a basket with me from the north. I would like to give it to you before I must go to the temple."

Curiosity overwhelming her, Istara followed Urhi-Teshub into a dimly lit storage room piled high with sacks of grain, right at the back of the royal stables. In the middle of the floor, set upon a blanket, a closed basket waited.

Urhi-Teshub knelt and unlaced its ties. Cautious, he lifted the lid and reached in to gather up something small and wriggling. He turned, his eyes warm, and held it out to her.

"She was birthed from one of my own bitches," he said, smiling at her. "The smallest and weakest are usually drowned since they will not be fit for hunting. But there was something about this one which reminded me of you. So I kept her, in the hopes you would take her as your own. Will you have her?"

"Yes! Oh yes!" Istara cried out, overcome with joy. "I will keep her by my side, always. Now I won't be lonely anymore." Her eyes filled with tears, she couldn't see the puppy, but it didn't matter, she was so happy. She hugged the little, wiggling bundle of life, feeling her tears escaping. The puppy licked them. She laughed, hiccupping, filled with delight. "This is the best day of my life so far in Tarhuntassa."

Urhi-Teshub said nothing. He bowed his head and turned away, busying himself with packing up the basket. The little brown pup, warm and solid, wriggled in her arms and tried to lick her some more. She lifted its face up to hers and kissed its soft nose.

"Your name shall be Anash," she whispered, "for happiness, because now, I am happy again."

FOUR

City of Tarhuntassa, Summer.
Reign of Muwatallis, Year 12

Urhi-Teshub pushed away his morning meal, his appetite gone. "I will not do it," he said, folding his arms over his chest. "I cannot. Even the thought of it makes me sick. I am nineteen, Istara is eleven, a child in mind and body and like a sister to me."

His father motioned for the steward to bring more mead. He waited until the cups had been filled and the steward had withdrawn before responding. "Perhaps now you understand what I suffered being forced to marry my own stepmother." He toyed with the stem of his wine cup, his lips turned downward. "It is no lie I cannot stand the sight of Tanu-Hepa. But for you it is not the same."

"You are right. It is not the same," Urhi-Teshub answered, tight. "Tanu-Hepa was eighteen, of equal age to you when grandfather married her to provide Hatti with a high priestess, her only purpose. He did not even allow her to live in the queen's palace."

"Yet, he knew her," his father replied, cold, "knowing he would force his son to marry her, knew her, and they had a child."

"The child died," Urhi-Teshub muttered, exasperated by his father's determination to make everything about himself, "and all know he never touched her again."

Over his raised cup, his father glared at him. "Why do you defend her? She is not your mother. Asuru is your mother."

"Tanu-Hepa is the only mother I have ever known," Urhi-Teshub said, feeling his temper beginning to rise, "and despite all she has suffered for Hatti, she has remained a kind and good woman. Even after you banished Lubarna to Hakpis, she loves you still."

His father eyed him, indifferent. "Just one time I had her," he muttered as he finished his meal. "I don't even remember it. Now I am burdened with her brat, but with Lubarna under your uncle's influence, the loyalists have been silenced and—don't look at me like that, you ingrate—I did it for you, to protect your inheritance to the throne. Enough of this. I expected you to be pleased with my decision for you to marry Istara since it is no secret how fond you are of her."

"As a sis—"

"Enough." His father tossed his napkin on the table and rose to his feet. "It is my command. Kadesh is too valuable to give to anyone else. I swore to Asuru I would make it right, and this is how it shall be done."

"By forcing your son to marry his near-sister?" Urhi-Teshub snapped, bitter.

"Before you return north," his father continued as he dipped his hands in a bowl of warmed water, ignoring Urhi-Teshub's question, "you will mix your blood before the altar of Arinna and seal your bond before the gods. None shall be able to break it."

"And I have no choice but to obey," Urhi-Teshub scoffed, eyeing his father, filled with hate. He leaned forward, his body vibrating with suppressed rage. "But in one matter you will have no power over me. I refuse to complete the bond with her until she is a woman, and even then, it will sicken me to take her to my bed. In this union, there can be no joy for me."

"You may thank me yet," his father said, waving away Urhi-Teshub's words as he took up a linen towel and dried his hands. "In a few years, when Istara has matured, I suspect you will be more than willing to take her to your bed. Her mother, as I recall, was astonishing."

Urhi-Teshub stared at his father, incredulous. "Do you not hear me? I will never thank you for this. Never. It is sick. No matter how much she matures, I will only ever see in Istara the broken-hearted, weeping child I carried away from Kadesh's square, the one who wet her blanket the first three nights of our march home." He leaned forward, angry, his words accusing. "The one I washed clean in the river in the dead of the night since there was no one else I could trust to do it."

"Go," his father shouted, pointing at the door. "Spend your time fighting for Nerik. When you return, a woman will be standing in the child's place. Tell me then you do not thank me. I can wait for your apology." He tossed the towel at a servant and stalked out, leaving Urhi-Teshub sitting alone at the table, furious and humiliated.

Urhi-Teshub slammed his fist against the table, bellowing the foulest curse he knew. He shoved his chair away from the table. Unseeing, he strode through his father's apartments, blinded by his anger and powerlessness. He plunged out the main doors into the crowded corridors of the palace, sending courtiers and servants scuttling to make space for him.

Istara was a sister to him, a child. An image, unwelcome and unbidden, flashed across his mind, of him taking her, the child, to his bed. Bile, bitter and burning hot, rose in his throat. He pushed his way into a garden, vomiting his morning meal onto a rose bush, uncaring of who saw.

Rubbing the back of his hand across his mouth, he watched the rose petals shrivel, blackened by the acid of his stomach. He recalled Istara's favorite flowers were roses. He turned. It was the only rose bush in the garden. Of all the places he could have been sick, it had to be here. A bad omen.

Gardeners came running, their heads bowed, and hurried to clean the mess before the king passed by. He left them to their work and headed for the training grounds. He longed for the familiar feel of his sword in his hands, and the deep ache in his muscles after a lengthy afternoon of sparring. His father might be able to force him to bind with Istara, but this much he could control—he would never touch her. Ever.

*   *   *

Istara gazed at her reflection in Tanu-Hepa's bronze mirror, admiring her new gown. It fell from her shoulders in elegant folds. White as winter snow, the linen had been woven with gold and silver threads, falling like rain from her shoulder to the hem. She turned, watching the material as it shimmered, catching in the torchlight. She smiled. The queen had ordered a gown for a woman, not a child. Istara's eyes had been made up, enhancing them, and a touch of color had been applied to her lips. A gold collar lay around her neck, and wide, jeweled cuffs encircled her wrists and upper arms. She could almost see the woman she was going to become in her reflection. She looked up at Tanu-Hepa standing behind her, her hands on her shoulders, a smile on her lips.

"Are you pleased?" she asked.

Istara nodded and stole another look at herself in the mirror. So pretty. She hoped Urhi-Teshub would approve of her.

"You must make certain not to get any blood on your gown in the ritual, it would be a bad omen," Tanu-Hepa said as she straightened one of the folds at the back of Istara's gown. She glanced up and met Istara's eyes. "I have sent a message reminding Urhi-Teshub to be careful."

Istara looked down at her right hand, feeling a faint sensation of unease, though not for the ritual. She had not seen Urhi-Teshub since his return from Hakpis almost two weeks earlier. She had waved at him from the queen's rooftop gardens. Instead of his usual pleasure at seeing her, he had turned away to speak to the men around him, and carried on walking, never once looking back. Since then, every invitation Tanu-Hepa had sent inviting him to dinner had been declined, with regrets.

Tanu-Hepa said it was to be expected, he would be busy preparing for the binding ritual, making sacrifices at the temple and offerings to Teshub to bless the marriage, but Istara wasn't as certain. Something felt different; he had seen her but looked away. She wondered if she had done something to displease him, perhaps she shouldn't have waved, it was quite childish. Soon she would know the truth, she could ask him at the feast. She bit her lip, trying to hide her smile as a thrill of joy rushed up her spine. Out of all the men she could have been forced to marry, the king had chosen her best friend, a man who could never hurt her, well, except for the part that was coming up.

"Are you afraid of the ritual?" Tanu-Hepa murmured, breaking into Istara's thoughts.

"A little. Will it be very painful?"

"It stings," Tanu-Hepa admitted with a sigh, "but as soon as the blood is mixed, Urhi-Teshub will put soothing oils on the wound and bind it. It will be his first act of protection as your husband. You must be brave and trust him." Tanu-Hepa's gown rustled as she knelt before Istara. "Remember, you must not pull back when he cuts your hand, it will be interpreted as a bad omen if you do. Just think of all the celebrations there will be afterward, and of how lucky you are to be betrothed to the Crown Prince of Hatti. You are fortunate, for you shall be loved."

A gentle knock at the door signaled the time for the procession to Arinna's temple had arrived. Istara hung back, the queen's words sending a sudden bolt of dread through Istara.

"Did you pull back?" she asked, pressing her palm against her dress, trying not think about what was going to be done to it.

Tanu-Hepa brushed a tendril of hair back into Istara's golden hair band. "Yes, when I was bound to King Mursili." Her eyes grew distant as she smiled, sad. "Only heartache followed after. No one doubts you are a brave young woman, but I will pray for you when the time comes, to give you the strength to see it through. Now. It is time. The goddess awaits."

Tanu-Hepa rose and nodded to her guards. The doors eased back. Across the sumptuous reception room, dozens of noblewomen came to their feet dressed in beautiful gowns, their throats and arms gleaming with gold, silver, and gems. In their hands, they carried little baskets filled with rose petals. They smiled at Istara, admiring her as they passed.

Careful not to tread on the hem of her new gown, Istara followed the queen out of her opulent royal apartments into the palace gardens. The noblewomen processed along the path, weaving back and forth in an intricate, slow dance, scattering rose petals and singing the hymn of love.

Despite her apprehension, Istara tried to remember everything, how her gown shimmered in the moonlight; the sweet scent of the rose petals as she walked over them; the noblewomen's song, rising and falling, more beautiful than any she had ever heard before.

They approached the darkened Temple of Arinna, lit only by the light of the full moon. At the end of the pillared colonnade, Urhi-Teshub stood alone at the altar, waiting for her, dressed in a white tunic, his long, dark hair tied back and held in place with a golden browband. Istara's apprehension faded. She wanted to run to him, drawn by his charismatic presence like a bee to a flower, but she kept to her slow walk, her heart pounding, overwhelmed by her good fortune. The Crown Prince of Hatti looked so handsome and strong, the most bravest, noble warrior in the whole of the empire. Her heart surged with pride. Soon she would be bound to him, would one day be his wife and future queen, and no one would ever be able to take him away from her, not even the King of Hatti, no, not even the gods.

Istara looked down at her hand, upturned and vulnerable in Urhi-Teshub's firm grip. He was going to cut it, very soon. He reached over and picked up the ritual dagger. She trembled, staring at the blade's sharp edge, glinting in the moonlight. It was going to hurt, a lot.

"Istara," Urhi-Teshub said, firm, "look at me."

She dragged her gaze away from the thing and met his eyes. He nodded at her. She understood. She kept her eyes on his and waited. He never looked down. The blade slid across her hand, burning, stinging, hot. She bit back a cry, but held still, willing herself not to pull back.

A collective sigh rose from the shadows. She blushed, knowing she had done well. Urhi-Teshub let go of her hand. Without taking his eyes from hers, he pulled the blade across his palm and took her hand in his. Their blood mixed together, warm and slippery. He lifted their clasped hands over the silver bowl on the altar, waiting for their blood to drip out from between their palms.

Fascinated, Istara watched their blood, black in the moonlight, slide down the side of the dish. Now it was over, she felt euphoric. She looked up at Urhi-Teshub, giddy with relief. She belonged to him. In a few years, when she became a woman, the full wedding celebration would take place, and she would become not only his wife but Hatti's queen-in-waiting. But that was years away, all that mattered right now was that she was safe and would never have to fear for her future again. She watched as he tended her hand, his ministrations gentle.

He looked up at her as he finished, nodding at her, acknowledging her bravery. Istara smiled at him, but he didn't smile back. He turned away, expressionless, and bandaged his hand, cold, silent and distant.

❄   ❄   ❄

A week after the celebrations ended, Tanu-Hepa took her evening walk in the gardens. Her guards had said she collapsed, falling to a strange, silent illness. Her heart tight, Istara knelt at the queen's bedside, waiting for the high priest to finish the incantations of healing and protection. At the foot of the bed, his arms crossed over his chest, Urhi-Teshub gazed at Tanu-Hepa, his expression grim. She lay so still, so pale, her breathing so faint, it was hard to tell if she still lived. The high priest fell silent. He turned to Urhi-Teshub.

"Your Highness, there is nothing more we can do. She is in the hands of the gods now."

"No," Urhi-Teshub answered, terse. "There is more you can do. Let the temples run red with the blood of sacrifices. Proclaim this day a day of prayer. Let every shrine overflow with offerings, and in each house, let every man, woman, and child pray for their queen. If we do these things, the gods cannot help but hear our cries."

The priest bowed. "It shall be done." The door closed behind him, soft.

"This is my fault," Istara whispered. "Ever since I left Kadesh, I have not been faithful to Baalat."

"Istara—"

She cried out, anguished. Clinging to Tanu-Hepa's hand, she lifted her eyes up to the deep blue of the sky, visible through the open doors to the terrace. "Lady Baalat, forgive me," she whispered. "I will make it right. Whatever you ask, I will do it. But please, I beg you, don't take Tanu-Hepa away from me, too."

Nothing happened. Istara lowered her face to the bedcover, her burden of guilt overwhelming. A creak of leather as Urhi-Teshub knelt beside her, his familiar, reassuring scent surrounded her; oiled leather, soap, horses.

"This is not your fault," he said. "I have seen it happen before. Sometimes people can recover, so long as they don't sleep too long."

"No," Istara persisted, determined to blame herself. "My mother told me to remain faithful to Baalat, but I worshiped your gods instead."

Urhi-Teshub covered her hand with his; it felt big, rough and warm. Reassuring. She felt his gaze on her, his concern.

"This house has been cursed for generations," he said, quiet. "My great-grandfather committed terrible, heinous crimes to become King of Hatti. When he died, the Wise Women foretold the gods would punish us for many years to come. You must not torment yourself. You are not the cause of this. Come." He pulled her to her feet and led her to one of the cushioned divans. "You have been up all night. Sleep. I will wake you if she stirs. I swear it."

Istara watched him as he turned and moved back to the bed, rubbing his hand over his jaw, listening to the soft rasp of his calloused fingers against his stubble. She lay back on the cushions, wondering what crimes his great-grandfather had committed. Her eyelids drifted down. Heaviness crept over her, numbing the fatigue in her aching muscles. Perhaps he was right and she should rest, just for a little while. She closed her eyes.

Istara sat up. From the terrace, early evening light filtered through the linen hangings. She had slept almost the whole day. Rubbing the sleep from her eyes, she turned toward Tanu-Hepa's bed. Her heart stopped.

Bathed in white light, the golden disk of her horned crown rising high above her, the goddess Baalat stood gazing down at Tanu-Hepa. Golden stars of light cascaded down the length of Baalat's silver gown, flowing in an endless stream. Her black hair, glimmering with little points of white light, cascaded in thick waves down her shoulders to her waist. She turned and looked at Istara, her eyes blazed, the color of gold.

Istara slid off the divan onto her knees. Baalat was the most beautiful woman Istara had ever seen, or could even imagine. She looked more real than real people. The goddess's lips curved into a gentle smile, sending little sparkles of white light darting across her face. She lifted her hand to Istara and beckoned her over, making thousands of tiny threads of light spiral around her.

At the goddess's feet, Istara prostrated herself, trembling, and waited. Baalat's voice came into her head, soft and compelling.

Daughter, you have offered whatever I ask in return for this mortal's life. If you wish to save her, you must learn to become a healer.

"A healer?" Istara repeated, perplexed, as she peeked up at the goddess. "To heal Urhi-Teshub?"

But Baalat did not answer. Instead, she reached out to stroke the queen's forehead. A little trickle of golden light left her fingertips and slipped into Tanu-Hepa's temple. Baalat smiled, soft.

To heal the one who will change the course of many destinies, including my own. If you agree to this, I will return your surrogate mother to you.

Istara didn't understand most of what Baalat said, but she understood enough. Baalat would save Tanu-Hepa if Istara learned to be a healer. It was an easy choice. "I agree, my lady, with all my heart. I will become the best healer in the empire, in gratitude and service to you."

Then, before this day ends, Tanu-Hepa shall be returned to you. I breached many boundaries meeting you here and have endangered myself. We will never meet like this again.

A flash of white light blossomed out from the goddess. The queen's apartment vanished, replaced by a formless, boundless space of gray. Beneath Istara's feet, a dark spot appeared and spread outward. Horrified, she watched, helpless, as an abyss opened under her, yawning, endless.

She threw herself away from it, clawing at the seamless gray surface, frantic. The abyss widened, tugging on her, dragging her down. She shrieked as she slid into it, her fingernails scrabbling against the impossible surface, finding no purchase. She spiraled down, falling deeper into the void, surrounded by darkness, the hole above dwindled to a tiny point of light. It vanished. She screamed. No sound came. A force slammed into her, flipping her over. Now she fell face first. Far in the distance, a tiny glimmer of light appeared. It grew into a circular opening, widening, spreading.

Shafts of sunlight pierced the darkness, beaming upward, distorted by the dense, oppressive, black nothingness. The opening widened.

She rushed toward it, crossing what felt to be a vast distance in mere heartbeats. The light blossomed outward, growing to an immense size, warping and bending around her, encircling her. She could see Tanu-Hepa's bedroom, distended as though viewed from within a sphere. She hurtled forward, bracing herself. The barrier loomed. She shut her eyes and thrust her hands out in front of her. A flash of light, so bright she saw it in the backs of her closed eyes. Then, nothing.

Istara sat up, her heart pounding, the remnants of her impossible dream merging with the ordinariness of the real world. She gazed at her surroundings, struggling to get her bearings. Out in the gardens, she could hear the servants brushing the gravel paths, smoothing them down into semi-circular designs of half a sunburst, the rhythmic swish of their brooms hypnotic. On the queen's terrace, little garden birds chirped, flitting back and forth, perching on the backs of chairs, oblivious to susurration of wails and cries rising from the city, begging the gods to spare the life of Hatti's dying queen. Several birds hopped past the open doors of the terrace looking for crumbs, eyeing Istara, chirping hopefully.

Bathed in the clean light of a new day, Tanu-Hepa continued to lay silent and still in the middle of the bed. At its foot, Urhi-Teshub looked back at Istara, his arms crossed over his chest. Dark circles shadowed his eyes.

"You barely slept an hour," he said.

Istara approached him, apprehension filling her. She would have to tell him. She turned over several openings in her mind before deciding on the simplest one. "My prayer has been answered," she said, quiet. Urhi-Teshub lifted a brow, skeptical, but remained silent. Istara pressed on, dogged, despite knowing how strange her words were going to sound to him. "Baalat came to me while I slept. She promised to save the queen if I become a healer."

Urhi-Teshub scoffed and pressed his palms against his eyes. "You had a dream, nothing more," he said, dismissive. "The gods never speak to us; they do not even speak to the Wise Women. You are meant to be a queen. You cannot become a healer; it would be beneath you."

"No. It was no dream," Istara insisted, thinking of her frightening return from the place where she met Baalat. "She said strange things about destinies and having to heal the one who would change everything. She told me she had endangered herself meeting me, and would never meet me like that again, and—" she paused, biting her lip.

"And?" Urhi-Teshub prompted, impatient.

"We have until tonight to save her, otherwise the gods will claim her," Istara finished, feeling her cheeks begin to burn, frightened by the sudden realization she had just given the Crown Prince of Hatti an ultimatum, a crime punishable by death.

Urhi-Teshub scoffed again, though he didn't say anything. He turned away, his hands clenching into fists, the muscles under his armbands rippling. He glanced at Tanu-Hepa, uncertain. Istara stepped toward him, meaning to reframe her words, to remedy her error, but he held up his hand and stopped her.

"You ask much of me to accept what you say is true," he said before falling silent, the muscles in his jaw working, betraying his agitation. He shook his head. "I cannot do that, but for Tanu-Hepa's sake, neither will I deny you. You may learn the healing arts, though I think you are just being fanciful."

Istara knelt before him, filled with gratitude. "My lord," she whispered, "if the gods have chosen me for a task, it means they have chosen you, too, because I cannot obey them without your permission."

He barked a scornful laugh. "You dare to presume to know the minds of the gods, a mere child?" He moved to the other side of the room and gestured at Tanu-Hepa. "Once this is ended for better or ill, I will leave Tarhuntassa and remain in the north. You will not see me again until our wedding, which I will hold off for as long as possible. You will not write to me, nor will I write to you."

Stricken, Istara followed after him. "I have said something wrong, forgive me. I beg you, do not cut me off. I live for your letters."

"It serves no purpose for us to write anymore," he said, cold. "My father forced me to bind with you against my will so Kadesh could never belong to Egypt again. But I will never love you as a man loves a woman. To me, you will always be a child, my little sister." He paused, his mouth twisting with distaste. "It sickens me, the thought of making you my wife. I will never know you. I cannot. I won't. If we must be married, it will be as brother to sister, our relationship chaste."

She stared at him, at his implacable expression. "It cannot be true," she breathed, "you would marry me and not know me? I will never have my own children? And what of your heir?"

"A concubine will provide one," he answered, abrupt. "My father asks too much of me and of you in his desire to keep Kadesh. You deserved better than this. I promise I will be kind to you and provide all you wish for, but there can be nothing more between us." He eyed the queen's bed, guilt slicing across his face. "I pray she cannot hear us, for this will break her heart, to know you will have to endure what she has endured at the hands of my father."

"You can't mean these things," Istara cried out, desperate. "Just wait a little, let me grow up and become pretty, like Adar. Maybe then you will like me, will want—"

His fist came down on the table. "Cease! Do not compare yourself to a whore. I cannot bear it."

Stunned, Istara fell silent. She had never seen him like this before. She wondered if she knew him at all. He departed, throwing open the doors so hard they slammed against the walls. Ignoring the astonished looks of the queen's retinue gathered in the reception room, he strode away.

Silence fell. Everyone turned to stare at her, judging her. Two guards came forward and closed the doors, their eyes lowered. Turning her back to them, she noticed the deep splinter running along the length of the table. What had she done wrong? She pressed her hands against her torso, trying to make sense of Urhi-Teshub's words. He did not want her, and would not love her. Her future lay before her, empty, bleak, lonely.

She returned to the bed and took hold of Tanu-Hepa's cold, limp hand. Baalat was real, no matter what Urhi-Teshub said. Istara had seen her, now all she had to do was wait. Tonight Tanu-Hepa would get better. Tomorrow, Istara would think about the rest.

❋   ❋   ❋

Just as Baalat promised, Tanu-Hepa returned, waking as though from a deep sleep, desperate for food and drink. Unwilling to leave her side, Istara stayed until dawn, curled up on the divan, dreaming fragmented dreams of Urhi-Teshub leaving, never to return.

She woke to the warmth of sunlight playing over her eyes. Panicking, praying she wasn't too late, she slipped from the room and hurried to the roof, her bare feet slapping against the cool marble as she took the stairs two at a time.

Bursting out into the drenching heat of the roof garden, she crossed it as fast as her legs would carry her. She lunged at a pillar, grabbing hold of it in time to stop herself from tumbling over the roof's edge. Her heart pounding, fearing she was already too late, she searched the vast palace square, bustling with activity.

She stopped. There they were, assembling outside the stables, two dozen of them, waiting by their chariots. Her heart thudded with relief. He had not left yet. She shaded her eyes, searching through the men. Where was he? She waited, fearful, maybe these were other men, and he was already gone after all. He emerged from one of the buildings, his commanding gait unmistakeable, his massive sword strapped to his back, its hilt standing proud above his left shoulder. On his hips, two daggers hung from his belt, in gold-embossed scabbards. She heaved a sigh of relief as he moved to the front of the group and stepped into his chariot, wrapping the reins around his forearms, fast and efficient.

She leaned forward, committing him to memory, for the long, empty years ahead. His powerful body, made solid after years spent on campaign, was nice, but she preferred his face; his strong, clean-shaven jaw, the curve of his lips that rarely held a smile, his dark green eyes with their golden flecks, his proud nose, and his long, dark hair, always held back with a leather thong.

Horns blasted, and she heard him shout, commanding his men to form up. She held her breath, willing him to stay just one heartbeat longer, hoping for something, anything, to delay his departure. He pulled away.

At the gates, he looked straight at her. Her heart somersaulted. She lifted her hand to him, to wave, but it was too late. He was already gone.

FIVE

City of Tarhuntassa, Summer.
Reign of Muwatallis, Year 19

Istara scrubbed harder, hurrying to remove the last of the blood from around her fingernails. From the corner of her eye, she caught Master Hurik, the Chief Surgeon of the School of Medicine, leaning over her unconscious patient, inspecting her work. He squinted in the flickering lamplight, following the long line of sutures along the man's torso. Istara eyed him as she dried her hands, nervous. It was a serious injury, a soldier from the training grounds. The Chief Surgeon stepped back, his lips pursed. He nodded.

"My lady, you have far exceeded our expectations," he said. "You are, without a doubt, one of the finest healers in all of Hatti. The gods have granted you a gift with your needle, one you have not wasted. When you have finished here, come to my office. I have something for you."

Pleased by his rare praise, Istara smiled and lifted a length of fresh linen from a neat pile to roll into a bandage.

"I shall not be long, Master Hurik."

He moved on, inspecting the work of the others. Someone must have displeased him, for his voice rose sharp and severe, full of reprimand. Istara grimaced, feeling sympathy for those still in training, remembering the days when she had faced his frustration and impatience; the humiliating tasks he meted out as punishment, her royal station irrelevant in the pursuit of the art of healing.

Something shattered. The scent of undiluted opium overwhelmed the enclosed space. Hurik shouted, furious. Opium tincture was precious, and to lose the contents of a whole vial— Istara cringed as he meted out the offender's punishment, a year of emptying and scrubbing the patients' waste pots. At least that was one task he had never given her. Perhaps her station had merited some benefits after all.

Her head beginning to ache from the smell of the opium, she hurried to lift a waxed piece of linen from the top of a stone jar. She dipped a wooden spatula into the honey and spread it over the puckered line of the man's torn flesh, to protect him from rot. She nodded to her assistants, waiting in the shadows. They eased him up, so she could bind his torso. Settling him back on the table, she looked him over, pleased with her work. Under her watchful eye, her assistants loaded him onto a stretcher and carried him away to the healing sanctuary.

She tidied her things and left the surgery, pulling off her bloodstained apron as she walked. It had been a good day. She had finally perfected her skill of sewing inner and outer sutures, bringing not only flesh but muscle back together. Today had been proof of that. So long as Baalat protected him, her patient would return to full strength.

She ducked under the exit's low lintel into the cramped, humid laundry where large vats of water sat boiling atop wood fires. Servants, naked but for a loincloth, stirred the linens, preparing them for reuse. She dropped her apron onto the pile of soiled linens and climbed the three irregular steps to the open door, emerging into the late summer heat of the apothecary's garden, her most favorite place in the whole of the school. Skirting the tidy beds of flowers, herbs, thistles, and thorny bushes she hurried through the gate and crossed the main square, passing the central pool, where the school's newest students lounged, splashing their feet in the water as they chattered and shared their food parcels during a rare break from their lessons. They waved at her. Smiling, she waved back. She remembered when she used to sit there during her first year, filled with excitement and anticipation. Those feelings had ended soon enough. She didn't envy them the path ahead; a long and arduous one. Not all of them would make it.

Passing through the grand facade of the medical administrative building, she entered its pillared hall, slipping past the long rows of desks, filled with scribes copying notes from wax tablets onto wet clay, for cataloging in the medical library. Over the last seven years, she had spent many long weeks studying in the library, learning everything from how to treat poisons, to relieving pressure in the skull. She wondered what Hurik had for her, perhaps another research assignment, she liked those. She quickened her pace, climbing the smooth stone stairs to the upper levels and knocked on Hurik's door.

"Come."

Istara slipped in. "Master Hurik, I hope I have not made you wait longer than necessary."

"Much longer and you would have." He set aside his stylus. "How fares your patient?"

"He returned from the opium unharmed. I have given him something for his pain. He should sleep now, until evening."

Hurik nodded and hefted his bulk from the stool, turning to his cupboard. He opened one of the cubby holes and reached in. "Lady Istara, I am delighted to tell you your education is complete. Tomorrow you will receive your commendation from the School of Medicine, granting you the title Surgeon, though I doubt you will ever have need of it. Also, a parting gift, from the school." He pulled out a small bundle, wrapped in blue cloth. Holding it out to her with both hands, he bowed his head. "It has been a pleasure to teach you, and to observe your progression into the healer you have become. You were just a child when you came to me. I really did not believe you would succeed, and I am not often wrong. But there it is. Here. Do take it."

Curious, Istara took the bundle from him. Unfolding the material, she found a large golden pendant nestled within, the length of the palm of her hand, shaped in the form of a staff with two serpents twining around it, facing each other. Perplexed, she looked up at him.

He cleared his throat, self-conscious. "It is said to be the ancient sign of the healer, from times long gone, when the hero Gilgamesh lived. A trader from Babylon had it among his treasures. I bought it, two years ago, to give to you upon the completion of your studies. Just a little something, to mark your time with us."

Her eyes drawn back to it, she smiled, delighted. "A wonderful gift, and so unusual. I will cherish it, as I have cherished my time here."

He nodded, brusque once more as he shepherded her to the door. "And for you, my lady, what comes next in your education? There must not be much left for you now?"

Placing the pendant back into its wrapping, Istara sighed. "There is always something to learn. The queen says I must learn Akkadian, though I am not keen to begin. Egyptian was difficult enough to master."

"Ah, but when you are crowned, the time you have spent in learning will be of immense benefit to the empire. Come, it is time for you to return to the royal residence, I have sent for your guards to escort you home. Please know you are always welcome here, your gentle presence soothes us all."

"Thank you, Master Hurik, I will visit as often as I am able." She paused at the door. "Thank you for teaching me the art of healing. It is a skill I have learned to love. I find because of it; my life now holds more meaning than it once did."

He didn't reply, nor did she want him to. She left the building, her guards flanking her, silent, protective. Clasping Hurik's gift in her hands, she began the long walk across the royal citadel to her apartments, lost in her thoughts, oblivious to the warmth of the late afternoon sun on her shoulders—and the children waving to her as she passed them by.

※　※　※

Urhi-Teshub inhaled the familiar leathery scent of the stable yard's office, glad to be home. It had been too long. To think the last time he had been in this cramped room was seven years ago. So much had passed since then. Nerik might still remain in the hands of the Kaskans, but with all the lands surrounding the city now fallen to Hatti, the Kaskans would not hold Nerik much longer. As soon as he could go back, he would finish this long campaign, and retake the holy city. He savored the thought, after more than one hundred years, Hatti would be returned to its former glory.

But, by Sharruma, he was tired, both in body and mind. He could not resent his father's command to return to Tarhuntassa, at least, not yet. After spending years living rough in the mountains, he welcomed the respite of civilization.

He bent over a basin of warm water and washed the dust and grime of the day's travel from his hands. Taking up a linen towel to dry them, he moved to the door of the office and gazed at the bustling palace square, watching as his father's nobles and officials hurried about their business, their advisors and attendants trotting after them to keep up. He smiled, wry, noticing how the years had treated some much better than others, their harried expressions telling him all he needed to know about the current political situation in Tarhuntassa.

A child ran in front of a chariot, making the horses rear, causing a ruckus. Chuckling, he watched the commotion, his hands stilling when a woman knelt before the boy, to check him for injury.

Satisfied he was unharmed, she sent him on his way and continued to walk across the palace square, flanked by two guards, the most beautiful woman Urhi-Teshub had ever seen. She walked on, gazing down at something she held in her hands, a small bundle wrapped in blue cloth, unaware of the admiring stares of those around her.

Intrigued, Urhi-Teshub leaned against the door jamb, his arms folded against his chest, his interest in her heightening. She was too far distant to see well, but her profile was clean enough, her cheekbones defined, her nose straight, and her eyebrows and lashes dark and full. She wore no jewelry; her gown plain, a deep green, edged with gold. Small and fine, her breasts and hips were almost hidden in the folds of her gown. Though she wasn't to his usual taste, he felt himself drawn to her. A servant came up to her, bowing, and held up a message. She took it from him and read it; nodding, she sent him away.

Without taking his eyes from her, Urhi-Teshub called one of the guards over.

"Send a messenger to Lady Astarte's house, asking for that courtesan there in green. I would have her brought to me."

"My lord, which courtesan do you mean?"

"Are you blind?" Urhi-Teshub pointed at her. "There is only one woman wearing green in the whole of the square."

The guard hesitated, uneasy. Urhi-Teshub glared at him. "Has so much time passed since I left men have forgotten how to obey a command?"

The guard glanced at the woman, then down at his feet. "I beg you. Forgive me, Your Highness, but I cannot fulfil your command. She is no courtesan. She lives in the queen's palace."

Urhi-Teshub turned back and watched, curious, as she moved further away, graceful and elegant. He tossed aside the towel and beckoned a messenger over.

Once he had seen his father, he would visit his stepmother, and find out who the woman was. He smiled as the messenger darted through the crowd toward the queen's residence. Tarhuntassa had become interesting indeed.

❋   ❋   ❋

Trying not to fret, Istara followed the twisting path through the queen's private gardens, forcing herself to keep to a dignified walk. Tanu-Hepa's message had commanded Istara to come without delay. Perhaps her surrogate mother was displeased with her. Istara had not seen the queen for almost a month; her work at the surgery had been taking all of her time. She scolded herself; she should have attended Tanu-Hepa. To be absent from her court for so long was inexcusable.

She came to the doors of the queen's apartment and announced her arrival, occupying herself while she waited with tidying her hair and brushing the dust from her gown. It was unheard of to go to the queen without bathing, but she dare not disobey her command. Looking down at her plain attire, Istara felt a twinge of regret, wishing she had chosen to wear a nicer gown that day.

The doors opened. The queen's steward called Istara's name. She followed him upstairs to a balcony overlooking the garden. Tanu-Hepa sat alone before a table laid out with refreshments. She gestured Istara over, a warm smile on her lips.

"You are just in time," she said. "Come, join me. I was just about to take my afternoon sweet. The bakers have made our favorite today, honeyed almond cake. There is more than enough for both of us."

Despite the temptation of almond cake, Istara bowed her head. "My lady, I beg you, forgive me for neglecting my duties. You have always been so kind to me, and in return I have been selfish, pursuing my own interests."

She heard Tanu-Hepa click her tongue, something she always did when she was amused. "You are not my nurse maid. I have more than enough women to attend me, though I will not lie, I have always preferred your company the most. Come, sit, I would like to eat this before the flies arrive."

Istara hurried to join Tanu-Hepa, feeling the queen's eyes on her as she served the cake.

"I sent for you so we could celebrate. I understand today was to be your last day at the School—Oh. What is that beside you, wrapped in the blue cloth?"

"A gift from Master Hurik for completing my studies," Istara smiled as she handed it to Tanu-Hepa. "It is the symbol of healing from the times of the hero Gilgamesh."

Tanu-Hepa held it up to the sunlight, inspecting it. "Lord Hurik is generous," she murmured, impressed. "It is a wonderful treasure. But who is to say if it is not even older? It could be from the Golden Age when the gods lived among men; there really is no way to know."

Taking it back from her, Istara cradled it in the palm of her hand, delighted by the thought. "I cannot help but imagine what path it must have taken to arrive here, into my hands."

Tanu-Hepa held up her cup. Istara filled it. The queen took a sip and looked out over the gardens, drenched in brilliant shades of purple, blue and pink. "Urhi-Teshub returned this afternoon," she said, quiet. "I received his message just before you arrived. He has requested to dine with me this evening."

Istara's heart lurched. After seven years of silence, he had finally returned. She set aside the pendant. "Did he ask to see me?"

Tanu-Hepa brushed some crumbs from the table, down to the little birds waiting at her feet. "He did not, but you shall dine with us as my attendant. I will not allow him to prolong this nonsense of his. I have a plan, or rather, a ruse. When he arrives, I will not introduce you. He knows well enough he cannot ask your name if I do not offer it, so let us see how he behaves toward you without his prejudices blinding him, shall we?"

"My lady, I should like him to know it is me as soon as he sees me. Perhaps, with so much time passed, he has forgotten the things he once said."

"Has he written to you, even once, in all these years?" Tanu-Hepa asked, soft.

Istara blinked at the blunt question. "He has not," she answered, her throat tight.

"We have one chance to show him he is wrong to cling to the past, of your being siblings." Tanu-Hepa set her cup aside. "Let us not waste it. Now, will you join me this evening, as my attendant?"

Istara bowed her head. "If it is your wish, I shall obey."

"It is my wish," Tanu-Hepa replied. "I would not have you live as I must live. Rather, I will do everything in my power to prevent it. Urhi-Teshub is a good boy, but he can be stubborn, so we must show him a way out of his stubbornness."

Istara blinked back the tears gathering in her eyes. All those years spent waiting, hoping, and at times dreaming of him—all of it, for nothing. After seven long, lonely years, he had returned and not asked for her.

Behind the queen's chair, Istara stood waiting, nervous. Tanu-Hepa had overseen every detail of Istara's preparation. The queen's own attendants had bathed Istara, scenting her hair and body with rose oil. A runner had been sent to bring Istara's best gown, white, edged in silver. Her neck and arms glittered with silver jewelry, and little sprigs of jasmine had been woven into her unbound hair. She wore no cosmetics, Tanu-Hepa decided Istara didn't need them.

When they were finished, Tanu-Hepa brought out her bronze mirror. Istara had stared at her reflection, disbelieving. The woman gazing back at her was beautiful. Istara's heart swelled with hope, perhaps Urhi-Teshub would change his mind, maybe once he had seen her, he would want—

Tanu-Hepa's voice broke into her thoughts.

"Forget who Urhi-Teshub was to you before, tonight you must see him only as your husband. When he has overcome his issues, you may recall the past, but until then, you must be the woman to the man. This is my advice. Follow it well, and he will be yours."

Before Istara could reply, the steward entered, announcing the arrival of the Crown Prince of Hatti. Istara's heart stopped, then juddered back to life. A dozen emotions surged through her, longing, hope, love. She pressed them down, striving to remain calm. She would not ruin this.

The door opened. Urhi-Teshub strode in and bowed. As he rose, his eyes went first to the queen, then moved to Istara, lingering, his interest clear. Istara felt a thrill course through her. He was nothing like she remembered. The years had hardened him; no longer was he a youth, but a man, full grown, his bearing regal and commanding. He turned his attention back to Tanu-Hepa and crossed the space to the dining table, to take his seat across from her.

They dined, with Istara serving them. She listened to their conversation, thrilling to the sound of Urhi-Teshub's deep voice, watching his strong hands moving as he ate, describing his adventures. When he was not looking, she allowed her gaze to travel over his hard, muscled body, his leather tunic taut against his chest, aware of delicious new sensations rippling through her.

She poured them more wine as they finished their last course. She handed him his cup. His fingers brushed against hers. She looked up, breathless. His eyes on her, he addressed his stepmother.

"How is it you have a goddess in your service, and I have not heard of it?"

Blushing, Istara looked away, a delicious tingling deep in her torso, spread outward.

"Am I to send a message to you in the mountains every time a woman joins my court?" Tanu-Hepa smiled as she lifted her fingers to her lips, elegantly stifling a yawn. "Ah. It has been a long day, and I am tired. Perhaps you would like to walk in my gardens? It is such a fine night."

Urhi-Teshub rose. "A walk will do me well after such a feast." He bowed. "It has been a pleasure to see you, my lady mother."

"Why should you walk alone?" Tanu-Hepa asked, rising from her chair. Her gaze moved to Istara. "The moon is full and the night is warm, on a night like this one should have company."

Urhi-Teshub blinked, taken aback. "I do not understand. Will you not have need of your attendant?"

"I have others to serve me."

"Are you willing to walk with me, unaccompanied?" Urhi-Teshub asked Istara, uncertain.

Istara met his eyes, dark green, the flecks of gold within them catching the lamplight. "I am."

A door closed, soft. Istara looked back. They were alone. Her gaze moved back to Urhi-Teshub, his longing for her plain. He touched her face, tracing the contour of her cheekbone and jaw.

"I would know your name, goddess, for you have stolen my heart."

When Istara didn't answer, he smiled at her reticence, mistaking it for shyness, his fingers drifted to her lips, tracing their outline. Istara shivered, trembling under his touch. "I saw you this afternoon in the palace square," he murmured, "and have been able to think of nothing else since, except to find out who you are. I beg you, tell me your name." He lowered his hand and caught her wrists in his grip, lifting her hands to his lips, palm upward. He kissed them, enticing her, sending shivers up her spine.

"Let me take you to my bed tonight," he whispered against her palm. "Let me love you."

He looked down at her hands as his thumbs traced the lines on her palms. He stopped and pulled back, staring at her right hand. Realizing her mistake, Istara tried to pull away, but he caught her wrist, holding her firm in his grip as he tilted her palm up to the lamplight.

He looked up at her, his face hard. "You bear the scar of binding upon your palm, and yet you would come to me? What game do you and the queen play? Who is the man she would have me dishonor?"

"There is no dishonor," Istara answered, her heart aching, taut with hope and fear. "This scar binds me to the man I love, who left me seven years ago, and has not written to me since."

"Istara?" he breathed, releasing her so abruptly, she staggered. He backed away from her, sinking down onto his chair, staring at her, disbelieving. "It cannot be. In my mind, you have always been a child, my sister, and yet, here you stand, a vision, my body betraying my heart. Even now, knowing what I know, I cannot stop myself from wanting you in my bed. No. It is wrong. I must go." In his haste to rise, he knocked over the chair. It fell against the marble floor, hitting it with a sharp crack, its gilded frame splintering.

Gathering up her gown, Istara followed after him, anxious. "I beg you, stay. Let us sit and talk. There is so much I long to tell you. I have missed you so much."

His breathing ragged, he took her by her shoulders, his hands hurting her. "No. I will not stay. I will not see you. Not now. Not ever. I carved a toy horse for you. I gave you a puppy. I washed you in the river when you wet your blankets. I cannot cross that boundary. Why could you not have been a plain woman? At least then we could have met as friends, but this, what you have become—it is unbearable. You shame me."

Pushing away from her, he stumbled to the door and yanked it open. She sank to her knees, his words cutting her deep, listening to his footsteps fade as he left her life once more. She choked, her eyes filling with tears. All those years she had waited for him to come home, gilding her heart with hope, believing he would have changed his mind. Now, she knew the truth. She loved a man who could never love her back.

A door opened. A rustle of material. Tanu-Hepa's arms came around her, holding her, hushing her, kissing her brow. Istara clung to her, understanding at all once Tanu-Hepa's awful fate and what it meant to have everything, and nothing.

SIX

City of Tarhuntassa, Autumn.
Reign of Muwatallis, Year 19

Alone in her apartment, Istara gazed at her reflection in Tanu-Hepa's full-length bronze mirror, loaned to her for this day. Istara, Princess of Kadesh, was no longer only bound but wed. She gazed down at the wide golden band around her right forearm, fastened in place by Urhi-Teshub, matching the larger one she had placed on his arm. She touched her lips, recalling the barest heartbeat his lips brushed against hers as they sealed their vows.

And now, the celebrations complete, the time had come for her to prepare for his arrival. She ran her fingers over her heavy gown, glittering with gems and tinkling with tiny rectangles of gold and silver, a tremor of anticipation rippling through her. He could not forsake her, not tonight, of all nights, when all eyes were upon them.

A knock at her door made her turn. The wife of the *Gal Gestin* entered, carrying Urhi-Teshub's wedding gift across her arms, a beautiful linen shift from Egypt, the hem and cuffs embroidered in golden thread. Istara touched its soft material. Long had she wished for something from Egypt, but she could never afford anything the traders offered. She held up the shift, examining its workmanship.

It was beautiful. An expensive gift, worth at least the price of two fine horses.

Her attendants helped her out of her gown. She stepped into the bath, letting them attend her, readying her for her husband, scenting her skin with jasmine oil. They left, indulgent smiles playing on their lips. Istara lifted her wedding gift, hope trembling in her breast. Perhaps in the last two months Urhi-Teshub had changed his mind, else why would he have given her such an intimate and extravagant present?

Before the bronze mirror, she put it on, watching it fall, accentuating the slight curve of her hips and breasts. She ran her fingers over the material, so fine it was almost transparent. She shivered. Her husband had chosen a sensuous gift.

She closed her eyes, imagining how it would be to be with him. Sometimes, she dreamed of him coming to her bed, his strong body lowering over hers, naked as he took her in his arms, kissing her face and mouth, murmuring words of love before entering her and becoming one with her. Those nights, she would wake, her body in an agony of arousal. With a whispered prayer to Baalat for forgiveness, she would touch herself and finish with a sigh what her heart began.

Taking up her best robe, she tied its sash closed, her fingers trembling despite knowing Urhi-Teshub would be forced to celebrate long into the night before coming to her. Pacing through her many rooms, Istara waited in a delicious state of anticipation; just to have him here, to be alone, together. She was determined to change his mind, and tonight would be her chance. She just needed to talk with him, to spend time with him, to prove to him she was no longer a little girl. She settled on a divan on her balcony, sipping her wine, listening to the drunken songs, blushing at the lewd phrases. Each time she heard footfalls approaching through the gardens, she hastened to the doors of her apartment. She knew her guards were watching her, pleased for her fortune. She tried not to look at them, to let them see her excitement.

The night wore on. The noise of the celebrations dwindled to the occasional shout from a drunken noble passing through the gardens. Silence descended, thick and claustrophobic. The palace slept, while she, the bride, remained alone, and awake.

Waiting by the brazier in the outer reception room, clutching her cup of wine, she watched the door, willing it to open; straining to hear his footsteps, uncertainty stalking her. She paced the rug, tracing and retracing her steps until the night guards passed outside, calling the hour.

She sank onto a divan. It was almost morning. He should have come to her hours ago. Her heart aching, she retreated to her sleeping room, glimpsing the sympathetic expressions of her guardsmen without. Her throat tight with unshed tears, she brought the door closed, quiet.

She slipped out of her robe and lay it across the gilded lid of the chest at the end of her bed. Smoothing down the material, she sensed her thoughts fragmenting, sliding into darkness. Moving to the mirror, she gazed at her hollow reflection, at her eyes, wide, haunted. Stifling a sob, she began the work meant for Urhi-Teshub of plucking the flower blossoms from her hair; dropping them one by one into the silver bowl on her dressing table, to be offered up to Arinna in the morning for the goddess's blessing.

Pulling her ivory comb through her thick hair with slow, deliberate strokes, she combed each tress until her arm ached. Putting the comb back, she stood before her dressing table, staring at it, her eyes unseeing, trying to think of something else she could do to occupy herself, but there was nothing.

Turning to the empty bed, strewn with sprigs of autumn flowers and fragrant herbs—now wilting—she brushed them aside with gentle movements, refusing to think of what might have been.

She sat on the edge of the bed, lonely, grief stalking her. Clenching her hands into fists, she suppressed her feelings, refusing to cry. He would still come. He could not shame her like this, by refusing to go to her on their wedding night. She could not, would not, believe he could do such a thing to her. Cocooned in luxury, raw with hope, she passed the time inventing stories to explain his absence, desperate to keep the awful truth at bay. She waited until all but one lamp had extinguished, before she accepted her fate, and yielded to the agony of her heart.

As the first tendrils of sunlight filtered between the hangings of her bed, Istara closed her eyes, gritty from crying, and succumbed to exhaustion. When she woke, she found Tanu-Hepa seated on the divan. She came to Istara, sorrowful, and took her hand, saying Urhi-Teshub had left Tarhuntassa at dawn to return to the north, in direct disobedience to the king.

Istara watched the queen's fingers stroking the back of her hand, feeling nothing. Urhi-Teshub's rejection was complete. By now, everyone would know, down to the lowliest stable hand, the crown prince did not want his wife, their next queen.

Clawing at the shift he had given her she tore it away and cast it onto the floor, ruined. Tanu-Hepa gathered her into her arms, and rocked her, stroking her hair, whispering soft reassurances. Numb, Istara stared at the ashes in the brazier. She could deny the truth no longer. Ever since the day she was taken, she had never been anything more than a token, her sole purpose to be used by kings to consolidate their power. Her meaningless, empty life stretched out before her. She closed her eyes, and gave in to her despair.

❄ ❄ ❄

A fresh wave of guilt pounding down on him, Urhi-Teshub looked back at the city, catching sight of the morning sun gleaming against the golden pillar of Teshub's temple. He should not have left Istara alone on their wedding night. He could have gone to her apartment and remained in one of the other rooms, sending her to their bed, alone.

Instead, he had chosen to go to the stables and sleep among the horses, where he knew no one would find him until morning. He sighed, tired of the circular route his thinking had been taking ever since he had woken. No, he had done the right thing. He had had enough sense to know if he had gone to her filled with wine, he would have taken her.

But to leave, disobeying even his father's command to remain, was too much. His father would not forgive him for this, not even if Urhi-Teshub reclaimed Nerik. He should go back, not just for his father, but for Istara. He could not leave her like this, drowning in humiliation before the whole empire. He had to try to make amends.

He pulled on the horses' reins, slowing them to a walk. It wasn't too late. He could still turn back. His men murmured behind him, hopeful. There were still two more weeks of feasts and celebrations planned. They wanted to be in Tarhuntassa, carousing, not traveling back to the mountains to continue the endless fight for Nerik. He gave in to his conscience, and called out the order to return, pushing his horses as hard as they could go, their leather-clad hooves pounding up the still-sleeping streets of the city until he burst through the gates of the royal citadel into the deserted palace square.

Stripping the reins from his arms, ignoring the banter of his men goading him on, he strode toward the queen's residence. He may never take his wife to his bed, but this much he would promise her: no matter what it cost him, he would never hurt her again.

❋   ❋   ❋

Istara stared at her reflection in the mirror, her face betraying the hard evidence of her weeping. Her eyes, swollen and puffy, gazed back at her, empty. She shivered, feeling as though the sun had fled from her inner world, leaving her lost in a realm of shadows.

She took in the luxury surrounding her, the opulence of Hatti's wealth satisfying her every need. Every need, except one. How long could she hide here, refusing to leave her rooms before the king ordered her out? A week? A month? A year? Forever?

Naked, she sank onto the divan, watching the linen hangings around her bed drift in the morning breeze, the air already warm. Listless, she followed their movements, thinking of nothing, grateful for the reprieve. Anash crept over and pressed her nose against her knee.

The door opened. Istara closed her eyes, willing whoever had invaded her sanctuary to leave.

"Istara . . ."

She scoffed. Now she imagined his voice. A creak of leather. The familiar scent of soap and horses. Fingertips, tough with calluses, touched her jaw. She opened her eyes, wary.

Urhi-Teshub knelt before her, his eyes dark with remorse. "I beg you. Forgive me," he murmured. "I should not have left you alone last night."

Her heart cold, she looked at him, feeling nothing. So, he had returned, but it was too late. He had already broken her heart, shaming her before the entire city. She saw concern flicker in his eyes. He leaned toward her, watching her.

"Istara? Can you hear me?"

Anger, hot and bitter, bloomed in her chest. She pressed her lips together and looked away, unwilling to give him what he wished for, his absolution. From the corner of her eye, she saw him petting Anash, distracted.

"You are angry with me, and I deserve it," he hesitated as he broached the subject, cautious. "But I could not come to you last night, full of wine. I would have taken you, blind with lust. It would have been worse after. Ah! I do not expect you to understand—" Agitated, he rose and paced to the terrace doors. He pulled one of them open. Sunlight flooded in, and a rush of clean air drove the staleness from the room. He looked back at her, his gaze flicking over the contours of her body, then away. "In only two months I have been expected to see you not as the child I knew for four years, whom I cherished as my own sister, whom I swore I would protect to the death—"

Istara laughed, hollow. "How you cling to the past, even when the past is long gone. Tanu-Hepa is right. You are stubborn." She stood up and walked over to him, bathed in the sun's golden light. "Look at me. I am a woman and have been for the last three years, thinking of you, longing for you. But it is over. You no longer need torment yourself for my sake. Your message yesterday was effective. For the first time since our binding, I feel nothing for you."

"No," he cried out, anguished. "This is not what I want, either. I would not have you indifferent to me. It would be unbearable."

"The crown prince has had everything his way all his life," Istara said, cold. "Taking women and casting them aside when they are of no more interest, disposable things, without feelings, existing solely for his pleasure. And so it has been with me, you knew I loved you, but you put your selfish, noble reasons before my heart and now you cannot accept what you have wrought. I am not a toy, nor were any of the other women you have dallied with. All of us, every one of us have feelings. Even as a child, I could see Adar had feelings for you, yet you forgot about her in the blink of an eye."

"Those women are courtesans and whores," Urhi-Teshub shrugged, dismissive, "it is not the same—"

"And yet, we are all women," Istara interrupted, "so it is the same."

Comprehension spread, slow, across his face. He sank onto a chair. "And so it is," he murmured, "I treat my horses better than this."

She did not answer him. Instead, she picked up the ruined shift and dropped it into his lap. Stricken, he lifted it up, running his fingers over the torn embroidery, trying to bring the sundered flowers and bees back together.

"Even if you decide you wish to have me, you never will." She went and stood by the open door to the terrace, letting the sun warm her body. "I belong to Baalat now."

He looked up from the rent shift; his eyes met hers, hard, determined. "I admit I have done great wrong, but in this one thing I will not concede defeat." He looked her over, this time taking his fill of her. "Seeing you before me like this, not only beautiful but intelligent and wise, it is fast becoming difficult for me to see the child anymore."

Istara folded her arms across her breasts, annoyed by his assumption he could change his mind, and she would come running to him.

"Before our wedding," he continued, dogged, "the queen advised me to spend time with you, but I would not listen. Now, far too late, I see you are a woman, both in body and mind." He left the chair and knelt before her. "I swear I will right my wrong and give you reason to love me again. May Teshub strike me down if I fail."

She stared at him, unmoved. "Then it is your god against mine."

His eyes darkened. "So be it," he retorted, rising to his feet, still holding the shift in his hand. "However long it will take, I will make this right. Until then, I vow there will never be another woman for me."

"As you wish," Istara snapped, irritated. "But do not fool yourself into thinking your sacrifice will win my heart, for I will never love again. I have learned the cost is too great."

"No," he breathed, taking a step toward her. "I pray you are speaking in anger. I could not bear to bequeath such a lonely existence to you. If you will not love me, then perhaps one day you will love another, you should not have to carry the burden of my crime to your grave."

Aghast, she stared at him. "You would permit your wife to love another?"

"If it somehow brought you back to me, yes. I have brought this on to us, why should I not suffer for it as well?"

Istara scoffed. "You have lost your senses. You cannot mean what you are saying."

"Then you do not know me," he replied, quiet. "Whatever it takes. I will make this right, even if I must lose you to another first."

Istara glared at him, disbelieving. He held her gaze, unflinching. "You would kill him," she spat, scornful.

"I swear I will not," he answered, steady. "We are bound before the gods. Nothing can break our bond, not even the love of another. The only thing I fear is what I am capable of doing to you myself."

When she said nothing, he went to the door, cradling her ruined shift in his hands. He paused, giving her the chance to stop him.

She turned her back, and let him go.

SEVEN

City of Tarhuntassa, Late Autumn.
Reign of Muwatallis, Year 19

Never before had Tanu-Hepa sent for Istara in the middle of the night. In her haste to obey, Istara had forgotten to put her hair up and had had to braid it as she ran across the silent gardens. At least none but her guards had seen her. Tucking away a stray tendril of hair behind her ear, she waited for the guard to push open the door to the queen's shadowy sleeping room. The guard backed away, his eyes lowered. Inside, on one of the side tables, the tenuous flame of a single lamp flickered. A soft sob slid out from the funereal quiet. Uneasy, Istara entered and knelt. The door closed, quiet, behind her.

Within one of the alcoves, obscured by the purple hangings drifting in the night's warm breeze, she glimpsed Tanu-Hepa, kneeling on a divan. The queen gazed through a lattice-covered opening toward the inky black sky, its canopy glittering with the cold white light of stars. She turned.

"Istara—" Her voice cracked. A tear slipped free.

Istara hastened to her, taking the queen's hand into her own, fearful. Never before had she seen Tanu-Hepa so undone.

"The courtesan from Byblos everyone speaks of," Tanu-Hepa began without preamble, her eyes returning to the stars, "you have seen her?"

"Only at the Court of the Sun," Istara replied, cautious.

Tanu-Hepa's gaze flicked back to her, sharp. "And is she as beautiful as the rumors say?"

Istara closed her eyes. She nodded. Silence fell, for a long time.

"And does the king parade her at court as though she is already his queen?" Tanu-Hepa finally asked.

Istara flinched, disturbed by the queen's directness. She shifted. Tanu-Hepa tightened her grip on her hands, holding her fast.

"Even though I have been barred from court for all but the most important religious ceremonies," she said, taut, "I still hear things. I must have the truth, from the only person I trust. Does he love her?"

Uncomfortable, Istara looked away.

"Your silence only prolongs my suffering," Tanu-Hepa murmured.

"I cannot say if he loves her," Istara replied, choosing her next words with care, "but there can be no doubt she has found great favor with him. I have heard rumors she is not even from Byblos, but Egypt, banished from Pharaoh's court for trying to usurp the first queen's place."

Tanu-Hepa laughed, a sharp, brittle sound. She left the alcove and poured herself a cup of wine, her hands trembling. Without drinking, she set the cup aside and fiddled with its stem. "He will send me away," she murmured, bleak. "I have dreamed of it many times since the summer. Tonight's dream was the most vivid. Soon he will banish me. Now I am certain of it."

Istara blinked, taken aback, for a heartbeat convinced the queen spoke the truth. She had seen the way Muwatallis behaved with his whore. At the last banquet, while fully drunk, he had placed his own crown on her head.

"He cannot," she said, recovering her composure, recalling that to remove a queen guilty of no crime, laws would have to be broken. Even a king couldn't overcome those. "It is unthinkable. You are

Hatti's queen, crowned twice over, chosen by the gods. No whore could ever take your place. My lady, none love her, she is a cruel, grasping, conniving woman. She has no ability whatever to rule beside the king. She is a temporary distraction, nothing more. It will pass."

Tanu-Hepa sank onto a divan and sipped her wine. Her gaze strayed to the tangled, twisted linens on her bed, evidence of the depth of her distressing dream.

"I hope with all my heart you are right. For it to end as I have dreamed, to be put on trial and stripped of my titles—" She shuddered and took another sip. "To be sent to Alasiya to live out my days alone, friendless and humiliated. Every night, to dream of him loving another, after all the time I have loved him and waited for him." Fresh tears slid, silent, down Tanu-Hepa's face. She looked up at Istara, desperate. "I loved him from the first time I saw him, when I was forced to marry his father, nineteen years older than me, who never loved me or wanted me. In those days, when Asuru still lived, Muwatallis was different. I know the love Muwatallis is capable of, have been waiting for him to see me, to love me . . . to think he could love that whore instead of me. It is unbearable, it is—"

Tanu-Hepa folded into herself, crying in earnest. Istara took her in her arms and held her. Despite her certainty, dread touched her heart. What if Tanu-Hepa's dreams were true? What would happen if Hatti's queen was sent away? Would the gods punish Hatti? What legacy would Muwatallis leave Urhi-Teshub?

Istara stopped herself. It was the darkest time of the night when the mind lay vulnerable to its deepest fears. She had learned enough from her study of medicine to know a healthy mind kept irrational thoughts from taking root, else madness soon followed.

She kissed Tanu-Hepa's hands, murmuring soon the sun would rise, and life in Tarhuntassa would go on. Nothing would change. It had been a night terror, nothing more. Tanu-Hepa could never lose her crown because she was blameless. There was nothing Muwatallis could accuse her of. Nothing.

❋　❋　❋

Urhi-Teshub set his cup aside and met his father's unyielding, determined gaze. "What you ask of me, to speak against Tanu-Hepa, to charge her with treason . . ."

"Tell me," his father leaned forward, intent, folding his ringed fingers together, "are you able to sit before me and say with a clear heart you have not seen the signs yourself? Of her allying herself with the houses of the north to raise her son above you as rightful heir to Hatti's throne?"

Urhi-Teshub searched his memories. When he had last been fighting at Nerik, he had heard vague rumors his birth mother's powerful family had been courting allies with bribes and favors across the north and east, but he had dismissed it, believing it to be stale information. For almost ten years they had sought to gather support to rise against his uncle Hattusilis, who had taken over their seat of power when Hatti's capital was moved from Hattusa to Tarhuntassa. But what his father was suggesting. No. It couldn't be.

He caught his father watching him, shrewd. It would be a disturbing development if his mother's family had aligned themselves with Tanu-Hepa and her son. Such an alignment would lead to nothing less than all out civil war—with Urhi-Teshub trapped in the middle.

He shook his head. "In truth, I have not seen or heard anything myself."

"Tanu-Hepa is clever," his father grunted, conceding. "But not clever enough. Last week, Hattusilis's spies intercepted a letter to her from your cousin. It makes grim reading. Your own blood has turned against you to support your half-brother Lubarna's claim to the throne."

Thinking of the close friendship he had developed with his cousin Sippaziti during their campaigns against the Kaskans, Urhi-Teshub dismissed his father's words. "I cannot believe it. Sippaziti would never turn against me. The letter cannot be legitimate."

"Sippaziti's seal is the first upon the letter," his father answered, stony, "then your grandfather's, followed by every one of your uncles'. They are unanimous in proclaiming their allegiance to Lubarna."

His head beginning to ache, Urhi-Teshub closed his eyes. He massaged his temples. It was a nightmare. If it was true, he would be forced to stand against his stepmother, banishing her from the empire, in an attempt to bring Hatti back from the precipice of war. He looked up at his father.

"I would see the letter."

His father rose, his tread heavy as he moved across the thick rugs of his office to one of the cupboards. Lifting out a leather scroll case, he brought it back to the table. "Beware," he said as he held it out, "what lies within is certain to take away your peace. I would prefer it if you took my word, as your father and king, but if you must see for yourself, I will not attempt to stop you."

Urhi-Teshub took the case and placed it on the table. He stared at it the ties holding the leather flap closed, hesitating, debating whether to open it or not, his emotions churning, angry, confused.

"They are my kin, my blood," he said, unable to understand. "Asuru was your wife. She gave birth to me. Why would they turn against me now, after all these years? Why challenge my right to the throne? What ill deed have I ever done to them? It is I who led them in those endless campaigns, living in the wilderness for years on end, driving back the Kaskans, bringing peace and prosperity to their lands. It makes no sense for them to repay me this way."

"The ill deed may be mine," his father answered as he gazed at the wall, thoughtful, his hands on his hips. "For these last ten years, your family has continually resented my decision to take away their seat of power in Hakpis. Of course, I gave them other, lesser cities to administer, but it seems they have not been satisfied."

Urhi-Teshub looked back down at the scroll case. "Then if this is their grievance, why now and not ten years ago?" he erupted, frustrated. "Sippaziti knows my plans, we have talked of it often enough, sitting by my campfire, how once I am crowned I plan to move the capital back to Hattusa. If they had asked, I would have returned Hakpis to them."

Silence fell. "And what of your uncle Hattusilis, once you have taken his seat of power from him?" his father asked, his voice low, dangerous.

Urhi-Teshub glanced up, wary. "Hattusilis may move south and administer Tarhuntassa, a far better prize than Hakpis by any calculation."

"Your uncle does not want Tarhuntassa," his father said, soft, though his words sliced through the air, sharp as blades. "He will not give up Hakpis without a fight."

Taken aback, Urhi-Teshub digested the veiled threat. "He cannot disobey a king's command."

"You would take away what your father, the king has given his brother?" His father's eyes narrowed, hostile.

His instincts prickling, Urhi-Teshub fell silent. Dark suspicions rose, circling him. There was more to the accusation against Tanu-Hepa than he was being led to believe. Lifting up the scroll case, he pulled the leather ties apart, determined to see for himself what his cousin had written to his stepmother.

He read through the letter once, twice, then a third time, searching for something, anything to confirm his suspicions. His eyes raked over the sentences, desperate to find the evidence he knew would be there. The words were damning, unequivocal, treasonous. Who would write such a thing, trusting it would not be discovered? It was too dangerous.

He skimmed over his cousin's seal, then stopped. He stared at it. It was not his cousin's seal, or at least it was not his most recent one. His cousin had added a trident to the hand of one of the hunters just this past summer to mark their triumph over Nerik, something Urhi-Teshub had been against since they had not yet taken the city. He lifted his eyes to his father's and rose to his feet, quivering, furious.

"You would have me stand in court against an innocent woman, banishing her for a crime she has never committed and condemn my entire family to their deaths?" he asked, his voice rising, outraged, uncaring of who heard. He threw the letter down, his hand going to the hilt of his dagger, ignoring the four *Mesedi* guards approaching him, prepared to protect the king to their deaths. "There is no crime, apart from this heinous forgery."

"You dare speak to your king thus?" His father waved the *Mesedi* back, scornful. "Do not tempt me; I can clip your wings until they bleed."

"Then do so," Urhi-Teshub said, his fingers tightening on the hilt of his dagger. "For I will never be a part of this."

"If you do not stand in court against Tanu-Hepa," his father said, his lips thin, "and support my charges against her, I will name Hattusilis my heir. He will stand with me. His testimony as Hatti's next king will be enough to condemn her."

Stunned, Urhi-Teshub stared at his father. "Have you lost your senses? Hattusilis is hated in the north; you would only give the northern houses a genuine reason to rebel and rally to me."

His father scoffed, dismissive, continuing, cold, "Think well before you answer, for this is your last chance. Do you stand with me or not?"

"She must ride you well, your Byblos whore, for you to accuse your queen of treason" Urhi-Teshub said, disgusted. "I will stand against you, for as long as I live."

His father roared, furious. He hefted the table up and shoved it over, sending its contents clattering against the wall. "So be it," he bellowed, spittle flying from his lips. "Hattusilis shall inherit Hatti's throne. Get out of my sight. I will not see you again."

Urhi-Teshub stood his ground, rigid, his own anger riding him hard. "As you wish, but I will never again bend my knee to your tyranny, or to my uncle. Teshub will protect me, for I am the rightful heir to Hatti's throne. I leave tonight."

✳ ✳ ✳

Istara smiled as Anash ran ahead into the writing room, she knew their routine well. Their afternoon walk over, Istara lay her cloak across the back of the divan and took a seat at her desk. Taking a sip of spiced wine, Istara waited for Anash to settle by her feet before beginning the translation of the three Akkadian tablets left for her by her tutor. Halfway through the first one, Anash stood up, her tail thumping against the desk's leg.

Gazing at a difficult portion, trying to puzzle out its meaning, Istara reached down, patting Anash, distracted. "Anash, lay down."

Ignoring her, Anash pushed out past her legs, whining. Istara turned around.

Her husband stood inside the door, gazing down at Anash, his expression distant and troubled. Istara came to her feet, apprehension clinging to her, they hadn't been alone together since the morning after their wedding night. Before she could ask why he had come to her he crossed the space and took her hands in his, his grip so tight, it hurt.

"I must leave. Tonight," he said, his voice clipped and rigid. "I would have you come with me. It will not be safe for you to remain here without me."

"What—"

"My father intends to banish Tanu-Hepa on false charges of treason," he continued, his words coming out hard and jagged. "He has forged a letter from my family implicating her in raising support for Lubarna's claim as rightful heir."

Istara staggered. Tanu-Hepa had dreamed true, and she had told the queen her fears were nothing more than night terrors. She pulled free and rushed to the door. "I must go to her and warn her."

Urhi-Teshub caught her arm, holding her back. "For your own safety, do not. Tanu-Hepa's fate is sealed, before the winter solstice she will be condemned and banished to Alasiya. Though I tried, I cannot stop this, even to the cost of my accession."

Istara stared at him. "Has the king gone mad?" she exclaimed, incredulous. "Who will take the throne if not you?"

Urhi-Teshub looked away, his profile etched with tension. "His brother, who seems more than willing to aid him in his treachery."

"Hattusilis. Ever the devious one," she scoffed, bitter, thinking how easily he had convinced Muwatallis to slaughter her mother all those years ago. Her husband's eyes came to hers, haunted. Uncomfortable, she averted her gaze and pulled free from his grip. "Where shall you go, what will you do?"

"I have sent messages to my mother's kin, warning them of my father's intentions, commanding them to gather their men and meet me in Karchemish." His hands slid up to her shoulders. "With all my heart, I would have you leave with me. If you will, then I will carry you to Kadesh, where you will be safe if Hatti falls to civil war. To leave you behind in this nest of vipers, alone and unprotected—" He turned away, unwilling to continue.

She went to her desk, her gaze falling to her unfinished work. Emptiness snatched at her as she traced the undeciphered cuneiform symbols—her efforts made redundant by the temporary lust of one man. No longer was she Hatti's queen-in-waiting. All her preparations, her memorization of protocol and ritual, her years of education, all of it had been for nothing unless Urhi-Teshub won his inheritance back.

She turned, catching her estranged husband watching her, waiting. She knew his thoughts. With Tanu-Hepa banished and himself standing against his father, Tarhuntassa would be unsafe for her, even dangerous.

Once again, just as when she was a child in Kadesh, her life and her path were being decided by powerful men without any regard for her feelings. A token, to be moved according to their will, or even tossed away, as was being done to Tanu-Hepa. Istara's heart constricted. She would not even have the chance to say goodbye to the woman she loved; two mothers lost in eleven years, because of Muwatallis. Her stomach clenched as old resentments, long suppressed, reignited. He would pay for this. One day, she would make him pay, twice over.

Urhi-Teshub's gaze moved to one of the braziers, his hand rasping over the stubble on his jaw. She knew his request was nothing more than politesse. If she refused, he would have to force her to come with him; he was oath-bound to protect her.

She sighed, grateful at least for the dignity he had afforded her in allowing her to consent despite his own turmoil, and for the respite of returning her to her father and home. He could have sent her to Babylon. Instead, he had chosen to keep her close and among those she loved. He thought of her welfare, even now, when he had lost everything. It counted for much.

She touched the pendant Hurik had given her, glad she had worn it today. She went to her cupboard and pulled out a dozen fat scrolls, filled with medical notes and packed them into a satchel. Hefting out her box of tinctures and ointments, she placed the satchel on top. She held the box out to Urhi-Teshub. He took it, hope igniting in his eyes.

Calling to Anash, she pulled the door open and collected her cloak. She nodded at her husband, still waiting, holding her medicine box, uncertain.

"I am ready," she said. "Please, take me home."

EIGHT

City of Kadesh, Late Summer.
Reign of Muwatallis, Year 20

Urhi-Teshub hurried through the temple gardens toward the torchlit pillars of Baalat's temple, the light of the full moon turning the graveled path blue-white. He had been asleep when Istara's message arrived, asking him to meet her in the temple's outer courtyard. In his haste, he realized he had forgotten his gift, bought in Karchemish from a trader traveling from the far east—a necklace of cascading silver, laden with creamy iridescent gems. The trader said the gems were called opals. Urhi-Teshub had never seen anything like them before. The necklace had cost a fortune, but when he saw it, he could not imagine it against any other woman's throat. He considered turning back. No, it would take too long, he didn't want her to change her mind.

Perhaps his many letters to her over the last nine months had softened her heart. She had even written him back several times. How he had savored those letters, even if she only wrote about her work in the temple, it didn't matter, Istara had written to him. It was a start. But her message tonight was another thing altogether. She wanted to meet him, alone, in the middle of the night. She said she had missed him. He hoped—

A trickle of sweat slid down his abdomen, beading with perspiration in the oppressive heat. Even after midnight, the heat continued to rise up from the city, relentless, the baking air thick with the thrum of locusts. He could not go to Istara like this. He looked around, searching the shadows for one of the temple's many pools. Seeing one a little distance away, he went to it and knelt by its edge. Cupping the cool water into his hands, he splashed it against his chest.

In the water's reflection, he caught the dying streak of a falling star. He looked up, uneasy, and scanned the canopy, uncertain whether it had been real, or a trick of his mind. Another fell, then another. For several heartbeats the sky was quiet, then one long streak slid across the full arc of the canopy. He shuddered.

"A bad omen," a woman murmured. "The gods are gathering, as men are gathering. Change is coming, whether we mortals wish it or not."

Startled, he turned and discovered a woman clad in a diaphanous blue gown, its edges embroidered in gold. She sank onto the pool's edge, her full breasts and hips visible through the thin material. She trailed her fingers through the water, creating little eddies in the pool's moonlit surface, a small smile playing on her lips. She reminded him of Adar, exotic, sensual, animal, but unlike Adar, this was a mature woman, older than him by several years, and reeking of sexuality. She continued her tracery, not looking at him, her every movement seductive, calculated.

Her voice, low, and smooth as honey, drifted across the pool.

"Were you in such a great hurry to go to Istara, you did not realize I was here, watching you?"

"Mistress, beware," he said as he rose to his feet. "Do you know to whom you are speaking as though you are an equal?"

She looked up at him, her dark eyes smoldering. She chuckled, throaty, sensuous. Despite himself, he felt his groin stirring.

"Urhi-Teshub, Crown Prince of Hatti," she drawled, languid, "do you not know to whom you speak as though *you* are an equal?"

She rose, slow. Her gown clung to her body, revealing the elegant shape of her legs as she stepped into the shallow pool. She slid through the water, closing the space between them, her steps measured, the transparent material of her gown molding itself to the shape of her crotch.

Unable to stop himself, his gaze fell to the space between her thighs, noticing the hair covering her mound had been groomed into a small, perfect vee. She stopped just in front of him. He caught her scent; opium, sandalwood, the musky scent of her sex. Her eyes on his, she slid the tip of her tongue along her upper lip, slow and inviting. His member tightened, straining against the bindings of his loincloth. Her fingertips drifted over his groin, caressing, teasing.

"I am Lady Rhoha, sister to Amunira, the High Priestess of Baalat, and Ba'al's consort in the mortal realm."

With each whispered word, she applied more pressure, stroking him, enticing him. He let out a ragged breath. He had never before known a priestess; it was forbidden in Hatti, but here, it seemed, things were different. In his filthiest fantasies, he had imagined taking a priestess. Aroused, he edged closer, letting her tantalizing fingers bring him erect.

Her nipples, dark and swollen, brushed against his chest. He cupped her breasts in his hands, feeling the weight of them, stroking her nipples until they hardened. She moaned, deep in her throat, her primal sound making his member twitch. Through the haze of his arousal, he remembered something she'd said. He pulled back.

"How did you know I was going to meet Istara?" he demanded, suspicious.

Rhoha smiled, seductive, continuing her work. An intense ripple of pleasure shot through him. She licked his nipple, sliding her tongue up his chest to his earlobe. She bit it. He groaned, realization sweeping through him. Istara had never sent for him.

"The message was yours?" he asked, his breathing turning ragged.

"You caught me," she breathed, amused, against his ear. "Now, will you accept my gift and taste the pleasures of the gods?"

Taking his earlobe between her teeth, she sucked on it, hard. The last shreds of his restraint fled. Lust, prurient and carnal, swept through him. Pulling off his kilt, he loosened the ties of his loincloth and freed himself.

Her fingers slid up and around him. He rocked his hips, moving in her grip, hungry, hot. She smirked, vindictive, and tugged on his testicles, hard. He moaned, aroused by the pain, willing her to continue. She acquiesced, and continued, her middle finger finding its way into his anus, penetrating him, pleasuring him even as she tormented him. Alternating waves of pain and pleasure shot through him, his member hard and throbbing within the tight fist of her hand.

"Don't stop," he panted, as she pressed the pad of her finger against the inside of his anus, sending deeps shards of pleasure screaming through him.

She stopped. He glanced down, angered by her disobedience. She smiled, seductive, as though she knew a delicious secret. Keeping her finger inside him, she knelt in the water, her eyes hot on his, and took him in her mouth, her tongue and lips sliding over him, devouring him. He groaned, wrapping his fingers into her thick, dark hair, watching her taking all of him deep into her throat, her expression drowning in pleasure.

Her mouth felt so good, hot, wet and tight. She sucked on him, so hard he staggered, groaning, desperate to make the experience last. Once, twice, three times she tugged on him, each time more intense than the last. He couldn't hold back any longer. He shifted his weight, expecting her to release him. Instead, she tightened her hold on him, her lips sliding over him, greedy. She closed her eyes, lost in her own pleasure as she sucked and licked him, her nipples protruding, large and erect through her gown. He realized she wanted to taste him, to swallow his seed. He let go, his member throbbing with the intensity of his release, enclosed within the hot, slippery warmth of her mouth.

He finished, panting, his jaw slack, his fingers still tangled in her hair. It wasn't enough. He needed more. He needed to take her, to be inside her. Within heartbeats, he was hard again. She led him into the shadows, to a concealed pavilion and a cushioned divan. He pulled her gown away, hungry, licking the place between her breasts, tasting the saltiness of her. Her fingers came around him again, urging him onwards.

Pushing her down onto the divan, he took one of her nipples, hard and slippery into his mouth. Parting the folds of her mound, slick with her arousal, he slid his fingers inside her, his thumb rubbing against the place of her greatest pleasure. Groaning, writhing, she clung to him. He mounted her, riding her hard until she cried out, sobbing with her release.

It was not enough. His hunger wasn't satisfied. She laughed, amused, teasing him, tormenting him. Unable to find relief, he gave in to her sordid, vulgar demands, pinching, choking, biting and slapping her, striking her so hard, her lips bled. She welcomed his brutality, even reveled in it.

Then, in the darkest part of the night, his blood burning hot with frustration and anger, she offered him her most secret place, where she was so tight, he dined on unbridled lust. He could not help but hurt her then, but she did not want him to stop, such was the depth of her pleasure in pain. Her demands escalated even as he savaged her, seeking greater agonies. Fuelled by her vicious taunts, he gave in to her, brutalizing her, pulling her hair, and choking and hitting her until she screamed in ecstasy, quaking with pleasure.

His release came soon after, the intensity of it stunning, unforgettable. Finally, he was satisfied. He had never been with a woman like her before; her appetites were relentless, insatiable, frightening. Still buried deep within her anus, he collapsed, exhausted.

He woke to the first streaks of dawn glimmering across the sky, the stink of sweat, blood, feces, and sex filling his nostrils. Rising from the divan, he looked down at the woman still asleep beneath him, a faint smile on her lips. His gaze drifted over her body, shame enveloping him at the sight of the ugly purple bruises around her neck and forearms; her buttocks and inner thighs smeared with feces, and blood. How could she have enjoyed him causing her so much pain? He looked down at himself, at the filth covering his member and groin, disgusted. He wanted nothing more than to get away from her, to wash himself, to forget this disturbing, sordid night ever happened.

His hands shaking, he pulled his loincloth around his hips. As he worked, his senses returned. What had he done? He had sworn to Istara there would never be another woman for him so long as she lived, yet while on his way to find her, he allowed himself to be sidetracked by this filthy whore of a priestess, Istara's own aunt. He had not even kept his vow for a year.

He caught Rhoha watching him, triumphant. He glared at her. "Wipe that look from your face. I concede you have seduced me. Now, name your price. What is it you want from me so this is never spoken of again?"

"Nothing," she shrugged. "Last night was a gift, a taste of what is to come."

He laughed, hollow. "Then it shall remain no more than a taste, for I will never touch you again. Your appetites sicken me."

She smiled, trailing her fingertips over the bloodstains on her cushion. "Hmm. I did not hear you complaining last night when you were buried in me, taking your fill of my appetites, relishing your power over me."

"I am not that man," he muttered, "despite what you may wish to believe."

Her eyebrow quirked, disbelieving. "If you say so. But, before you leave, I have one final gift for you, son of Muwatallis. The goddess has shown me what is to come. You shall have your throne after all—but at a price."

"And what price is that?" he asked, sharp.

"Istara will never be your queen," she answered, soft.

He narrowed his eyes at her. "You dare speak her name with your filthy mouth?"

She stretched, examining the numerous bite marks on her breasts. "If it is, it was soiled by your member, Prince of Hatti."

Her rebuke cutting him hard, he fell silent. From behind the encircling barrier of bushes, the crunch of footsteps neared on the graveled path. The footsteps slowed.

"Urhi-Teshub?" a woman's voice asked, aching with disbelief.

He turned around. Resplendent in a gown of pure white, Istara surveyed the scene of his debauchery, her gaze lingering on the bloodstained cushions. Behind her, a retinue of servants carrying food and offerings prepared for Baalat stood with their backs turned, sheltering the sanctified goods against the filth of the pavilion.

He moved in front of her, in a vain attempt to block her view. "Do not look at what has been wrought here. I cannot even bring myself to beg for your forgiveness, for I deserve none."

Ignoring him, she swept past him and ran up the steps to Rhoha. "You promised me," she cried. "You swore you would not seduce him like all the others. Why have you done this? Why!?"

"I did promise you," Rhoha admitted, a semblance of guilt flickering across her features. "And I intended to keep my promise, but the goddess came to me in a vision, commanding me to lie with the Crown Prince of Hatti. She has foretold I will be the one to give him his son and heir. The babe that quickens now within me shall be his only child."

"No. I cannot believe it," Istara staggered, backing away, horrified. "Why would Baalat betray me? I have been faithful to her, obeying her every command—"

Rhoha raised her hand, stopping her. "Child," she said, though not unkindly, "the goddess has said your husband will never know you."

Urhi-Teshub had heard enough. He lunged into the pavilion, his hands sliding around Rhoha's throat, choking her. "Cease your lies, you serpent-tongued whore," he bellowed, blind with rage. "Even if you do carry my child, he will never be my heir. Never. I will not recognize him." Through his haze of fury, he became aware of Istara weeping. He shoved Rhoha aside and turned to his wife. "I beg you, leave. If you can ever bring yourself to look upon me again, send for me, I will come." He pressed his hand against his chest. "No matter where I am, no matter how far, I will come to you."

Her eyes fell to his hand. She backed away, disgusted. He looked down at his fingers, coated in dried blood and feces. She turned and descended the pavilion's steps, unsteady. One by one, the servants followed her, their hostile silence damning.

His throat aching, Urhi-Teshub watched her go. After a year of trying to win her back, he had lost her in one night. It was over. It was—

Rhoha touched his shoulder, murmuring something in an incomprehensible language. Roaring with frustration, he caught her wrist and threw her aside. She tumbled down the steps, laughing, hysterical, her eyes wild.

He backed away. The woman was insane. He gathered up his kilt as her laughter deepened, turning malevolent, frightening him. Dread climbed up his spine. She had cursed him, he was certain. He shuddered and left the pavilion, desperate to get away from her and her taint. He could put his kilt on elsewhere.

❋　❋　❋

With Anash beside her, Istara entered her father's lavish dining room. He looked up from his mid-morning meal. "Daughter," he said, leaving the table to embrace her. "Come, sit. Have you eaten yet?"

"I am not hungry," she answered, suppressing a gag as the sharp tang of fried mullet reached her nostrils.

"No, I imagine you must not be." He poured her a drink. "Are you able to take a little wine?"

She accepted the cup, but could not bring herself to drink; she set it aside, untouched. Sensing her mistress's unhappiness, Anash pressed her nose against Istara's thigh. Istara stroked the dog's face, remembering when Urhi-Teshub had brought Anash from the north in a basket, a wiggling little puppy. It seemed a lifetime ago. Was he different then, or had he always been violent and dark, keeping his true nature hidden from her? Perhaps his predilections were the real reason he had not wished to marry her, or why he had not come to her on their wedding night, perhaps he feared what he would do to her—

"I could send you to Egypt. You would never have to see him again."

Startled, Istara looked up, catching the set of her father's jaw as he swallowed the last of his wine, the hardness in his eyes.

"Ramesses will just send me back," Istara sighed. "He will want no part of this."

Her father made a sound of annoyance. "You are probably right. Muwatallis was clever to marry you to his son, ensuring Kadesh could never escape Hatti's leash." He paced the room, agitated. "Ah! How I wish to be free of that tyrant and repay him for the crimes he has committed against us, for what he did to Azfar—"

A knock came to the door. Her father looked back, irritated as his steward entered.

"Your Majesty, the Crown Prince of Hatti has requested an audience."

Istara met her father's eyes and saw the question in his. She inclined her head. She would stay.

"Send him in," her father said, tight.

The steward left. They waited, tense. Footfalls approached. Istara recognized Urhi-Teshub's tread—strong, determined, purposeful. Nervous, she rose, hating herself for feeling the old, familiar thrill of anticipation he ignited within her. Until this morning, she hadn't seen him in almost nine months. Their journey to Kadesh had helped repair some of the damage between them, but Istara had kept herself aloof, unwilling to let him hurt her again. Then, there had been the letters.

Over the months, safe in Kadesh, her heart had begun to thaw, caught by the romance of his words. And when she heard he had returned, despite the lateness of the hour she had put on her best dress and made her way to his apartment. When he did not answer, she realized he might be coming to her. She had hastened back to her rooms, but the knock never came. Now she knew why.

The door opened. Urhi-Teshub's gaze went to her, enigmatic. Her heart betrayed her, beating faster, drawn to the familiar smooth planes of his jaw and the curve of his lips—the corners turned down ever since they fled Tarhuntassa. Despite herself, she admired his long dark hair, tied back in a leather thong, and his powerful, muscled body clad in leather and bristling with weapons; his two-handed sword strapped to his back, its hilt rising above his left shoulder, the grip wrapped in strips of oiled goatskin. She hated herself for her reaction. How could she still long for him when she knew what he was capable of?

He inclined his head to her, then bowed to her father. "Your Majesty," he said, his deep voice sending a fresh, treacherous thrill through Istara's breast. "I come to request your permission to depart from Kadesh. I must travel to Babylon."

"Indeed?" Her father raised an eyebrow. "And what takes you all the way to Babylon?"

"My lord," Urhi-Teshub stepped closer to her father, "may I suggest we hold our interview in private?"

"You may not," her father answered, abrupt. "Istara is my daughter and your wife. She is entitled to remain here with us, unless what you have to say concerns your gross indiscretion with my sister?"

The muscles in Urhi-Teshub's jaw twitched. "It does not. It has to do with matters of state and of my father's command."

"I see." Her father eyed him, cold. "One failed attempt to stand against him and you crawl back, a whipped cur."

Urhi-Teshub crossed his arms. "You hate me, and with good reason. I violated your sister and dishonored your daughter. I accept your abhorrence, even welcome it, for I deserve nothing less. But know this, even though my father believes he has brought me back under his heel, I intend to rise again and continue my fight. I will have my throne, and Kadesh can help me."

Her father barked a derisive laugh. "Your arrogance is astounding. It is clear who sired you. To suggest such a thing after what you have done. I would rather become a vassal of Ashur than lift a finger to aid someone like you."

"As would I, in your place," agreed Urhi-Teshub, unprovoked by the insults. "But, if you support me, once I am crowned I will leave you in peace to rule your kingdom. I have no interest in holding on to Kadesh."

A tense silence fell as her father considered. He nodded, terse. "Say what you have to say."

Urhi-Teshub hesitated. He turned. "I beg you, Istara, please leave us. I would not—"

"She stays," her father interrupted, "if she wishes to. You have kept enough from her already. Daughter?"

Istara sank onto her seat. "I will stay."

"So be it," Urhi-Teshub muttered. "My lord, next summer, my father intends to confront Egypt once more, here at Kadesh. He has commanded me to remind you of your allegiance to Hatti's throne."

"Our formal allegiance is still with Egypt," her father replied, his expression hardening, uncompromising. "Kadesh can provide supplies to Hatti, but my men are still oath-bound to support Ramesses."

"I cannot be explicit enough what your role will be," Urhi-Teshub persisted, stubborn. "You must deceive Ramesses into believing you will support him. But, when the day comes, you will ride with Hatti. If you do not, there will be severe consequences."

"I will not," her father erupted, bridling. "You may tell your father Kadesh stands with Ramesses, and to the Under Realm with his consequences."

"You will oblige," Urhi-Teshub answered, dogged, "for if you do not, the cost will be too great to bear."

Her father glared at him, unimpressed. "He threatens to destroy Kadesh? Let him try; we are Ramesses's vassal. Egypt will defend us."

"It will not be Kadesh who will pay, but another," Urhi-Teshub said, low. He looked down and traced the binding scar across his palm.

Stricken, her father stared at Urhi-Teshub then at Istara. "No, it cannot be."

Frightened, Istara watched them, desperate for one of them to break the lengthening silence. She rose, unsteady, filled with apprehension. "Muwatallis will send me to the gods if Kadesh does not support him against Egypt?"

The silence deepened. "No. I will." Urhi-Teshub finally said, soft. "If I do not, my father has vowed to execute all my supporters and their families. I swear, if it must be done, I will use the same blade to end my own life and follow you into the Under Realm. I will not leave you alone."

Istara choked, incredulous. Sinking down onto her knees, she stared at the stone-flagged floor, numb, disbelieving. Urhi-Teshub knelt beside her. His hand touched hers, uncertain. She pulled away, burying her hands in the folds of her gown, unable to bear his touch.

Her father cleared his throat. "It seems, as usual, we have no choice," he said, quiet. "Whatever he asks, Muwatallis shall have it. Kadesh will obey. But tell me, how does any of this help you in the fight for your throne?"

Urhi-Teshub turned back to her father. "My father intends to use my cousin Sippaziti and uncle Teresh as misinformers on the day of the battle. To ensure they do not fail, he has imprisoned their wives and children, vowing their lives will be forfeit if they do not convince Ramesses of my father's deception."

"But Ramesses will torture and kill them," her father said, perplexed. "What deception could be so important it must come at the cost of men's lives?"

"Their deaths will convince Ramesses our armies are still in Aleppo." Urhi-Teshub said, expressionless.

"And," her father asked, narrowing his eyes, suspicious, "where *will* Hatti's armies be?"

Urhi-Teshub crossed his arms, his muscles rippling under his leather armbands. "Waiting in the valley on the other side of the river behind the ridge," he answered, "ready to ambush Ramesses as he encamps his division, alone and separated from the rest of his army." He lowered his voice. "Make no mistake; my father intends a slaughter. None are to survive—not even Pharaoh Ramesses."

Horrified, Istara came to her feet. "Your father cannot force honorable men to take part in such a dishonorable act!"

Urhi-Teshub shrugged, resigned. "I have come to learn my father has no honor. You should expect this, and much worse from him in the days to come."

Her father broke the troubled silence. "And Babylon?"

"I must go to recruit mercenaries," Urhi-Teshub answered, "but while I am there I will seek King Kadashman-Turgu's support, as I now seek yours. Karchemish supports me still. I am not quite alone, and after the crimes my father intends to commit here next year, I believe the tides will turn in my favor."

"And why you must be seen as the obedient, chastened son until then," her father murmured. He nodded, slow. "A treacherous and dangerous path to navigate. So be it. Kadesh will stand with you."

Urhi-Teshub bowed his head and murmured his thanks. Istara expected him to leave. He did not. He hesitated. Her father raised his brow.

"Is there something else, Prince of Hatti?"

"There is," Urhi-Teshub said as he knelt before Istara. "My lady, it is my great regret to have lost so much at Karchemish because of my haste. I shall not make the same mistake again." He leaned toward her, his elbow on his knee, his leather armor creaking. "I cannot bear to leave you as things are between us, so I must ask, will you support me after all I have done to you, or are my crimes so great, you no longer wish to remain by my side?"

Stunned, Istara sank onto the floor. "You would let me go?"

"It would grieve me hard to lose you," he admitted, a look of remorse slicing across his face, "but neither will I force you to remain by my side as my wife if you no longer wish it."

She stared at him, taken aback, the only purpose she had was to be his queen. Without it, who was she? He looked down. A thought slid through her mind, dark, insidious. She pushed to her feet, jealousy clawing at her.

"Or perhaps you have found another," she said, cold, "someone who suits your tastes better than I?"

"There is only you," he said, his eyes meeting hers, sincere. "I did not make this offer because I wish for another. I swear it."

"As you swore there would never be another woman?" she blurted out, bitter.

He lunged to his feet, agitated. "I admit I made a terrible mistake, one I will regret for the rest of my life. I sought to remedy it by offering you your freedom, but I have failed you so much, now you only see evil in me—" He stopped, at a loss for words.

She waited, saying nothing, watching him, suspicious.

"Come with me," he reached for her hand. "I have a gift for you, from Karchemish. Let me at least prove to you it has always been you I have thought of. Always."

She pulled back. "Apart from last night, that is."

"I remained true to you!" he bellowed, frustrated. He stalked across the room, his voice rising, sharp, aggravated. "I ignored the women who came to me in Karchemish, wanting no one but you. Rhoha sent a message, pretending to be you waiting for me. I came to meet you, Istara. You! She seduced me. The whole night was nothing like I have ever known before. I only wish to forget, and never think of it again."

Seething, Istara stepped toward him. "Only a coward would blame a woman for his actions. You could have walked away, but you did not. You stayed with her. All night."

Her father's hand touched her arm, holding her back. "Do not be so quick to discount Rhoha's abilities," he said, quiet. "As Ba'al's consort, she is able to practice powerful sorcery. Though I am loathe to speak of it, she once came to me deep in the night. Under her influence, I lost my senses, reveling in her depravity and my brutality. When she left, the spell ended, and I became myself again. Everything we touched, I burned. I have never allowed myself to be alone with her again."

Aghast, Istara stared at her father. "Since then," he continued, uneasy. "I have learned her body belongs to Ba'al. His cravings have turned her into what she has become, sick, insatiable, and addicted to pain. She is lost, a slave to Ba'al's desires."

Urhi-Teshub moved back to join them. "I knew I was not myself," he muttered, relieved. "I have not been able to find peace, so deep has been my torment over what I became with her. I could not believe I was that man."

"Under her spell," her father resumed, disgust turning his mouth downward, "Ba'al overcomes you, experiencing her through you. It is he who is that man, not you. It is he she is fornicating with, who she longs for, night and day."

Urhi-Teshub shuddered, his face tight with revulsion. An uncomfortable silence settled over the room; Istara's thoughts spun away, clashing, conflicted, as she tried to make sense of her father's words. Anash stood up, whimpering for attention. Istara patted her, distracted.

"I hear Rhoha has proclaimed she will give birth to your son who will be your only heir," her father said as he poured himself a fresh cup of wine. He drained it and gazed into the empty cup, continuing, thoughtful. "In all the time she has been Kadesh's high priestess, Rhoha has never been wrong. Should this come to pass, it would give her immeasurable power over you, and one day, over all of Hatti."

"By all the gods, I will not allow it," Urhi-Teshub vowed, angry. "If your daughter will remain with me, I will make certain we will have sons enough of our own." His eyes came to Istara's once more, his torment plain. "I beg you, what is your answer? Will you remain with me, or have I lost you?"

"I must have time to consider," Istara answered, longing to escape, to have time to think.

"I can delay my departure until tomorrow morning," he said, taut.

"Then come to me this evening," she sighed, "and you shall have your answer."

She left them, her heart battered, exhausted. There was only one place she could go, where she would be able to find refuge from her inner storm. She would go to Baalat's sanctuary, and pray.

❋   ❋   ❋

Istara stirred. She gazed at the golden statue of Baalat, wreathed in thick plumes of opium incense. Rubbing the back of her neck, Istara wondered how long she had been unconscious. Her hand stilled; there had been a vision. She closed her eyes, the vision's vivid images returning, filling her mind: a tent, lit by the feeble light of two lamps. A man, unconscious, filthy, and naked apart from a loincloth, lay before her; his powerful body covered in injuries packed with mud. Two men assisted her, silent, as she washed the dried mud from his wounds.

She sank deeper, immersing herself in the vision, experiencing all of its sensations, the biting hunger pangs, the grinding drag of total exhaustion, and the stinging, bitter cold. Despite her great discomfort, she held on to the vision, watching herself working to save the man's life.

There, an odd detail: she was wearing her best gown, but it was ruined, torn, and bloodstained, and on her arms, a fortune of gold and jewels, incongruous against the misery of the tent. Her left calf hurt. It was bound up tight, the linens stained with blood, she felt the tug of sutures. The man moved, rousing. She leaned forward to look at his face. A brief glimpse, and the vision ended, abrupt.

Istara stared at the sanctuary's floor, trying to recall the man's face. Was he Urhi-Teshub? An image flitted through her mind, brief, tantalizing. She lunged after it, but it slipped away, leaving behind just one detail. The man's eyes had been kohled black. An Egyptian. Despite the heat, she shivered. An aura of prescience enveloped her. She held herself still, waiting, hoping for more.

Sensing someone behind her, she peered into the shadows, and heard a voice, faint, distant, speaking in Egyptian; two people materialized. She blinked, astonished, realizing she was looking at herself when she had been a child. Before her child-self, a young Egyptian man knelt, giving her his rations. She watched, dismayed by how thin and ragged she had been as she devoured his food, starving. His ration pack emptied, he stood and smiled at her. Istara's gaze drifted over him, curious. He was taller and bigger than Urhi-Teshub. An aura of easy confidence radiated from him. He walked away, fading into the shadows, her child self trailing after him, trusting.

Istara came to her feet, trembling, staring at the place where her long-forgotten savior had once stood, all those long years past, and again, only heartbeats ago. Was he the man in the tent? Why had Baalat shown her these things when she had asked about Urhi-Teshub? Istara shook her head, perplexed.

She waited a little while longer, but the atmosphere in the sanctuary became mundane once more. Outside, she heard the watchmen's horn announcing the evening hour. Urhi-Teshub would be waiting for her answer. She pushed the doors open, letting the hot evening air rush inward, heavy with the fragrant scent of jasmine. The hiss of locusts filled her ears. She looked back at the statue of the goddess, waiting, hoping for something more. Baalat's eyes gazed back at her, blank. Istara sighed and closed the doors. The goddess had given her answer, and it meant nothing.

Istara saw him before he saw her. She slipped behind a pillar and gazed at Urhi-Teshub as he leaned against the wall beside her door, his arms crossed over his chest, waiting. Footsteps approached. He pushed away from the wall and looked down the corridor, expectant. An attractive courtesan approached, a flirtatious smile playing on her lips.

He nodded at her, terse, his gaze moving back down the corridor. Several others approached, and each time, he looked up, expectant, hopeful, his disappointment increasing as they passed. Though she knew it was wrong, Istara felt reluctant to give up her vantage point. She continued to watch him, curious.

For a while, no one passed. He fidgeted, nervous, straightening his tunic—his best one, she noticed—brushing the dust from it, his expression tight with worry. She realized he feared she would not come to him at all, that her answer would be no answer.

She stepped out, ashamed of herself. He looked up, and for a heartbeat, his face lit up. Recovering himself, he bowed as she approached, formal once more.

Moving past the guards flanking the entrance to her apartment, she opened the door. "Please, come in. I have kept you waiting."

He followed her into her sumptuous reception room, filled with the scent of fresh cut roses, and closed the door. It came to with a quiet thud. Anash woke and greeted them, her tail wagging. For a little while, content to avoid what was to come, they gave all their attention to Istara's companion, making light conversation until Anash tired and returned to her basket, curling up to sleep.

Istara poured wine. She sipped, watching the movement of Urhi-Teshub's throat as he swallowed. From nowhere, Baalat's answer came to her, clear as pure water. She set aside her cup, catching her husband's gaze. Uneasy, he lowered his cup, his fingers tight against it.

"I have come to a decision," she said, quiet. "Too much has passed. I cannot remain with you."

He paled. Within his crushing grip, the golden cup succumbed. "I beg you," he murmured, "please reconsider."

She prised the ruined cup from his hand and placed it beside her own, trailing her fingers over the cup's deep indentations. "It is the will of Baalat. I have asked, and this is her answer."

His eyes dark, he moved closer, his chest rising and falling under his linen tunic, agitated. She caught the scent of him, soap, leather, horses. Familiar, old feelings stirred deep within, betraying her. She stepped away from him, seeking distance. He caught her, his fingers sliding into her hair, wrapping around her skull. He stepped closer, so near she could feel the heat of him. She closed her eyes and held still, struggling to suppress her feelings.

His lips brushed against her forehead. "But is it your will?" he whispered.

Before she could answer, he tilted her face up to his, his lips touching hers, gentle as a breeze. "Now it has come to this," he murmured against her mouth, "I cannot bear the thought of losing you. My wife, my queen-in-waiting, bound to me before Arinna. If it is not too late, let me love you, just once—"

He kissed her harder, his grip on her tightening, possessive. Her knees trembled, and the last of her resistance fled, her arms sliding up his chest and around his neck. He eased back, taking his fill of her, worshiping her, his eyes black with desire.

"By all the gods," he breathed, "I swear you are the most beautiful woman in the world."

His lips, gentle once more, touched her face, caressing her eyelids and brow. They drifted down to her ear, tracing the line of her throat to her shoulder. He stopped at the curve of her breasts. She moaned, caught in his thrall, sagging in his arms. He lifted her up and carried her through her apartment, kicking aside the doors, searching for her sleeping room.

He found it. Beside her bed, he knelt and lowered her onto its cover. His eyes never leaving hers, he loosened his belt and dropped it on the floor, the hilts of his daggers clattered against the stone flags. He lay down beside her and gathered her into his arms. He stroked the hair from her face, his tenderness exquisite, heartbreaking.

"Are you willing?" he asked, low, intimate.

Surrounded by his body, lost in his arms, she nodded, trembling.

He began undressing her, taking his time, removing her jewelry, setting each piece aside with care. His fingers moved to the ties of her gown, opening them one by one until the material fell open and she lay atop it, naked, shy. He gazed at her, filled with adoration, tracing his fingertips from her lips, down her neck, to her nipples; circling them, lingering until they grew taut. He moved lower, stopping just before her most secret place. His thumb slid between her legs and touched the place of her pleasure. She yelped, startled. He pulled away.

Mortified, she covered mouth, her cheeks burning with shame.

"It has been an age since I have known a virgin," he murmured as he brushed his lips against her brow. "I should not have rushed you."

He lifted the jug of wine from the side table and filled a cup. He handed it to her, watching as she sipped, his expression veiled. When she finished, he took the cup from her and turned it around, his eyes holding hers as he drank from the same place her lips had touched. She shivered, savoring the private intimacy of his act.

He handed her the wine and pulled his tunic over his head, the muscles of his chest and abdomen rippling, the lamplight highlighting the silvery lines of his battle scars. She stared at him, taken aback by the extent of his injuries. He had suffered much for Hatti.

She sipped, watching as he untied the leather thong holding his hair back; it fell around his shoulders, thick and dark. She drank in the sight of him; she had waited so long to see him with his hair down, as only a woman intimate with him could. Savoring the delicious feeling of their intimacy, she shivered with anticipation, an ache growing in her groin, intensifying. She lifted her hand to him, and he took it, intrigued. Pulling him toward her, she let him kiss her, her inhibitions melting away. Her hunger, long suppressed, breaking free of its restraints.

He pulled on the ties of his kilt, the material ripping as he shed it, impatient. Their fingers met at his loincloth, tangling, tearing at its knots, urgent. It fell away. She looked at her husband, at the smooth planes of his lower abdomen, the flat hardness of his muscles, at his erect member, its head swollen. She looked back up at him, catching his gaze, dark, hot, hungry.

His hand came around her head, firm, hard, possessive. He pulled her to him, his lips meeting hers, no longer gentle, but rough, passionate. He groaned, deep in his throat, and her body twitched in response. She clung to him, her back arched, her breasts pressed against his chest, letting him carry her down onto the mattress, sending the cushions scattering onto the floor. The wine cup toppled over and rolled across the floor, noisy.

His mouth went to her throat, his teeth nipping her. Spasms of pleasure surged through her. He moved to her breast, and took her nipple between his teeth, pulling on it, until it stood, hard and proud. The ache in her groin escalated, tightening. She moaned. He let go, his tongue flicking down her smooth belly, toward her secret place. Her eyes widened, her innocence fleeing as she writhed against him, encouraging him as he brought her, quaking, to the brink of release.

He looked up at her from between her thighs, his eyes hard on hers, the question clear. She nodded and licked her lips, hungry to taste him again. He moved up, slow, positioning himself, just as she had always imagined he would, covering her, possessing her. She felt his member pressing against her, probing. She opened her legs, longing for him to penetrate her, desperate to fill the hollow, throbbing ache inside.

He stopped moving, falling unnaturally still. His eyes unfocused. In her arms, his heat evaporated, his flesh turning colder than stone in winter. Movement on the ceiling caught her eye; shadows gathered, coalescing into the shape of a man, wearing a crown with a horn protruding from the front. Ba'al's crown. The thing looked at her, its yellow eyes malevolent, hungry. It crawled, sinuous, across the ceiling, and down the wall, toward the bed, watching her. Horror clawed at her as it crept onto the bed and slid into her husband. Urhi-Teshub stiffened, his pupils dilating, turning black. He blinked and looked at her again. Cold, malicious intent hardened his features. She shrank away from him, horrified.

"I beg you," she panted, terrified, "let me go."

He sat up, his weight crushing her, pinning her down. A brutal smile twisted his lips. She panicked, scrambling to escape. He laughed, cruel, his hand slamming against her jaw. Stunned, she fell back against the mattress, tears burning her eyes. Pain came, cascading over her, waves of cold fire. She tasted blood. He watched her, aroused, his eyes glittering. She cried out, pleading for him to stop.

He raised his fist and hit her again, sending her unconscious. She came to, his blows still raining against her head and chest, vicious, brutal. Anash barked, frantic, clawing against the closed door. She screamed for her guards, fearing for her life. Urhi-Teshub flipped her over, shoving her face into the mattress, his hands rough against her bruised and broken body. Taking hold of her hips, he brought her buttocks up against his groin. She felt his member probing against her anus, forcing his way past the barrier, tearing her open; blood ran down her inner thighs, hot and sticky. Sobbing, she begged him to stop. He laughed, cruel, and shoved his way into her, harder.

She retched, vomiting the wine they had shared onto the mattress, enduring her agony as he rotated his hips, burying himself deep within her, grunting.

The door to her reception room crashed open. Guards shouted, calling for her. She cried out again, desperate to be heard over Anash's urgent barking. The sound of running feet. Her door slamming hard against the wall. The hiss of daggers drawn. Anash growling. A violent struggle behind her. Urhi-Teshub's grip on her hips releasing, his member wrenching free, tearing her anew.

She collapsed, shuddering, into her vomit. It was over. Urhi-Teshub's ragged breathing slowed. Something dark and cold crawled over her, slithering across the bed, dissipating into the wall. Urhi-Teshub cried out, anguished.

"No!" he bellowed, disbelieving, horrified. "What have I done? Istara . . . my love. It was not me. It was not me!"

Ordering the soldiers to find a surgeon, he fell to his knees, his hands shaking as he tried to wipe the blood away, still pouring from her bottom. Sobbing, grieving, cursing, he ran his fingers over her injuries, vowing to kill Rhoha for what she had done to them.

Istara closed her eyes, her body drowning in a sea of pain, its dark waves lapping against her, sharp and cold. Darkness beckoned. She clawed her way to it, desperate to escape; her husband's pleas for forgiveness following her as she crawled, battered and broken into oblivion.

❋ ❋ ❋

Urhi-Teshub lowered the note, his throat tight. He had broken two of Istara's ribs and beaten his beautiful wife's face into an unrecognizable pulp. The violence he had done to her had given her blood sickness. She had fallen to a raging fever. She might not live. By Amunira's command, he was forbidden to see her. Maddened by grief, he searched for Rhoha, tearing the temple apart. When he learned she had fled Kadesh for a destination unknown, he raged, uncontrollable, destroying everything in sight. It took six guardsmen to contain him.

Desperate to bring his wife back from the brink of death, he sacrificed a dozen bulls to Teshub, bought with the last of his gold. He wouldn't eat, and slept only in broken snatches, waking whenever he heard footfalls approach. For five days and nights, as the surgeons remained by her side, dosing her with willow bark and opium, he remained on the temple's cold stone floor, keeping vigil, praying for a miracle.

On the sixth day, Amunira sent for him. The message was brief. Istara would live and was asking for him.

Flanked by two guards, Urhi-Teshub walked through the rooms of Istara's apartment, recalling how he had carried his wife, trusting in his arms to her bed. He stopped at the threshold of her sleeping room, the memory of how he had left her returning, vivid, brutal.

He willed the image away, forcing himself to look at her, fragile and still against the bed's white linens; the air thick with incense and the scent of roses. Amunira stood over her, gazing at her swollen, bruised and broken face.

She stirred. Her eyes, swollen almost shut, opened a crack.

Hesitant, Urhi-Teshub moved closer, his guards followed him, alert, gripping the hilts of their daggers. He sank down beside her, taking in her injuries, sickened by what his hands had wrought.

"I will make this right," he vowed, tears burning in his eyes. "I swear it."

Her lips moved, swollen and scabbed. "I cannot remain with you," she rasped. A tear slipped from the corner of her eye, sliding down the side of her ruined face onto the cushion. "I loved you," she whispered. "So much."

He choked, waves of loss and regret crashing over him. At a signal from Amunira, the guards took hold of his arms and hoisted him to his feet, escorting him back to the door. Amunira moved in front of him.

"I have read your messages," he said, "and I believe you. Go to Babylon. When I find Rhoha, I will imprison her until your return, so you may punish her as you see fit. I owe you this much at least, for what has been done to you, and to my daughter."

Urhi-Teshub nodded, though it was too little, too late. He paused at the door.

"I accept I have lost Istara," he murmured, his throat tight with grief, "but when I die, I swear I will wait for her at the threshold of the Under Realm so I may protect her against the dangers she will face as she journeys toward the Immortal Realm. I might have lost her in life, but in death there still remains the hope I might make amends."

"What grieves me most," Amunira said, grim, "is I believe you."

Urhi-Teshub caught Istara watching him, fresh tears leaking from her eyes. His heart aching, he turned and walked away.

NINE

The Immortal Realm

Baalat leaned over the vision pool, intent, watching as Urhi-Teshub took refuge in a quiet alcove. He fell to his knees and wept, grieving, begging Teshub to restore Istara's heart to his. She glanced up as her consort, Horus, entered the hall, a small smile lifting the corners of his lips.

"You must be bored, to come here." He moved to her, curious. "What are you watching?"

She turned away. Without her gaze upon it, the scene faded, and the surface of the pool solidified, turning silver.

"Nothing of interest."

He lifted his hand to her, and she went to him, letting him take her into his embrace, his lips meeting hers, as fierce as the first time they touched, eons ago. He broke away, nodding at the pool.

"The others are talking, saying you are spending too much time here. You know it is useless to watch. You only torment yourself, seeing what we no longer have."

Baalat scoffed, dismissive. "I was curious to see what the mortals have made us into. I have a new name now, in the empire called Egypt, I am Hathor."

"And, are you still my consort, or have you gone to another?"

Baalat smiled. "I am still yours."

"At least our love remains sacred," Horus said, dry, eyeing the dormant vision pool, "even when all else is lost."

As he led her from the room, Baalat looked back, her heart filled with longing. Soon, she promised herself, she would return.

Hundreds of thousands of years ago, soon after their self-imposed exile, she had created the vision pool, yearning for the mortal realm. In its awakening, the pool had granted her a gift. She had seen the future. Her future. At first, she had been afraid, but as the epochs passed, she found her feelings shifting toward anticipation, then impatience.

At long last, the mortal Istara, had been born, and Baalat had watched her grow into a woman, suffering each agony with her, locked inside the immortal realm. Now, after eons of waiting, the time was approaching when everything would change.

Soon, Istara would set Baalat free.

PART II

EMPIRE OF EGYPT

Autumn 1275 - Late Spring 1274 BCE

ONE

City of Waset, Autumn.
Reign of Ramesses II, Year 5

"In the beginning, there was no land; the whole world was nothing but water. From outside the heavens, the Great God Re-Atum spoke the secret word, forming the foundation of the world. Deep below the surface of the primordial waters, a small hill awakened and began to rise.

"After an eon, the hill grew into a mountain and breached the surface of the waters, a solitary pyramid. Re-Atum entered the heavens and rested upon it, thinking of all he wished to create. When he was ready, he spoke a secret word. The mountain's foundation lifted from the four corners of the world, rising through the waters, becoming valleys, plains, deserts, and cliffs, the waters draining into the depths between them.

"But the land was barren, so Re-Atum covered it with grasses, flowers, and trees. Pleased with his work, he spoke another secret word and brought forth the birds, to fill the sky with color and song, and from within the waters of the river, the creatures who breathe the wet air sprang to life.

"He spoke the final secret word and brought forth the gazelles, and lions, and all the living things which breathe the dry air. He looked upon his creation and was filled with joy. From this sacred mountain top—the first pyramid—Re-Atum brought forth life from nothing.

"His heart was so overcome with joy, he wept. His tears fell to the earth, mixing with the dust. Out of the mixture, beautiful men and women rose to their feet. But these men and women had not been created with a secret word, so they were flawed. Re-Atum could not see them, and they could not see him or understand the wisdom of his creatures.

"Because the men and women were flawed, they became hungry and cold. They longed for the flesh and skins of the wise animals, so they slaughtered them.

"When Re-Atum discovered what had been done to his companions, he fell to his knees and tore his garments to shreds. Who would dare destroy what he had created? Filled with wrath, he spoke the secret word to bring to life a daughter to avenge him. From out of the ground, the lion-headed goddess Sekhmet rose, growling.

"She ran, roaring, after the men and women, hungry for their blood. Astonished to see a woman with the head of a lion, they fell to their knees, worshiping her. Sekhmet read their thoughts and understood what her father could not. She decided to spare them and teach them the way of the Creator, so they might atone.

"Though the men and women were blind to the wisdom of Sekhmet's teachings, they were willing to obey. As they studied her teachings, and their hearts opened, it became their greatest hope to be able to commune with Re-Atum as they could with Sekhmet, sharing in the wisdom of the other creatures.

"For one thousand years, under Sekhmet's guidance, they labored to build a vast temple to honor Re-Atum. When all was ready, they raised an obelisk in the temple's center court, marking the place where they had first awakened, its golden cover reflecting the brilliance of Re-Atum's light. They waited, hoping, and praying for Re-Atum to notice their monument to him, but because their hearts were still impure, he could not see them. Then, one terrible day, still heartbroken from the loss of his companions, Re-Atum stepped onto his barque and sailed into the heavens, leaving them behind, unseen and unheard.

"In a sacred court, far to the north of Waset, at Iunu, there stands an ancient weathered obelisk still capped with gold. No one knows how old the obelisk is, but the sages say it must be hundreds of thousands of years old. It is said this obelisk may be the very one raised by the first men and women to atone for their crimes. If this is so, then Iunu is the place where Re-Atum himself once cried with happiness, bringing us to life, flawed though we are.

"Since he left and ascended to the heavens, the ancient texts have taught our true purpose is to purify our hearts, so when the Creator sails in his sky barque, he will be able to see us. On that day he will descend from the heavens, and walk among us, granting us the wisdom of his first creations. Together we shall walk through scented gardens, side by side with the gods and goddesses, and speak of wondrous things. Egypt will be filled with peace, wisdom, and understanding, once more becoming the beloved home of Re-Atum."

Meresamun's voice faded away. Utter silence descended on the banquet hall. She bowed, her golden hairband glittering in the torchlight, and backed away from the royal platform.

"Priestess of Sekhmet," Pharaoh Ramesses called from his throne, imperious. "You will wait."

Meresamun stopped, uncertain.

Ramesses rose and descended the steps of the platform. He circled the priestess, appraising her. Taking hold of her chin—the golden armbands on his forearm and biceps gleaming in the torchlight—he tilted her face up so he could see her. She kept her eyes lowered. On each of her eyelids, someone had painted the eye of Horus, the effect pleased him well.

"Look at me."

The smallest shake of her head. "Your Majesty. It is forbidden."

"I command it."

Hesitant, her eyes met his. He caught his breath. Blue, the color of lapis lazuli. How rare. The scent of her washed over him—lilies, his favorite. He looked over the hall at his guests, watching, excited, whispering, hoping he would do something outrageous. He would not let them down.

"Priestess of Sekhmet," he said, raising his voice so all could hear, "in your telling, you have given the creation story beauty and life, moving our heart as it has never been moved before. We cannot let such a telling go unrewarded. Therefore, you shall have anything you wish." He heard the gasps, rippling outward. They would talk about this for the next week. He hoped she asked for something extravagant so he could show his wealth. She trembled in his grip, terrified. He leaned closer. "Whatever you ask, it will be yours. Do not be afraid."

"Great Pharaoh, Blessed of Re," she whispered, so low he had to strain to hear, "if it pleases you, I would have my freedom."

"The temple sent a slave to tell our creation story?" he asked, incredulous.

Those closest to the royal platform heard him, their murmurs, fearful, spread through the hall.

"I . . ." she faltered, quaking.

He half-turned, taken aback, catching his wife, Nefertari glancing at her sister, Imtes, smug, savoring his sudden humiliation. He bristled. How dare she.

"We have promised what you wish," he called out, catching his wife's eye, his heart cold, "and so you shall have it. It is done. Meresamun, Priestess of Sekhmet, you are free. The papyrus naming you a full citizen of Egypt will be sent to the temple tomorrow."

A collective sigh of relief rippled through the hall. Shouts of approval filled his ears; fists pounded against tables. Laughter. He ignored his guests, watching Nefertari as the color drained from her face. She looked away, disgusted. Good.

He turned back to the priestess who stood swaying, overcome, and took her arm. "You must stay for the banquet, as our guest." He escorted her to his oldest, most trusted friend, seated close by. "Lord Ahmen-om-onet, Meresamun, Priestess of Sekhmet will join you at your table."

Ahmen's eyes lit up. In his haste to rearrange his table, he knocked over a cup of wine. Ramesses turned away, amused. Never in his life had he seen Ahmen lose his composure. His mood improving, Ramesses returned to his seat and raised his gold-embroidered napkin into the air, holding it high. A hush fell. He could feel everyone's eyes on him, waiting, expectant. He let it go. It fluttered to his feet. Horns blared. His guests roared, cheering and clapping, welcoming the start of the feast.

From the shadows of the pillared hall, servants emerged carrying golden platters laden with sweet and savory breads, and from the perimeter, the soothing chords of harpists eased in between the conversations and laughter.

Ramesses leaned back, pleased, looking over his guests, wearing their finest, mingling, toasting, and greeting one another. Henufkhet, his steward, approached, offering a selection of delicate breads. Ramesses chose a piece and took the first bite of the feast, granting his subjects permission to join him. They cheered and raised their cups to him.

Idle, he sipped his wine, watching Meresamun as she looked around, filled with wonder, staring at the women's finery, holding a drooping piece of bread to her lips. He felt a familiar stirring within, a longing. She was extraordinary, untouched, delicious. He knew he wanted her for himself, to take her to his bed, where he could watch her beautiful mouth moving as she told him more stories. He stopped himself. She belonged to Sekhmet. Not even he, a pharaoh could trespass there. The hall's great doors opened; he turned his attention to it, grateful for the distraction,

The outline of a tall, powerful man appeared in the corridor, sending a ripple of excitement through the crowd as Egypt's commander, Sethi, entered, resplendent in his finest kilt, wearing golden armbands embossed with the Eye of Horus. Ignoring their husbands, the women preened, trying to catch the eye of the enigmatic hero of Egypt.

Sethi was never late. Ramesses knew there would be a reason, and a good one. He lifted his hand, permitting Sethi to join. His commander bowed low, his fist against his chest, the rings on his fingers gleaming. He retreated to the back of the hall, taking an empty table. Before long he was surrounded by admirers, male and female, vying for his attention.

Ramesses watched, uneasy, as his commander made polite conversation, turning his cup round and round in his hands, his wine untouched. Ramesses recognized that behavior. Something was wrong. He sent Henufkhet to him.

He waited, as his steward worked his way through the vibrant, noisy crowd and delivered the message. *Tomorrow, after the lion hunt. My private office.*

Sethi looked up and nodded, his dark eyes sharp with warning. Ramesses dithered. Perhaps he should meet him now. No. If he left, the feast would end. His subjects had waited weeks for this celebration.

He settled back in his seat. There was always something demanding his attention. He had to stop and enjoy himself sometime. He would have this night and celebrate his successful campaign in Amurru. Tomorrow, as planned, he would go on the lion hunt. Then, he would face his responsibilities. Whatever Sethi knew, it could wait a day.

The second course of fish arrived. Ramesses looked over the trays, deciding which piece he would take when he glimpsed Ahmen leaning toward Meresamun to tip a morsel of almond bread into her mouth. Ramesses narrowed his eyes. Was Ahmen *flirting*? Ahmen's fingers touched Meresamun's lips, intimate. She licked them, by accident. She pulled away, blushing and covered her mouth, shy. Jealous, Ramesses watched his friend—once more exuding his usual charm and elegance—pour Meresamun more wine.

Ahmen held out the cup, his fingers lingering on hers as he passed it to her. Ramesses scoffed. Ahmen *was* flirting, the scoundrel. Meresamun pointed at the embroidered hieroglyphs on Ahmen's kilt, tracing their outlines, following the length of his thigh, her actions innocent and seductive all at once. Ahmen's eyes darkened, aroused. Spikes of envy pierced Ramesses. He sent the fish away, no longer hungry. *He* was the one who had freed her. He finished his wine, and waited, impatient, for Henufkhet to pour another.

The feast progressed. Ramesses continued to drink. Trying to ignore Ahmen and Meresamun, he occupied himself searching for a woman to share his table, and later, his bed. There were several tempting candidates. One met his eyes, brazen, daring. She ran her fingers over her bare breasts, her nipples covered with little disks of gold. He almost sent for her, but then Meresamun laughed, and his gaze snapped back to her, hungry. She was the one he wanted. No one else would do.

He felt the judgmental eyes of his vizier, Paser, watching him, alone at his table, sober and boring, as always. Ramesses raised his cup, unsteady, in a toast, the wine sloshing over his hand. Paser raised his cup in return, his face impassive. He knew Paser disapproved of his whoring, especially in front of Nefertari, but that grievance was old. Paser had brought it up, once, years ago, to his detriment. He had learned never to mention it again.

Ramesses drank, on and on, sinking deeper into the comforting arms of the wine. Meresamun was clapping, delighted as Ahmen acted out an animated tale. Ramesses scoffed, certain Ahmen was telling the only humorous anecdote he knew; the one about the donkey and the oarsman. Ramesses emptied his cup and held it out for Henufkhet to refill. Meresamun was still clapping and laughing. Ramesses continued drinking, bitter. The story wasn't that funny.

The night wore on. Ramesses realized he was drunk. It felt good. He felt good. He turned and looked at his wife. Her table overflowed with platters, all of her food untouched. She sat, quiet, her hands in her lap, watching the guests. She looked tired. Imtes offered her some wine, Nefertari shook her head, waving it away.

A glimmer of understanding flickered. Remorseless, he stamped it out, denying it the chance to ignite. Hers was the lesser suffering. Nefertari's lot was to envy other women, while he was being forced to envy a god—there could be no comparison.

His appetite returned in time for the last course, the sweet. He ate, ravenous. Dancers filtered through the guests, making their way to the open space before the thrones. They took up their positions. The harps quietened. The guests lowered their voices. Someone belched, so loud, it echoed. Giggles erupted. Drunken shushes. Quiet fell. Hidden within the smoky plumes of the burning incense, the sensual sounds of an arghul pipe rose. The dancers began to move.

Ramesses leaned back, his cup cradled in his hands, following the seductive poses of the men and women, his gaze straying to Meresamun watching them, her lips full, slightly parted, aroused. The dance sped up, and the dancers' moves progressed to a fantastic display of acrobatics, accompanied by the beat of a dozen drums. An intense crescendo brought the dance to an explosive ending as the acrobats somersaulted high in the air. One of them landed on the royal platform, right in front of Nefertari. The dancers stood still for a heartbeat, like statues, then came to life, bolting away. Taking up baskets of flower petals, they scattered them through the crowd as they ran back into the pillared shadows. The hall erupted in thunderous applause. Laughter and shouts of approval filled the hall.

Ramesses drained the last of his wine, his gaze gravitating back to Meresamun, laughing, her eyes bright as Ahmen plucked rose petals from her hair.

His head throbbing, Ramesses rose and lowered his hand to Nefertari. She joined him, subdued. He staggered, her hand tightened on his, holding him steady.

He ignored her and glanced back at Ahmen's table. It was already deserted. A lone flower petal slipped free of the table and drifted to the floor. The sight depressed him. He turned, his gaze raking over the throng making their drunken way toward the vestibule. There they were—hurrying to the front of the press—Ahmen's hand resting on the hollow of Meresamun's back, guiding her.

Her body was so full. How could he have forgotten that? Ramesses closed his eyes, imagining removing her gown, carrying her naked to his bed—

"My lord?"

Annoyed, he yanked Nefertari to him. She stumbled against him. He shoved her back, rough. "First of all queens," he sneered, contemptuous, as she struggled to gain her balance, "the pharaoh cannot help but envy Sekhmet tonight."

Nefertari blinked at his blatant humiliation. "It is dangerous to attract the anger of the gods," she said, rallying, though her voice trembled, "especially for the pharaoh."

He ignored her rebuke. He was the king; no one could tell him what to do. He looked her over. She would suffice. "Come to my apartment. Do not keep me waiting."

She left, her head bowed. He knew she knew what he intended, to use her in place of the woman he wanted, but he didn't care. He could have sent for any one of his women. She should be grateful.

The image of Meresamun, naked, slid back into his thoughts. He licked his lips. He had her in his arms now, his body covering hers. He entered her, making love to her, imagining the feel of her full, seductive lips pressed against his. His member stirred, awakening, despite the wine.

He closed his eyes and forced the images away. He was insane; he had to forget her. She was forbidden, even to him. Drunk, he cursed the gods, and went to fuck his wife.

✳   ✳   ✳

Ahmen went to the terrace's wooden shutters and cracked open a panel. Cool night air washed over him. He opened the panel wider, to cleanse the room of the smell of sex. A beam of moonlight cut across the floor, leading to his bed; where drunk with wine and desire, he had committed a terrible crime.

He paced, crossing and re-crossing the moonbeam, shimmering motes of dust spiraling in his wake. His tangled thoughts collided, condemning him. It was more than lust, why he had taken her, despite her obvious appeal. She matched him. He felt alive with her. Connected. And she was clever. The women he usually bedded were vapid and uninteresting beyond the shape of their breasts and the fullness of the hips. They all wanted one thing—not Ahmen himself—but to be the wife of the closest friend of Ramesses. Ambitious, social climbing, empty-headed women. And then Meresamun happened.

She had stolen his heart halfway through the telling of the creation myth. He had already fallen in love with her before she even came near him. A priestess. He shook his head. Typical.

He shouldn't have brought her to his villa. He should have taken her straight to the temple and said goodbye to her forever, grateful for their brief time together. But no, his feet went the other way, to the district of the high nobility, and before he knew it, they were in his villa, in his sleeping room, naked, making love. It had been perfect.

Movement came from the bed. Meresamun sat up, her hair tumbling over her full breasts. He watched, entranced, as the linen sheet slid down to her hips.

"Ahmen?" she called out, soft.

He crossed the room and knelt beside her, drinking in the sight of her.

Her fingers traced the contours of his jaw. "I must return," she sighed as she slid from the bed, her nakedness enhanced by the moonlight.

Ahmen moved aside and picked up his kilt, pleating its folds around his hips, watching as she lifted her dress from the floor and tied it in place, her movements precise, elegant, regal.

"I wish we could see each other again," she murmured, catching his eye.

"You are a free woman," Ahmen said as he fastened his belt. He smiled at her. She looked away, biting her lip. Thinking perhaps she didn't fully understand the legality of Ramesses's gift, he explained: "Once you have the papyrus, no one can forbid you to leave the temple, unless—" He stopped. He didn't want to know if she had given herself to Sekhmet, a different problem altogether.

Her gaze lifted to the diagonal scar slicing across his chest. She trailed her fingers along it.

Ahmen looked down, then back at her. "A Libyan blade," he said, recalling the moment it happened, the brutal agony of his flesh tearing open, his muscles sundered, his organs exposed, how he'd believed he would not survive.

"A terrible injury," she whispered. "The gods protected you."

"And . . . do they still?"

She sank onto the side of the bed and patted the mattress. He joined her.

"I was not always a slave," she said, her eyes meeting his, dark. "When I was a child, my father, a rich and powerful prince of Babylon angered our king. In retribution, my sister and I were taken away, placed with a great caravan and sent to Egypt—part of a diplomatic gift from Babylon's king to yours.

"My sister, fifteen years old and beautiful beyond compare, became Pharaoh Seti's concubine, and I, at five, went to Sekhmet's temple to serve the goddess. I felt no gratitude for being spared a life of menial servitude, only anger. I refused to accept my lot, scorning the kindnesses of the priestesses who cared for me. So, I was punished, and often."

She paused. Her fingers, which had been tracing the folds of her gown, stilled. Ahmen waited, sensing Meresamun was leading him down a path of no return. He hoped he was wrong.

"Three years later," she continued, "my sister, a favorite of Pharaoh Seti, came to visit me. She told me she had asked him to free me and send me home. He had laughed and said a pharaoh never releases slaves, Egypt's greatest commodity. She said she had done all she could and told me to focus on being a dutiful servant, to accept my life in Egypt.

"Six months later, she died giving birth. I never felt as alone as I did then. I gave in to my fate, and in time found a small measure of peace in my new life. The years passed and the rhythm of the temple became my whole world. Then tonight, when the priestess who was to go to the banquet fell ill, I was sent in her place."

Ahmen braced himself. He knew what was coming. Even so, he could not bring himself to regret his actions even as he spiraled toward his destruction. Their souls had touched, and he had been whole, just for a little while. No matter what she said next, having her in his arms had been worth it.

"Tonight I left the sanctuary of the temple's walls for the first time in eighteen years," Meresamun sighed, her fingers straying back to the folds of her gown, pressing them down. "I knew nothing of the pharaoh's court, or of men, or how my heart could tremble in the presence of one. Thus how could I have imagined such a thing: by the simple telling of the creation story, I would be granted my freedom and be sitting here beside you, a known woman?"

Ahmen took her hands in his. "Meresamun, have you—?" He stopped. She looked back at him, stricken.

"Less than a month ago," she whispered, "I performed the ceremony and gave myself to Sekhmet. I realise now I should have told you."

Ahmen sensed a door slam closed behind him. There was no going back. He had stolen from the goddess. Death was the penalty. Forever cut off from his safe, ordered world, he entered the shifting, treacherous world of chaos. Meresamun's fingers touched his arm.

"I went willing to your bed," she said, quiet. "I longed for you to know me. The fault and guilt are mine to bear. I chose this. I wanted it. I am ready to suffer for what I have done."

He covered her fingers with his hand, protective. Her honor took his breath away. He knew now, more than ever, his heart could never belong to another. "No, the guilt is mine," he said, firm, refusing to allow her to carry the burden of their crime alone. "I knew better. I will pay the price. Restitution can be made."

He went back to the shutters and gazed down at the waters of the lotus pool, sparkling, innocent, in the moonlight. What was he saying? Meresamun belonged to Sekhmet. There was nothing he could do, restitution at this point was impossible. The temple would execute both of them; even Ramesses could not protect them. A dark thought skittered across the surface of his mind, the dishonor of it blinding him. He looked back at Meresamun, an enslaved princess, doomed to a brutal death for the unforgivable crime of loving him. He could not let her die; he had to stop it.

"Does anyone else know?" he asked, his words gritty with shame.

"No," Meresamun answered, moving to join him at the shutters. "I performed the ceremony alone. Why?"

If no one knew . . . he plunged into the darkness.

"Once you have the papyrus from the pharaoh," he said, striving to overcome his dread for the crime he knew he was about to commit, "tell the high priestess you intend to leave. Pack your things and return here. No one must ever know of your ceremony. Today, I must accompany Ramesses on the lion hunt. But when I return, I will offer restitution for the temple's loss. No one needs to die."

"The goddess knows," Meresamun whispered, reaching up to caress his cheek. In the moonlight, he saw his troubled eyes reflected in hers. "If the temple does not exact my punishment," she said, soft, "Sekhmet will."

"No," he murmured, anguished, taking her into his arms, holding her tight against him, fierce. "I will remedy this, I swear it. Somehow I will find a way to make this right."

TWO

Bored of staring at the hieroglyphs painted across the ceiling, Ramesses tore at the sheet caught around his waist, irritable. Despite Nefertari's visit, and having taken enough wine to fell an ox, sleep still eluded him. It was the priestess, he was certain of it. He couldn't stop thinking about her.

He slipped out of the bed and pushed aside the gold-embroidered linen hanging separating his sleeping room from the main apartment, thinking of what he had done during his wife's brief visit; tearing her gown open and pushing her onto the bed, taking her from behind, rough, brutish. He might even have hurt her. When he had finished, he had left the bed and commanded her to leave, listening, impatient as she gathered the remnants of her ruined gown around her, her breathing ragged.

He rubbed his hand over the firm muscles of his abdomen, experiencing a rare twinge of shame. He had used Egypt's first queen as though she was less than Waset's lowliest whore. Nefertari, the woman he once loved to the exclusion of all others—when he was still capable of love. If not for his father, perhaps he would still love her.

It was . . . he closed his eyes and calculated the numbers, twelve, no, thirteen years ago. He was fifteen, wed to Nefertari for just a handful of months when his father summoned him before the high council and forced him to endure a humiliating lecture before Egypt's elite.

My son, why have you not sent for any of the women from the harem I gifted you at your wedding? Could it be because you are in love with your wife?

Amused, condescending laughter had surrounded Ramesses. Through the haze of his humiliation, his father continued, relentless.

This is unacceptable, even unthinkable behavior for the heir to Egypt's throne. No pharaoh has ever been faithful to one woman like a common man. Not even the heretic Akhenaten.

You know your responsibility—to ensure the royal line is secure. Your wives and concubines exist for this purpose and this purpose only. By all means, take your fill of them, but do not give them your love, unless you wish to invite intrigue and treachery into your court.

This nonsense of yours ends today. In ten days, we will travel to Pi-Ramesses—without Nefertari—to meet Iset-Nofret, whom I have chosen for you to wed and bed. And, until you learn what it means to be Pharaoh of Egypt, Nefertari will remain here, in Waset, out of your reach. This I so swear, by the light of Re, to uphold for as long as I live.

Ramesses had erupted, furious, refusing to acknowledge his father's decision, vowing to do as he pleased with his life. He was restrained, and confined to his apartment for the next ten days; his father's guards sending back Nefertari's gifts and messages unopened, cutting off all contact between them.

The day they left Waset, Ramesses was not granted permission to say farewell to his wife. Instead, his father had him escorted like a criminal to the docks. Once aboard the royal barque, Ramesses stood alone and watched the city where the woman he loved more than his own life, disappear on the horizon.

In Pi-Ramesses, his father arranged the introduction to Iset-Nofret, a girl nothing like Nefertari. At first, Ramesses could not stand her, but as time passed, he found her witty, daring, and at times, outrageous. They were wed, and drunk on wine, he took

Iset-Nofret to his bed, but she left him dissatisfied and lonely. He sent her away, to later learn she carried his child.

After his wedding, his longing for Nefertari heightened. Desperate to ease the ache in his heart, he turned to the harems and courtesan houses, sampling the countless women of Pi-Ramesses along with Ahmen and Sethi until his heart grew cold, and Nefertari's no longer called to him.

The next time he saw Nefertari, over a year later, holding his firstborn son in her arms, he allowed himself to feel pride, she had fulfilled her duty. He took her to his bed several times before his father's siege against Kadesh. On his return, he learned he had fathered another son, her second, and his third.

During those early years in Waset, whenever he had brought Nefertari to his bed, he would wake in the night, savoring the feeling of her, naked in his arms, his heart crying out to love her again. Angry with himself, he would wake her, commanding her to leave, terse, and impatient.

How many times had he sent her away deep in the night, rejecting her for the crime of rekindling feelings he had believed were long dead? Dozens, at least.

He had stayed away from her for the next three years, using the harems whenever he was in Waset, surrendering to his concubines' wantonness until he had driven the last vestiges of love from his heart. The next time he permitted Nefertari to see him, she was an elegant woman of twenty, and by far the most beautiful woman in the empire, admired by all.

His attraction to her was sudden and intense, he summoned her to his apartment. She had learned to reconcile herself to her fate and demanded nothing of him. For the first time in the six years since he had left her behind in Waset, Nefertari remained with him for the night and shared his morning meal with him.

There had been a brief reprieve for them in their new, controlled way of relating. Though he slept with dozens of other women, he favored her in the three years leading up to his accession to the throne. She had become clever, keeping herself at a distance, using their children as her connection to him, never speaking of love, even when he saw it burning in her eyes as he made love to her.

Then, he had been crowned, and the sumptuous harems of the pharaoh were opened to him. For a long time, as he explored the extensive rooms of the harems, he forgot Nefertari, and when he summoned her once again to him, almost two years later, she had changed. Though she tried to hide it, jealousy had sharpened her edges, and her cleverness had turned to cunning. He had pushed her too far. Uncomfortable, he had sent her away and had not summoned her again until tonight. It had been four years.

He glanced back at the disheveled bed, recalling her suppressed sob at his terse dismissal. A stab of remorse shot through him. He should not have misused her. He would send her a gift after the hunt, perhaps one of his leopard cubs, he recalled she liked cats—or did, years ago. He scoffed; he had no idea what she liked anymore. He decided to send a message to Imtes. She could choose a gift. It would be enough.

He poured himself a cup of beer and strode out onto the terrace, naked. It was still dark, but the subtle shade of gray on the horizon promised Re-Atum's barque would soon rise from the Under Realm to begin a new day. He gazed over the quiet city spreading away beneath his terrace, its streets and lanes cloaked in silence. Apart from the pools of torchlight surrounding the palace and temples, Waset lay shrouded in total darkness.

Above, the stars glittered within the canopy of a clear, black sky. Spotting the constellation of Osiris, he admired the three bright stars of the god's crown, before turning east to view the constellation of Isis, the eternal love of Osiris. A love they could no longer know, having been torn apart by the violence of Set during Egypt's Golden Age.

His thoughts moved back to Meresamun, her talent as a narrator, of her grace, bearing, and elegance. She was as near to a goddess as a mortal could be. It had been a very long time since he felt this way for a woman. He wanted to learn more about her, where she came from, who had been her father, and how she came to be a slave. She was well-bred, he was certain.

His hands came to rest on his hips. He gazed, unseeing, at the whitewashed stone beneath his bare feet, seeking to find a way past the walls of her unattainability. He could keep her at court and give her a title. *Keeper of the Histories of the Gods.* He nodded, pleased by the sound of it, imagining her at court telling stories, entertaining visiting envoys, and when he could not sleep, she could come to him—he stopped himself. Would he be able to be near her and not touch her? Would others? He scoffed. He could not have her at court; it was too dangerous. Sooner or later someone would take her, and the wrath of the goddess would be upon Egypt.

His focus returned to the stars, searching for a solution, but the insight he hoped for eluded him. He returned to his apartment and caught a glimpse of his reflection in his bronze mirror. He gazed at his image as he continued to fight his internal battle. He turned away, unable even to face himself as he came to his decision. Though he should not, he would see Meresamun one last time before giving her the papyrus. Before setting her free.

✳   ✳   ✳

Her hand in his, Ahmen led Meresamun through the darkened lanes and alleys of Waset, toward the Temple of Sekhmet. As they neared, torchlight from the outer pylons of the temple spilled into the mouth of the alley.

Ahmen stopped in the shadows and took in the bright square. "It is almost morning," he said, his gaze moving to the temple's entrance. "It is dishonorable to send you back like this, alone, I should come with you, to explain—"

Meresamun pressed her finger to his lips. "To explain what? A lie?"

He caught her as she moved to go. "Swear to me you will come to my villa once you have the papyrus from the pharaoh. I cannot bear the thought of losing you now I have found you."

"I swear it," she pulled away, though she let his hand capture hers, her fingers sliding along his until only their fingertips touched. "Be safe on the hunt."

Reluctant, he let her go. She moved into the firelit square and passed the solitary guard, vanishing into the pillared shadows beyond. Ahmen turned away, filled with misgiving. Now she was gone, the full weight of his crime bore down on him. Soon he would go on the lion hunt and kill the very creature who represented Sekhmet. He shuddered. He had seen what a lion could do to a man. He shook his head, banishing the thought. There would be dozens of others on the hunt. He had nothing to fear. For now.

❈   ❈   ❈

Ramesses moved out from the deeper shadows of the alley and glared at the place where Ahmen and Meresamun had just been. The one he trusted more than any other had trespassed where even he dared not go. Why would Ahmen do something so foolish? Out of Ramesses, Sethi, and Ahmen, Ahmen had always been the sensible one, the last person in all of Egypt Ramesses would have believed could do something like this. When Ramesses was still a boy, his father declared every man had at least one fatal weakness. It seemed a beautiful priestess was Ahmen's.

Ramesses cursed. Why had he not left Meresamun with Paser. All knew the vizier's heart belonged to a woman he could not have, though none knew who she was. Meresamun would have been safe with him, the bore. Anger pushed through his shock. He stared at the lane Ahmen had taken. So, this was how their friendship would end—over a priestess. How small and insignificant. His fingers closed around the hilt of his dagger. He would end Ahmen. How dare he take what even he, Pharaoh of Egypt could not have? A thought cut through the red noise of his anger. A murder committed by a pharaoh could only be punished by the gods—famine, plague, or even worse would be certain to follow.

No. He would not risk endangering his empire over jealousy. He let go of the dagger's hilt. Better to let the high priestess deal with it. Ahmen was beneath him now. His mood sour, Ramesses strode across the temple square, flanked by his guards. He stopped before the lone temple guard, who leaned on his spear, dozing.

At a prod by one of Ramesses's guards, the temple guard woke, blinking and bleary-eyed. His gaze moved over the small party, coming to a halt on Ramesses. He gaped, incredulous. "Great Isis, what a dream!"

Ramesses's guard stepped forward, blocking his view. "This is no dream, fool," he muttered, giving the temple guard a shove with his spear. "You keep the pharaoh waiting. The High Priestess Amunet. Now."

The blood draining from his face, the temple guard bowed and stumbled away, leading them past the dark waters of the sacred pool and into the heart of the temple. They entered just as the high priestess slipped out from the temple's inner sanctum, the home of the goddess herself.

Startled, Amunet looked up. For a heartbeat, alarm flickered over her features. "Your Majesty," she murmured, inclining her head, "how may I serve you?"

"High Priestess Amunet of Sekhmet," Ramesses answered, looking over her bowed head at the closed door to Sekhmet's sanctuary, "last night at the banquet we granted a gift to the priestess Meresamun. We would give her this gift our self."

Amunet bowed, sending the temple guard to fetch Meresamun. He set off at a run, his sandals slapping, loud, against the smooth stone floor of the Second Hall. His head beginning to ache from all the wine he had drunk, Ramesses followed Amunet past the towering pillars of the Hypostyle Hall into the moonlit courtyard, out along a paved lane past the sacred lake and down a palm-lined path into an elegant courtyard, through a colonnaded vestibule and into a sumptuous reception room.

Clad in a plain temple gown, her feet bare, Meresamun waited. Her eyes widened, fearful, as he entered. She sank to her knees, trembling. The door closed, quiet. Ramesses caught her hand and brought her to her feet. When she wouldn't meet his eyes, he reached out and grasped her chin, lifting her face up to his. As he looked at her, a memory from his youth returned, recalling the time when he had explored the forbidden ruins of Amarna and happened upon a workshop. Within, half-buried in the sand, he had discovered an unfinished bust of the most beautiful woman he had ever seen. Meresamun, with her straight nose, high cheekbones, full lips, and piercing eyes framed by long lashes and arching brows, reminded him of the long-lost, forgotten woman.

He traced the outline of Meresamun's cheekbone, his fingertips hovering over her lips. "I would have you as one of my queens if I could—" he pulled his hand away, abrupt, "—but you are the property of Sekhmet. Forbidden." He lifted the papyrus from his pouch and held it out to her. "The papyrus, granting your freedom."

She unrolled it and read its contents. Her lips parted in a breathless smile.

Ramesses couldn't bear it any longer. "Ahmen has known you, hasn't he?" he asked, blunt.

Her gaze still on the papyrus, she blanched.

"You will answer the King of Egypt," he commanded, the pain in his head beginning to throb.

Her voice came to him, so low he might have imagined it. "Yes."

He endured the molten heat of his fury. Through the burning haze he saw her lick her lips, sensed her fear. "And were you willing, Priestess of Sekhmet?" he pressed, his words sharp as daggers.

She lifted her eyes to his. "I was, Your Majesty."

His frustration spiked. He caught her chin in his hand. She had already been taken, he could have her now, and no harm could come to him. He felt her quaking in his grip, perceiving his intention. Shame bit him hard. He let her go.

"He intends to make you his wife?" Ramesses demanded, harsh.

"I do not know," she answered, quiet, her fingers tightening, almost imperceptibly on the papyrus.

"I would have made you my wife," he said, low, watching her, gauging her reaction.

"My lord," she breathed, her eyes flicking to meet his, astonished, "I am not worthy of you."

Seething at her veiled rejection, he slammed his fist against the table beside him, making the golden platters rattle. "Ahmen is not worthy of you!" he bellowed, furious.

She flinched, fear snapping, sharp, in her eyes. Fear, not for herself, but for Ahmen. Slow, like the drip of honey from its comb, he realized the truth, and it sickened him.

"Do you love him?" he asked, incredulous.

Her gaze fell away, her lashes sweeping down against her cheeks. "I feel something I have never felt before," she answered, soft. "Perhaps this is what love feels like."

Ramesses scoffed as his thoughts scattered, ricocheting between the rising pain in his head and her impossible, foolish words. He bit back a curse, annoyed a mere temple slave had undone the Pharaoh of Egypt. He caught her watching him, wary.

"Has Ahmen arranged to see you again?" he asked, cold, certain Ahmen would never attempt something so insane.

She nodded, hesitant. "Once I received this," she said, cradling the papyrus against her chest, "I was to return to his villa. He has vowed to make restitution to the temple, whatever the cost."

Restitution? Ramesses almost laughed out loud. Ahmen, in his ignorance, had left her to the lions. He looked at Meresamun, gazing once more at the papyrus, looking at it as though she couldn't believe it was real. He had to tell her. She deserved to know the truth.

"Ahmen is mistaken," Ramesses said, matter-of-fact. "There is a temple law still in place, an old, obscure one from earlier, harsher times, one you should know of before you ask for permission to leave. Before you are allowed to depart, you will be subject to inspection by a surgeon for purity."

"And my fate, if I am impure?" she asked, paling.

"Facial mutilation—the nose and ears cut off—then sold to the highest bidder at the slave market. Whoever buys you may use you as they please, a fallen priestess, maimed for life. It is a fate worse than death."

She sank onto a bench and looked once more at the papyrus, still open in her hands. Ramesses waited. A tear fell onto her knuckle. He caught the slight nod of her head as she reconciled herself to her punishment. His anger fled, shamed by her quiet courage.

"If you do not ask to leave, no harm will come to you," he offered, seeking to show her a way around her dilemma. "As a free woman, you would have permission to attend festivals. You would not be a prisoner."

"No," she shook her head. "I am prepared to admit to what I have done. I cannot live dishonestly."

He lifted an eyebrow, impressed despite the madness of her words; the temple had indoctrinated her well. "Last year in Libya," he began, knowing what he was about to do was reckless, dangerous even. He forced his misgivings away, unwilling to leave her alone to face the consequences for Ahmen's crimes. "Ahmen saved my life, taking what would have been, for me, a fatal blow. In return, I told him he could have anything he desired. Although he has not yet asked anything of me, I consider my debt paid in full. A life for a life. I will take you with me when I leave. Because none would dare confront me, you will not be inspected."

She looked up at him, uncertain. "I have committed a crime, why should I be spared, when others must abide by the laws?"

"It is my command," he said, his admiration for her deepening. "Let me answer to the gods for this." He helped her to her feet. "Do you have any items you wish to collect?"

She rose, her voice quiet. "Yes, there are a few."

"Come with me, then." He led her into the vestibule where Amunet stood, waiting, tense.

"We have granted Meresamun her freedom," he declared, officious. "She will leave with us once she has collected her belongings. Please let Lord Sethi, the King's Treasurer know how Pharaoh should compensate the temple for its loss."

"Pharaoh is a god who walks among us," Amunet murmured, her eyes downcast, "who are we to ask anything of him in return?"

"Then ask the goddess what she wishes," Ramesses snapped, his head aching and his patience wearing thin.

Amunet closed her eyes and communed with Sekhmet. She looked up, pale. "Your Majesty, I am powerless in these matters. Sekhmet will take whatever she sees fit."

Meresamun's eyes met his, fearful. He turned away, enduring his own deep spike of dread. "What will be, will be," he muttered, resigned. "What is done, is done."

THREE

Ahmen took a quick step back, catching Haran's head before the horse could bite him. "You bit me once," he smiled as he stroked the horse's nose. "Never again. You are just going to have to get used to having your girth tightened."

A curse erupted from one of the storerooms just as a heap of baskets tumbled out the doorway and toppled over, sending little rivers of grain and corn spreading across the flagstones. From amongst the wreckage, the boy Dhet burst free, two peacock plumes in one hand and a three-legged stool in the other. He settled the stool beside Haran and scrambled up to fasten the feather onto the top of the horse's bridle, wobbling on his perch when Haran shook his head.

"By Horus, what a morning," he said, yanking his arm aside just in time to avoid Haran's snap. He glanced at Ahmen, the dark color of his cheeks betraying his earlier exertions. "Haran's very excitable this morning. It took three of us to get him yoked to the chariot. Wekhra took the worst of it when Haran stood on him not once, but twice."

Ahmen caught the look of satisfaction sliding over Dhet's face, quickly concealed. Despite himself, Ahmen smiled. Wekhra was a terrible bully, especially to Dhet, the youngest and most talented of the grooms in the royal stables. He patted Haran and told him he was a good boy.

Dhet finished his task and ran round in front of the horses, dodging a fresh nip from Haran, to climb up beside Haran's companion. "Kerkhem at least knows to save his energy for the work he has in front of him." He gave the quiet horse's ear an affectionate tug.

While Dhet finished his work, Ahmen carried on with his inspection, his fingers moving over the burnished buckles and straps of the equipment. Kerkhem's crupper was too long. He shortened it. He caught Dhet watching him. Ahmen tilted his head at the offence. His face flushing with shame, Dhet murmured an apology. The boy rarely made mistakes; Ahmen could let it go.

"Haran has not had a chance to run since he boarded the barque at Pi-Ramesses," Ahmen said, nodding at the horse, who pawed at the ground, impatient. "He will be much calmer when we return, you will see."

From behind Kerkhem, Dhet let out a disbelieving scoff. It was well known Haran had been testing the boy hard. Suppressing a smile, Ahmen stepped into the chariot's box and wrapped the reins around his forearms just as Re-Atum's barque approached the horizon, tinting the sky a deep shade of pink. Leaning back, he tested the reins' tension. After several adjustments, he nodded to Dhet to let the horses go. They burst out of the stable yard onto the empty avenue, frisking, happy.

At the edge of the palace's square, he slowed the horses, apprehensive. The square lay completely empty. Confused, he looked up at the sky, wondering if he was late. No, he was early. Ramesses walked out of the palace gates, flanked by his guards.

Uneasy, Ahmen brought the horses to a halt. Ignoring Ahmen, Ramesses went to Haran and ran an appreciative hand along the horse's flanks, patting him with murmurs of approval.

"You have my weapons?" he asked, still looking over the horse.

"Yes, Your Majesty," Ahmen answered, his uneasiness escalating into certainty. Something was definitely amiss.

Ramesses stepped into the chariot, his eyes sliding over Ahmen, unseeing, as he took his stance. "You may proceed," he nodded at the horses, terse.

Ahmen eyed the deserted square. "Have the others been sent ahead?"

"No. Today we hunt alone," Ramesses replied, crossing his arms over his chest. "I have no desire for an escort of guards, or to be slowed down by hordes of attendants, water bearers, and provisioners. I wish to hunt as we did as boys, unfettered by the trappings of court."

Ahmen stared at him, incredulous. They couldn't go on a lion hunt, *alone.*

"We are seasoned warriors, are we not?" Ramesses glanced at him, then away, scoffing. "It is only a lion we must face, not an ambushing party of Libyans."

Ahmen blinked, taken aback by Ramesses's callous remark. He had almost died when he took the blade in Ramesses's stead. Wary, he waited, searching for the others. It had to be diversion, with Ahmen being played the fool.

"I have decided I will not die this day," Ramesses tilted his head at the way ahead. "Proceed. I command it."

Not as certain of his own survival, Ahmen called to the horses and set them to a brisk walk, wondering at the sudden change of plans. Even if Ramesses wished for a day without the encumbrances of court, his decision would leave many disappointed—today's lion hunt had been greatly anticipated by Waset's nobility, even more than last night's feast.

They passed through the gates onto the open road. The horses pulled, eager to run. Ramesses gestured toward the eastern horizon, turning golden in the distance. "Reports confirm the lion keeps his den near the Me'ddja quarries. We go to Bekhen."

Ahmen struggled to hide his dismay. Was Ramesses insane? More than two long iters of blazing desert heat separated them from Bekhen, and they carried no water. Filled with misgiving, Ahmen eased the horses into a trot and turned them onto the road leading away from Waset. He looked up at the sky and calculated. Re-Atum's barque had only just left the horizon. If he paced the horses and conserved their energy, allowing them breaks at the settlements along the way, they might still be able to reach the base of the mountains before the killing heat of midday.

He began the prayer of protection to Horus, then stopped. Guilt flooded him. He could not petition the gods, not when he had stolen from one of them. His conscience gnawed as he fell into a troubled state, alienated and alone. Beside him, Ramesses stood still as a statue, ignoring him, gazing into the distance, preoccupied, withdrawn, silent.

The horses passed the outer boundary of Waset's shady plantations, emerging onto the dusty, hard-packed quarry road. The desert's dry air slammed into Ahmen, leaching the moisture from his body. He drove on, into the glare of Re-Atum's barque, pushing the horses deep into the desert, a solitary chariot in a wilderness of sand. Anxious, he watched the unchanging, barren iters flee under the horses' hooves. Haran began to labor, frothing at the bit, gobbets of foam hanging from his muzzle. Ahmen fretted, searching the horizon, willing the flat-roofed buildings of Iskhet to appear. When at last he saw them shimmering in the distance, he cried out in relief, calling encouragement to the horses, promising them water and rest.

Driving into the speckled shadows of a cluster of date palms, he ordered the women nearby to hurry and bring skins of water. As he watered the thirsty horses, Ahmen sensed someone's eyes on him. He looked over his shoulder. Seated on a bench under the trees, Ramesses watched him, cold.

Troubled, Ahmen continued his work. There was more to this hunt than Ramesses was telling him. Perhaps he had displeased the pharaoh. Ahmen reviewed his duties over the last days. Nothing stood out. He refilled the empty skins and tied them onto the chariot, resigned. He had no choice but to wait.

They continued, moving from one village to the next, racing against the encroaching midday heat. As the empty iters passed, only the creak of the chariot, the steady breathing of the horses, and the rhythmic thud of their leather-clad hooves on the desert road occupied Ahmen's senses.

In time, the sandy landscape began to change, becoming rockier; the faint outline of cliffs shimmered low on the horizon, tantalizing. They drew nearer, the evanescent wall of rock rising, its heights solidifying into a reassuring mass. Beneath its rugged face lay the abandoned settlement of Bekhen. Ahmen eyed the cliff wall, stretching away into the distance. Apart from a handful of valleys leading out to the sea, the mountains extended all the way south to Nubia and almost as far again to the north. The mountain range served both as a barrier and a wealth of raw materials, a gift from the gods.

He turned the horses into the courtyard containing the workshops and slowed them to a walk. They limped into the deep shade of a mud brick building, its floor dotted with piles of raw quartz. Ramesses stepped down from the chariot and gazed around the building, curious. Lifting one of the water skins from the chariot, he drank, noisy. Wiping his mouth with the back of his hand, he gestured toward the abandoned yard.

"While we were in Amurru, the lion killed three men and a half-dozen oxen. The quarries were evacuated, ending all gold mining until our return." He nodded at one of the dense piles of quartz, half hidden in the gloom. "Those are filled with veins of gold. My father spent years trying to find a method to extract it, but it was I who discovered the secret."

Bending over, he picked up one of the crystals, weighing it in his hand. With a grunt, he hurled it out into the courtyard, where it smashed against the base of the well. His mouth twisted. "By the light of Atum, these should already be broken, and more besides. Almost an entire season of gold production lost. This lion has cost me enough."

He surveyed the other buildings, displeasure emanating from him. He left and crossed the yard, leaving Ahmen to breathe a little freer, grateful for the reprieve.

Sliding the bridles from the horses' sweat-stained faces, Ahmen stroked their noses, vowing they would never have to make such a journey again. He watered them and rubbed them down, leaving them hobbled, their heads hanging as they dozed.

Leaning against the chariot's box, he wiped the sweat from his brow and took a deep pull from the waterskin, eyeing their meager store of weapons. Two men against a lion. Not impossible, but very dangerous. He refused to allow himself to think of those who had not survived the previous hunts.

He went out to find Ramesses. The settlement was empty. At the boundary of the buildings, he shaded his eyes, searching along the base of the cliffs. Half a short iter away, his body distorted by shimmering heat waves, Ramesses gestured for Ahmen to join him.

Beside a breach in the cliff wall, Ahmen handed over Ramesses's weapons. Ramesses jerked his head toward the opening as he adjusted the quiver's position against his torso.

"It is as I suspected, the lion keeps his den within. This crevice leads to a gully. Inside there is fresh spoor, not even an hour old."

He took up his bow and spear and slipped inside. A few steps behind, Ahmen followed, moving into the narrow channel, no more than an arm span wide. He looked up. High above, he glimpsed a narrow ribbon of blue sky.

They reached the mouth of the gully. Ramesses slowed and sank into a crouch. He tilted his head, listening. Silence greeted them. Creeping out of the shadows into the gully's white glare, he followed its smooth contours to the far side. He turned and stopped. He lifted his spear, slow, pointing it at the curved wall beside him, motioning for Ahmen to move in. As Ahmen drew closer, he saw it too, another crevice hidden by a fold in the gully's walls, burrowing deeper into the cliffs.

They entered a small basin where the crevice separated into two channels. Ramesses jerked his chin toward the largest one and slipped, silent, into its dense gloom. Gripping his spear, Ahmen followed, despite his instincts prodding him to turn back. He pressed on; he was no coward. The channel ended at the mouth of an enclosed circular canyon, its sheer vertical walls towering up to a brilliant blue sky. Heat hit him, hot as a baker's oven. Along the perimeter, more than a dozen caves, some of them deep enough to remain sunk in shadow, even at midday. Further down, Ahmen spotted the other channel's opening. His instincts prodded once more, warning him, urgent, insistent. He silenced them.

Ramesses motioned toward the nearest caves. They would start there. He gave the hand sign to separate, his spear moving back and forth as he picked the caves out one after the other, the nearest to the furthest.

Ahmen nodded his understanding. They would check the caves one by one. When they found the beast, one would flush him out, striking him with their spear as he emerged and the other would bring him down with their arrows. They had done this once before, with success, although not alone. There had been a dozen more men with them, all armed with bows and spears. He bit back another prayer and slipped away to the right, measuring his steps to match Ramesses's.

The nearest openings proving to be far too shallow to be of any use to a lion. They moved deeper into the canyon where the shadows of larger grottoes held more promise. Ahmen reached the first cave. He listened for the sound of breathing, counting, slow, to thirty. Nothing. He turned to Ramesses and shook his head. As they crept toward the next grotto, a shriek—faint, high and thin—broke the silence. Another scream followed, then another, crescendoing, riven with terror and pain.

Cursing, realizing too late what his instincts had been trying to tell him, Ahmen bolted across the canyon's uneven ground into the channel, the butt of his spear clattering against its sides. He darted through the gully, his sandals sliding on the loose rocks. Ducking into the crevice, he choked back yet another prayer as he tumbled out onto the burning desert floor.

Ramesses burst out after him. "The lion must not escape," he bellowed, "or we will be next."

Ahmen ran, his stride lengthening, his feet barely touching the ground, the desperate cries of the horses maddening him. He darted into the settlement, the buildings sliding past, a blur. Ramesses raced past him and vaulted up onto a workbench, pulling himself up onto the building's roof. Ahmen clambered up after him, pieces of mud brick falling away under his feet.

They were too late. Kerkhem stood trapped, quaking, between the workshop and what was left of Haran. Ahmen stared, disbelieving. Somehow, Haran was still alive. The muscles of Haran's shoulder were gone. Ahmen could only see bone. Through the torn openings of his abdomen, Haran's internal organs lay exposed, his ribs protruding from his flayed flesh. Ruptured intestines slid out, trickling onto the ground, the foul stink of them saturating the air. Deep in the act of feeding, the lion tore into Haran's abdomen, Haran grunted, tears running from his eyes.

Ahmen dragged an arrow against his bowstring. "I must end his pain."

"No." Ramesses shoved the bow down. "We have one chance. We need Haran to hold the lion in position until we can mark him. Aim for the beast's spine, sever it so he cannot run away. We must not fail. On my command."

Ahmen's gaze slid back to the suffering, eviscerated horse. He had never seen such a thing before. Why did the lion not kill Haran first? Ahmen aimed, pulling his bowstring taut. Long heartbeats passed as the lion continued to feed, Haran's cries of suffering unbearable.

"The lion is not moving," Ahmen persisted, aiming at Haran. "I beg you, let me end Haran's pain."

"If you release before I give the command, we will all die." Ramesses cursed as Haran cried out again. "There! Mark the beast, he's about to shift."

The lion moved to the right, just a little, enough to expose his spine. A perfect mark. Ahmen concentrated his aim until there was only the mark and the point of his arrow. From far away he heard Ramesses give the command to release. Ahmen's fingers opened. The bowstring snapped free, cutting into his forearm. He felt nothing. He slammed another arrow against his bow, automatic. Ramesses shouted for spears, jostling Ahmen as he jumped from the roof.

Hefting his spear, Ahmen joined Ramesses. He eyed the paralyzed lion, his arrow protruding from the base of its neck. Haran's eyes streamed with tears, and with every labored breath, black blood bubbled out of his mouth and nostrils. Ahmen's hand went to his dagger. Rage, vicious and vengeful, spilled free. He would skin the lion alive.

"Finish it," Ramesses ordered, shoving him forward. "Haran needs you."

Fury consumed Ahmen. The scream burst from his torso, a living thing. He rammed his spear into the lion's side, past its rib cage and deep into its heart. The lion grunted, his eyes widening with pain and shock. His head drooped onto his front paws. A quiet shudder. The light in his eyes, gone.

Ahmen dropped to his knees beside Haran. Gently, he lifted the horse's head onto his lap. "Can you hear that sound?" he asked, his throat taut with grief. "That is Re, calling for you. You must run to him. Do not make him wait."

His heart constricting, Ahmen lay his dagger against Haran's throat. He pulled the blade, deft, quick. Haran lay quiet in his lap, looking up at him, his blood pumping out, slow, viscous. The light in his eyes flickered and dulled, a heartbeat later, it extinguished. Ahmen lowered Haran's head onto the ground. He rose, his blood-soaked kilt clinging to his legs. For several heartbeats he stared at what was left of the horse, trying to piece him back together. He could not. Haran had become a macabre thing. Only his face remained intact.

He looked up at the sky, Haran's *ka* was up there, flying away to the gods; he would be able to see Ahmen, looking down at his remains. Something glimmered in the sky. Ahmen choked. Haran.

High overhead, vultures circled, patient. His throat aching, Ahmen looked back at Haran's body. "I cannot leave him like this, to become the food of scavengers."

Ramesses wrenched Ahmen's spear out of the lion. "Do as you see fit," he said, callous, the slain beast's blood pooling against his feet. "When Re's barque descends, we walk."

With the chariot's yoke on his shoulder, its weight almost as heavy as his burden of guilt, Ahmen turned to look one final time at the mound of rocks covering Haran's broken body. It wasn't until he had placed the last rock on the makeshift grave that the realization came, swift and brutal. Haran was Sekhmet's price. Just as Meresamun had predicted, the goddess had meted her punishment. An innocent had suffered and paid for their crime. Guilt beat down on him in sickening waves. He welcomed his suffering, prodded it even, forcing himself to relive Haran's final moments.

Above, twilight stars breached the sky's dusky canopy, their twinkling light beautiful, deceptive. He glared at them; all knew the stars were where the gods lived. Where they looked down upon the doings of men, judging them. Punishing them.

Ignoring Ahmen, Ramesses walked ahead, leading Kerkhem, who limped, stoic despite the ragged claw marks in his flanks. Ahmen followed him for almost an hour, the silence between them taut, stretching out, claustrophobic despite the vast open space surrounding them. Just as Ahmen had begun to resign himself to Ramesses's hostility, the pharaoh halted, abrupt. He turned, his face black with suppressed rage.

"I know what passed between you and Meresamun last night," he seethed as he bore down on Ahmen. "How dare you take what belongs to the goddess."

Clarity came. So this was why Ramesses had taken him alone on the hunt. Ahmen was to be a casualty. He dropped to his knee. "Once you granted her freedom," he babbled, hating himself for bleating like a coward, "Meresamun no longer wished to remain a priestess. Temple law—"

"Of which, it seems, you know very little" Ramesses interrupted, severe.

Dread clawed at Ahmen as fear for Meresamun bolted past his own trepidation. He waited, desperate for Ramesses to continue. The silence dragged out, thick with tension. Ramesses exhaled, slow, his gaze moving over the dry dunes of the desert.

"You saved my life from a Libyan blade," he said, finally. "I consider my debt paid. Meresamun is waiting for you at your villa, safe from the law you believed would protect her. Had I not intervened, she would have been found guilty of impurity, maimed, and sold into a life of the meanest slavery where even I could not have helped her."

Ahmen sagged. He had utterly failed Meresamun. Without Ramesses's intervention, she would already be mutilated. Shame bore down on him, unbearable.

"And now, Sekhmet has taken Haran as her price," Ramesses continued, relentless, his gaze moving to Bekhen. "Have you not asked yourself why the lion did not kill Haran first before feeding as all lions do? It was unnatural. The mind of the goddess was upon that animal. None of us have been spared from her wrath today, not even Kerkhem. He will never pull my chariot again. But Haran—a gift from the King of Amurru—Haran was my greatest hope for breeding a royal line of horses, lasting longer than my reign. I have never before seen such a creature as perfect or as well made as him, nor do I expect to again. Sekhmet chose her price well."

Ahmen stared at the ground beneath his filthy kilt. There was only one honorable choice for him. He pulled his dagger from its scabbard and held it up with both hands, hilt forward. "Great Pharaoh, by my selfish and dishonorable actions I have made myself unworthy of you and of Egypt. I await your command."

Ramesses said nothing. In the distance, a hyena howled. Time stretched, slow. Ahmen's arms began to ache. Kerkhem whickered and shook his head, the metallic rattling of his bridle mundane, ordinary.

"No. I will not command you to end your life," Ramesses finally muttered, pushing the dagger down. "It is a better punishment for you to continue to live and take responsibility for your actions. Carry the memory of this day with you for the rest of your life. Never forget what Haran suffered for your crime. I have said what needed to be said. Put your dagger away and let us walk to Waset in peace."

His hands shaking, Ahmen sheathed his dagger. He had been certain he would join Haran. He bent down to pick up the chariot's shaft.

"Ahmen, wait."

He turned. Ramesses looked down and rubbed his thumb and forefinger along Kerkhem's rein. "I would speak to you as a brother—just for this one brief space of time."

"Your Majesty—"

"No," Ramesses held up his hand. "I am guilty too. I cannot lay all the blame on you. I wished to take Meresamun to my bed. I used my power to prevent her inspection and, because of her I cursed the gods."

Ahmen stared at Ramesses. The pharaoh had cursed the gods? Had he lost his mind?

"Though I envy you," Ramesses continued, a taint of bitterness tingeing his words, "I honor Meresamun's choice."

Ahmen shook his head, disbelieving. It was all too much, too fast. Ramesses looked at him, waiting for him to respond. Ahmen raised his fist to his chest. "I will honor her always. There will be no other but her. If she goes to the gods before me, I swear to live the rest of my days alone." He met Ramesses's gaze. "My lord, I will never fail you again."

Ramesses's face hardened. "No. You won't."

His demeanor becoming distant once more, the pharaoh turned and led Kerkhem into the glittering white sands of the desert, sparkling in the light of the full moon.

A long time passed before Ahmen picked up the chariot, and followed them home.

FOUR

Nefertari woke. The flame of Re-Atum's lamp still burned bright. She smiled and stretched, pleased. Until the oil in the sacred lamp ran out at dawn, she would be alone, a rare treat.

She slipped out from under the jasmine scented sheets and padded barefoot to a cedarwood cupboard. Opening an empty alabaster unguent jar, she dipped her fingers inside and probed for the wooden key. Turning it in the locking mechanism of the cupboard, she listened for the quiet click of the lock's release. She eased the key out and pulled the door open, careful to stop just before the point where it always creaked. Reaching in, she pulled out a linen pouch, containing three precious rolls of papyrus. Holding the pouch against her chest, she went to a divan and lifted out the scrolls, careful of the aging papyri's fragmenting edges.

Savoring the pleasure of holding the very papyrus Ramesses had once touched, she unrolled the first scroll, her lips moving to his words as she relived the brief, fleeting months when happiness had filled her life with light. As she read, the thirteen years separating her from a vanished past melted away, and she once more walked the corridors of Pharaoh Seti's court, when she had loved Ramesses and had been loved in return.

Unrolling the second scroll, she smiled at the memories Ramesses's words brought back. She hesitated before opening the third, his most passionate declaration of love. He had written it on the night of their marriage while she slept, after he had shown her the full meaning of what it meant to be loved by him. When she had woken, still in his bed, she was alone. On his cushion, his words waited for her.

Her gaze lingered on the scroll as she remembered reading it for the first time, her heart bursting with joy. She unrolled it and skimmed to his final words, her favorite ones, hearing his voice, warm and intimate as she read.

My love is unique—no one can rival her, for she is the most beautiful woman alive. Just by passing, she has stolen away my heart.

Lifting the papyrus to her lips, she kissed his words, savoring the memory of how he had loved her then. She eased the scrolls back into their pouch with care, the memory of their last encounter returning, unbidden.

He had been quick, and rough, taking her from behind. He had not even looked at her. She had had to return to her apartment with her dress in tatters, her breasts exposed. A fresh wave of humiliation crashed down inside her. She waited it out, used to the feeling, though not the pain it brought.

Catching her reflection in the bronze mirror, she went to it, turning her face from side to side, examining her features, trying to see herself as Ramesses would. Her almond-shaped eyes, the color of copper and flecked with gold, gazed back at her. Perhaps they were not as wide as she would have liked, but she had long, thick lashes, and enviable, well-shaped brows.

Her thick, black hair had been plaited into dozens of braids, the ends tipped with golden cylinders. She liked this latest style; it framed her high forehead, long, narrow nose, round cheeks, and full lips very well. Apart from a few fine wrinkles around her eyes, her complexion was still smooth, though not as firm as it once was. Tugging on the skin at the sides her face, she brought the younger version of herself back to life. She stared at her reflection for a long time, seeing how beautiful she had once been, wishing she could have her youthful beauty back. She let go and watched her face settle into place, her jaw a little heavier, the skin under her eyes no longer tight. She sighed, disappointed, and turned away.

What did she expect to see at twenty-seven? A woman in the full bloom of youth, ten years younger?

Before he was crowned, she recalled Ramesses would take pains to keep the visits of his companions private, sparing her feelings. However, once he took the throne, he changed, behaving as he pleased, taking whomever he wished. One favorite followed another, sometimes two or three at once, all of them with full, high breasts. He would have them seated on cushions at his feet during feasts, sharing the food from his table with them. And after, she would return to her apartment alone, to be tormented by thoughts of her husband making love to those women as he once did to her.

Thinking of her most recent public humiliation, Nefertari looked down at her body, comparing the priestess's to her own, running her hands over her once youthful breasts and hips, cradling the curve of her small, round belly, distended after delivering five infants.

No, there could be no comparison, the priestess was far more desirable than she. Meresamun's body was young and firm, full and voluptuous. Her face was as perfect as a goddess's—and those blue eyes—astonishing. Even the sensible and level-headed Ahmen had been smitten by her.

The flame from Re-Atum's lamp flickered. It would soon go out, its oil matching the lamps placed outside the doors of her sleeping room. When it extinguished, her guards would open the doors, and her sister Imtes, followed by Nefertari's attendants would come in, carrying trays of food and drink.

Nefertari hurried, placing the scrolls back into their hidden drawer. She locked the cupboard, secreted the key, and slipped back into her bed. She had just laid her head upon her cushion when the lamp guttered out.

Her door opened, quiet. A whisper of material as Imtes moved toward her, the train of her sister's gown trailing along the polished travertine floor. Familiar sounds followed, the linen hangings around

Nefertari's bed being drawn back and the terrace shutters being folded away, unobtrusive and gentle.

Nefertari's nose itched. She ignored it, forcing herself to lay still, waiting for her sister to speak the formal words of awakening.

"Great Queen, Beloved of Isis, Re-Atum has arrived," Imtes intoned, quiet. "Let us greet him together and give thanks for his light."

Nefertari sat up, rubbing her nose.

Imtes leaned closer. "The pharaoh returned during the night from the hunt. He is unharmed, thank Re." She looked over her shoulder before continuing, "But he went straight to his private office, sending for the lords Paser and Sethi."

Nefertari left the bed, and slipped into the robe Imtes held up. "Such urgency can only mean one thing," she sighed, resigned, "another campaign. Let us pray the gods will allow him to stay, at least until the end of Akhet."

Imtes's hand clasped hers. "I will arrange offerings of gold, and a barge to take us to Hathor's temple. The goddess cannot help but hear our prayers."

"I do not expect you to give up all your offerings so Ramesses will remain until the winter solstice," Nefertari smiled, squeezing her sister's hand. "You may keep back a little for your own petition."

Her sister blushed. "I saw Lord Paser on my way here," Imtes whispered, her eyes shining. "He looked at me. I think he smiled. Although we were in the shadows, so it is hard to be certain."

Unable to stop herself, Nefertari laughed. "I do not believe it. Paser does not smile."

Her cheeks burning with humiliation, Imtes bowed and went to the terrace, busying herself with inspecting the platters; moving two of them so the courses were in the correct order, her movements elegant and graceful.

A ripple of shame shimmered through Nefertari for laughing at her sister's hopes. Imtes had suffered in silence, loving the vizier from afar for the past four years, her subtle interest seeming to go unnoticed, though it was difficult to tell with a man like Paser, who revealed nothing.

Rumor had it he loved a woman, one he could not have, though no one knew for sure if it was true, or just a tale. Regardless, even if it was true, it was foolish, Egypt's vizier should have a wife and children of his own.

Nefertari decided Imtes would have her heart's desire. At twenty-one, it was past time for her sister to be wed. Until now, Nefertari had insisted on keeping her as her companion, while Imtes waited for Paser to realize her interest. But it had been four years. The man needed a push.

Nefertari watched her sister—whose heart brimmed with romance for the vizier, fourteen years her senior—prepare the morning meal, laying it out on the queen's golden platter. Nefertari would miss Imtes's company once her sister moved to Paser's villa. It would be lonely without her. She shook her head, banishing the selfish thought, she had stayed her hand long enough thinking only of her own needs, while Imtes waited, patient, hopeful and good.

Nefertari considered what to do. It would take some planning, and perhaps a little cunning, but she would find a way to see them wed. Somehow an opportunity would present itself, and she would make certain to take it. Where she had failed in her own life, she would succeed in her sister's. At least one of them should know happiness.

She went to the terrace and sank onto the divan just as Re-Atum's barque left the horizon, its warm, golden light illuminating Imtes's face, almost identical to Nefertari's. Though where Nefertari's beauty was considered regal, Imtes's was filled with innocence.

Nefertari lifted her golden cup to the east and took a sip of the mead offering, honoring Re-Atum's return. As she uttered the prayer of thanks for the god's gift of a new day, she gazed across the palace gardens toward her husband's apartment, thinking of him still filthy from the hunt, holding council.

How she longed for him. It had been like this for almost her entire marriage. The man she loved, so near, yet so far. Still holding her cup, she walked to the edge of the terrace and gazed at the empty terraces of his apartments, its blue awnings rippling in the river's cool morning breeze.

She closed her eyes, and whispered a prayer to Isis, entreating the goddess to move the pharaoh's heart so he would send for his queen—just for one night—before he was gone.

❋ ❋ ❋

As the door closed behind Sethi, Egypt's commander bowed low, his fists crossed over his chest.

Tired, hungry, and sore after walking all night, Ramesses beckoned for Sethi to join Paser, nodding at the men to sit. Wood creaked as they settled onto the chairs. Silence. Ramesses leaned back in his chair and eyed his commander, noting the tension in his jaw, the dark circles under his eyes.

"Commander. Tell me what you know."

Sethi leaned forward, resting his elbows on his knees, the muscles in his arms and shoulders flexing, the movements annoying Ramesses.

"My lord," Sethi began, his voice gritty from lack of sleep, "on the night of the feast, I received an urgent message from one of my mercenary captains in Babylon. The Crown Prince of Hatti has been gathering men in preparation for a great battle against us."

Ramesses lifted his brow, surprised. He turned his attention to his vizier. "Lord Paser?"

"Your Majesty," Paser bowed his head, "I have no firm intelligence on this matter. However, yesterday I received word from one of my spies in Tarhuntassa's court of an intriguing development. The High Priestess of Kadesh, King Amunira's sister Rhoha, has taken up residence in Muwatallis's court."

Ramesses stared at Paser. "Kadesh is ours, what treachery is this?"

Paser looked uneasy. "My lord, it is my great shame to have failed you. Rhoha's presence revealed intelligence which has eluded my spies for years . . ."

"Get on with it," Ramesses muttered, resigned. "I'm tired."

"Of course," Paser cleared his throat. "As you know, one month after you and your father captured Kadesh twelve years ago, Muwatallis arrived with his armies—"

Ramesses waved his hand, dismissive. "Yes, and took their gold and food to punish them for becoming our vassal. Then Muwatallis left and never returned. Kadesh has continued to send her tribute every year since then. Why are you telling me this?"

"Because Muwatallis took Amunira's seven-year-old daughter— his only child—with him when he left. Her name is Istara."

A finger of dread touched Ramesses. He had heard that name before. He searched his memory. Realization dawned, cold, sickening.

"The same Istara the Hittite ambassador informed us was wed to Urhi-Teshub last autumn in Tarhuntassa?"

"Yes, Your Majesty."

Ramesses rose. His men came to their feet. He paced, agitated. "Muwatallis was clever to keep Istara's true lineage quiet. Now he has raised her in his court and married his heir to the daughter of Amunira. Though Kadesh pays lip service to me, there is no question to whom she truly belongs." He moved to the front of his desk and crossed his arms over his chest. "I will not give up my plans for next year's campaign. I will have Karchemish. Lord Sethi, can it still be done without Kadesh as our base?"

"It is possible, but the news from Babylon has revealed Muwatallis knows of your intentions for Karchemish. He plans to stop us at Kadesh, with the whole of his empire rallying to his call."

Ramesses gritted his teeth. "So be it. If it is a fight Muwatallis wants, then Egypt shall give him one. Paser, find out his numbers and keep Sethi abreast of your intelligence." He turned to Sethi. "How soon can you recruit more men and have them equipped to march?"

Sethi rubbed his hand over his head, considering. "I can ensure we will still leave Pi-Ramesses on the First Day of the Second of Shemu, as originally planned."

Ramesses nodded. A thought crossed his mind. "And the treasury?"

Sethi shook his head. "Not enough for an undertaking of this size. We will have to borrow."

"Then we borrow," Ramesses said, decisive. "Lord Paser, send out letters to our vassals in Amurru and raise advances from them. When we have received their tribute, write to them again and ask for more."

Sethi and Paser looked troubled. He was asking much of them. Despite the extravagance of his ambitions, he knew he had their support, loyal and unquestioning. Still, he sought to reassure them.

"I have long dreamed of making Egypt as great as it was during the reign of Thutmosis III," he said as he walked to the door. "Let us meet Muwatallis at Kadesh and defeat his rag-tag army. The gods are with us. With the defeat of Muwatallis, it will be no hardship to take Karchemish. By the end of next summer, Egypt's empire will stretch from the deserts of Nubia to the borders of Assyria, and your names, the heroes of Egypt, will be remembered for all time."

Their eyes dark with ambition, Sethi and Paser pressed their fists to their chests. Ramesses nodded, satisfied, and left. War might be coming, but first, he needed to sleep.

FIVE

Ahmen strode through the drenching heat of his villa's pleasure gardens into the deep shadows of the vestibule. Tuy, his steward, met him. He eyed Ahmen's bloodstained kilt as he bowed.

"Lord Ahmen, welcome home. We rejoice to see you safe." He turned, and gave a sharp clap. Servants emerged from the kitchens, holding trays laden with refreshments.

Ahmen moved along the trays filled with sweet and savory breads, cheeses, fruit, and sweet confections, pausing beside the last one, bearing a whole swan's breast stuffed with dates and goat's cheese. He lifted an eyebrow. "Swan? To what do I owe this honor?"

"You have a guest, my lord, one escorted here by the pharaoh's royal guard," Tuy answered, uneasy. "Not long after, the king's steward, Henufkhet arrived, carrying a message from the pharaoh. The message was a command instructing me to order garments, headdresses, sandals, cosmetics, perfume, jewelry, fans, games and a palanquin for her in the name of the king. This afternoon, trays prepared in the palace kitchens arrived with a message signed by Henufkhet—another gift from His Majesty, sent from his own table."

Ahmen clenched his fists. Ramesses might have yielded to him, but only just. He looked up at the guest terrace, its linen hangings billowing in the breeze. His aggravation melted away. Behind those hangings, Meresamun waited. Nothing else mattered. He glanced down at himself, filthy with desert dust, sweat, and dried blood. He could not let her see him like this.

"Lay out the food on my terrace," he said as he walked into the inner courtyard and unfastened his belt, "and have my best kilt brought down."

Movement on the guest terrace caught his eye. At its edge, Meresamun smiled down at him, her relief tangible. He stopped, drinking in the sight of her. Her smile faded. He looked down, seeing himself with her eyes. Ashamed, he turned into the privacy of the enclosure and sluiced away the worst of the grime before stepping into the warmed waters of the pool. Attendants added scented oils, and as they scrubbed the filth away, Ahmen felt his confidence returning.

A barber arrived. With meticulous care, he shaved the stubble from Ahmen's jaw and scalp. When he was done, Ahmen rose out of the waters, his body drying almost immediately in the desert heat. His servants hastened to rub myrrh oil over him, before tying his kilt around his hips. As an attendant applied kohl to his eyes and eyebrows, Ahmen selected several rings from a tray, placing them on his fingers, while another attendant fastened a pair of golden armbands to his forearms. Slipping his feet into a pair of white sandals, he lifted his bronze mirror, inspecting their work. He nodded, pleased, he was himself again.

In the courtyard, he moved among the flowerbeds surrounding the central pool, collecting cornflowers, poppies, jasmine, daisies, and irises into a lush bouquet. His heart filled with anticipation he climbed the stairs to the terrace. Shaded from the glare of Re-Atum's barque by an indigo-dyed canopy, Meresamun gazed at the boats jostling for position at the docks. Arrayed before her on several low tables, the delicacies from the palace awaited. Ahmen went to her and took hold of her hand. Sekhmet's price had been paid. Meresamun was his.

"I am so glad to see you safe," Meresamun smiled, soft. "It has been a long wait. I feared something terrible had happened."

"The hunt was a success," he answered, forcing himself to find a reassuring smile.

"My heart is glad to hear it." She breathed in the scent of the flowers, looking up at him from under her lashes. "I confess the scent of jasmine is my favorite."

"Then I shall tell my gardeners to plant more jasmine." He gestured to the tables. "You must be hungry, I have made you wait long enough. Let us enjoy the feast the pharaoh has sent to us."

Meresamun watched him in silence as he prepared their platters, placing the choicest pieces upon hers. He took up his own and ate, ravenous. Half-way through, his hunger abating, he realized Meresamun had eaten nothing.

"Are you unwell?" he asked, setting aside his platter.

She didn't answer. Instead, she rose and walked to the edge of the terrace. He followed her, anxious. "You must tell me. Has something happened?"

She looked up at him, apprehensive. "Yesterday morning the pharaoh came to see me at the temple. He brought the papyrus to me himself. I do not know what he has told you. I do not know what I am permitted to say."

Ahmen took her hands in his. "He told me some of it at least, but I would know all of what happened when he met you unless he forbade you to repeat anything."

She shook her head. "He did not."

When she did not continue, he offered, "I know enough to understand what may be troubling you." Her eyes met his, waiting. He pressed on. "He is not happy you have chosen me over him, but he honors your choice. We are in no danger of retribution from him."

"And Sekhmet?" she breathed.

The image of Haran's mutilated body flashed across Ahmen's mind. Forcing himself to keep his eyes on hers, he answered, "Sekhmet has taken her penalty. You are free."

Stricken, Meresamun backed away. She sank onto the divan. "My shame is too great to bear."

"The shame belongs to Ramesses and me. We both knew better; it was our penalty to pay."

"No. It is my fault you took me to your bed. I encouraged you," she said, desperation edging her words. "The price is mine to pay. Not yours, or the pharaoh's. I have been waiting for Sekhmet's retribution—have been wishing for it—so the waiting would end. Instead, I am protected by the pharaoh and escorted by his guards to your villa. Then I learn I am to be given a fortune in gifts. How is it I am to be rewarded while others must suffer?"

Ahmen didn't like where her thoughts were going. He searched for a suitable reply. "Who of us can understand the heart of Sekhmet?" he asked, gentle. "She alone knows the minds of her subjects, knows who should be punished and who should be spared. You must stop thinking this way, to question the decision of the goddess is a dangerous path."

He took Meresamun's chin in his hand, tilting it up so her eyes met his. It was time to change the subject. Her hand touched his.

"I would know just one thing more. I would know Sekhmet's price."

He looked away. He did not want her to know, nothing good could come of it. Her hand tightened.

"Please."

He sighed, relenting. "Our horses were taken by the lion at Bekhen. Kerkhem will never pull a chariot again. Haran was eaten alive. He—"

"No. It is unbearable," Meresamun cried out. "An innocent animal. She killed an innocent animal and maimed another. Why not punish me? How shall I reconcile this in my heart? How shall I ever live well again?"

Her desolation unnerved him. She began to weep, quaking with shame. He took her in his arms, fearful. He should not have told her. It was a long time until she quieted.

"Whatever you must do," he murmured, kissing her brow, "we shall do it. I cannot bear to see you suffer. Tell me how to help you find peace again." She nodded. He brushed the hair from her face. "Tell me, and it shall be done."

Her eyes, still wet, met his. "Tomorrow morning, when Re-Atum's barque rises, you shall have my answer."

SIX

Her heart pounding, Meresamun hastened past the deeper shadows of Ahmen's pleasure garden toward the compound's gate, warm and bright in its pool of torchlight. She stepped from the gloom.

A guard glanced up, startled, his hand darting to the hilt of his dagger. "Lady Meresamun, is something amiss?"

"I have a task to which I must attend," she answered, "and would have the door unbarred."

When he hesitated, she moved into the torchlight, letting him see her temple gown.

He dithered, uncertain. "I will have one of my men accompany you." He gestured to one of the others.

"An escort is coming for me," she said, holding up her hand to stop the other guard from approaching, "you need not ask one of your men to leave their post. I shall be quite safe."

"My lady, we have received no notice of an escort arriving at this time."

"It is a matter of some discretion." She found a faint smile for him. "I assure you, I shall be quite safe. Please, I will be late."

He turned, still uncertain, to heft the bar aside. Meresamun hoped he would not be punished for yielding to her deception. It was wrong of her to lead him to believe she was going to the temple, but after hours of lying awake turning over the possibilities, she knew of no other way she could convince him to unbar the door.

He opened the door and looked out. His arm came out, stopping her before she could pass. "There is no one waiting for you. I do not like this, not one bit."

She pushed his arm aside, gentle. "The goddess will protect me."

Uneasy, he drew back. She stepped into the lane and looked back as the door swung closed; the torchlight within reducing to a narrow band, then a sliver. A quiet thud. Darkness surrounded her. Inside, the wooden beam settled into place, soft, so as not to attract attention.

She shivered. It was cold in the alley. Wrapping her arms around herself, she peered along both directions of the lane, pressing down a tremor of fear. It had been easy to see the northern gate's location from atop the terrace of Ahmen's apartment, but down here between the high compound walls with their overhanging canopies, she could only see a thin strip of sky. All her bearings were lost.

She could only guess. Resigned, she set out for where she hoped the northern gate lay. Trailing her fingers along the outside of Ahmen's courtyard wall, she waited for her eyes to adapt to the shadows. Coming to the wall's corner, she halted. The lane opened up into a small courtyard. At its opposite end, three merchant alleys branched away. With their overhanging awnings, the alleys lay shrouded in an even deeper gloom. Uncertainty assailed her; she had no idea which way to go. She was traveling blind.

She looked back along the wall, toward Ahmen's gate. It was not too late to change her mind, she could go back. She turned halfway, then stopped, shame filling her. No, she had made her choice. There was no going back.

Hoping the middle alley would lead to a main thoroughfare, she decided to take that one. Soon, Re-Atum's barque would ascend, and Ahmen would wake to find her gone. She hurried along the alley, keeping to her chosen path, even as it curved back onto itself. It led to a dead end. A chicken coop filled the space. Within their baskets, the chickens looked up at her in the leaden pre-dawn light, their feathers flattening. Turning back the way she came, she stopped. Two men, elegant and well-groomed, blocked her way.

Despite the dim light, she could see their white kilts were immaculate, the linen a fine, smooth weave; the hems embroidered with a band of hieroglyphs sewn in delicate silver thread. Their belts bore gems, and the leather scabbards of their daggers were inlaid with silver and lapis lazuli.

Meresamun swallowed, these were not Ahmen's men. Whoever they belonged to, however, was powerful and very rich.

"My lords, please allow me to pass."

One of them bowed, graceful. "You must come with us, Lady Meresamun," he said, as charming as a palace courtier. "Our lord has commanded us to bring you to him."

Alarmed, she edged away from them. The backs of her legs touched the low walls of the coop. "I would know who is commanding you to bring a free woman to him against her will."

"You will know when you arrive," he answered, still full of charm. "We have been told to use any means necessary, though we would prefer not to have to force you." He gestured behind him and smiled, his teeth white and even. "There is a closed palanquin waiting for you where you may ride in comfort. We will carry you to him."

"I am afraid I cannot oblige," Meresamun replied, striving to maintain her calm, though her heart pounded so loud, she feared they could hear it in the claustrophobic, oppressive silence. "I have somewhere else I must go, someone is waiting for me and will know I am missing if I do not arrive on time."

"There is no one waiting," he said, his smile tightening as his patience thinned. "Please, do not make this difficult for yourself, you will come with us, whether you consent or not."

"I will never consent," Meresamun panted, terror taking her in its grip. "I beg you, do not carry out this dishonorable command. Think of the day of your judgment, when your heart must face the scales of *Ma'at*."

The men exchanged a look. The other man moved forward. His hand shot out, quick as a viper and caught the back of her head, his fingers wrapping in her hair. With gentle but firm tugs, he pulled her head backward. The fingers of his other hand clamped onto her jaw, forcing her mouth open. Panicking, she cried out for help, her voice loud in the enclosed space.

"Open her mouth wider," the first man said, terse. "Good. Now swallow, my lady, and quickly, for the essence is vile."

She tasted a bitter liquid at the back of her throat. Gagging, she struggled, trying to spit it out. She choked. Unable to stop herself, she swallowed the foul, viscous fluid, her eyes watering. A heartbeat passed, two. A dullness settled over her, the sensation spreading from her torso to her extremities. Her legs folded beneath her.

One of them caught her and lifted her up. "Forgive us," he murmured as he carried her away, "but our lord must be obeyed. You have been given a sleeping draft, used by surgeons for operations. It will not harm you, though when you wake you should drink plenty of water, it will help to ease the pain you will have in your head."

The softness of cushions underneath her. A blanket came over her, warming her cooling body. A whisper in her ear, "Sleep well, and may Horus protect you."

Darkness.

✳   ✳   ✳

His eyes burning with unshed tears, Ahmen lowered the papyrus. Numb with disbelief, he let it go and watched it flutter to the floor. He looked back at the rumpled linens of the bed, struggling to understand Meresamun's words. She could not accept his offer of marriage or be at peace living in wealth and privilege, knowing she did not deserve it.

But out there, alone, without the protection of guards—a woman like her. He shuddered as his mind began to list the unsavory people who gathered around the fringes of decent society: mercenary soldiers, criminals, and unscrupulous slavers. His thoughts skidded to a halt as he recalled the recent reports of foreign sex slavers who kept captured women chained in filthy desert pits, forcing them to suffer terrible things.

Jagged with fear, he tied his kilt around his waist and unlocked the cupboard containing his weapons. His gaze lingered on his *khopesh*, tempted despite knowing it was against the law to wear one outside of the training grounds.

Lifting out his dagger, he pulled the blade from its scabbard, checking its sharpness before fastening it to his belt. As the reassuring weight of it sank onto his hip, he looked back one last time at the bed, where Meresamun had lain beside him. She had just been there. The bed was still warm.

He turned away. He would tear the city apart. He would find her. He had to find her. To lose her was unthinkable.

❆ ❆ ❆

With a start, Meresamun returned. She sat up, her head aching.

An oppressive, thick silence filled the air, ripe with the absence of life; no sounds of servants sweeping, or the quiet murmur of their conversations drifted past the closed terrace panels; no breeze from the river rustled its way through the palms, no plaintive heron cries lifted up to the skies.

Wary, she looked around. A sleeping room, lit by lamps burning smokeless oil. Beautiful pieces of gold-inlaid furniture, arranged in perfect symmetry. A soft and luxurious bed, piled high with cushions. She pressed her hand against the mattress, feeling the spines of small feathers poking between the linens. It was a real bed like Ahmen's, set upon a wooden frame, only this frame's exotic, warm scent told her it was made of precious cedarwood, imported from forests two hundred long iters away, far to the north. Her gaze moved over the fortune of furniture in the room, its lowliest piece far exceeding anything Ahmen possessed. She bit her lip. Whoever had taken her possessed vast wealth, and judging by the obedience of the men who had done the deed, great power, as well.

On a low table beside the bed, a tray holding a silver jug and cup waited, accompanied by an assortment of sweet breads and dried fruits. Her mouth dry as dust, she poured herself a drink of water, rubbing at the dull ache pressing against the inside of her forehead.

She drank, taking in the colorful band of hieroglyphs painted around the room's perimeter, just under the cornice. One of its phrases caught her attention. She re-read the text. It was a declaration of a forbidden love, unreturned, yet the heart of the unloved one vowed to carry on alone, locked in silence. She lowered her eyes. It was too unhappy; she would not finish reading it.

A click as the latch of the door released. She rose, her heart thudding, the cup clutched against her chest. From within the alcove's shadows, the door closed. A man's voice, pleasing and refined, addressed her.

"So you have returned at long last. It is almost time for the evening meal. I had begun to fear my men had given you too much of the draft."

She waited for him to step out from the alcove's gloom. He did not. Nor did he say anything more. She moved closer.

"Who are you," she asked, hesitant, "and why have you ordered your men to take me? What do you intend to do with me?"

"Your first two questions," he replied, "I will not answer. However, I intend to do with you whatever I am asked to do. Your future is not for me to decide."

The cup slipped from her hand and bounced off the bed, clattering against the stone floor, its noise rude against the smooth elegance of the room. "My lord," she protested, frightened, "I have done nothing wrong, the pharaoh himself delivered the papyrus releasing me, granting my freedom. Who are you to gainsay the King of Egypt? What would he say to this act of yours?"

A heartbeat of quiet as he considered her words. "You have done one thing wrong," he answered, his tone turning colder, "you left the safety of Lord Ahmen's villa, and by doing so, made my task easy. You are far outside Waset. If you scream, no one will come to aid you, so save your strength.

"In the meantime, rest, eat, read if it pleases you, I have a library full of scrolls. I do not expect you will have to wait long before a decision is made. If I were in your position, I would appreciate what little time I had left to enjoy such comforts and luxury as are being offered, for very soon—I assure you—it will end."

The door opened and closed once more, soft and discreet. His footsteps faded away. Silence returned. Meresamun sank onto the bed, numb. She bent over and picked up the cup from the floor, setting it back onto its place on the tray.

Her gaze drifted back to the text painted around the perimeter of the room. She forced herself to finish it. The lover dies alone, the name of his forbidden love the last word on his lips. It was depressing, this tale. Who would put such a thing on the wall of a sleeping room? She had been captured by a madman.

Bolting to the door, she pounded her fists against it, pleading to be released, but her cries, just as he had promised, were ignored. She stumbled back to the bed, putting her back against the wall, her arms around her knees. The hieroglyphs taunted her. She closed her eyes, shutting them out, and waited.

※　※　※

Paser hurried through his courtyard gardens, preoccupied, not allowing himself any time to appreciate the beauty of its flowers. Ahead, on a low platform protected by the shade of date palms, his palanquin waited. Eight men, their skin gleaming with oil, knelt beside its support poles. Paser settled onto its cushioned chair and gripped its armrests, bracing himself for the ascent as his bearers rose to their feet. They lifted him up in one fluid motion. He quirked an eyebrow, pleased. A good omen. His guards opened the gates to his villa, proceeding ahead, clearing the way.

Paser settled back for the ride to Waset, his thoughts returning to Meresamun, locked in his guest room. A dilemma. Yesterday, his spies had confirmed Ramesses had freed her himself before the lion hunt, taking her with him from the temple. But in a peculiar twist, he sent her to Ahmen's villa, under the protection of his own guard.

Paser shifted, uneasy. What if, for reasons he could not yet know, Ramesses had relinquished Meresamun to his oldest friend? If he had, Paser was committing a foul crime, breaking the twenty-ninth of the forty-two laws of *Ma'at*.

He rubbed his hand against his kilt, smoothing down its pleats as he considered the law: *I have not acted hastily or without thought.* Wrestling with his conscience, he reviewed what he had observed on the night of the feast. While it was clear Ramesses desired the priestess, there was also no doubt there had been a strong attraction between Ahmen and Meresamun.

But Ahmen was a law-abiding man, courageous and honorable, a model Egyptian, Ahmen would never take a priestess to his bed, even while full of wine. And, of course, there was the fortune's worth of gifts Ramesses had bestowed upon Meresamun. No, she must belong to Ramesses, Ahmen's villa nothing more than a resting place for her until a villa of her own could be had, where Ramesses could visit her, discreet, an ex-priestess. Yes. She had run away to escape her eventual fate, a life of loneliness and imprisonment in a gilded cage, a slave to Ramesses's lust. Paser nodded, congratulating himself for his foresight to keep his men outside Ahmen's villa.

He spread his fingers out, examining his manicured nails. A memory returned, irking him. More than once he had caught Ahmen and Meresamun sharing their food, intimate, like lovers. Maybe Ahmen *had* bedded her, and Ramesses was covering it up to protect his lifelong friend. If Paser was wrong and had misjudged, then no matter where he sent Meresamun, if she belonged to

Ahmen, she would find a way to return. Questions would be asked, answers demanded.

Uncertain, he glanced back at his villa, its buildings and colonnades gleaming white, surrounded by verdant fields of green. If he were to be found out, he would lose everything. He still had time to undo the damage, Meresamun did not know who her captor was. She could be drugged and returned to Waset's alleys, but it would be the queen's decision, not his. He had done his work; the rest would be up to Nefertari.

In the distance, the walls of Waset shimmered in the light of the lowering disk of Re-Atum. Nefertari would be pleased, as she always was whenever he removed another of her competitors from court. But what if this time he had been too eager to protect his queen? Meresamun could not be handled the same way as the courtesans. Those women were sent to one of the eleven fortresses of The Horus Way, far to the north in Lower Egypt. Surrounded by long iters of burning desert, they soon realized there was nothing else for them to do but make their fortunes servicing the soldiers.

They did not remain long in the fortresses; often they were claimed as companions by the most senior members at the post. Many fell in love or married, a few lived in wealth beyond their dreams. Others retired in luxury in the vast city of Pi-Ramesses, or were taken on as a companion by one of the capital's elite.

There was one who had achieved great success. Nerit, stunning, ambitious, and devious, her heart set on a crown. Paser sent her to Byblos, where she became King Bentesina's favorite courtesan, making a fortune. Not satisfied with her lot, she traveled to Tarhuntassa, and enthralled Muwatallis so much, he charged his queen with treason, banished her, and crowned Nerit instead. Yes, Nerit had been worth the effort and expense to send far away. A heartless, conniving woman, she was the perfect match for the cold-blooded King of Hatti.

Paser's guards called out to make way as Waset's eastern gate came into view. A path opened through the bustling crowd. Nobles and commoners bowed before Egypt's vizier, murmuring with excitement. Ignoring them, Paser continued with his thoughts: In many ways those women were better off for his intervention. Once Ramesses grew bored with his conquests—which he always did—there could be no return to society, not once a woman had been known by a god in the flesh. For each discarded unfortunate, a life sentence awaited her in one of the harems, where she would be left to pace her gilded cage, surrounded by jealousy and hate, forgotten and unloved, waiting for the day her heart would stop beating.

His bearers turned down the market street, passing the empty meat stalls, closed for the day. A cat ran in front of them, a dead rat dangling from her mouth. Flies swarmed, thick in the fetid air. Paser hated the meat market; such a filthy place. He held his breath, flicking his fly whisk back and forth, willing his bearers to move faster. Another cat bolted under the palanquin. Paser narrowed his eyes, watching it as it pounced. A terrified squeal. His men moved on.

The cat reminded Paser of Ramesses, to whom women were prey; creatures to be caught, played with, then cast aside as soon as another captured his attention. Paser scoffed. Yet, women went to him willing enough, dreaming of being made a queen. In four years, not one of them had been crowned. All of them forgotten, discarded, replaced.

Paser wondered how many frightened, weeping women his clandestine actions had saved? He did a quick calculation. The number was almost four dozen. He felt a stab of pride; all those women, spared.

His bearers climbed upward, entering the walled citadel of the nobility. Paser looked toward the palace walls, glowing pink in the evening's light, recalling Nefertari's hollow expression at the banquet, as Ramesses, drunk, flaunted his lust for the priestess.

If only she were mine—

Paser cut off the thought. It could never be, it was impossible. It was dangerous even thinking it. But it was in his power to do this one thing: To his dying breath, he would protect the woman he loved from Ramesses's humiliations. Anything for her. Anything. Even to the cost of his eternal soul.

※　※　※

At this time of the evening, the scents of the pleasure garden pleased Nefertari most. She caressed the soft petals of a poppy, distracted. Ramesses had not sent for the children after his evening meal. How disappointed they had been. She learned he had been closeted with Ahmen and Waset's chief constable the whole day, runners coming and going.

None knew what was happening, or if they did, were unwilling to speak of it. She considered asking Paser; he would be certain to know, though whether he would tell her was another question altogether. A rustle of material. She turned. Imtes approached, her eyes filled with excitement.

"My lady," she breathed, "Vizier Paser requests permission to approach the queen's presence, what shall I tell the guard to say?"

"Granted," Nefertari smiled, pleased, then added, "instruct my attendants to fall back."

She turned as Imtes departed and continued through the gardens, aware of her attendants slowing their steps. She savored the space. From the corner of her eye, she caught Paser's arrival, his fists crossing over his chest. He bowed.

She picked a cornflower. Lifting it to her nose, she smiled, glancing sideways at him. "Lord Paser, I was just thinking of you. How convenient you should arrive just now when I have had thoughts of you in my mind."

His composure deserted him. His hands moved to the pommels of his daggers, a stance forbidden in her presence. He caught himself and murmured an apology.

Still holding the flower, she turned toward him, curious. "Your distress is quite noticeable. Do you come bearing bad news?"

"No, my lady." He pressed his palm to his heart. "Forgive me. All is well, though there is an urgent matter I should like to discuss with you."

She moved along the path. He fell in beside her. She kept her tone light. "Is it to do with Ramesses shutting himself away all day today?"

He hesitated. Then: "I have not been part of his meetings, though I suspect I may be the cause of them."

She stopped, intrigued. He stepped closer. "I have Meresamun. My men found her outside Ahmen's villa, alone, before Re-Atum's barque ascended this morning."

Nefertari blinked. Familiar, bitter jealousy pooled in her torso. "So," she snapped, "he refrains from his duties to search for a runaway priestess. She must have a firm hold upon him indeed, to cause him to refuse his children." She moved on. "Should he uncover where she is, your wealth and power will not protect you. Ramesses will send you to the gods."

Paser nodded, solemn. She walked on, catching Imtes watching them, her eyes full of hope. She turned her back to her, irritated. Now wasn't the time.

The vizier cleared his throat and leaned closer, his voice low. "I have come to seek your counsel. Meresamun may be Ahmen's woman, or Ramesses might be keeping her at Ahmen's for himself. Yesterday, he sent her a fortune of gifts, which favors the latter possibility. I am prepared to resolve this once and for all. Anything you ask of me, it shall be done. Anything."

Plucking the cornflower's petals one by one, Nefertari considered his offer. She looked up at him, watching her, his expression unreadable. She shook her head. No. It was monstrous even to think it. She walked on.

"You say your men found Meresamun alone in the lanes of Waset," she said, pausing to sniff what remained of the cornflower. "I would know why. I must speak with her."

Paser's eyes darkened. "Impossible. I cannot bring her into the palace, and you cannot visit my villa without bringing half the palace with you."

"Then I shall not leave as the queen," Nefertari said, bristling at his tone, "but as my sister. Imtes will stay with me tonight. When it is late, I will cover my face with a veil and leave as her. You will have a palanquin waiting for me at the gates."

His eyebrow quirked. She suppressed a smile. He hadn't expected that. She waited. He looked over his shoulder, inspecting Imtes as though she were a horse at market. Her sister blushed, shy under his perusal.

"I beg you, reconsider," he murmured. "Apart from the terrible risk you would take, Lady Imtes's reputation will be ruined if it becomes known she has visited my villa unescorted. What of the price she would pay for such a scandal?"

Nefertari smiled, pleased to offer the prize herself. "Then it is as I have long suspected. You are a blind man. Imtes only has eyes for you and would welcome the implication as your lover. Unless you would rather not have the queen's sister as your wife?"

Something deep within his eyes flickered. He veiled it almost instantly. His composure returned. He backed away, bowing, formal. "Your Majesty. As you wish, it shall be done."

Tossing aside the ruined cornflower, she gestured for Imtes to join her, forcing a smile for her sister's sake. At least one of them would have her heart's desire. It would be enough. It had to be.

✳ ✳ ✳

Outside Meresamun's room, Nefertari adjusted her veil, her heart tight with trepidation. It had been far more difficult to leave the palace than she had expected. She had almost been unveiled not once, but twice. Never again would she underestimate the diligence of the palace guards.

Paser unlocked the door, his expression thin. Nefertari pressed her lips together, a spear of guilt impaling her as she realized just how much she had asked of him. Her ill-considered plan had put both of their lives in mortal danger. He pushed the door open and nodded at her. It was time.

Upon the bed, Meresamun lay huddled in a ball, a cushion clutched against her chest. Even in her disheveled state, the priestess's beauty was flawless. Nefertari felt a childish, jealous urge to slap her. She raised her hand. Meresamun's eyes opened. She cried out and scuttled to the other side of the bed, still holding the cushion. Paser had said they had little time. Nefertari went straight to the point.

"Where were you going in the dead of the night, alone and unescorted?" she demanded.

Meresamun's fingers tightened on the cushion, defensive. She shook her head.

"You will answer me," Nefertari said, low, irked by the woman's refusal, "for it is I who shall decide your fate."

A heartbeat of silence. "To make my atonement," the priestess whispered, her gaze falling to the bed cover.

"Atonement?" Nefertari asked, taken aback. "For what?"

"I encouraged Lord Ahmen to know me," Meresamun answered, quiet. Her blue eyes lifted up, filled with shame. "My lady, I have committed a terrible crime. I am—was—a priestess."

"Ah," Nefertari nodded, understanding. "You were on your way to confess."

"No," Meresamun whispered, her fingers toying with the cushion's tassels, nervous. "I cannot go back to the temple."

"And why not?" Nefertari demanded, perplexed.

A long silence. Then: "Pharaoh Ramesses, Blessed of Re, took me from the temple to protect me from my punishment. If I were to go back, he would face retribution."

Nefertari leaned forward, tendrils of jealousy rising anew, tightening around her heart. "He protected you because he intended you for himself?" she asked, taut.

"No, because he pitied me," Meresamun answered, low, after an uncertain silence. "I was prepared to face my punishment, but he intervened and sent me back to Ahmen."

Nefertari couldn't keep up. She went back to the beginning. "If the pharaoh has reprieved you, why would you need to make atonement?"

Meresamun cast aside the cushion. "How shall I live in peace when my crimes have been paid for with the blood and suffering of innocents?" she cried out, anguished. "I cannot. I prayed to Sekhmet. Last night I sensed her answer: Until I have atoned, until she has forgiven me, Ahmen will not find me again."

Nefertari frowned. What blood and suffering? She tried to make sense of Meresamun's words. Ah. The lion hunt. She was talking about Haran. "Then where were you going? Where *could* you go?"

"Back to my mother and father in Babylon," Meresamun said, soft. "I pray they still live."

Nefertari stared at the woman, incredulous. Babylon was on the other side of the world. Meresamun would never make it. She had chosen death, the true path of atonement. Learning Meresamun had chosen Ahmen over Ramesses was enough to make Nefertari's journey from the palace worth every risk. The woman should be rewarded, not punished.

Nefertari had heard enough. She moved to the door. "Your honor compels me to aid you. A private barque will be arranged to carry you to Pi-Ramesses."

"My lady—"

Nefertari raised her hand. "Right now, the pharaoh is tearing the city apart searching for you. I have it in my power to ensure there will be no trace left of your departure, but if I do so, at great risk to myself, you must never speak of this to anyone. Do you agree?"

Meresamun nodded. Their eyes met, and for the briefest heartbeat, Nefertari recognized herself in the woman before her; caged, powerless, their paths decided by men and their gods. She pulled the veil away.

Meresamun's eyes widened, fearful. "Your Majesty, I . . ."

Nefertari opened the door. "I admire your courage," she murmured. "I pray you will find your absolution. I believe you, above all others, deserve to know peace."

❋   ❋   ❋

"You have not found her, then?" Ramesses asked.

Ahmen shook his head, numb. "No, my lord. It is as if she has vanished."

Ramesses gestured to the chief constable to give his report.

"Your Majesty," he said as he unfurled a scroll and read over the notes, "no building in Waset has gone unsearched over these last three days. If she is still alive, Lady Meresamun is not in Waset. According to the dock master's records, two barques left for Pi-Ramesses the day she went missing. She may be traveling with one of them, though there is no record of her booking passage."

Ramesses looked at Ahmen. "What do you say, had she any way to pay for her passage?"

Ahmen handed a papyrus over to Ramesses. "Everything in my house is accounted for. As for the gifts you acquired for her, they have all been left behind."

Ramesses looked over the notations, silent.

Ahmen looked down at the floor as the chief constable departed, hearing Ramesses as though from a great distance, imagining watching himself from the other side of the room, none of it happening to him. He realized he had not heard what Ramesses had been saying. He forced himself to pay attention.

" . . . I will dispatch a courier to the mayor of Pi-Ramesses. If Meresamun somehow took one of those barques, we still have a chance of finding her and bringing her home."

Ahmen rubbed his eyes. Pi-Ramesses was three times the size of Waset. How would he ever find her? He sensed Ramesses was waiting.

"My lord, thank you."

Ramesses grasped Ahmen's shoulders. "Speak your mind," he said, "I can see you are suffering. At such a time as this, you need not hide your feelings from me."

Ahmen looked up and saw the friend of his youth. The barrier he had sustained for three days disintegrated. "We have no idea where she is," he said, sick with despair. "She could already be on her way to the Nubian mines, bound in chains, forced to be a water bearer—or worse. What if we never find her, never know if she is alive or dead? How can I go on, eating and living if she is suffering? It is unbearable."

Ramesses patted Ahmen's shoulder, his movements awkward. Silence fell and lengthened. Ahmen closed his eyes. It was hopeless. A tear escaped.

Ramesses cleared his throat. "Have faith. I am the Pharaoh of Egypt. I have the resources to find her, though it may take some time. I too do not sleep or have an appetite to eat. There can be no satisfaction until she is brought back to us. I will not leave you alone in this, I swear it."

Ahmen met Ramesses's eyes. "Unless this is the true punishment of Sekhmet," he whispered, haunted.

For a heartbeat, Ramesses did not reply. He turned away. "In my darkest thoughts," he answered in a low voice, "I have wondered the same, myself."

SEVEN

City of Pi-Ramesses, Late Spring.
Reign of Ramesses II, Year 5

Sethi woke and stared at the ceiling. It was his dream. Again. Always the same. It never changed. For thirteen years, he had dreamed of her standing alone in the midst of a violent battle, surrounded by fire, her gown torn and bloodstained. Jewelry covered her arms and neck. Her dark hair, tangled, blew around her face in the heated updrafts. Her eyes, wide, fearful, searched, desperate, through the men dying around her.

In every single dream, he fought his way to her, his arms bloody, his body wracked with pain. And just as he was about to reach her, a blade, from behind, delved into his heart, the pain agonizing. Stricken, she fell to her knees, her hands coming to his face, but he had never felt her touch. Not once in thirteen years.

He sat up, agitated, and rubbed his hand over his scalp.

"You have dreamed of her again."

He looked down. Edarru lay naked atop the linens watching him, her green eyes highlighted by the malachite painted on her eyelids. She got up and poured him wine.

"It is more frequent of late," he admitted as he took it from her.

Her hand came to his forearm. She stroked it, soothing him. He turned the cup in his hands, thinking of the dream, of the woman, of his death. He drank the wine, wiping his mouth with the back of his hand, grateful it was Edarru who shared his bed this evening. She was the only person who knew of the dream, and she never judged him, was never jealous.

He cupped one of her breasts in his hand. She arched her back, and let him feel its fullness. He brushed his thumb against her nipple, watching it harden, despite the oppressive heat. She was perfect. Why could he not just take her as his companion? He let go.

"Though I would stay and have you again," he said, brushing her hair, damp from their lovemaking, back from her brow, "I must go. My captains are waiting. What would you have of me for this evening?"

She smiled and lifted his fingers to her lips, kissing them. "Whatever pleases you."

He watched her, his groin stirring as she bit his thumb. He groaned. "Would you like a villa of your own?"

She scoffed but did not cease in her seduction. "It is cruel to tease."

He pulled her onto his lap. "You are my favorite courtesan, have been my woman in Pi-Ramesses for these past five years. I owe you more than gold for the time you have wasted on me."

She knelt, straddling his groin and slid her hips against him, making him hard. "And will you come to visit me in this villa?"

He entered her, and let her ride him, her breasts pressing against his chest until his release was close. "Every day," he promised as he flipped her over and found the spot she loved. She arched her back, crying out. He followed close after. He rolled away, pulling her into his arms.

"You won't," she sighed. "I understand what you are doing. I will miss you, all alone in my fine villa."

"You should have a husband," he said as he brushed his lips against her forehead. "I have kept you long enough from motherhood."

She fell silent. Tears glinted in her eyes. Guilt sliced through him. "Please don't. You have ever known my heart."

"And yet, after all we have shared together," she said as she collected her gown from the floor, "how can you blame me for hoping? I am real, I am right here . . ."

He took her in his arms and held her as she wept. Was he wrong to send her away to find another man just because of a dream? He realized he was tired of waiting too. "Give me until after the campaign against Hatti," he murmured, "then I will be yours."

She looked up at him, fearful, hopeful. "With all my heart, I pray you do not find her before then."

He looked away, ashamed his feelings for a woman he had never met were stronger than the ones he had for the woman who had loved him for five years.

He watched her dress, her movements subdued, quiet. He ordered her a chair and saw her off, her green eyes meeting his, filled with longing, and dread. He closed the door to the lane. The night was still young. Once he had met with his captains, he would drink until he forgot the woman in his dream. Just for one night, he would have peace.

❋   ❋   ❋

Meresamun hefted the tray of dirty crockery over her head and pushed her way back to the kitchens, struggling to escape the drunken groping of the tavern's boisterous patrons. Someone snatched at the back of her gown, sending her stumbling down the steps into the kitchen, the tray's contents dangerously wobbling. One of the cooks, naked apart from a loincloth, rushed over and took the tray, a look of sympathy on his face.

With a nod of gratitude, Meresamun sank onto a ledge and plucked her sweat-soaked gown from her damp breasts, the unrelenting heat and still air making her feel as though the gods had turned Pi-Ramesses into a bread oven. Her gaze drifted around the smoky low-ceilinged kitchen bustling with workers, the air thick with the smell of roasting meat. Teret, the tavern's owner, hefted a fresh jug of wine and settled it against her hip; her heavy breasts and thick torso beaded with sweat. She sidled over, nimble despite her girth. At the door's lintel, she surveyed the room, packed with carousing soldiers and even a handful officers.

"I don't care how hot it is," she said, sliding a sideways look at Meresamun, "make sure to smile—and if one of the pharaoh's officers asks to take you home, you don't be saying no again like last time. For the love of Isis, do you think offers like that happen every day?" She pulled apart the ties on Meresamun's gown, deft. "If I had those big, perky tits, I'd have them right out, showing them off—"

"Teret!" Meresamun cried, pushing her away. She hastened to cover her breasts, noticing several of the soldiers were watching them, their eyes dark. A fat, hard pinch lanced her buttock. Meresamun yelped, furious.

"I'm only trying to help you," Teret tutted, unapologetic. "If you ever want to get back to your family, you are going to have to start spreading those fine long legs of yours, unless you want to end up an old woman like me, pouring wine until the day you die."

Meresamun rubbed her backside, certain it would bruise. "There must be another way. I can tell stories—"

Teret laughed, sour. "Ah, that you can, I heard you well enough when I found you, starving and shivering in the slums. Fine, fancy stories no one down here in the gutter cares to hear."

"But they are the only stories I know."

Her eyes softening, Teret brushed a loose tendril of Meresamun's hair back into place. "I'm fond of you, though I don't know why, with your funny airs and high morals. Ah, but there it is. If you don't ever save enough money to leave, you will always have a home at The Falcon's Wing, here with me."

A deafening cheer filled the tavern. Teret turned, her eyes narrowing, listening to the men hailing one of their own, the name almost drowned out by the pounding of fists on tables. Teret's eyes widened. She pulled Meresamun back into the shelter of the kitchen.

"Clean yourself up," she said, no longer playful. "This is your night."

Curious, Meresamun leaned over to see, but Teret yanked her back into the shadows, her strength surprising. "You listen to me. One of the most powerful men in the empire has just walked into my tavern. You will serve his table, and if you are very lucky, he will take you home. If he asks, I forbid you to say no."

Nervous, Meresamun licked her lips, hopeful, yet fearful. "Is he . . . Lord Ahmen-om-onet?"

"Who?" Teret asked, distracted by the cheers. "Never heard of him. No, he is none other than Lord Sethi, Commander of the Army. I knew him when he was growing up in this slum, street fighting to survive. Now he has risen to power and wealth almost as great as Pharaoh himself."

She turned, hustling Meresamun through the kitchens toward her quarters in the storerooms. "Put on a fresh gown, wash your face, and tidy your hair and cosmetics," she ordered, brusque. A sharp slap landed on Meresamun's backside, making her jump. "And you'd better be quick about it or I'll have you scrubbing pots for the rest of your life!"

Lord Sethi, the Commander of the Army was drunk. As Meresamun poured more wine into Sethi's cup, she caught Teret watching her, hawkish.

Patting the bench beside him, one of Sethi's men, the one called Naram, gestured for her to sit, his actions clumsy and uncoordinated.

"Come an' sit with us," he slurred, his face flushed from wine.

Clutching the jug against her chest, Meresamun glanced at Teret, uncertain, who nodded, making frantic shooing gestures. Meresamun sank down, catching the one called Sethi, sitting across from her, look up from his cup, his movements heavy and languid. He gazed at her for a while, curious, unsettling her.

"You are no tavern maid," he muttered in a deep, rough voice. "You are a princess from another land."

Meresamun stared at him, astonished, wondering how he could possibly know. His gaze turned blank. Leaning on his elbows, he gazed at the table, chuckling.

Naram leaned over, his breath hot against her ear. "Lord Sethi's far gone, don't mind him. Wha' are you called, oh flower of the Nile?"

"Mere—" she stopped, and forced a smile.

Naram raised an eyebrow. "Mere? Thassa strange name."

Sethi's head lifted up, his eyes unseeing. "Meresamun? Ahmen's missing woman?"

Naram shook his head, wagging it back and forth as he replied. "No my lord, she's jus' Mere. She's not Ahmen's woman. Or—lessee—are you Ahmen's woman?"

Stricken, Meresamun said nothing. She couldn't. Sekhmet had to send Ahmen to her, and so long as he did not come to her, the goddess's message was clear. She was not forgiven.

One of the others, less intoxicated, laughed and held out his cup to her. Grateful for the diversion, she refilled it.

"She's just a tavern maid," he chided Naram. "Leave her alone." He gestured at Meresamun. "Come, sit with me. I'll protect you from our first captain's nonsense."

Naram waved her away, almost knocking over the cup beside him. Meresamun moved to the other side of the table to join her rescuer, catching Teret's smile of satisfaction as she slipped in beside Sethi. Her rescuer leaned over, elegant and attractive, his interest plain.

"Mere, I am Khutu, third captain of Lord Sethi's division, the second division of the pharaoh's army known as Pre." He nodded at the others around the table. "These are Commander Sethi's other captains, each of us command one thousand men."

She sensed he was waiting for her reaction. She nodded, showing what she hoped was a fair imitation of admiration. She poured more wine into Naram's cup. "I have heard rumors the pharaoh intends to go to war," she said. "Is it true?"

His eyes on hers, Khutu took a drink. "It is." His hand moved to her thigh. "We leave next week to retake Kadesh from the Hittites."

He began to stroke her leg, up and down, higher and higher, his fingers drifting toward her crotch. She edged closer to Sethi. "Kadesh?" she asked, pushing his hand back down. "Is that close to Babylon?"

Sethi laughed again, to himself. She looked at Khutu, who shrugged at Sethi's behavior, answering, "Much closer than Pi-Ramesses, but still quite far." He leaned closer. "Why? Do you have a lover in Babylon I should be jealous of?"

"No my lord," she answered in a small voice, losing the fight to his probing fingers. "I was just curious."

He smiled, pleased, his fingers sliding between her thighs until his middle finger touched her crotch, light. "I would pay much to take you to my bed this night. I am not a poor man. Ask whatever you wish, and you shall have it."

"I . . ."

His other hand slid around her head. He pulled her to him, his lips touching hers, soft. "I have been told I am talented in the art of love."

She pulled back. "My lord, I cannot."

Undeterred, he stood, bringing her with him. "Come now; I will pay whatever you wish, there is no need to play games."

"There are no games," Meresamun protested, trying to free her arm from his grip. "I beg you, cease."

He hesitated. "Are you another man's wife?"

"No . . . but I love another."

He laughed, though it was not unkind. "Mere, I love my wife, she is the mother of my sons. But what I ask for is not about love, but pleasure. There is no crime in taking pleasure when the body is crying out for it, so long as the heart remains faithful to the one they love."

She pulled back, bumping against Sethi's shoulder, it felt like hitting a wall. "I cannot. Please," her eyes raked over the tavern, desperate to find her replacement, "take another for your pleasure. I am unwilling."

She felt Khutu's strength as he took hold of her arms, possessive. "I do not want another," he persisted, his eyes darkening with desire. "I swear upon Re's light I will not harm you. I shall spend the night pleasing you, whatever you wish will be my command."

"Then my wish is to return to serving your lord and his captains their wine," Meresamun pled, struggling to escape his hold.

He stared at her, disbelieving, his warmth cooling to irritation. "Enough of your nonsense," he snapped, "you are a tavern maid, the next nearest thing to a whore. How dare you refuse me."

He pushed his way out from between the tables, pulling her after him, dragging her to the kitchens. She cried out, begging him to stop. Above the din of laughing and shouting voices, one cut across them all, sharp, commanding.

"Captain Khutu. My cup is empty."

The tavern fell quiet. Khutu halted, the blood draining from his face. His grip lessened, uncertain. Meresamun pulled free and hastened back to the table, the tavern's patrons turning raucous once more. Her hands shaking, she refilled the commander's cup.

"Sit down," he jerked his head at the seat beside him, "you will remain with me until I leave."

She sat, trembling. Across from her, Khutu took his seat, diffident. "Commander, had I known you wished Mere for yourself—"

Sethi drank, shrugging, non-committal. Murmuring an apology, Khutu averted his eyes from Meresamun, turning to seek out another companion. From under her lashes, Meresamun watched him call Retan over. Her eyes shining, she came to him, brazen, baring her breasts as he settled her onto his lap. He flirted with her, making her laugh at his bawdy jokes. Before long, they left.

Meresamun filled Sethi's cup. He turned it in his hands, round and round, watching the wine swirl. A little of it sloshed over the edge, down his hand, onto the table. She wiped the table, careful not to touch him.

He took the cloth from her and wiped his hands, his movements slow, exaggerated by the drink. He pushed the cloth back to her. "My mother was a serving woman," he muttered, "and she was no whore. When I was seven, a patron raped her when she refused to service him."

He drank deep, falling silent for a long while. Meresamun poured more wine. He looked up, staring at nothing. "She died from her injuries."

"My lord, my heart aches for your loss," Meresamun said, soft, and meant it.

He shook his head. "I cannot change the past, and perhaps, not the future, either . . ."

Meresamun waited for him to say more, but he remained silent. The night wore on, and he said little else, apart from his thanks for her services. He drank, on and on, emptying three jugs of wine, never once looking at her.

She waited for him to fall unconscious, but he carried on drinking, silent, morose. As he ruminated, she occupied herself with listening to his men speak of the ordeals they would face during the long march ahead, and of their hopes the quality of whores amongst the followers would be better this campaign.

At times, they talked to her, asking about her past. She was careful in her replies, diverting them with questions about the march, seeking answers to the ones burning within her breast. She learned much. The night waned. One by one, they left.

His thick, muscled arms crossed over his chest, Sethi dozed, still upright. Meresamun gazed out the open door, at the pale blue light which always arrived just before morning began. It had been a long night. She stifled a yawn.

From the kitchens, the smell of Sethi's order, roasted chicken, wafted. Her stomach growled, hollow. Apart from a servant opening the shutters, and another cleaning the tables, the tavern was empty. Even Teret had long since taken to her pallet.

While she waited to serve the commander's morning meal, Meresamun thought of Egypt's army gathering, preparing for its thirty-day march to Kadesh, how each division would be joined by one thousand paid followers—tradesmen, cooks, leatherworkers and armorers. With so many civilians in the rearguard, she was certain no one would notice one more. A storyteller might make a welcome diversion after a long day of marching.

Nourishing her kindling hope, she unfolded her fingers and looked down at the small gold ingot Sethi had given her before he dozed off. She hid it in the folds of her gown. It was worth more than two months wages. She thought of the six months she had spent surviving on scraps within the roughest slums of Pi-Ramesses before Teret took her in, saving her life and giving Meresamun the chance to save for her passage to Babylon. An exorbitant, impossible price, she soon learned.

Over the next two months, as she labored in The Falcon's Wing, she had hoped after all she had endured, Sekhmet might forgive her and allow Ahmen to find her. The days blended together, unchanging in their monotony. Though a surprisingly high number of officers and nobles drank at The Falcon's Wing, Ahmen never once crossed its threshold.

A familiar feeling of despair pulled on her. She fought it, forcing herself to think instead of her parents, imagining their joy when they would see her again, of her return to her opulent childhood home, set within a vast estate on the banks of the Purattu River.

The roast chickens arrived, their skin crisped golden and bubbling with grease. Her mouth watering, she laid the food out and prepared the commander's platter. He roused, tearing a leg from one of the chickens. She poured him a cup of beer. He nodded his thanks and waved her away.

Grateful to be relinquished from her duties, she slipped into the kitchens. Deserted and dark, its silence felt strange, unnerving. She collected her covered platter of roast meat, long cold—her wages for the night—and hurried to her pallet in the storerooms to eat.

Pushing aside the linen hanging into her private quarters, she looked down at her dinner, grilled goat shank. Despite it being congealed white in its fat, she felt a wave of gratitude. After months of deprivation and hunger, she had food and a place to sleep. She was safe here, and Teret, though crude at times, was kind to her. But Meresamun could not stay. If she did, she might never have another chance to return home.

Shredding the shank into strips, she devoured it, her resolve firming as her hunger abated. She would march to Kadesh with the army, and once there, with what the commander had given her, she might even have enough to pay for a place in a caravan.

She looked around the cramped storeroom as the first light from Re's barque filtered in through the opening in the low ceiling. It moved across the wall toward the small stone statue of Sekhmet, nestled in an alcove. Meresamun set aside her empty platter and knelt, asking the goddess if she should stay in Pi-Ramesses to give Ahmen more time. She peeked up just as the light touched the goddess's leonine face. Sekhmet glared back at her, implacable. Meresamun bowed her head, tears burning her eyes. Though she had nourished her hopes, she knew what she sought was impossible. Sekhmet would never forgive her; her crime was too great.

Meresamun closed her eyes and lay down. Sekhmet had given her answer. Go to Babylon. A tear slipped out. It was over. She would never see Ahmen again.

PART III

KADESH
Summer 1274 BCE

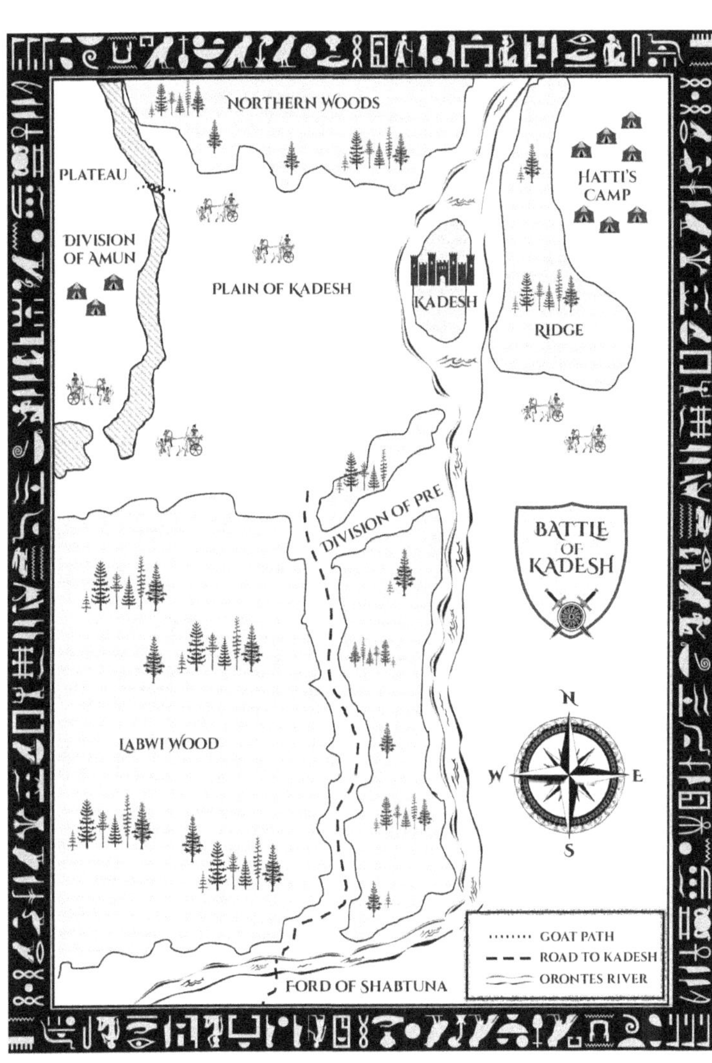

NORTHERN WOODS
PLATEAU
HATTI'S CAMP
DIVISION OF AMUN
PLAIN OF KADESH
KADESH
RIDGE
DIVISION OF PRE
BATTLE OF KADESH
LABWI WOOD
N
W
E
S
GOAT PATH
ROAD TO KADESH
ORONTES RIVER
FORD OF SHABTUNA

ONE

Summer. Reign of Ramesses II,
Year 5 / Reign of Muwatallis, Year 21

From the distance, a blast of horns sounded, breaching the quiet calm of Istara's afternoon meal. She lowered her eating knife, listening. The horns sounded again. Her skin prickled. A long buried memory returned, vivid. She knew that sound. Thirteen years ago, at seven, she had heard it the first time—when the armies of Egypt arrived and her people starved.

She pulled the terrace's wooden doors open. Damp afternoon air rushed in. She shivered. Reaching for a cloak, she wrapped it around herself as another sounding of horns came, louder, closer.

The sky hung low and oppressive, its dark clouds reflecting in the puddles on her apartment's terrace. Summer had not come, nor even spring. Instead, an unnatural cold stalked the land as incessant, heavy rains fell, cold, sharp, relentless.

She had heard the whispers. Kadesh was being punished for Rhoha's return as high priestess. Two months ago, her aunt had arrived at the palace with Urhi-Teshub's infant son Hartapu in her arms. Surrounded by Muwatallis's soldiers, she flaunted the King of Hatti's protection, reveling in Amunira's powerlessness over her. But the months she had lived in Tarhuntassa had changed her; a strange, sudden illness had left her beautiful hands misshapen, her fingers twisted. Some murmured her disfigurement was her punishment for what she had done to Istara through Urhi-Teshub.

Despite her illness and her pregnancy, Rhoha had lost no time in Tarhuntassa. She trained in the dark arts, devoting her time to seeking augurs and omens, becoming so adept at seeing the future, she gained the favor and trust of the King of Hatti. Now, with his protection, none dared challenge her, not even Urhi-Teshub, though it was said he had refused to see his son.

Istara closed her eyes, forcing away the nascent thoughts of her husband. After he had left for Babylon, it had taken half a year for her body to heal. Two months more had brought her strength back, though the ache in her heart remained. A month after Rhoha returned, Anash lay down in her basket and went to sleep. She never woke up. She was old at eleven and had had a good life, but Istara was inconsolable.

With Anash's companionship gone, Istara felt alone, vulnerable. And as Rhoha paraded her son through the corridors, behaving as though she was Urhi-Teshub's wife already, Istara accepted with the loss of Anash her last remaining connection to her husband was gone. He had sent her a letter the day after Anash died, from his camp across the river. She burned it, unopened, like all the others. His letters had regained her trust once. Never again.

A heavy pounding erupted at her door. She jumped, startled. Hasurna, Kadesh's commander entered in full battle armor. He bowed.

"My lady, the king wishes to see you before he departs."

❋   ❋   ❋

Huddled against the wall of the roof garden, Istara watched, wary, as Rhoha circled the king, sprinkling chicken blood onto his weapons and armor, murmuring low incantations. A biting wind gusted down from the mountains, making the tassels of Rhoha's tunic flap into the bowl, splattering blood over her robe. With a deft movement, she warded the evil.

Istara turned away, shivering within the folds of her cloak. At the far side of the Plain of Kadesh, the pharaoh's golden chariot began its ascent up the southern slope of the wide plateau at the base of the mountain range. The Egyptian column, five chariots abreast, stretched away behind him for almost an iter to where it emerged from Labwi Wood. As Ramesses's white horses—their legs stained black with mud—made the long climb up the slope, the line lengthened. Soldiers continued to emerge from the forest's edge, endless. Istara watched, fascinated, morbid, knowing what was to come.

Her father joined her, his gaze moving past the Egyptians to the distant mountains, where, beyond their girth, the kingdoms of Amurru lay. A hiss of metal as he sheathed his weapons, followed by the quiet creak of leather as he leaned his weight against their hilts. She looked up at him. He nodded toward the plateau.

"This clash has been going on for almost two hundred years. But tonight, unless the gods intervene, Egypt will fall to Hatti once and for all. Muwatallis has laid his plans well, down to the last detail." His gaze slid to Rhoha, his expression cold. "To think he can control me so much, I cannot even punish my own sister for what she did to you. Instead, she watches me, sending messages to him, while parading that bastard son of hers though my palace as though you do not even exist. By Baalat's crown, it is a nightmare."

He fell silent, brooding, lost in his thoughts.

Istara touched his hand. "I will go to Baalat," she whispered, glancing at the lengthening column of Egyptians, "and beg her to intervene before it is too late. While there is still time, justice may yet be done."

He father scoffed, bitter. "Baalat abandoned us when my sister returned and dirtied the temple with her presence. No. It is far too late now to hope for divine aid." He turned to Istara, eyeing her. "If I fall, you will leave at once for Babylon. King Kadashman-Turgu has agreed to take you into his court until it is safe for you to return. Commander Hasurna has his orders; he will escort you there."

Istara pulled her cloak tighter against her torso, defensive. "Urhi-Teshub arranged this, didn't he?"

Her father looked at her, unapologetic. "He is only trying to protect you." He glanced at his sister again, his lips twisting with loathing. "You must know Rhoha intends Hatti's throne for herself. Had your guards not arrived in time that night—"

Bitterness filled Istara. "Rhoha has Hartapu, why can she not be satisfied with being the mother to Urhi-Teshub's firstborn son?"

"I know her heart," her father answered, resigned. "She will not stop until she has what she believes is meant to be hers." Horns blared within the city. He glanced up. "I must depart. Will you do as I command should I fall today?"

Istara looked away, frustrated, angry, resentful. Again, she would be moved, a piece on a game board. Babylon was far. She might never come back. The horns blew again.

"I must leave. Give me your word."

She sighed, quiet, resigned. "You have my word."

He nodded, satisfied.

From within the folds of her cloak, she reached out to him. "I will pray for Baalat to protect you. Return safe, Father."

He took her hand and pressed it against his chest, his hardened leather armor unforgiving against her palm. "In these darks days, I fear the gods have abandoned us. But my heart thanks you for your prayers." He let go of her hand. "Go. Take shelter in Baalat's sanctuary. May the goddess protect you just as she did when you were a child."

A sudden apprehension came over Istara. She took a step toward him. "Father—?"

He tilted his head toward the temple grounds, his eyes dark. "Go, and do not look back."

She bowed her head, her apprehension increasing. She turned, catching his gaze flickering over her, pride hardening his features. She left, her heart aching, and didn't look back.

❋   ❋   ❋

Alone within Baalat's sanctuary, Istara lit a stick of opium and inhaled its sweet, resinous, earthy scent. Against the cold flagstones, she prostrated herself, praying for the protection of her father and her people, her head becoming light as the incense permeated the enclosed space.

"Child, the battle will soon begin. Why are you still here?"

Istara came to her knees, peering at Baalat's golden face, astonished. She leaned closer, curious. A soft chuckle came from the shadows. Rhoha emerged, her gemmed necklaces glimmering in the flickering lamplight as she sank down and prostrated herself before Baalat.

"She doesn't talk," she said, nodding at the statue, "and she never will. She is just a thing made by men, used to control other men. The gods do talk; you just have to know how to listen." Rhoha pressed her palm to her chest, her beauty marred by her gnarled and twisted fingers. "When they do, they speak to us here, in our hearts."

Outraged, Istara stood up, trembling with anger. "Do not speak to me of the gods," she seethed. "You are an abomination with your worship of the black arts. How many innocent creatures have you caused to suffer, mutilating them to seek your filthy augurs?"

"What little things you care about," Rhoha smiled, unconcerned. "Those small lives are worthless, but the augurs they give are worth a fortune. Muwatallis has paid me well for the things he has learned. And, he has promised me more. Much, much more."

"Even if you send me to the gods," Istara spat, "Urhi-Teshub will never have you. He will never give you what you want. Ever."

Rhoha plucked at her gown, indifferent. "Except I have his son, and you have—" she glanced up, "—nothing."

Seething, Istara took a step closer to her aunt. "How arrogant you are. You do not even try to hide your ambitions. I loved him, but to you he is nothing more than a footstool to stand upon while you gorge yourself on your insatiable hunger for power."

"Perhaps," Rhoha admitted. "But for women of royal blood, love is a lie. There is only power. Urhi-Teshub will be mine, you will see. The augurs have shown it, over and over."

"And yet, I am still his wife."

Rhoha glanced up, sharp. "Who refuses all contact with him."

Istara crossed her arms. "Your brother and your king are about to face battle. Should you not be preparing the sacrifices instead of tormenting me?"

"I do not mean to torment you," her aunt murmured as she came to her feet, brushing at her gown. "I am just impatient when I know what is to come and must wait while others fumble their way to their destinies. I came to tell you of a prophecy, and of your part in it."

Istara lifted her brow, dubious.

"The augurs have shown what is to come if Muwatallis is not stopped today," Rhoha continued, meeting Istara's eyes, cautious. "Egypt will fall, never to rise again."

"How pleased you must be," Istara said, wishing her aunt would hurry up and leave. "Since it is the outcome Muwatallis wants."

"But he has not seen what I have," Rhoha persisted, a faint shudder whispering through her. "I have seen our future if he successful, and it is dark indeed."

Istara uncrossed her arms. "Go on."

"I know well the people of Kadesh blame me for the cold and the unending rain," Rhoha muttered. "But I have learned it is the same all across Hatti, even to the gates of Ashur. The cold, the rain, and the failed harvests are just the beginning. There is much worse to come."

"There is nothing worse than famine," Istara retorted, crossing her arms again.

"There is. Total collapse across the empires," Rhoha said, warding herself against evil, uneasy. "Only the lands of Egypt will remain unscathed. But if Ramesses does not survive today's ambush, the empire of Egypt is destined to fall with him."

"And?" Istara prodded when her aunt fell silent.

"And the entire world will fall to anarchy and darkness."

Istara stared at her aunt, disbelieving.

"I have seen things I long to forget," Rhoha continued, apprehension shadowing her features. "For the next one hundred years plagues, famines, fires and powerful earthquakes will tear the kingdoms apart. The glittering island capital of Ahhiyawa will sink into the sea and disappear forever. For tens of years, there will be nothing but barbarism. I saw mothers kill and eat their own children, they—"

Istara held up her hand. "It is an annihilation; none could survive. But why are you telling me, what part could I possibly play in all of this?"

Rhoha licked her lips, nervous. "You must go to Ramesses and warn him of the ambush."

Istara stared at her aunt. "Are you insane? I will not do it. It would be my death sentence. You go and tell him."

Rhoha winced. "I cannot. After I witnessed the augurs, the goddess came to me in a vision, saying the messenger must be you. Ramesses will heed no other."

"I do not believe you," Istara said, cold. "Baalat would never speak to you. If you value your augurs so much, prove it, and take the risk upon yourself."

"I know you have no reason to trust me after all I have done to you," Rhoha admitted, glancing at the goddess's statue as though seeking her aid. "But there is more. Baalat granted me a vision, one she said I must tell you if you resisted. She said you would understand."

Istara scoffed and looked away.

"I saw you in a tent," Rhoha continued, dogged, "tending an Egyptian soldier, washing and sewing up his many injuries, aided by two more Egyptians. Though you were wearing gold and jewels on your arms, you were cold and trembled with hunger. Ah, yes, there was one more thing—your left calf was bandaged, a deep injury, sewn back together."

Istara's flesh tingled. She had told no one of her vision. She looked down at her fingers curling into fists. Her aunt waited, silent and uncertain. Istara looked at Baalat's image. Keeping her tone non-committal, she asked, "And does the goddess say how I should do such a thing?"

"Only this—you must go to Ramesses alone."

Istara reached for another stick of opium. "I will ask the goddess to confirm your words."

"There is no time," Rhoha said, harsh, slapping Istara's hand away from the offering table. "Do you recognize the vision, or not?"

Istara turned away, refusing to answer.

"Think of your people," Rhoha pressed, urgent. "If you do this, Kadesh will be the first to benefit from Egypt's protection—it is your duty."

Istara glared at her aunt, resentful. "I know well what my duties are; I need no lectures from one such as you."

Rhoha turned away. "I have done what I came here to do. I must go and attend the sacrifices." She paused at the door. "You have one chance to change the course of history, to save the lives of thousands. I envy you. The power you hold in your hands today is enormous."

As the door closed behind Rhoha, Istara sank to her knees. Why would the goddess send her into the heart of the enemy's camp on the brink of battle? Why her and not someone else? A wave of nausea washed over her. How could she manage such a feat, a woman, alone? Istara rose, unsteady, the burden of responsibility bearing down on her, crushing, oppressive.

Outside the thick doors of the sanctuary, the horns of the Egyptians echoed once more, repeating across the plain. She thought once more of the vision, and of Rhoha's words. She had to decide, and quickly. She turned to the doors, dithering, uncertain. She would be a traitor, could never come back, would never see her father again—but what greater purpose could there be than to save her people? She stopped. Ramesses would kill her. She reached for the handle of the door. So be it. Her whole life had been nothing but loss. Kuma. Her mother. Her home. Tanu-Hepa. Anash. Her throne. Urhi-Teshub. She had always been a token on a game board, moved by men. No more. The goddess was granting Istara the chance to choose her own path, a chance of freedom. She pushed on the door, suppressing a wave of terror, and made her decision. Today she would change the destinies of kings and empires, and die a free woman.

Alone in her apartment, Istara fell to her knees, naked, and rifled through her clothes chests, searching for her best gown and tunic. In her haste, she knocked over her jewelry box. An armband—a gift from her father—hit the stone floor with a dull snap. She cried out, dismayed, and lifted it up. It was broken beyond repair.

She set it aside, angry at herself. Righting the box, she noticed her pendant from Hurik wasn't in its clamp inside the lid. She dug through her jewelry, becoming frantic when she couldn't find it. An intense urge to hurry overcame her, warning her there was no time; she would have to leave it behind. She dressed, her fingers shaking as she fastened a veil over the lower half of her face. Drawing her plainest cloak around her shoulders, she picked up her bronze mirror and inspected her reflection; her golden browband glimmered in the lamplight, betraying her. She pulled up her hood and concealed her crown. Now, to anyone who cared to look, she was just an ordinary woman.

As she passed her writing desk, she caught sight of her agate seal, without thinking, she tucked it within the folds of her gown.

Leaving her apartment, she slipped through the palace, meeting no one; not even the guards stood at their usual posts. She pressed on, foreboding clawing at her.

At the edge of the stable yard, she hesitated. Nothing moved. In the middle of the yard, a lone helmet lay on its side, forlorn. She cut across the open space and slipped into the storeroom containing the supply gate. It opened with a soft creak. She glanced behind her, her heart pounding, fearful someone had heard. Silence greeted her. Stepping into the tunnel, she pushed her way through the stacked supplies, emerging onto the lane leading to the palace square. Following the lane to its final bend, she stopped, stunned. The gateway to the square seethed, chaotic, the palace guards overwhelmed, struggling to hold back Kadesh's elite, demanding sanctuary within the palace walls.

A fresh melee erupted. Without pausing to think, Istara bolted into the crowd, squeezing herself into a narrow gap between two women. The horde surrounded her, frantic, clawing their way toward the guards, desperate. She shoved them back and broke free, stumbling out into the palace square where she staggered to a halt, astonished by its transformation.

Across the expanse of the once-regal square, families huddled together, their meager belongings piled into carts or tied in bundles to their backs. All through the square, livestock milled, frightened, the ripe stink of their urine and feces making Istara's eyes water. She clambered through the press to the edge of the square only to find every street and alley crammed with carts, animals, and people. She pushed her way through, desperate, fearing the far worse fate awaiting them should she fail to deliver Baalat's message.

As she neared the city's wall, cries erupted, filled with panic and fear. Soldiers on the ramparts gestured for those still outside to fall back. One soldier leaned over, his hands cupped around his mouth.

"The city is full," he bellowed into the mob swarming below. "By King Amunira's command, the gates must be closed. Move back!"

The cries crescendoed, peppered with pleas for mercy. Istara pushed her way into the gate's courtyard just as the heavy wooden gates groaned, beginning to close. A fat blockade of carts stood before her, barring the way. She stood on her toes seeking a way through, finding none. Falling to her knees, she looked under the carts. There. A way through. Uncaring of her dignity she crawled, scrambling through the narrow gaps between the carts' wheels. Her hand came down on a broken piece of crockery. She bit back a cry, feeling the sudden warmth of blood spreading across her palm. Ignoring the pain, she scuttled forward, bursting out from under the carts. A solid wall of refugees, at least twenty deep, barred her way through the gate's barbican. One of the wooden doors juddered to a halt, its ropes caught. Soldiers on the ramparts hurried to free the snag. The pressure in the crowd eased, and from within the crush, more than two dozen people freed themselves, pushing their way into the city, clambering over the carts.

For the briefest heartbeat, a space opened. She threw herself into it, shoving with all her might against those still trying to get in. On either side of her, the doors—as thick as the length of a man's arm—were near enough to touch. The stalled door began to move again, closing in on her, blocking the light. Terror took hold of her. The doors bore down on her, relentless, threatening to crush her in their grip. She screamed, panicking, clawing her way up onto the shoulders of the man in front of her, scratching his face as she climbed over him. The space between the gates narrowed to the width of an arm span. Currents of air caught by the momentum of the doors brushed against her. Panting with fear, she dragged herself over the shoulders of the crowd. A man grabbed hold of her waist and cast her aside in his rush to save himself. She tumbled, helpless, caught by the momentum of the crowd as they tossed her to its edge. She slid to the ground, shaking, and tried to stand. She couldn't. Her legs had turned to water.

The cries escalated, becoming a deafening roar, filled with urgency. Caught in the grip of the closing doors, a man and woman struggled, panicking. The doors slammed together with a heavy boom. For the smallest breath, the pair continued to live, their eyes wild with pain and fear. Istara stood up, horrified.

Something heavy struck her chest. She recoiled, stumbling back against the wall of the bridge. Bloody entrails clung to her cloak. Gibbering, she shook them off, her gaze darting back to the bloodstained gates, splattered with the remains of its trapped victims. The men and women left outside surged up against the city's walls, crying, begging, pleading to be let in. Women held up their babies, imploring the guards for mercy. Istara stared at the scene, horrified by the chaos, the misery, the desperation. This was the future, for the next one hundred years—for everyone—if she did not reach Ramesses in time.

She worked her way over the bridge, weaving around the carts and livestock. At the forest's edge, she scanned the dripping shadows, a tremor of fear rippling through her. The cries of the people escalated. She turned, watching, sickened, as the guards turned away, abandoning the helpless people to their fate. With sudden clarity she realized even queens had no more power than those left outside the safety of the walls. In the empires of men, all were tokens, disposable—just like Tanu-Hepa; just like her mother. It was enough. She would be a token no more; she gathered up her gown, and ran.

TWO

His hands clasped behind his back, Ramesses stood at the edge of the plateau and gazed at the towering stone walls of Kadesh, its purple flags hanging limp under the leaden sky. He narrowed his eyes, appraising the improvements made to the city's defenses since Egypt's siege thirteen years earlier. Back then, three of Kadesh's walls had been surrounded by groves of olive trees, its eastern wall butting up against the bank of the Orantes River.

Ramesses had heard the reports, of course. But to see the changes for himself was another thing altogether. The olive groves were gone. Now, a wide, stone-lined channel encircled the walls of the city. From the city's three gates, stone bridges crossed the moat. No longer did the city sit vulnerable on three sides: Kadesh had become an island, surrounded by the river's deep, fast-moving waters.

When he believed Kadesh had been Egypt's, these improvements pleased him. Now he faced the unpleasant possibility of another time-consuming siege. He glared at the city, infuriated. He had sent masons to help build those bridges. Kadesh would pay, and this time Egypt would take more than just gold.

He caught sight of Paser approaching. "You bring news of Amun's encampment?" he asked as his vizier bowed low.

"Yes, Your Majesty," Paser replied, glancing back at the spreading camp. "The commanders of Amun's companies report good progress.

At our current rate of effort, we will be established before Re-Atum's barque descends."

Ramesses sniffed, pleased. His gaze returned to the island city. "Has a rider been sent to the holding position of Na'arn's division with the order to join Amun when Re-Atum's barque rises tomorrow?"

Paser bowed his head. "I despatched the rider myself."

Ramesses crossed his arms, continuing to search the city's walls for signs of weakness. A random thought crossed his mind. "What was done with the two Hittite deserters once they confessed Muwatallis's location?"

"They were tortured until they succumbed to their injuries," Paser answered. "They never recanted their words, though mercy was promised if they did."

Ramesses turned, raising an eyebrow. "So, we killed honest men?"

Indifferent, Paser brushed a fly from his arm. "Does it not strike Your Highness how fortuitous it was for Egypt to find Hittite deserters so close to Kadesh, and carrying such useful information?" he asked, his tone suggesting the opposite. "With your permission, I would like to send scouts out to confirm we have not been deceived. If not, we have at least nine days to prepare—"

"And if we have," Ramesses interrupted, impatient, "we will not be caught with our kilts around our ankles."

Paser bowed his head, embarrassed. Ramesses ignored his vizier's discomfort, continuing his surveillance of the city, his gaze moving beyond its walls to the landscape surrounding it. "Look there," he nodded at Kadesh, "do you see that long ridge on the other side of the river? Its forested flanks rise higher than the royal citadel. I must know what lies behind those woods. Perhaps Muwatallis's armies are already here, and he is watching us from Kadesh's walls as we speak." He glanced up at the dull sky, his mood souring. "Those cursed clouds have rendered our sundials useless, but it must be close to the tenth hour by now. If so, we only have four hours until Re-Atum's barque descends. Commander Sethi's division should arrive by the thirteenth hour and Na'arn's by the first hour tomorrow—" He stopped, his senses prickling. "If Muwatallis has deceived us, and intends to attack tomorrow, we would be outnumbered even with Pre and Na'arn—almost two to one if the numbers your spies have given are correct." He paused, considering. "Send riders to the commanders of the divisions of Seth and Ptah to be here no later than the sixth hour tomorrow."

Paser bowed low. "As you command."

Over Paser's shoulder, Ramesses caught a glimpse of movement in the woods to the north-east. It appeared again. He pointed at it. "Do you see that—there—in the woods?"

Within a clearing along the edge of the woods, a dark figure stumbled to a halt no more than an iter's distance from the base of the plateau. Ramesses narrowed his eyes, straining to see. The figure transformed into a blur of color, the cut of her garments leaving no doubt he was looking at a woman. She spent some time adjusting her attire, before disappearing deeper into the forest. Soon, only brief flashes of color could be glimpsed between the gaps of the trees.

"In Kadesh, only the highest nobility may wear the color purple," Paser murmured. "A woman fleeing the city alone? It bodes ill."

"Send Ahmen for her," Ramesses snapped, suddenly irritable, "I would see her myself."

Paser brought his fists to his chest. "As Pharaoh wills, it shall be done."

As his vizier departed, Ramesses watched the woman's rapid progression toward his camp, uneasy. First, the treachery of Kadesh, then the Hittite deserters, and now this. Nothing was as it seemed. He looked at the sullen sky, searching for Re's barque. He could not find it. Within his heart, he called out to the god.

Lord Re, your servant needs your light. I beg you, reveal the truth to me.

He waited. There was no answer. He watched the woman run.

THREE

A dozen bronze-tipped arrows in one hand and his bow in the other, Ahmen eyed the four empty chariots lined up before him. Despite the rugged terrain, he decided on the lightest one, the fastest. He pulled it out and stowed his bow and arrows in the box's containers. A groom arrived with horses, their legs still muddy from the day's march. Ahmen helped fasten their harnesses to the chariot's yoke, his fingers moving swift on the buckles. He stepped into the box and hastened to wrap the reins around his forearms. He looked around; the others were almost ready. He ordered them to fall in.

Outside of the relative calm of the nobles' enclosure, the Division of Amun was in chaos. Ahmen pushed his way through the encampment, slowed down by obstacles at every turn. Navigating around an ox-drawn wagon, he just missed two men carrying goats to the royal enclave for the sacrifices. He bit back a curse, catching the frustrated oaths of his men as they avoided their own pitfalls.

Picking his way through the camp, his horses sped up and slowed down until the tents finally began to thin out. He gave the horses their heads, letting them plunge past the last of the tents out onto the barren, windswept plateau. At its edge, he pulled up, searching for a way down. The slope was steep and strewn with rocks, terrain impossible for their chariots to traverse. Cantering ahead, he spotted a goat path. It would have to do.

Impatient, he waited at the plateau's base until the rest of the chariots arrived. Calling out the order to take the arrow formation, he surged ahead, plowing through the deep furrows of the muddy plain. As he drew near the forest, he narrowed his eyes, searching for his target. There. Between the trees. She stumbled. He veered toward her, wary, searching the sparse woods for others. Finding no one, he pressed on.

❋　❋　❋

Istara stumbled to a halt, panting. Black spots cascaded across her vision. Groping her way to a tree, she leaned against it, grateful for its solidity.

The pounding in her head became the thundering of hooves. She leaned out, clinging to the tree. Five Egyptian chariots, bristling with weapons, galloped toward her. Terrified, she pushed back from the tree and considered fleeing into the depths of the forest, where the chariots could not follow. An archer pulled an arrow from his quiver and fixed it to his bow. He drew its bowstring taut and aimed at her, his eyes cold. Istara froze.

One of the men, the one in front and riding alone, bellowed a command. On either side of him, the chariots came to a rough halt, black mud spattering around them. Another sharp word from their leader, and the man aiming at her lowered his bow. She watched the Egyptians, wary, their hostility promising death for the least provocation. She held herself still, and waited.

The one who had given the order to halt called out to her, his use of Akkadian basic, though sufficient.

"Come out. Hands before you."

She stretched her arms out, her hands turned palm upward and looked up at him, uncertain. He nodded, impatient.

"Yes. Come."

Her arms extended, she struggled to clamber over a fallen tree, tearing her tunic on one of its branches. She left the woods, her sandals sinking into the cold mud of the plain.

The leader eased his horses ahead, his kohl-darkened eyes riveted on her as he drove his horses in a wide circle around her, inspecting her from all sides. She glanced at the others. Only one kept his attention fixed on her; the rest scanned the woods, alert, defensive.

One of the horses snapped at her. She cried out, shielding her face. The man said something in a low voice. The horses came to a standstill. He continued to watch her. The silence stretched. Hesitant, she lowered her arms. He narrowed his eyes, suspicious.

"Who you be?"

Cautious, she removed her veil. He looked at her, impassive. She sought courage.

"Lord of Egypt," she said, suddenly grateful for her years of training in international diplomacy, "I am able to speak your language. I am Istara, Princess of Kadesh, daughter of King Amunira. I carry an urgent message from the goddess Baalat for the Pharaoh of Egypt."

His brow quirked, though his mien remained implacable. After a heartbeat, he leaned his weight against the reins, backing his horses until they were at a safer distance from her.

"How is it you are able to speak Egyptian?" he asked, wary.

"I am the wife of Urhi-Teshub, the firstborn son of King Muwatallis," Istara answered, trying to keep the tremor of fear from her voice as his expression shifted from suspicion to utter disbelief. "I have learned several languages in preparation for my crowning as queen of Hatti."

His gaze drifted over her, impassive, lingering on the details of her gown, the opulence of her gold and gems. "Lady of Kadesh," he said, his mouth twisting with distaste, "your claim is absurd and offensive." When she said nothing, he leaned forward and said, "Unless you carry proof, you will cease with your lies and tell us who you truly are."

For a heartbeat, Istara found herself at a loss. She had believed her royal garments, jewels and her ability to speak Egyptian would be enough. Suddenly remembering her seal, she reached into the folds of her gown. The creak of arrows being drawn filled the air. She looked up at the men.

"Peace. I only wish to show your commander the evidence he seeks."

She unfolded her fingers palm upward and held her hand up to him, showing him the seal of the Princess of Kadesh, Hatti's queen-in-waiting. The man's eyes darkened, uncertain. She stepped toward him.

"My lord," she said, quiet, "I am the only child of Queen Azfara and King Amunira of Kadesh, once a hostage of King Muwatallis, later bound to his son to retain Hatti's power over Kadesh. Before my father left today to join the Hittite king, he bade me take shelter in the Temple of Baalat. While in her sanctuary, I received the great lady's command, demanding of me a task so terrible I confess I resisted. Yet though I have faced significant peril doing so, and expect my life will be forfeit before the day is over, I have obeyed. I swear this is the truth on my very soul. I beg you, take me to the pharaoh, and allow me to deliver my message."

※　※　※

In the wake of her words, an ominous silence fell. The horses fretted, uneasy. Ahmen looked at the others and tilted his head toward the woods. A terse shaking of heads. She was alone.

He caught the woman who called herself Istara gazing at the agate seal. She looked up. For the barest heartbeat, he glimpsed her urgency and fear. Though she challenged everything he believed to be the correct order of things, he sensed she might be telling the truth.

"You must give up your weapons," he said, tight. "They will be held by Egypt until the pharaoh decides what will be done with you."

"I have no weapons."

"We must search you, regardless."

He waited while one of the men searched through her gown. She had told the truth. He nodded at the space in front of him.

"You will ride with me."

Skirting the reach of his horses' hooves, she clambered into the box beside him, her knuckles whitening as she gripped the edge.

"Lady of Kadesh, have you never learned to ride in a chariot?"

She shook her head. "Not one as small as this."

"Then," he said, "if you don't wish to fall out, you must stand in front of me between my arms and lean back against me as I drive. You may hold on to the box as well if it pleases you."

She eyed his bare chest, uneasy. "There must be another way."

He felt a muscle in his jaw twitch. The pharaoh was waiting.

"Could I not stand in front of you and hold on to the reins as well, without touching you?" she asked.

He lifted an eyebrow. "You may try."

Before they were halfway across the plain, her hands began to slide along the reins. He felt a twinge of admiration for her. Her fingers would be on fire. She let go of the reins and lunged forward, catching hold of the front of the box. Dragging her arms over its edge, she anchored herself against it, hunched down into an awkward crouch.

They had almost reached the crest of the plateau when a hare burst out from under a bush and darted under the horses. The horses shied, bolting across the slope. The box climbed up onto a boulder, tilting to one side, careering to a steep angle. A sickening crack, followed by a snap, as one, then two of the opposite wheel's spokes succumbed to the box's weight. Splintering sounds spread, ominous, along the length of the axle.

Ahmen threw his weight sideways, bringing the wheel back onto the ground, sending Istara pitching against him, scrabbling against the interior of the box, searching for a handhold. Within a heartbeat she would be out of the box, tumbling down the rocky slope. He sawed on the reins, his arms aching, fighting to stop the panicking horses.

Her hands slammed against his legs, her fingernails sliding over his flesh, tearing into him, seeking purchase. Gritting his teeth, he held firm, waiting, hoping. Her weight hit him. He swayed backward, grunting.

His knees and shoulders aching, he lay back on the reins. The horses scrambled onto the plateau and stumbled to a halt. Panting, he looked down at Istara, clinging to his calves, shaking. She had lost a sandal, and her foot bled. Across her calves and shins, a score of dirty gashes bled out, one of them deep enough to need sutures.

"Lady, you are injured."

She rose, pale and trembling, taking her place in front of him once more. "It is of no matter now."

His admiration was genuine. She was courageous, this woman of Kadesh. He called to the subdued horses, easing them into a limping trot. His men caught up to him, concern on their faces. He sent them ahead, reassuring them the chariot would last long enough to get them to the royal enclosure.

"Lord of Egypt, perhaps you will allow me a name to remember you by?"

He noted the faintness of her voice. She was in great pain, he was certain.

"I am Ahmen-om-onet," he answered, "son of Wennefer, First Prophet of Amun. I am Pharaoh's Royal Charioteer and Chief of the Archers."

When she said nothing, he continued, "Even if you are who you claim to be, your kingdom betrayed Egypt's treaty and allied itself with Hatti, which makes you the pharaoh's enemy twice over. You had better pray whatever you have to tell him is of the greatest value for if it is not, your life will be taken from you—even if you are the future queen of Hatti."

They passed over a dip in the ground. She tightened her grip on the box. "What I have to say carries far more weight than even what my life would be worth as queen of Hatti."

He waited.

"I am prepared to go to the gods," she continued, low. "I only hope I am not too late." She paused to shift her weight, then said, "The men you found this morning were no deserters of the army but men of noble blood, allied to my husband in his fight for the throne. They were sent with false information to mislead the pharaoh. My lord, upon my life, the King of Hatti is riding with a host of thousands to your camp even as we speak."

Ahmen shook his head, pitying her. It was almost evening. Her information had to be wrong. No battle would ever commence at this hour; it was against the rules of engagement. But how could she know such things, a woman?

"Those men were tortured by amputation," he said, terse. "They died from their injuries. They would not have told us lies when they could have saved themselves with information like this."

She looked back at him, bleak. His instincts prickled. He slowed the horses. "Are you suggesting they lied even to their deaths?"

"Over a year ago," she answered, low, "their wives and children were made Muwatallis's hostages. Giving up their lives today was the only guarantee those men had to keep those they loved alive." A tear slipped down her face. "They were good men. They died with great honor."

Ahmen stared at her, astonished. Muwatallis had been planning this for a year? To hold women and children hostage for so long, just to ensure Ramesses was misinformed—her earlier words returned, seizing his full attention. *Before my father left today to join the Hittite king, he bade me take shelter in the Temple of Baalat.*

Realization gripped him, cold. Muwatallis had never intended to meet them in an honorable battle. It was always to be an ambush. His flesh crawling, Ahmen bellowed at the horses and shook the reins. Startled, the horses burst into a gallop.

As they raced across the plateau, Ahmen caught fragments of the woman's prayers drifting back to him, recited in her native tongue. Ever since he had lost Meresamun, he had never prayed again. He couldn't begin now. He hoped this woman's prayers were powerful enough to grant protection not just to her, but to Egypt—in this, her darkest hour.

FOUR

They came to a juddering halt within the royal enclosure. Ahmen took hold of Istara's arm, his fingers pinching the flesh between her arm bands, and escorted her past the royal guard. He pulled her, limping, into the vestibule of the pharaoh's tent, where a dozen others stood waiting in the cramped space. Several gazes drifted to her, some hostile, others curious.

"You must not speak until you are spoken to," Ahmen said in a low voice, tightening his grip on her arm, "neither will you look at the pharaoh's face unless he commands it."

He stopped before a white linen panel, opaque with columns of gold-embroidered hieroglyphs. Istara stared at it, horrified. That piece of material was all there was left between her and the Pharaoh of Egypt. Her small store of courage evaporated. She clenched her fists, fighting her escalating quail. She would not be able to find the right words, would not know—

A guard called Ahmen's title. Her captor tugged on her arm, pulling her after him. Istara slipped past the material, blinking in the sudden glare. A fortune of golden plates and cups gleamed on narrow wooden tables arranged along the tent's walls, the furniture's polished wood reflecting the light from the hanging lamps burning a clear, smokeless oil.

Benches, stools and three gold-inlaid chairs fanned out around several glowing braziers. Colorful cushions and soft animal pelts layered every seat. Thick rugs covered the cold, damp ground. Rich, fragrant incense curled upward. In the tent's center, a table the size of her bed overflowed with scrolls, maps, and stacks of papyri. Despite Ahmen's warning, her gaze moved to the man standing behind the table, surrounded by men of various ages; lean and powerful, they regarded her, cold, some of them dropping their hands to the hilts of their sickle-bladed *khopesh* swords strapped to their belts.

Engrossed in a map, Ramesses rested his palms against the table, his eyes, kohled black, moved over the map, examining it. On his shaved head, he wore a brilliant blue crown, adorned with a golden uraeus—the cobra's hood open, its head pulled back, ready to strike. Over his shoulders, a wide pectoral collar of gold and lapis lazuli, and around his immaculate linen kilt—as white as the purest alabaster and edged in gold thread—a leather belt embossed with gold held his dagger and a *khopesh*.

Though he was not as large as those surrounding him, he had the build of an elite warrior, every muscle defined. He was nothing like any man she had ever seen, with his smooth, oiled skin and exotic regalia. Oblivious to her, he surveyed the map, preoccupied, intense, his movements elegant, refined, his face expressive, arrogant, regal. Without even speaking, his presence commanded her attention, dominating her, striking fear into her. Unlike the King of Hatti, the Pharaoh of Egypt emanated power, charisma and beauty, a god in the flesh. She sank to her knees and lowered her face, her heart quaking. Soon she would die just like her mother, struck down by the blade of a king. Silence fell.

※　※　※

It was the quiet that made Ramesses look up. Just inside the entrance, a woman knelt, her head bowed, Ahmen waiting beside her, expressionless. Ramesses pushed the map aside. "Tell me what you know."

"Your Majesty," Ahmen said, bowing his head, "for reasons so far known only to her, this woman brings you intelligence of the movements of Hatti's king. She claims the scouts we found were made to give us false information—their families hostages to be put to death if the informers failed."

Intrigued, Ramesses moved closer, eyeing the woman's purple gown, noting the fortune of gold, silver, and gems. "Indeed?" he replied, his heart cold, suspecting a trap. "And who is this woman?"

"She claims to be the daughter of King Amunira," Ahmen answered, bland, "Princess Istara, wife of Urhi-Teshub, Crown Prince of Hatti, and the future queen of Hatti. My lord, she also speaks fluent Egyptian."

Ramesses scoffed. How tacky. Kadesh expected him to believe the Hittite queen-in-waiting was the woman kneeling before him?

"Has she any proof?" he asked, then regretted it immediately. This was a waste of his time. Whatever Kadesh was playing at would soon end, on the blade of his dagger.

"She carries the seal of the Princess of Kadesh," Ahmen replied.

A quiet murmur of interest rippled through the tent. Ramesses remained silent, suspicion filling him. A dark game was being played; he wished Paser was present—

Ahmen moved closer. "Your Majesty," he murmured, "the woman carries a message worth hearing."

Ramesses caught Ahmen's private look, filled with warning. So be it. He would hear the woman out.

"Lady of Kadesh," he said, resting his hands on his hips, "despite your evidence, I do not believe you are who you claim to be. By coming to us, you have made your life forfeit. You are granted enough time to tell us your message, then you will die by our hand. You may rise."

She lifted her head and came to her feet. Despite her disheveled state, the woman was a rare beauty; her features a captivating blend of fragility and strength. Defensive, he crossed his arms over his chest, refusing to let himself be swayed by her obvious charms. Her gaze drifted to the dagger on his hip, then continued up until her eyes met his—as an equal. He held her gaze, challenging her to look away. When she didn't, he rode the feeling she ignited within him, a blend of outrage and pleasure, secretly admiring her fearlessness.

"Taker of my life," she began, her command of Egyptian flawless, her accent regal, "know the woman before you is Istara, Daughter of Baalat, firstborn child of King Amunira and Queen Azfara of Kadesh, wife of Crown Prince Urhi-Teshub, son of King Muwatallis. I have been chosen by the goddess Baalat to deliver her prophecy to you. On this day, the goddess tells us men have reached a crossroads, and if they continue on their current path, a great calamity will befall all of us, friend and foe.

"This cold, dark weather is just the beginning; the gods will soon send plagues, fires, famine, and earthquakes. Cities and kingdoms will burn. Mothers will eat their children. Every empire, except one, will be brought to its knees. That empire is Egypt. She will provide succor to those fleeing the devastations of the north. But today, Egypt is in great peril, and if she does not heed our warning, she too will be destroyed—and without Egypt, the world will fall into anarchy.

"The two men you met this morning, pretending to be Hittite deserters, were not mere soldiers, but powerful lords, rulers of cities themselves. They threatened the succession of the usurper Hattusilis when they supported Urhi-Teshub's right to Hatti's throne; it was *they* who came to Pharaoh to misinform His Majesty. Their entire households made hostage to ensure their lie would not be recanted. Your calm arrival today proves those brave lords suffered unspeakable agony, lying to the end, to protect those they loved, granting Muwatallis the advantage he now presses.

"As we speak, twice the number of your men are fording the Orontes River with the intention of ambushing this camp while you are unprepared and isolated from the rest of your divisions.

Muwatallis has ordered his men to kill every man, woman, and child. No one is to be spared, not even the royal family."

She sank to her knees before him, her face turned upward, her eyes never leaving his.

"If His Majesty is able to survive this day, then I will have done what I have been asked, ensuring the survival of many others in the years to come. If my life is the price to be paid for this act, then I accept my death with honor. My lord King of Egypt, I am ready to meet your blade, but as you take away my final breath, please do not forget my last words, given at the cost of my life. Arm yourselves. I beg you."

A stunned silence descended. No one moved. Astonished, Ramesses stared at the woman kneeling before him, her eyes sliding down to the floor, awaiting her execution, quiet as a lamb.

Everything she revealed had been coherent, much of it agreeing with his earlier suspicions of Muwatallis's deception and possible location. But to attack now, just a few short hours before darkness fell? It was unheard of to engage a battle at this time of day, madness even, and yet he had asked Re to grant him the truth before it was too late. Was this the god's way of warning him—from the mouth of his enemy, a mere woman?

His fingers slipped around the hilt of his dagger. The silence thickened, filled with trepidation. He let go. If she had been sent by Re and he killed her, would Egypt be destroyed? He dared not risk it, at least not yet. He turned to Ahmen.

"Bind her hands, and leave her in the vestibule of the queen's tent, under guard."

Ahmen took hold of her arm, bringing her back up to her feet. Caught in the thrall of shock, the woman, who called herself Istara, sagged in Ahmen's grip. Ramesses rubbed his jaw, regarding her with renewed interest. So it had not been an act. She had prepared herself for death, even expected it.

He returned to the table, deep in thought, considering her words. Either he was being played for a fool, or she was saving his empire from annihilation. If she was lying, he would give her a long and painful death, but if she was telling the truth—

He slammed his fist against the table, scattering the neat piles of papyri. It galled him a woman could force his hand. But would he have listened to a man? No. He would have killed him. Re had chosen his messenger well. His throat tight, Ramesses looked up at his men, waiting for his decision, the tension in the air so thick he could have cut it with his dagger. Fighting against every principle of war, every rule of battle he had ever been taught, he made his decision.

"Sound the battle horns. We prepare for attack."

※　※　※

Istara's wrists hurt. The queen's Nubian guards had bound them tight. The ebony-skinned men stood on either side of the entrance to Nefertari's accommodation, staring straight ahead, their bronze-tipped spears butting against the vestibule's carpet. Istara recalled Nubian men were the most powerful and dangerous warriors in the world, hence their privileged role as the Egyptian queen's royal guard. Their home lay far to the south of the empire of Egypt, an exotic land still unconquered, apart from the contested land where the rich gold mines lay, *those* were overshadowed by bristling Egyptian garrisons.

Wary, her gaze moved over the men. Each sported a dagger, and a long, curving sword, even more vicious looking than the Egyptians' *khopeshes*. Blades meant to remove an enemy's head in one brutal strike. She looked away.

In the distance, shouts, horses whinnying. Close to, outside the sacred space of the royal enclosure, chariots thundered past. So, Ramesses had heeded the warning. A small part of her wished she could see Muwatallis's face when he discovered he would not have everything his way.

She waited, filthy and bleeding, for her execution, her thoughts tangling between hope for Kadesh and despair for herself. Time passed, slow as the drip of honey. Thirst overcame her, her mouth turning dry as wool. A wave of nausea swept through her, then another, stronger. A cold sweat broke out across her chest. She shivered as she looked down at her filthy legs. The pharaoh might not have to dirty his dagger after all. If no one attended her, the blood fever would be certain to take her. She staggered, trying to stay on her feet. An upwelling of bile, foul and bitter, filled her mouth. Falling to her knees, she vomited onto the beautiful rug. From above, a sound of disgust. A man stared down at her, his handsome, elegant features pinched with revulsion.

"Princess of Kadesh or not," he said, "no woman should be left thus." He turned to one of the guards, his deep, eloquent voice edged with irritation. "You. Send for a surgeon. For all we know, if she dies, we die."

FIVE

Sethi drove his chariot out from under the towering canopy of Labwi Wood, emerging from beneath a ragged line of ancient cedar trees, their boughs glistening with damp. He drew a deep breath, savoring the sudden reprieve of open air as he scanned the sky, still laden with dense, dark clouds.

For days, the Division of Pre had endured a constant state of near darkness as it crossed a land of perpetual gray; the further north Sethi led them, the colder and darker the skies became. Since his campaign thirteen years ago at the siege of Kadesh, the once verdant lands of Hatti had become cold, bleak and depressing. He wondered what the Hittites had done to anger their gods. With weather like this, they would have no harvest and would starve come winter. And yet Muwatallis had chosen to pour his waning resources into war, mustering the able-bodied men of his empire against Egypt so he might cling to next year's graveyard. Sethi scoffed, incredulous. Hatti's king was nothing less than a madman.

Leaning his weight against the reins, Sethi slowed his horses, eyeing the vast deforested area to his right, the trees' stumps broken apart and pulled free, left to rot in heaps along the clearing's perimeter. The cleared ground angled away, an open, gentle slope extending all the way up to the horizon. He gazed at the open space, suspicious. Forest surrounded the field on all sides apart from the east. Why would anyone go to all the effort to carve out a swathe of forest in the middle nowhere? No one lived here. This land would never be used for farming. He narrowed his eyes, filled with misgiving. There had to be another reason.

He pulled his horses to a standstill, signaling for Naram to order a halt. His captain shouted the order down the line and approached Sethi's chariot, pressing his fist against his chest.

"Your orders, Commander?"

"We wait until a scout returns from the top of the clearing," he said, nodding at the rutted ground, his instincts sharpening. "I would know what is beyond the crest before bringing Pre through."

The scout soon returned, his face ashen. "Commander," he said as he knelt in the mud, "at least two thousand Hittite chariots have massed on this side of the river. On the opposite side, hundreds more still wait their turn to cross the ford."

Sethi digested the scout's intelligence, grim. Pre would never make it to the plateau in time, which only left one option. So be it. If Muwatallis wanted an unfair fight, Sethi would give him one. He turned to his captain. "Naram, Scorpion Formation. Shields two lines deep, spearmen to the front, archers to the rear, split the soldiers into two companies, one at each flank. Make certain to use those piles of rotting trunks to our advantage. We must hold them here for as long as we are able."

He left Naram to his work, and drove the horses up the slope, their leather-shod hooves sliding in the thick mud. Halfway up, one of the box's wheels snagged against a sunken boulder. The horses lurched to a halt, dragged backward as the box slid sideways into a pit. A sickening crack shot upward. A heartbeat later, the hardened axle snapped, sharp. Under Sethi's weight, the box's floor sagged, caving in. Biting back a curse, he quit the ruined chariot, his feet sinking ankle deep in the cold muck. He grabbed onto the offending boulder and hauled himself free, his legs and kilt blackened by the mud. Near the top of the slope, he crouched down. The clear-cut's scar swept all the way to the bank of the Orantes River where dozens of Hittite war chariots struggled to ford the river's rising waters. As he watched, several teams of horses burst out from the churning river, cantering onto the plain, the drivers organizing into ragged battle lines fifty wide. On the opposite bank, those still waiting swarmed back and forth, impatient for their turn to cross.

A suspicion came to him. He sifted through the mud, extracting several pieces of blackened, charred wood. His suspicion confirmed, he tossed the pieces aside, disgusted. He eyed the walls of Kadesh, wondering how Amunira had felt as the ancient wood—worth a king's ransom—burned at Muwatallis's command.

His heart cold, Sethi watched the Hittite chariots plowing their way across the ford; the frightened whinnies of the horses carrying across the ruined land. He narrowed his eyes, searching for the royal chariot of Muwatallis. There. Leading from the center of the third line, he spotted the king's chariot, the crests of the horses' bridles sporting the royal plumes of the peacock. Despite hundreds still waiting to cross, the Hittite king raised his arm and signaled their departure. Horns blew, thin with distance. The front lines advanced, moving out at a canter.

Slipping back down from the crest, Sethi half-ran, half-slid back to his chariot, black mud splattering his chest. Using his dagger, he cut his horses free. They surged away from the chariot, eager to escape the muddy pit behind them. His muscles straining, he held them steady as he unbuckled the girth of the nearest one and yanked its gold-embossed harness away, sending it tumbling into the ooze. Pulling himself astride the horse, he galloped back to his men, the reins of the second horse caught tight in his fist. Cantering up and down the line, he inspected Pre's formation, bellowing orders, tightening the ranks. Pride hurtled through him; in almost no time, Pre had formed a perfect Scorpion. The ground tremored. He turned, his skin prickling, his senses awakening at the drumming of thousands of hooves. His blood burned, hot with anticipation. *This* was what he lived for.

He gestured to a soldier he knew could ride, beckoning him over. Throwing him the reins of the second horse, he gave him the message for Ramesses. In a heartbeat the soldier was gone, absorbed into Pre's lines, disappearing down the road to Kadesh. Sethi grunted, satisfied.

Horns blared from the crest. A slew of Hittite chariots streamed over its edge at full speed, careening down the slope, reckless, arrogant, fearless, determined to smash through the bristling Division of Pre.

Sethi pulled his *khopesh* free and screamed Egypt's battle cry, raising his sword in the air, giving the signal to fire. A thousand barbed arrows hurtled into the oncoming wall of horses. Equine screams rent the air. The wounded, blinded horses bolted, colliding into each other, scrambling over the fallen, dragging their broken chariots behind them. He bellowed the command to fire again, and another thousand arrows exploded from the wall of Pre. The second line of chariots came over the crest at full speed, plunging into the stricken first line, trampling their own men. Fresh screams tore across the ravaged land.

The men of Pre roared, savage. Sethi shouted for the pincer offense before the third and fourth lines arrived. Swarming into the roiling mass, the soldiers slashed their way through the chaos, their *khopeshes* despatching the survivors with ruthless efficiency.

As Pre's soldiers scrambled back to their positions, Sethi surveyed his men's work. Hundreds lay dead or dying among the fallen chariots, the bodies and wreckage forming a grisly barrier between his men and the Hittites still to come. He clenched his jaw, gratified. Now, Muwatallis would have to drive over his own men to get to the pharaoh. Sethi eyed the oncoming line, his heart cold. He would hold Pre in position as long as he could. They would never win this battle, foot soldiers against war chariots, but before they died, his men would take down as many Hittites as possible, each Egyptian death granting Ramesses a little more time to prepare.

He lifted his *khopesh*, waiting to give the order for the next attack. A rush of adrenaline coursed through him. He would die soon, but he would die protecting his king and empire. A noble death, one worth having lived for. He looked up at the crest, catching the King of Hatti staring down at him, his face black with fury. The third line tore down the slope, the massive war chariots slewing their way toward Pre. Meeting Muwatallis's eyes, Sethi shoved his *khopesh* high and gave the order to fire.

❋　❋　❋

The last strap tightened on his breastplate, Ramesses's armorer stepped back, his head bowed. Ramesses moved in front of Pre's kneeling soldier, noting his mud-spattered body. The man was still panting.

"You bring a message from Commander Sethi?" he demanded, terse.

"Yes, Your Majesty," the soldier nodded, gasping, struggling to catch his breath long enough to deliver his message. "One short iter distant, on the road to Kadesh, the Division of Pre stands—" he gulped at the air, "—against twenty-five battle lines of chariots, led by the King of Hatti."

"And the numbers?" Ramesses asked, terse.

The soldier snatched at a breath before answering, "Commander Sethi reported four to a chariot."

Ramesses stared at the man, stunned. Ten thousand men. Twice Pre's numbers, and twice his own. Comprised of foot soldiers, Pre would be crushed by the Hittite chariots, which meant Ramesses stood alone, isolated, and unprotected, his men outnumbered two to one. Anger, cold and hard, washed over him. The King of Hatti had no honor. None at all. If it were not for the woman from Kadesh warning him, Egypt's first division would have been annihilated. Thank Re he had spared her.

He looked at his commanders, waiting for their final orders, their faces grim. He met his vizier's eyes. "Lord Paser," he said as his vizier bowed his head, "send another rider to King Bentesina, commanding him to bring Na'arn's division to us with all haste. The last five companies of Amun are now yours to command. Prepare the defense of the camp. If the line is breached, fall back to the royal enclosure. You will protect our queen to your death." He paused. "The woman from Kadesh has spoken the truth, to the last detail. If she truly is the wife of the Prince of Hatti, we have been granted a valuable hostage. Move her into the queen's presence, commanding the royal guard to protect her. Go, there is little time. May Horus protect you."

Paser bowed from the command tent. Ramesses looked over his men. "Right now, Commander Sethi is buying us time with his men's lives. However, I suspect Muwatallis will not remain long with Pre; we are the prize he is after. He may be on his way to us even now." Ramesses turned, and pointed to spot on a map of the plateau tacked against the tent's wall. "We will wait for them at the top of the slope. One-third of the way down from the crest, the slope narrows, where only four chariots abreast may pass. We will hold them there until we run out of arrows. When we do . . ." He moved his finger to point at a position on the plateau halfway between the crest of the slope and the camp. "We fall back here. Hawk formation. Keep the enemy in small groups as they take the crest. If they cannot form up, we will hold our advantage. Equip the horse burrs, but do not use them until the command is given, those vile things are, and always will be, a means of last resort." Pacing in front of his men, he eyed them one by one. "We have one priority, to hold them until Na'arn comes from the north, and those who still remain from Pre arrive from the south. If we can hold until then, victory will be ours. Muwatallis may believe he is about to grind us under his heel, but today it will be Hatti who will be annihilated, not Egypt. Do not fear, do not waver, we will overcome. The gods have proven they are with us. With them by our side, we cannot fall. Men, to battle."

He strode out of the tent to his gilded chariot, watching his men as they lined up, their fists against their chests. He stepped into his chariot. "Look now upon the Pharaoh of Egypt, Ramesses, Keeper of Harmony and Balance, Strong in Right, Blessed of Re," he called out, imperial, waiting as their eyes came to his. "We will triumph this night. Know Ptah, Osiris, Horus, and Re are with us. We are Egypt. We cannot be defeated."

His men, all of them veterans of war, gazed at him, their eyes hard, glinting with purpose. They lifted their fists, saluting him, united, fierce, their message clear. They would not fail him.

Ramesses nodded, satisfied. Tonight, Hatti would fall.

※　※　※

Bellowing orders to strengthen the weakest points of the Scorpion, Sethi bit back a foul oath as another section of Pre collapsed. His men rushed in to fill the breach, huddling under their shields. Everywhere, the clearing swarmed with Hittites pushing through the muck seeking a way past their fallen, goaded by Muwatallis. Their desperation to find a way through made clear by their recklessness, as Pre added more bodies to the growing pile of the dead.

Still, despite the onslaught, Pre continued to hold, a wall of men, against a horde of war chariots, protected by a grisly wall of flesh and bone. Unless the Hittites left their chariots and met his men on foot, all the Hittites had left to them were their slings, spears, and arrows. Yet, despite their limitations, they had still managed to bring down almost half of Pre's men. Sethi eyed the formation, so thin in places, it was only three men deep. He gritted his teeth. Hold. Just a little longer.

Muwatallis signaled. Sethi narrowed his eyes, watching as the Hittite chariots pulled back from the dead, organizing at the crest of the slope. Surrounded by a square of chariots, Muwatallis pulled to the front, shaking his reins, forcing his horses to gallop straight at the weakest part of the Scorpion.

Sethi screamed over the noise of the chariots as they drove over the bodies of the fallen, pulping them.

"Retreat! Retreat! Let them through!"

The retreat orders fanned out, Pre's soldiers scrambling to escape the wall of thundering horses gouting into what was left of the Scorpion. A bloody swathe opened. Helpless, Sethi watched his men fall to the onslaught, the Scorpion torn to shreds, the mud under Pre's feet no longer black, but red.

It was a long time before the last of the Hittite chariots galloped down the road and disappeared into the forest. Sethi called his captains to him. Only three arrived. Idri and Khutu had gone to the gods, along with most of their men. He harnessed his rage, saving it for later. They were good men. Their lives had been needlessly taken, because of the dishonor of one man.

"We have no time to waste," he said, eyeing his captains' injuries, "the severely wounded are to remain with the followers, out of sight. Naram, send scouts to find a way through the forest to the plateau since we cannot use the road anymore—at least not while there are still Hittites fording the river. Gather your men. We depart in a quarter hour. Go."

As they left, he surveyed what remained of his division. After thirty days of marching, Pre was just one short iter from Kadesh—a mere one hour's march—and within what felt like heartbeats Pre had lost almost half its men. There had been no honor in this battle, none at all.

He slid off his horse and slogged through the carnage toward an eviscerated Hittite, still living. The man held up his hand in supplication, crying out in his incomprehensible language. Ignoring his pleas, Sethi lifted his *khopesh* high and brought the blade down, a clean kill. Hot blood sprayed onto his legs and kilt. Picking up the man's head, he kicked a broken chariot shaft free and ascended the blood-soaked slope. At the top, he impaled the man's head on the shaft, and wedged it between two rocks. He looked down at the remains of his division, his men sifting through the fallen. Burning with rage, he raised his bloody hands up to the black sky. Warm rivulets of the Hittite's blood slid down his arms.

"We will avenge our dead!" he bellowed, his voice carrying, harsh, across the grisly clearing. "May Ammit devour me if they have died in vain!"

The shouts of Pre's survivors rose, ragged. Raising his bloody *khopesh* in the air, Sethi dined on his fury, screaming Egypt's battle cry, tasting blood.

Looking up from their dead, the survivors of Pre found their voices and roared.

❋   ❋   ❋

Muwatallis fumed over his losses—almost two lines fallen to Ramesses's tenacious commander when Hatti should have lost none. He would make the Egyptians pay, and when he found that arrogant commander—

The road widened. He burst out from the woods at full speed onto the muddy plain. Hauling on the reins, he turned the horses hard to the left, the chariot's wheels dragging in the heavy muck, slowing.

He cursed the horses, blaming them for the mud, the delay, and his losses to Pre, slamming the metal-studded reins against their flesh, tearing their flanks open. Roaring with pain, they lunged ahead, desperate to escape.

With a lurch, the chariot pulled free, the horses galloping, frantic, panicking, toward the plateau. Muwatallis gazed at the slope, beckoning to him like one of his filthiest whores, his long-awaited triumph so near he could almost taste it. Soon Hatti's chariots would overrun the pharaoh's camp, and even if Ramesses had been warned, he would have had no time to prepare. No, tonight, Egypt would fall to Hatti like wheat to a sickle.

Cracking the reins against his horses' ravaged flanks, Muwatallis bellowed at them, impatient to begin the butchery. Their blood flew back on the wind, splattering against his face. He roared, bloodthirsty, and whipped them harder, ignoring their shrieks of pain, driving them far ahead of the others, straggling behind, stuck in the mud.

He was a god. Nothing and no one could stop him now. He would begin the onslaught alone.

※　※　※

His gaze fixed on the plateau's edge, Ahmen flexed his fingers against the grip of his bow, waiting. To either side of his chariot, the front lines of the Division of Amun spread away, ten lines of archers, one hundred across. Behind them, three thousand five hundred soldiers stood in their companies, battle-ready. All of them hungry and tired.

Khu, his driver, fidgeted, making the horses restive. Ignoring him, Ahmen scanned the edge of the plateau, his instincts prickling. Soon now. He leaned forward. There. The faint drumming of hooves. Bows lifted, arrows nocked, and bowstrings creaked. He drew an arrow, just as the peacock plumes of the Hittite king's horses crested the plateau. Ahmen lowered his bow, incredulous. The man was beyond arrogant. Ahmen longed to shoot, but to kill a king was forbidden, unless one was a king himself. He hoped Ramesses would fire.

Their eyes bulging, Muwatallis's horses scrambled over the crest, plunging, reckless, straight at the bristling lines of Egyptians. Muwatallis hauled on the reins, roaring. His horses turned hard to the right, rearing, gobbets of foam and blood flying from their mouths. One lost his footing in the mud and fell backward, his neck twisting, caught in the harness. Muwatallis jerked on the reins, savage, yanking the horse's neck back. A sickening snap, and the bloodied horse thudded to the ground, dead.

"King of Hatti," Ramesses's voice rang out cold, and imperious, "you are defeated. The gods have abandoned you for your dishonor."

Muwatallis tore the reins from his arms, the wind carrying his foul invectives against Ramesses's mother across the short distance. Ahmen paled. A creak, as Ramesses pulled his bowstring taut.

"Honor?" Muwatallis sneered as he clambered from his stricken chariot. "All you speak of is treachery. It takes no diviner to see Hatti has been betrayed by Kadesh. As Sharruma lives, Amunira's head will be my footstool, his daughter my lowliest slave—" He stopped and scoffed. "Is this all you have to stand against my might? If you are hoping for aid, it will not come. I left your second division writhing in the mud like maggots." His face darkened, sinister, triumphant. "You are alone. Prepare to face your gods, because tonight you will die."

Ramesses murmured an order. A stone flew from a sling, striking Muwatallis behind his ear. The King of Hatti staggered, his legs buckling. He stumbled a few steps, and fell to his knees, slamming face down into the mud. Two soldiers ran out and collected him, dragging him, his feet trailing in the mud, to the camp.

Ahmen glanced at the pharaoh. Ramesses stood utterly still, his attention fixed on the crest. A muscle in his jaw twitched, a tell Ahmen recognized and feared. Restrained fury.

The ground began to thrum, quiet at first, then louder, vibrating from the drumming of hooves. Ahmen eyed the crest, tense. Shouts. Whips cracking. The roar of thousands. Five, ten, twenty chariots poured over the crest, mad for the slaughter.

Ahmen fired. A spearman scrabbled at his neck, Ahmen's arrow in his throat. A hundred more arrows fled the Egyptian line, followed by another hundred, then another. The Hittites roiled backward, men and horses falling, screaming, maddened by pain. The survivors fled back to the crest, desperate to escape. The arrows continued to fall, relentless. None survived. Hatti's first line had fallen.

Horns blew. Ahmen nodded at Khu, who brought the horses to a canter, leading the archers to the plateau's edge. At the barrier of the fallen, Ahmen quit the chariot and pushed his way through the abandoned Hittite chariots to the edge of the slope. He dropped to his knees, stunned.

Hundreds of chariots pushed up the slope, struggling to reach the crest. In their rush to begin looting, all order had been lost. The slope seethed, reminding Ahmen of a swarm of scarabs crawling over a new dung heap. The second line broke through the choke point, hurtling toward them. His men fired, littering the slope with the dying.

A warning shout. Ahmen slammed down into the mud, dodging a spear. It thudded into the corpse of a fallen horse behind him. Ahmen eyed the quivering shaft, his heart cold. This was no battle. This was nothing less than genocide. No one would escape judgment for their crimes tonight, Muwatallis's dishonor had forced every man, friend, and foe, to become a cold-blooded murderer.

Another spear flew past him, slamming into the dead horse, missing him by a hair's breadth. He rammed an arrow against his bowstring, shoving his qualms aside. To do nothing would mean the end of Egypt. They had no choice. He looked down into the eyes of the man beneath him, and fired.

❋   ❋   ❋

Shoving his way through the thick undergrowth, Sethi led Pre's survivors through Labwi Wood. Hampered by the bushes and fallen branches, he cursed for the hundredth time. The pharaoh needed Pre up on the plateau, not down here fumbling through a dark forest. He glanced back at his men, their wounds packed with mud, enduring their private agonies in silence.

A scout approached. Sethi slowed and gestured him over. News, at last.

"Tell me everything."

"When I left," the scout answered, breathing hard, struggling to catch his breath, "the Hittites had not yet breached the crest of the plateau where the pharaoh holds. He is using his archers to exploit a choke point in the slope, which has caused an immense crush of chariots as the full force pushes its way up from the rear. I saw men killing their own in their desperation to clear a way forward."

Relief flooded Sethi. His message had arrived in time. Ramesses might be in control for now, but it would not last. Pre had not taken down enough men to offer any true advantage to Amun. Once Amun ran out of arrows, the Hittites would abandon their chariots and climb over their dead to meet the Egyptians face to face, crushing them with their sheer numbers. Gesturing to the scout to fall in, he pushed on through the woods, his thoughts organizing.

"And what of Muwatallis?" he asked.

"I did not see his chariot," the scout replied, "although it is very difficult to see in this accursed near darkness. He may be there, he may not, I cannot say for certain."

Sethi grunted, resigned.

"The slope is a gorge," the scout continued, his hands moving, describing the terrain. "Attack is only possible from the rear or by joining Amun at the crest. At this pace, you will reach the base of the slope in less than an hour. From there, it is a little more than half an iter up the slope to where the pharaoh stands. Further along the eastern side of the plateau, there is a goat track, but to reach it, your men would have to run out onto the plain."

Sethi climbed over a fallen tree and slipped on something slimy. Pain lanced into the back of his thigh. He yanked it free from the shaft of a broken branch. Blood gushed. He smeared mud into the wound and pressed on, ignoring the pain.

"Are there any advantages we could use to pull the force apart at the rear, separate them?" he asked, his thoughts returning to strategy.

The scout shook his head. "Once you leave the woods, the terrain is open all the way to the plateau."

Sethi considered. To attack a force so much greater in number on an open plain would be madness. If he could not engage the Hittites from the rear, then he needed to get his soldiers into the camp, by the goat path. A thought occurred to him.

"If there is only open plain ahead, how did you manage to gather so much information about the battle?"

The scout glanced at him. "I used the forest's cover to get as close to the slope as I could."

"And how close was that?" Sethi demanded, sensing an opening.

"Close. Where the plain and the forest meet, it is near to the base of the slope. I could have reached out and touched the wheels of the chariots before me. The undergrowth is much thicker there than here."

Slapping aside a thorny bush, Sethi wondered how that could even be possible. He stopped, and stared at the undergrowth. The strategy came to him, its simplicity, stunning. Yes. It would do. He pushed on, a smile darkening his lips. Tonight, Pre would have her revenge.

Istara opened her eyes. Shadows from the flame of a single lamp danced across the vestibule's ceiling. Hampered by her bound wrists, she leaned on her elbows and pushed herself up, her fingers brushing against the place where she had vomited. She recoiled, shuddering and looked down. The ruined rug had been taken away. A new one lay in its place, just as beautiful. She stared at it, incredulous, marveling at the priorities of the Egyptians.

Leaning against the support pole, she winced as a sharp pain lanced through her left calf. Lifting aside her tattered gown, she ran her fingers over the clean linen bindings, feeling the bumps of the sutures where they held the flesh of her calf together in neat rows, catching the sweet scent of honey. She lifted an eyebrow, impressed, they had granted her an expensive antiseptic.

A sudden clamor startled her. Horses bellowed and men shrieked. Battle commands rang out, sharp, insistent. The wind shifted and the noise faded. She shivered, it had been so clear, as though they were right outside.

An elegant man, dressed in gleaming leather armor ducked into the vestibule. Two *khopeshes* hung from his belt, one at each hip. She recognized him, the one who had sent for a surgeon.

"Princess Istara," he said, inclining his head, "you return to us, and just in time. The surgeon informed me you were given a strong dose of willow bark tincture to halt the blood fever. Are you feeling stronger now?"

"I am," she answered, quiet. She gestured at the linens wrapped tight around her leg. "Thank you, Lord—?"

"Ah yes, forgive me," he replied, pressing his palm against his chest. "Paser, Vizier of Upper Egypt, son of Neb-netjeru, Prophet of Amun. I was with the pharaoh when he saw you. It was I who relayed his command for you to be brought to him. It seems you have told the truth."

He took hold of her bound wrists, bringing her to her feet with ease. She looked at him, impressed. He was strong, his fine looks deceived.

"I would have preferred to meet you under less difficult circumstances," he said, stepping back.

"And I, you," Istara answered. "Your kindness will not be forgotten."

The wind shifted once more, carrying the cries of the dying; sharp, jagged, bloody. Paser's gaze slid to the exit, distracted. "The pharaoh has commanded me to move you within for the duration of the battle—" he stopped to listen to a round of shouted orders cutting through the noise, his expression tightening, "—to be kept under the protection of the queen's guards."

Without waiting for her reply, he pushed aside the linen hanging separating the vestibule from the queen's private residence. Istara followed him, one foot bare, and limping. She came to a stop, stunned. The luxury of the queen's tent far surpassed the pharaoh's. Thick, colorful rugs covered the ground in soft layers. A variety of gold-inlaid stools and several piles of tasseled cushions surrounded two bronze braziers, the heated air above the glowing fuel shimmered, distorting the gleaming tables lining the tent's walls, their surfaces arrayed with golden pitchers, cups, and platters. Hung between the tent's support poles, oil lamps burned a smokeless oil, filling the space with clear, warm light. At the rear, an embroidered linen hanging hung before a real bed, the wooden frame paneled in gold, its thick mattress heaped with cushions and woven blankets dyed a deep indigo. Beside the bed, a table held a bronze mirror in a stand, surrounded by an assortment of alabaster bottles and jars, a gilded brush and comb, hair ornaments and earrings. Gowns and jewelry spilled out of baskets on the rugs. From another smaller brazier by the bed, languorous trails of sandalwood incense curled away, lazy and sinuous.

Seated upon a gold and lapis lazuli inlaid chair, Egypt's first queen eyed Istara, impassive. She sipped from a golden cup, her gaze drifting over Istara, listening, disdainful, as Paser delivered Ramesses's command.

She set aside her cup and folded her hands together on her lap, the jewels on her rings glinting in the lamplight. A long, taut silence stretched, punctuated by the distant cries of the dying. "We are the pharaoh's humble servant," she finally said, cutting a look at Istara, cold. "It is our duty and honor to obey. Princess Istara may wait by the entrance. The two who guard without shall be her protectors. The rest are dedicated to us, their queen. Should we die because we lack two of our guardsmen, this shall not be Princess Istara's responsibility but our own lord's who has decided this shall be so."

Nefertari's eyes left Istara's. None of the rigors of traveling seemed to have taken their toll on the queen's smooth, flawless complexion. Her long hair had been woven into hundreds of small braids, the ends of which were held together with golden cylinders. She wore a close-fitting golden crown fashioned in the form of a vulture, its wings enveloping either side of her head, protective. Her eyes and brows had been elegantly kohled in black, and her eyelids, accented by long, black lashes, glimmered with a dusting of golden powder.

Paser leaned over. "You are not Hatti's queen yet," he said, low. "Please lower your eyes in Her Majesty's presence."

Istara looked down, though the intimidating image of Egypt's first queen remained. A gesture from Paser and a guard brought a stool. Grateful, Istara sank onto it.

"Return to your men," Nefertari said, rising to her feet with a crisp rustle of expensive material. "And may Re go with you."

"Your Majesty," Paser bowed, his fist against his chest, "my life is yours."

He left. The guards moved, quiet and efficient, rearranging the tent for the queen's defense. Istara huddled on her stool, her leg aching, shivering when the fires in the braziers were extinguished and cold air seeped inward. No one looked at her or addressed her. It was as though she did not even exist.

The wind rose, carrying the escalating sounds of battle, the agonized screams of butchered men and horses rent the air, tearing into her. Trembling, Istara closed her eyes, and prayed.

Thick twilight shrouded the plateau as the last arrow left the Egyptian lines. At a gesture from Ramesses, Ahmen slid down onto the slope and crouched behind a fallen chariot. Around him, nothing moved. Further down, a horse cried out in pain. Wood snapped. Someone sobbed.

Beyond the carnage, repeated crumps, as chariots collided. Whips cracked, horses screamed, men shouted. Cautious, Ahmen looked around. Spread across the entire width of the slope from the edge of the plateau until nearly one-third of the way down—the furthest reach of their arrows—lay the bodies of hundreds of Hittites. He divided the area into equal sections and counted the empty chariots within one section. Calculating the totals, he clambered back up over the edge, joining the group of commanders surrounding the pharaoh. Ramesses nodded at Ahmen.

"Your report," he said, terse.

"My lord," Ahmen answered, "you have sent almost two and half thousand Hittites to the gods."

"Which leaves more than seven thousand alive," Ramesses muttered, bleak, looking across the darkening plateau, "and without our archers, Amun numbers only four thousand." His gaze moved to the darkness beyond the slope of the plateau. "Sethi, I do not accept you have fallen. It is time. Amun needs you now." He waited, scanning the horizon, as though expecting Pre to arrive. Ramesses looked back at his men. "Re will not abandon us. Prepare for hand to hand combat. They will soon reorganize to meet us on foot. Once again, they will find us ready and waiting. Time is short, send out the orders. We will prevail."

His fist against his chest, Ahmen turned away, a wave of fatigue washing over him. What if Pre was gone, and they were alone? Ahmen hoped he would die with honor, defending Egypt to his last breath.

A thought crossed his mind. Perhaps Meresamun was already there, in the afterlife, waiting for him. He closed his eyes, willing it not to be so, willing her to be alive, and safe. He would fight to his last breath so he could continue to search for her, yet he suspected as the shadows closed around him, he would never see the light of another day again.

❇   ❇   ❇

Urhi-Teshub gritted his teeth. By the time he would arrive, there would be nothing left to accomplish. He cursed, frustrated once more by the maneuverings of his father. Behind him, the three lines of chariots allocated to him carrying a paltry twelve hundred men, straggled to keep up. The river had risen during the fording of the earlier lines, and by the time his men were able to cross, the fast-moving, high waters had made their crossing exhausting and time-consuming. It was impossible to ignore the plight of the horses, stumbling as they slogged through the muddy fields. He bit back another curse.

In the distance, the roar of thousands rose and fell on the wind. He searched the horizon, frustrated by the darkling light until he glimpsed the crush of chariots milling at the base of the slope. He scoffed, bitter. His uncle and cousin had died for nothing. The pharaoh had not been fooled after all.

He shouted new orders to his driver. His horses veered away from the slope and cut across the plain, past Kadesh's walls. Behind, his men peeled away from their intended path, thundering through the mud behind him.

He grasped the shoulder of his driver and pointed at the exposed limestone of the goat track, faint in the gloaming light. He would show Hatti who should be king. Unlike his father, he knew how to defeat the pharaoh. He would capture his queen.

※　※　※

The noise of hundreds of chariots thundering across the plateau from the north filled Paser's ears. He cursed. The Hittites were coming at Egypt from both sides now. Faint cries of terror filled the air as the Hittite chariots slammed into the northern edge of the camp. Shouting orders down the line, Paser pulled his men inward, tightening the circle, abandoning the outer reaches of the camp to the Hittites.

He listened. Ten, no, twelve war chariots crashed inward, their destruction unrelenting as they pushed their way toward the center of the camp. Further out, screams of terror and pleas for mercy pierced the darkness. The raping of the camp women had already begun, he cursed the foulest oath he knew. He needed more men, five hundred to protect a camp made for six thousand was madness. Forcing himself to ignore the women's cries, he gave the order to fall back.

※　※　※

A woman's scream, sudden, desperate, raked Istara's ears. Another followed soon after, then another, and another, until dozens of cries rent the air. She glanced at Nefertari. The queen exuded calm. She gazed, impassive, into the middle distance, her fingers resting, light against the gemmed hilt of a sheathed dagger.

Their eyes met. Her heart pounding, Istara dropped her gaze back to her bound wrists. It could not be. She must have imagined what she had seen. She looked up again. The queen, rigid with hostility, still stared at Istara, her fingers tightening, slow, around the dagger's hilt, her look menacing, meaningful, and riven with hate.

※ ※ ※

Thick black smoke drifted over Paser. He looked up at the sky. The heavy, low-slung clouds glowed a dull orange, their roiling surfaces flickering, turbulent, as the tents across the northern edge of the camp succumbed to flames. He glanced over his remaining men, bloodied, gripping their *khopeshes*, their eyes moving back and forth, searching the shadows, wary. The group of soldiers he had been tracking continued to move through the camp, determined, uninterested in rape or pillage. Paser listened: at least fifty by the sound of them, their language guttural and discordant. One voice cut across the others, commanding, giving orders. The Hittites fell silent and pressed on, organizing, changing their course, veering away from the fires toward the center of the camp and the royal enclosure.

His throat tight, Paser motioned to his men. They fell back, leaving the wives and children of the followers to the rest of the Hittites that had come from the north; the women's desperate cries for help going unanswered, just so he could save one.

Hastening through the opening into the royal enclave, Paser looked over his remaining men—fifty, left from five hundred—panting from their flight through the camp. The Hittites had moved fast, staying hard on their heels, his men had only just made it in time. His chest constricting, he eyed Nefertari's tent, his long-suppressed love for her threatening to undo him. She would not go to the gods this day. To lose her. No. The thought was unbearable. Outside the enclosure's linen wall, the creak of leather, and the hiss of swords sliding from scabbards, stealthy. He gave his men hand signals. They surrounded Nefertari's tent in total silence, a wall of flesh and bone.

He turned to face the enemy, alone. Crossing his arms in front of him, he pulled his *khopeshes* free. He breathed, once, twice, calming himself, finding his focus. Movement at the enclosure's opening. A shadow coalesced from within the thick drifts of smoke, forming into the bulk of a powerful warrior: leather tunic, leather kilt, a pair of daggers on his hips, the hilt of a two-handed sword over his left shoulder. Breathing a prayer to Horus, Paser narrowed his eyes, smoked-burned and gritty, and waited.

❋   ❋   ❋

Urhi-Teshub eyed the one wielding the pair of hateful sickle swords, standing between him and his destiny. Motioning for his men to remain hidden in the shadows, he stepped into the enclosure, smoke wreathing around him. "We are Urhi-Teshub, Crown Prince of Hatti," he called out to the man in Egyptian. He paced closer, cautious, closing the distance between them. "Submit and live, or meet our blade and die with honor."

His black-lined eyes hostile, the Egyptian said nothing. He lifted his swords, angling them up in front of him, taking the defensive stance.

Urhi-Teshub waited, but the man remained silent, refusing to give his name and title in return. Pulling his sword free, he eyed the Egyptian. Two *khopeshes*. Unusual. And deadly. They were well matched at least. He would enjoy the challenge.

Pulling his sword free, he moved forward, hefting his blade, preparing to engage. A sharp cry came from the queen's tent. He glanced up, wary. The material over its entrance yanked open. A woman staggered out, shoved from behind, her wrists bound. She tripped and fell onto her knees, her once elegant gown torn, dirty and bloodstained. She raised her head, her eyes meeting his. His grip on his sword slackened. Disbelief, then rage poured through him. He glared at the Egyptian.

"I will skin you alive for this."

The Egyptian didn't answer. He stared at Istara, watching, horrified as a warrior followed after her, his skin dark as night, carrying a dagger, its hilt laden with gems. The warrior grabbed a fistful of Istara's hair and pulled her head back, rough, baring her throat. He lay the blade against her neck and looked at Urhi-Teshub, his eyes glittering, cold. The warrior flicked the dagger, a tight movement, contained. Istara cried out. A trickle of blood slid down her neck.

"Crown Prince of Hatti," a voice, cold, calm, imperial, called from the tent, "we are Queen Nefertari, first queen of Pharaoh Ramesses. If you do not take your men and retreat from our camp, we will send your wife to the gods."

Urhi-Teshub tore his eyes from Istara and glared at the tent, seething. How dare she threaten him. He glanced back at Istara, bound, bleeding, trembling, separated from him by a distance of no more than two strides. She caught his eye and shook her head, warning him not to save her. His heart clenched, fierce, proud of her courage.

"I will only agree if the princess comes with me," he shouted back, tightening his grip on his sword.

Silence. A tear slid down Istara's face.

"Princess Istara stays until the battle ends," Nefertari answered, speaking as though from her throne and not in the midst of a battlefield. "Pull your men from the camp, and you shall have her returned to you as you see her now. Fail, and she will not see the light of another day."

He scoffed at Nefertari's impossible request; he had lost control of most of his men the moment they entered the camp. He called out a terse command. An arrow snapped out from the shadows and sliced through the smoke, just missing his shoulder. A dull thud. The Nubian gurgled, clutching at the shaft in his throat. The Egyptian rallied, rushing at him, his blades raised. Urhi-Teshub slammed his sword against them, using his weight to shove the Egyptian back, granting a mere heartbeat of time.

Dropping the weight of his sword into one hand, he reached down and pulled Istara to her feet, putting her behind him, keeping one hand on her, unwilling to let her go. The Egyptian bolted back at him, baring his teeth, savage, intent, ruthlessly exploiting Urhi-Teshub's handicap. He was fast, like a viper. A complex feint and one of the Egyptian's *khopeshes* carved into Urhi-Teshub's upper arm, biting deep. Bellowing an oath, Urhi-Teshub let go of Istara and hefted his sword with both hands. Two more Nubians burst from the tent, aiming their spears.

He screamed Hatti's battle cry. His men roared back, bursting out from the shadows into the enclave, falling onto the soldiers surrounding the queen's tent. A dozen arrows slammed into the Nubians; they staggered, their spears sliding from their fingers, tumbling, useless, into the mud. The Egyptian's eyes darted to the tent, his concentration wavering as the Egyptian soldiers struggled to hold against the onslaught of Urhi-Teshub's men. Grim, Urhi-Teshub pounded him backward, forcing his way through the melee to the queen's tent.

A strangled cry. Something struck Urhi-Teshub from behind. Shoving aside a brutal slash, he glanced down. Istara lay at his feet, senseless. He bellowed and slammed the flat of his sword against the Egyptian's kneecap. The Egyptian reeled, his swords flailing. Urhi-Teshub balled up his fist and punched him in the face. Hard. The Egyptian stumbled, struggling to remain upright. Urhi-Teshub punched him again, harder. This time, the Egyptian fell.

Panting, Urhi-Teshub staggered, leaning on his sword, watching as his men dispatched the last of the Queen of Egypt's defenders. The enclosure was his. He glared at Nefertari's tent, furious. He longed to end her for what she had done—

Istara moaned. He dropped to his knee and cut her bindings. His men gathered around him, putting their backs to him, giving him time and what little privacy could be afforded.

Her eyelids fluttered open. He caught his breath. It had been so long.

"Istara," he murmured, reverent, bringing his hand, bruised and bloody to her face. He brushed a tendril of her hair away, tender.

Smoke burned his eyes, but his tears were real. Almost a year had passed since he had had no choice but to leave her side. He had missed her so much. His wife. His love. He drank in the sight of her, safe. Alive.

"How can you be here?" he breathed. "No. It does not matter. I have you now."

"It does matter," she answered, quiet, sitting up and rubbing her wrists where the bindings had dug into them. "I betrayed your father to save thousands. I can never return."

Urhi-Teshub stared at her, incredulous. His wife was the reason for Ramesses's preparedness? A wild thrill of pride cascaded through him. Taking her face between his hands, he pressed his forehead against hers, intimate, possessive. "Even so, I will die defending you."

"I beg you, do not," she said, her eyes glistening with unshed tears. "There can be no future for us."

"Do not say such things," Urhi-Teshub cried out, anguished. He grasped her shoulders. "Let me protect you from my father. I will send you to Babylon, tonight. You will be safe there until I am crowned. Istara you are mine, you will always be mine. We are bound in blood. Only the gods can take you from me."

"My lord," one of the men said into the dense silence that followed, "we are not alone."

Reluctant, Urhi-Teshub let Istara go and rose to his feet. He listened. Horns pealed, faint with distance. "Amurru comes," he said, abrupt, "from the mountain pass." He took up his sword. "It is time to capture Egypt's queen—and him, take him as well—our brave defender of the queen. Whoever he is, he will be more valuable to us alive than dead. Bind his hands, and see if you can wake him up. It will be better if we don't have to carry him."

He turned back to Istara, bringing her to her feet. "I must finish this. Once I have captured Nefertari, my sword and my life will be yours." He brushed his lips against her brow, savoring the nearness of her. "I swear to see you safe from this. From all of it."

She pulled away, distancing herself from him. "May the gods protect you," she said, hollow.

Uneasy, he backed away. She met his gaze, her remoteness robbing him of the last of his hope. No. He could not lose her again. Tonight he would earn his second chance. He would prove himself by spilling his blood to keep her alive, by seeing her safe to Babylon, away from his father. The horns blew again, from the plateau. He strode to Nefertari's tent, its white linen walls splattered with the blood of her last defenders.

Within, all was silent. He plunged his sword into the tent's fabric and tore it open. Nefertari stood surrounded by her five remaining guards, her dagger poised in readiness to impale her breast.

"Queen of Egypt," he said, seething with hate, "you are now a hostage of the empire of Hatti. You will remain our hostage until the King of Egypt accepts Hatti's terms and his defeat. Egypt has lost. Lower your dagger and submit."

"We will not submit," she answered, defiant, "we will die first."

"As you wish," Urhi-Teshub muttered as he lifted his sword.

The horns sounded again, from within the camp. Nefertari's lips curved into a satisfied smile. "My husband has yet to lose a battle, Prince of Hatti. Tonight will be no exception."

Her arrogant look provoked him. His blood boiling, Urhi-Teshub lunged into the tent, skewering the nearest guard onto her ridiculous dressing table, sending her perfume jars and cosmetics scattering. He stood on one of the jars, felt its thin structure collapsing under his weight. An overpowering scent of lilies filled the air, sickly-sweet. His sword lost to the table, he pulled his daggers free. From behind, the shaft of a spear came over his head, slamming down against his throat.

He shoved his daggers behind him, feeling the drag as they sliced across flesh. His captor grunted and yanked on the spear, pulling Urhi-Teshub backward. Pain mushroomed, jagged, blinding him. Hands caught his wrists, their grips vicious. They twisted his arms back and up behind him, rough. The daggers fell, one after the other, thudding against the thick rug. The pressure on his throat increased. He couldn't breathe. Black spots encroached, filling his vision. The shaft dug deeper, he jerked backward, gagging, saliva flying from his lips.

Someone kicked him in his back, hard. He staggered, choking, desperate for air. They kicked him again. He tumbled to his knees, struggling as leather bindings slid around his arms, tightening. He couldn't see, couldn't hear, darkness beckoned, soft, welcoming. The pressure on his throat eased. Pinpoints of white light burst into his skull. He sucked at the air, starving, his chest and throat on fire, his lungs screaming. His vision cleared. The roar of sound returned, deafening. Small, light chariots overran the enclosure, emblazoned with the sigils of the allied kings of Amurru. Strewn across the space, the butchered bodies of his men.

Frantic, he strained to see past the melee of men, horses, and chariots to the place where he had left Istara. There. The bodies of two of his men, beheaded. Panic filled him. He screamed her name, tasting blood. A rain of violent blows fell onto him. He felt nothing. He cried out for her again, searching, desperate, struggling against his bonds, even as the blows continued, relentless.

She would not survive long without him. He had to protect her. Summoning all his strength, he rose and shoved his oppressors aside. One step, two steps. Pain exploded from the back of his skull, so intense it blinded him. His legs crumpled.

He breathed her name, a prayer. He hit the ground.

Another blow.

Oblivion.

⁂ ⁂ ⁂

Hidden in the shadows, Istara watched Urhi-Teshub fall. They tied him up, like a beast, and left him lying in the mud. A voice called her name, quiet. She turned, defensive. His hands bound before him, Paser pulled himself up, wincing.

"Do not go to him," he said, lifting his muddied kilt to inspect his swollen kneecap. "I cannot protect you if you do."

She moved toward him, keeping to the shadows, cold mud seeping into her bandages. Her fingers brushed against the hilt of a fallen dagger, buried in the slick earth. She pulled it free and gestured at his bound wrists. Wary, he held out his arms. Shaking the mud from the blade, she sawed at the leather straps.

She met his eyes, watching her, intrigued. "Muwatallis may be his father," she said as she pulled away the bindings, "but Urhi-Teshub is nothing like him. He wanted no part of this."

Paser said nothing. He rubbed his wrists, his expression unreadable. She turned to leave. His fingers came around her arm, holding her back.

"You will die out there, unprotected," he said, his grip tightening. "You must remain here. It is Pharaoh's command."

Istara glanced at the queen in her ruined tent, taking her seat, rigid, icy, murder in her eyes. "If I stay, I am certain to die."

His gaze slid to Nefertari. His grip loosened, uncertain. Istara pulled free, darting through a rent in the enclosure's wall, ignoring his cry of dismay. She hesitated outside the fluttering opening, her gaze lingering on Urhi-Teshub for the last time, her heart clenching. Her name had been the last thing he had said.

Paser's voice rose over the tumult. A soldier rushed over and helped the vizier to his feet. Limping, Paser turned and gestured at the torn barrier, ordering the soldier to find her. Pulling his sword free, the soldier moved to the opening, cautious. Her heart pounding, she drew back and slipped across the open space separating the enclosure from the rest of the camp.

Where the shadows were darkest, she plunged into the smoke-filled night, the dagger tight in her hand.

EIGHT

Amunira didn't care if the second assault was going to be late. Muwatallis might be a god, but even he could not control the rising waters of a river. Despite his efforts to save them, Amunira had lost twelve men, though, thank Baalat, they were not his own. Muwatallis's suspicious, untrusting nature had dispersed the men of Kadesh across both assaults, leaving Amunira to lead men who hated him.

The driver struck the horses again. One of them stumbled. Amunira gripped the driver's forearm and shook his head. There was no point in whipping the horses; they were already done. The man from Hakpis shot him a look filled with loathing before lifting the reins from the horses' bloodied flanks, yelling colorful insults against Kadesh at the laboring animals instead. Ignoring him, Amunira glanced back at the five hundred chariots pounding past the western walls of his torchlit city, impatient to join the battle. Only one hundred of the two thousand men behind him were his.

The horses turned, cutting across the plain toward the goat track. Above the plateau, the leaden sky glowed orange; white flurries of ash drifted down, light and gentle, settling on the horses' backs like the first soft fall of winter snow. Amunira gritted his teeth. Soon, the dishonor would begin.

❋ ❋ ❋

Ahmen shoved aside a spear and gutted the man in front of him, enduring the screams of his horses as they lashed out, trying to escape the sharp points of the leg burrs. Several thuds followed as three more of the enemy fell, struck by the horses' hooves. Khu cursed, his arms shaking as he fought to control the horses.

Another Hittite staggered toward Ahmen, his eyes glazed. No reinforcements had come. They could not last much longer. For every Hittite they felled, two more emerged from the darkness, pushing the soldiers of Amun back step by bloody step into the soaring flames of the burning camp.

His arm aching, Ahmen lifted his *khopesh*, preparing to defend himself, but the man fell to his knees, already dying, a spear protruding from his back. Afraid, he looked up at Ahmen and reached out, his hand bloody, trembling. Ahmen lowered his *khopesh*, understanding. He held his enemy's gaze, until the light in the other man's eyes flickered out and died. The man toppled over. His heart tight, Ahmen turned and killed another, then another, and another. All the while, the eyes of the one below looked up at him, silent, empty, alone.

❋ ❋ ❋

A line of Amurrite chariots thundered across the plateau toward Amunira's men. He bellowed for the archers to release. A mere few dozen arrows flew past him. He turned. Only fifty chariots remained with him, those driven by his own loyal men. The rest had dispersed into the flames of the camp, hungry for the spoils, the wheels of their abandoned chariots tangled in the support ropes of the tents. Trapped between the fires, the horses squealed in terror, struggling to escape.

Amunira slammed his fist against the chariot's box and pulled his sword free, shouting new orders. The drivers called to their horses, forming up on either side of him, a solid line. Pounding across the muddy plateau they plunged into the Amurrites, smashing into flesh and bone.

He parried a strike and cut his attacker down. Their eyes met. Amunira staggered, recognizing him—Lanarta. When Amunira had been Crown Prince of Kadesh, Prince Lanarta had visited with his father, the King of Byblos. Over long evenings spent playing games of strategy, they had become friends.

He stared at his dying friend, panting, maddened. His driver roared, fevered with battle lust, driving the horses over Lanarta, malicious. The vizier's agonized cries clawed into Amunira, tearing him apart. He tightened his grip on his sword. He had been a coward for too long. No more.

He brought up his bloody sword and drove it into the Hittite's back, ending his laughter. Vaulting over the side of the chariot, he cut low, hamstringing the Hittite in front of him, dispatching him as he fell. He knew he would not last long, but until he was cut down, he would take as many of Muwatallis's whoresons with him as he could. Kadesh would not be a part of this. If he could not live with honor, he would die with honor.

His men rallied to him, their swords no longer used for Hatti but against it. They stood with him against the greater number of Hittites, valiant in the face of their oppressors. One by one, his men fell. He stood alone. Four Hittites closed in on him.

A blade pierced his armor. Its point emerged from his torso, glistening red-black in the firelight. He fell to his knees. The blade withdrew, the pain exquisite, unbearable. He pressed his hands against the opening. Blood coated his fingers. He looked up, another sword hurtled toward his neck.

He closed his eyes. Azfara's image filled his mind. The blade struck, sharp, fast. Excruciating pain. Silence.

In the darkness, an opening, filled with white light. Warm. Beckoning. Bright. He shed the weight of his body and fled, free.

※　※　※

Istara scrambled through the camp's turmoil, searching for a place to hide, desperate to escape the horror surrounding her. In every open space, soldiers fought, looted, and raped. Hidden in the shadows, she crept past a group of Hittites surrounding a man coupling with a dead woman. The woman's vacant eyes met Istara's. Beside the woman, a dismembered child spasmed in his death throes.

Horrified, Istara stumbled away, scrabbling over the wreckage of a fallen tent. She felt the shape of a head, still warm. Recoiling, she scuttled over the body, aiming for an overturned chariot. A soldier approached. She slid around the chariot and pressed herself against the belly of a dead horse, holding her breath. The soldier staggered past, his eyes glazed, a bloody sword in one hand and a small golden statue in the other. Paser was right. She would die out here. Pushing away from the fallen horse, she darted into the shadows, moving from one tent to the next, avoiding the knots of soldiers locked in conflict. A wave of panic washed over her, almost submerging her. Nowhere was safe. It was an unending nightmare.

Her eyes fell to the dagger, her knuckles taut and white around its hilt. If they caught her, she would not die like the others. She came to a halt in the shadow of a tent, searching for a way forward. The way ahead was far too bright, lit by fires burning all around. There had to be a way through—

A scream, close by. She peered around the tent's edge. A soldier dragged a weeping woman from a tent and threw her down into the mud. Kneeling over her, he reached up under his leather kilt and freed himself. He tore her gown away, the rending of the fabric loud in the enclosed space. Her breasts spilled out. She cried out, pleading, begging, weeping, struggling. He laughed, smashing his fist into her face. She spasmed and went limp. He mounted her, grunting like an animal, his face savage as he took his pleasure.

Further down, others searched tents. Finding new victims, they hauled them out, mocking their pleas for mercy. Istara pulled back, panting, behind her the shadows had vanished, lost in the light of the spreading fires. She had nowhere left to run. She would be next, raped by soldiers who would have been her subjects had she become their queen.

Huddled against the tent, she brought the dagger's point to her chest. Her hand trembling, she positioned it against her heart. A hand touched her arm. She flinched and scuttled backward, the dagger held up before her, defensive. The tent flap moved, easing back a fraction. The frightened kohl-lined eyes of an Egyptian woman met hers. She beckoned to Istara

"Hurry," she whispered, urgent.

Her feet sliding in the mud, Istara slipped inside, scrambling past the woman to the center of the tent. Shaking, she huddled into herself. Her fingers cramped. She let go of the dagger.

The Egyptian woman's eyes darted toward the escalating screams. "I could not leave you out there to face the unspeakable actions of those men." Fresh screams tore into the air, frantic, pleading. One by one their cries ended, silenced by the soldiers' blades. Despite the heat of the fires, Istara shivered.

The other woman's gaze fell to the dagger. "Do you know how to use that?"

"Only to find my own heart," Istara answered, low.

"May I use it after you, should the time come?"

Stricken, Istara nodded.

Screams. Close by. The woman cut a look at the tent's flap, her hands clenching into fists, catching the thin material of her dirty gown between her fingers. Without taking her eyes of the flap, she whispered, as though to reassure herself, "I am Meresamun."

Her gaze flicked back. Istara caught her breath. Blue eyes, how rare. Meresamun had good reason to be afraid, they would keep her alive until every last one of them had used her.

The sound of soldiers drew near, closing in on their tent. The blood drained from Meresamun's face. The soldiers pressed on, toward the glut of plundering Hittites. Swords clashed, men screamed. Istara pulled the dagger closer and prayed.

❇ ❇ ❇

At Sethi's signal, over one thousand of his men streamed out of the woods and sprinted across the dark plain heading for the goat path. The remaining thousand would stay and fight with Pre's commander, cutting into Hatti's rear lines, tearing a swathe up the slope to the pharaoh. Sethi glanced behind him, sensing rather than seeing the men of Pre, spread out in the darkness. They were ready. Now, the Hittites would pay.

Across the plain, the last of his men's shadowed forms slipped out of sight. It was time. He stood up and threw his arms wide, his battle cry so fierce he tasted blood.

"For Egypt!"

Pre thundered his cry in return, bursting out from the undergrowth into the startled Hittites, hacking and slashing. As he dispatched the men in the chariot before him, Sethi heard the satisfying sound of bodies hitting the ground all around him.

He dragged the corpses from the chariot and grabbed hold of the reins, driving into the melee. Behind him, his men took their own chariots. In the darkness and confusion, unable to separate friend from foe, the men of Hatti panicked and attacked each other.

His sword slick with blood, Sethi smiled, cold, and butchered the butchers.

✳ ✳ ✳

In the distance, Ahmen heard a single cry rise into the heavens.

For Egypt!

A Hittite rushed at him. He struck him down, straining to hear over the grunts and thuds of men deep in the act of killing. Had he imagined it? A heartbeat later he heard it again, not a solitary voice, but the roar of a thousand men, cutting across the smoky air.

His *khopesh* drenched with the blood of the dead, Ramesses met Ahmen's eyes and grinned, triumphant.

Lifting up his spear, Ahmen screamed back the cry.

The soldiers of Amun bellowed in return. The Hittites wavered, uncertain. Then, as the roar faded, from behind the stricken camp the cry repeated, by a thousand voices more.

Pre had arrived.

NINE

It was over. Khu slumped face down, dead, over the front of the chariot's box, a spear buried deep in his back. Ahmen staggered. A sharp pain lanced through his thigh. He looked down. An arrow impaled it, the shaft snapped off. He stared at it, unable to remember being hit, or breaking off the arrow. He grasped the stub, and pulled, bellowing as the barbed arrow tore away from his flesh. Lifting the arrowhead up, he frowned at it, making sure he had pulled it out intact. Its point glistened, black in the firelight.

He tossed it aside, smearing a fistful of mud over the gouge. Limping to his fretting horses, he released the leg burrs, their legs soaked in blood. Guilt sliced through him. They had suffered much for Egypt. He loathed the burrs—their purpose to turn horses into weapons—a relic of the barbaric inventiveness of the *hekau khaswet*, who had overrun Egypt in her time of weakness. The burr hung between the horses' front legs, harmless until they moved. When they did, the burr would cut into them, making them strike out. In close fighting against striking horses, even a spear was useless, the horses always connected first. Ahmen wondered how many men had fallen to their maddened striking. He looked around. Many, by the look of it.

Stumbling full circle, he caught sight of Muwatallis—brought back from his confinement—and Hattusilis being taken away, subdued, their arms bound.

Ahmen watched them go, recalling how abrupt the end had been. With the arrival of Pre and the chariots of Na'arn from Amurru, the disorganized and exhausted Hittites panicked. Some ran into the darkness, fleeing for the city of Kadesh, others threw down their weapons and surrendered.

Horns had blared, and Ramesses, bathed in a pool of torchlight, had shouted in triumph. Beneath the pharaoh, Muwatallis had knelt, bristling with defiance. Ramesses brought his *khopesh* high, his eyes cold, aiming for Muwatallis's neck. A man cried out Hatti's surrender. Hattusilis, the king's brother, emerged from the darkness, bloodied and battered. He fell to his knees and dropped his weapons. His eyes narrowed, Ramesses had lowered his sword, sparing Muwatallis, and in a heartbeat, it was done. Horns blared once more, sounding the triple staccato pulse signalling the end of battle. After hours of combat, men stumbled, disoriented, dazed. Many had blacked out.

Ahmen gazed over the firelit plateau covered with the bodies of the fallen, so thick in places, men lay piled one on top of the other. Blinking a trickle of blood out of his eyes, he tried to estimate the number of the dead. He lost count and tried again. No. There were too many. He tasted bile. He coughed and tried to spit. He couldn't; his mouth was dry as desert sand. He needed water.

Down on the slope, hyenas cackled. He shivered; he hadn't realized it was so cold. He heard the hyenas again, closer this time. Sounds of distress rose from the injured Hittites still on the slope. They would have to be brought up to the plateau for their safety. It was the honorable thing to do.

He picked up a fallen dagger and salvaged a burning torch from a toppled chariot. Dropping over the plateau's edge, he moved, wary, onto the slope, toward one of the men trapped under a fallen chariot. He walked a little past the Hittite and swept the flame in a circle. In the burst of firelight, a pair of eyes gleamed back at him. Startled, Ahmen shoved the torch at the beast with a grunt. The hyena moved further back into the shadows, giggling as it went.

Turning back to the Hittite, Ahmen heaved on the chariot. It was so much heavier than any of his own. He bellowed, cursing, and threw all his weight against it. It slid to the side, enough for him to pull the man free. The Hittite met Ahmen's eyes, his gratitude plain. Uncomfortable, Ahmen looked away.

Together, they stumbled toward the firelit plateau, clambering over broken chariots, shattered weapons, and the still-warm bodies of fallen men and horses. The hyenas' snickers edged nearer, growing in confidence, closing in on their little pool of torchlight. Uneasy, Ahmen glanced back, his foot catching between the spokes of a wheel. He staggered, slamming into something hard. Pain lanced across his shin as he tumbled forward. The Hittite grabbed his arm, jerking him back. He pointed. Ahmen looked down. An upturned chariot shaft, its splintered point deadly, aimed straight at his heart. The man had saved his life. Ahmen nodded to him, grateful.

They reached the plateau's rocky edge. Ahmen climbed up onto an overturned chariot and stepped onto the firelit safety of the plateau. The Hittite followed, clambering up onto the box. A snap, and the chariot's floor gave way. The Hittite tumbled, chest deep into the gap. He cried out. Ahmen leaned over the edge, bringing the torch closer. Blood gushed from the man's leg. Ahmen reached down, and took hold of the Hittite's forearms, pulling, then dragging the soldier toward him, his muscles screaming with exertion. Finding purchase against a rock, he braced his foot against it. With a final, shuddering heave, the Hittite emerged. Ahmen tumbled backward, slamming against the blood-soaked ground. He tried to get to his feet, but the last of his strength had been spent. The Hittite rose and offered Ahmen his hand. Ahmen joined him. Panting, they stood and looked at the plateau's carnage.

The Hittite scoffed. "We deserved to lose this battle."

Ahmen looked at him in surprise. The man spoke Egyptian. "You are not a Hittite."

"I am not."

"You are no common soldier either."

The man shook his head again. "That is also true."

Intrigued, Ahmen blundered on. "I would know your name."

"If you will do me the same honor," the older man answered, "and allow me to know yours."

Ahmen nodded, terse.

"I am Commander Hasurna of Kadesh," he continued, his voice worn from shouting, its edges rasping and harsh. "Yesterday, my men numbered seven hundred, though after this, I suspect almost none are left. We were separated, told not to worry. It would be a slaughter. Plenty of spoils for every—" He spit. A bloody molar landed on the ground, the top cracked almost in half, the pain must have been agonizing. He rubbed his jaw, grunting.

"Commander Hasurna of Kadesh," Ahmen said, pressing his palm against his chest, struck anew by the ruthless machinations of Hatti's king, "I am Ahmen-om-onet, son of Wennefer, First Prophet of Amun, Pharaoh's Royal Charioteer and Chief of the Archers."

Hasurna tilted his head. "Should I have known I would be rescued by so illustrious a person, I would have put on my best armor."

Unable to stop himself, Ahmen's lips quirked into a half-smile. Taking Kadesh's commander by his arm, Ahmen led him to the prisoners, surrounded by a circle of torches.

Ahmen cleared his throat. "I will not forget you."

"Nor I you, for what you have done for me this night."

"Perhaps one day, we might meet as—"

Hasurna shook his head, a look of warning in his eyes. Ahmen blinked, hardly believing what he had almost said. The words were treason. He stumbled away, back to the top of the slope, exhaustion slamming into him, thickening his movements. He rubbed his eyes, trying to clear his blurring vision. There would be others waiting for help.

At the plateau's edge, he waved his torch. The slope teemed with packs of hyenas climbing over the dead, frantic from the scent of blood. Their blood-curdling cries, dripping with savagery, echoed up the slope's rocky walls. Deep within the darkness, agonized screams sliced through the air. The hyenas turned, swarming as one toward those still living. The cries of those left behind spreading down the slope, brutal, primal. Sickened, Ahmen stumbled backward, his feet sliding in the mud. The desperate screams of the dying men haunting him.

He lurched toward the burning camp, his steps leaden, numb with fatigue. It began to rain, hard. He couldn't see. He staggered, pummeled by the rain, and tripped on a body. His legs gave out. He fell, shuddering, into the mud, succumbing to senselessness, dreaming of the battle, of his horses, and as always, of Meresamun, safe within his arms.

Alone at the command table, Ramesses looked over Amun's report. Without exception, every one of its companies had taken enormous losses. Fourteen of its commanders were dead, men who had taught him many things, their tutelage shaping him into the battle commander he had become. And he had lost them. In one night.

He picked up a reed brush and made a note in his journal, writing down their names, titles, and the date of their deaths. He stared at the wet ink, depression overwhelming him. Everything they had done, all they had achieved; all of it amounting to nothing more than a few marks noting their passing. And in the passage of time, they would be forgotten, men who had once meant much to him, and to Egypt. For him—one day—it would be the same. Morbid, he dwelled on the thought, determined to prevent the same fate from happening to him. He would be remembered. Even the passage of thousands of years would not erase his memory. He would make certain of it.

He pushed his journal away, and waited to receive the wax tablet containing the final tally of Amun's losses. The scribe handed it up to him. He looked down, quick; then again, disbelieving.

Two thousand six hundred and fifty-six dead, one thousand four hundred and nineteen more injured, at least two-thirds of the camp's followers butchered. He stared, numb, at the figures, unable to process the enormity of it. The scribe shifted his position, wincing with pain. Ramesses eyed him, noting the blood-soaked bandages wrapped around his torso. He gestured toward the camp.

"Go. Help Amun, and change those bandages. Egypt will not lose you, too."

Ramesses's gaze drifted back to the tablet. In all of Egypt's history, even during the invasions of the *hekau khaswet*, never had a pharaoh lost so many lives in so short a time, and for so little. Egypt was barely breathing. He unrolled the scroll Paser had prepared before the battle, outlining Egypt's terms to Hatti, and perused it. His vizier had been thorough as usual. He set it aside, watching it curl back into a scroll. By the wings of Horus he was tired. He closed his eyes. He would rest, just for a little while.

※　※　※

Paser ducked into the command tent. At the table, Ramesses sat alone, leaning his forehead against his fingertips, his eyes closed. Paser backed away, quiet, deciding his report could wait. He was in no hurry to tell Ramesses he had lost Istara.

He crossed the enclosure. Within her bloodstained, torn tent, Nefertari paced, her arms wrapped tight around her torso. She looked up. He lifted his fist to his chest and pressed on, his head bowed as he passed the spot where Istara had freed him.

Nefertari had been furious when she found out Istara had escaped. She had wanted to kill her in front of Urhi-Teshub to punish him for what he had done to her guards. Paser scoffed. He had no idea Nefertari could be so vengeful. He hurried across the charred open space separating the royal couple's residences from the rest of the camp. While he had his reprieve from Ramesses, he would continue the search for Istara. He looked back, his attention drawn by the bright blue flags atop the royal tents, snapping, loud, in the cold air. He stared at them, offended by their exuberant undulations. Someone should take them down. They looked ridiculous, flying proud over the scorched tents of the pharaoh and his queen; the ruined enclosure a mockery, perched alone and vulnerable in the middle of a bloodied, burned wasteland.

Paser rubbed his hand against the back of his neck, thinking of what he had endured after Istara had disappeared. Even with King Bentesina and his men from Amurru, they had been hard-pressed to protect Nefertari. The Hittites' numbers had been endless. They had just kept coming, right up until the horns blared Egypt's victory. But even then, it was not over. The camp burned out of control. Fire surrounded them on all sides. The flames drawing so close he had been forced to wipe a dagger clean, in preparation to obey Nefertari's brutal command. She would not burn to death.

She had waited until the last heartbeat, when the scorching heat of the approaching fires had turned the interior of her tent a dull orange, the heated air suffocating and almost impossible to breathe. Still regal, she had come to him and knelt, her back pressed against his thighs, her breasts rising and falling, rapid, betraying her fear. His eyes burning with tears, he had wrapped his fingers in her hair and tilted her head back, gentle, tender. Her eyes, streaming, met his, trusting, frightened. His heart clenched at the memory. He had been so close to confessing his love for her.

But Horus had been watching over them. Just as Paser laid the blade against her neck, rain, cold, sharp, and heavy pounded down onto the stricken camp, thundering against the tent's roof. The flames succumbed.

He had snatched his dagger away and helped Nefertari, shaking, to her feet. Neither of them had looked at the other for the rest of the night.

The flags snapped, sharp. He blinked, and pushed the dark memory aside, stepping over the still-warm embers of the nobility's enclosures, cautious. His own tent was out there somewhere, lost in the cinders.

Ahead, the fire line ended, and a wall of broken tents stood between him and the way out. He shoved through the wet material of a sagging tent and emerged into the chaos of Amun's vast barracks.

Wounded soldiers sifted through the wreckage. Their eyes widened when they recognized him. Sagging with exhaustion, they stood up and lifted their fists to their chests. He gestured for them to carry on, picking his way past them, clambering over broken chariots and fallen horses. Other horses, still living, stood trapped and exhausted in their harnesses, their heads hanging. Atop an overturned Hittite chariot, he paused to catch his breath, turning full circle. The devastated camp stretched away in every direction, blackened, broken. Unrecognizable.

A group of camp women—their gowns torn open, their breasts and faces battered—hauled broken stakes, poles, and tattered lengths of tents toward the camp's edge. Nearby, a knot of soldiers, their faces hard, dragged aside the remains of a burned-out tent, pulling out the charred body of a decapitated woman. In grim silence, one of them lifted her up and carried her away.

A little distance away, a bloodied follower struggled to heft a fallen support pole. Paser scrambled down from his perch and hastened over to help him. The pole cast aside, the man scrabbled through the remaining debris. With a broken cry, he found the ones he sought. Crying out their names, he dragged the eviscerated bodies of his wife and child to him.

His heart tight, Paser turned away, giving the grieving man his privacy. A group of soldiers passed by, carrying the corpses of Hittites toward the blazing fires outside the camp, where thick billows of greasy black smoke gouted up into the sky. Paser glared at the dead men, bitter. Without their hearts, they could not enter the afterlife. It was what they deserved, for what they had wrought against innocents.

He carried on, stumbling through the debris of dozens of rows of charred tents, overwhelmed by the magnitude of what Hatti had wrought. Ahead, a wall of ruined chariots barred his way, he clambered over them and broke free of the camp.

He staggered to a halt, gaping.

Row upon row of injured men and women fanned out across the plateau, laid out in irregular lines on the muddy ground. Between each line, fed by the women carrying out the broken tents of Amun, fires burned. Groans and cries for help rose over the crackle of the flames, the voices of the wounded mingling, a susurration of desolation and misery, rising and falling in the cold gusts of air.

He moved forward, thinking he might find Istara there, among the wounded. He stopped. No. If Istara had been found alive, dressed as she was, she would have been taken to the prisoners. If she had been found dead—he glanced at the fires of the burning Hittites, shuddering. She deserved better. Bleak, he turned away, sensing the souls of Egypt's dead brushing past him, flying away to the gods, as soft as a summer breeze.

<h1>ELEVEN</h1>

Istara sat back on her heels and pressed her palms against her gritty smoke-sore eyes, waiting for Meresamun to finish. A cold gust bore down on her, carrying the cries of the wounded. She shivered, despondent, noting the fresh losses surrounding them. In the time they spent saving one, ten had succumbed to their injuries.

"He will live thanks to you," Meresamun said, tying off the last suture on the soldier's chest. "By Isis, you are as accomplished as any of Egypt's foremost surgeons." She reached into the satchel loaned to her by the surgeons and pulled out a length of linen, rolling it into a bandage.

Istara hefted the unconscious soldier up, struggling to hold him steady as Meresamun bound the linen tight and tied it off. Breathing a prayer for his protection, Istara packed her satchel and rose, working the kinks from her back, scanning the wounded for those they still had time to save. She stopped, abrupt. The soldier was unconscious, filthy with mud and covered in dried blood, but he still lived.

"The one there, without a pallet," she pointed, her voice tight. "I know him."

Meresamun stood, shading her eyes, curious. A sharp intake of breath and she was gone, stumbling through the men, falling to her knees beside him, holding his bloodstained face in her hands. She pressed her forehead against his, tears in her eyes.

Istara knelt beside him, assessing his condition, eyeing the gouge in his thigh where an arrow had been torn free, the gaping hole packed with mud.

She touched Meresamun's shoulder. "He is your man?"

Meresamun's eyes met hers, then fell back down to Ahmen. "Once, for a short time," she whispered. She looked back up, taut, pale. "Will he . . . ?"

Gesturing to a passing woman to bring them a pan of warmed water, Istara emptied her satchel. "His injuries are many," she answered, nodding at his leg, "but this one in his thigh needs urgent attention. We will begin there. So long as the blood fever has not yet taken hold of him, he will return to you."

She kept Meresamun busy cleaning and bandaging his wounds while she closed the torn muscles of his thigh with fine inner and outer stitches. It was painstaking work. The arrow had been torn fee with brute force, severing the major fibers of connecting tissue. Mid-afternoon came and went, the cold wind intensified, driving in hard gusts across the plateau. Huddling into herself, she carried on, enduring.

As the sun lowered its weight onto the horizon, she sat back and inspected her work, wiping her hands on a linen cloth. His injuries would heal, and cleanly. She felt the back of his neck. No fever. Meresamun had found a pallet and a thick blanket for him. Cleaned and bandaged, she covered him, wrapping him tight against the chill. There was nothing left to do but wait.

As she collected her things, Meresamun asked, hesitant. "How is it you know Ahmen?"

Istara paused in her work, catching the flicker of uncertainty in the other woman's question. "Do you see the city there, across the plain?" Istara nodded at the walls of Kadesh. "That was my home until I was sent here by the goddess Baalat. It was Ahmen who brought me into the camp, who defended me before Pharaoh. I pray you will not have to wait long until you are reunited."

She continued her work, soothed by the familiar actions of stoppering vials of ointment and rolling up the remaining linens into new bandages.

"We cannot be reunited," Meresamun said, hollow, "at least not like this. I must leave before he wakes."

Istara stopped rolling the linens, intrigued despite her exhaustion, but Meresamun said no more. Returning to the bandages, Istara murmured, "Then you should depart before the evening falls."

Meresamun nodded. Pressing her fingers to her face, she wiped away a tear, discreet.

"You mentioned you intend to return to your family in Babylon, but did not yet know the way." Istara pulled off two golden armbands and held them out to Meresamun. "March with the Egyptians until they pass through the Great Wood of Amka, then take the road to Damas. These will more than cover the cost of your passage home from there."

Meresamun drew back, embarrassed. "It is too much. I cannot accept such a gift. I do not even know your name."

Reaching over Ahmen's prone form, Istara took Meresamun's hand, filling it with the heavy weight of the armbands. "My name is not important. You saved my life. Be safe on your journey." She rose, catching Meresamun looking up at her, cradling the golden bands, her expression drowning in gratitude. Istara's chest tightened, a stab of loneliness lancing into her. She would miss her sudden companion. "I will pray for your safe return home," she said, soft. She didn't wait for Meresamun's reply. Looking over the field of the wounded for her next patient, she turned and walked away.

❋ ❋ ❋

Meresamun watched the woman from Kadesh slip behind one of the fires, her satchel tucked under the crook of her arm. She had never once given any hint of her name or her family. She could be anyone.

Meresamun wondered if perhaps she was a surgeon, disgraced in her own kingdom, slipping away to seek her fortune in a new empire. She didn't believe the story about a goddess sending her. She knew enough from her years in the temple to know the gods never spoke to mortals. No, she must be a surgeon, and a wealthy one, to be able to give away her gold without a care.

A cold gust of mountain air penetrated Meresamun's thin gown. Shivering, she tucked the blanket tighter around Ahmen and stroked his forehead, drinking in the sight of him. She sat beside him, her legs turning numb in the cold mud, willing the evening not to come, but the sky darkened, and beyond the light of the fires, the shadows deepened. Her heart clenched. Her time was coming to an end. It was too soon. She couldn't leave, not yet. Just a little longer.

She brushed her lips against Ahmen's, remembering the last time they had touched, how he had held her against him, fierce, as he made love to her. A tear slipped free, landing on his cheek. He stirred. Alarmed, she shrank back. There would be no atonement if Sekhmet had not sent him to her. Ahmen had to seek her out and find her. She lifted her satchel, the arm bands tucked safe within, and slipped into the shadows.

He sat up, disoriented, and called her name, uncertain, a question, cracking with hope. She stifled a sob. He had not forgotten her. He lay back down and slept once more. She crept back to his side, tears glittering on her cheeks, bright, stars in the firelight.

Ramesses pushed his platter aside. It was good to have food again. He sat back and sipped his wine. Henufkhet cleared the table and lifted the tray. He paused, uncertain. Ramesses set his cup aside.

"You have something you wish to say?"

"My lord, a request." Henufkhet bowed. "May the people have your permission to eat now Pharaoh has dined?"

"You are following protocol, even now?" Ramesses demanded, sharp. "Does my queen still wait to dine?"

Henufkhet's knuckles whitened against the tray. "I thought it best to wait until you had finished," he answered, paling. "I did not wish to anger the gods, especially when things right now are so . . . difficult."

"Until we march," Ramesses said, terse, "my people are to eat until they can eat no more. With the arrival of the other divisions, Horus knows we have more than enough rations."

He dragged a stack of fresh reports closer, eyeing Henufkhet as he departed. Low voices drifted in from the vestibule. He waited for an announcement. None came. He rose, wary, his dagger ready. A filthy, bloodied soldier ducked inside and dropped to his knee.

"Lord Commander Sethi," Ramesses said, relief cascading through him, "you live, thank Re. I had counted you as one of the lost. Never before have I been so pleased to be wrong. You bring Pre's report?"

Sethi raised his fist to his chest, his knuckles scabbed over and grimy with mud. "Great King," he answered, hoarse, "forgive me. I returned to those I left on the road to Kadesh. The accounting is done. Pre has lost two thousand, two hundred and eighty-seven men, and of the remaining men, one thousand two hundred and twelve are injured. Unless the gods intervene, it is certain almost a third of them will not live to see Re's barque rise tomorrow."

Ramesses turned away. "Which means between Amun and Pre, Egypt has lost five thousand men. An entire division, gone, in one night." He clenched his fists. "By Osiris's blood, for what purpose did we endure all this? What has been accomplished here at Kadesh? Nothing but an honorless battle, with Amun's camp turned into a pit of carnage, soaked with the blood of the innocent. It is beyond comprehension."

"Your Majesty," Sethi said, ragged, "you have defeated Hatti, and reclaimed Kadesh."

Ramesses swiveled back around. "Have I? Paser's scouts returned this morning from across the river, and what did they find beyond those hills, but Muwatallis's camp seething with twenty thousand soldiers more. Muwatallis may have used all his chariots in last night's assaults, but he is not defeated. Not yet. So here we lay, weak as a newborn, while the leaderless Hittite hordes sit and fight amongst themselves over what to do next. How long will they wait before they come at us once more, twenty thousand of them against the thirteen and a half thousand I have left?" He stopped, calming himself. "I still have at least one advantage. I hold the lives of Muwatallis, Hattusilis, and Urhi-Teshub in my hand. The entire royal line of Hatti is mine for the taking should the need arise."

He caught Sethi's oblique look. "What?"

Sethi eyed him, cautious. "You know you cannot, the gods—"

"I know the prohibitions of battle well enough," Ramesses interrupted, aggravated, "but do they even apply now? This was no true battle. It was an ambush. I would have his blood after what he has wrought upon my men, women, and children!" Furious, he kicked one of the stools. It hit the tent's wall with a dull thud.

"Your Majesty, I too long for his blood. I will never forget what he did to Pre. But we cannot kill him now. The battle is over, and he has surrendered." Sethi grunted, shifting his weight. "The gods will punish Hatti for his crimes."

Ramesses crossed his arms and stared into the flames of the brazier, annoyed. He knew Sethi spoke the truth. He had hoped he could match dishonor with dishonor, but beneath his rage, the burden of his crown prevailed. He could not justify the risk of angering the gods, Egypt was in enough danger as it was. But neither would he let the Hittites go, not when they could return to their men and regroup.

An idea struck him. It stretched the spirit of what was permitted after a battle to the limit, but so long as no blood was spilled, he was not breaking any of the prohibitions. He looked back at Sethi, still kneeling, his head bowed.

"Then they will remain with us until we have marched to the road to Damas. A contingent from Amurru can escort them back to Kadesh. Muwatallis will not come after us once we have twelve days' march between us."

Sethi nodded, grim. "How soon do you wish to depart."

"The day after tomorrow," Ramesses answered, "when Re's barque ascends the horizon."

Sethi raised his fist to his chest. "Pre will be ready to fol—" He broke off, coughing hard, coming to his feet. He bowed. "My lord, forgive me."

Ramesses stared at his commander, seeing for the first time the extent of Sethi's injuries. Deep gashes covered his arms, legs, and chest, all of them taut with dried mud. "By Horus," he said, "your injuries need attention, and soon. You put yourself at great risk of blood fever."

A cold draft of air swept in, making the lamps' flames waver. Henufkhet entered. In the vestibule, a woman waited, obscured by the half-closed material.

"Your Highness," Henufkhet murmured, bowing, "I have brought a surgeon for Lord Sethi."

Ramesses nodded at Sethi. "Go. I will send for you before I depart."

Sethi's fist came to his chest. "Your Majesty."

He left. Ramesses turned to Henufkhet. "Make certain Commander Sethi is brought hot food and wine." Henufkhet bowed and turned to leave when Ramesses bid him wait. "It seemed to me the surgeon was dressed in purple. Is she the woman from Kadesh?"

Henufkhet paled. "My lord, forgive me, I could find no others on the field. The men around her swore to her abilities as a surgeon. Shall I fetch her back?"

"No," Ramesses answered after considering, "but send men to keep an eye on her. Once she is finished, have them bring her back to me."

As Henufkhet hurried away, Ramesses rubbed his hand across his jaw, sifting through the details of Paser's report. Istara had been used as a bargaining tool to force Urhi-Teshub to withdraw his men, but during the melee, she had fled, and despite Paser's efforts to find her, was assumed dead. Ramesses wondered anew why she would have fled into the camp, a woman, alone, instead of remaining in the enclave, protected by the queen's guards.

Taking up his wine, he thought of all the courtesans who had gone missing over the years, to reappear months later in Pi-Ramesses. Nefertari thought he didn't know. He just didn't care. There were always more women to be had. He let her play her little game, it kept her occupied, and amused him.

But Paser had not met his eyes when he spoke of the incident in the enclave, and Ramesses had suspected there was more to the story. Now he was certain. He swallowed the wine, tasting bitterness. It seemed he had greatly underestimated his wife.

Her medical satchel clutched tight to her chest, Istara clambered over a fallen support pole, struggling to keep up after the filthy, bloodstained soldier stalking through the ruins of Amun.

He passed a bonfire. Despite the chill in the air, his body gleamed with perspiration. A multitude of injuries seeped blood, all of them untended for far too long. Almost a whole day had passed since the battle, plenty of time for the blood fever to take hold, even of this man, as strong as he looked, pushing his way through the camp toward a destination known only to him.

Istara felt a ripple of fear. She had never lost a patient before, and this one, a confidant of the pharaoh could not be her first.

The soldier left the stricken camp of Amun and crossed the plateau toward another camp, its perimeter bright with the light of fires and torches. He plunged into it, navigating through the maze of tents. Deep inside the camp, he headed to a darkened tent and ducked inside. Scrambling to keep up, Istara closed the distance, and with a quiet call announcing her arrival, slipped under the flap.

In the shadows, she heard his breathing, ragged and shallow; his silhouette, massive in the confines of the small tent, turned toward her. He coughed, hard. When he recovered, his voice came to her, harsh.

"Light the lamps."

She tightened her hold on the satchel, defensive. "My lord, my talents lie in healing, not lighting lamps."

He took a step toward her, the stench of him—stale urine, feces, blood, and entrails—overwhelming. Another step and he was close enough for her to see the whites of his eyes, glittering, despite the gloom.

"You dare disobey my command?" he asked, quiet, dangerous.

"I am no slave," she retorted, though a tremble of fear touched her words. "Another can light the lamps, so I may tend to you sooner—unless you are in a hurry to join the host of thousands already on their way to the gods?"

He stared at her, working through her reasoning with painstaking slowness. A grunt, and he leaned past her, pushing aside the flap, calling to one of his men; the startling heat of his fever blasting through her gown, hot as a blazing brazier. She shivered as the cold fled her bones, her respect for him growing, realizing his ability to withstand both his injuries and his fever meant he was no ordinary man.

Slipping out from under his broiling bulk, she knelt and laid out her supplies, what little she had left. A soldier came in and lit the lamps. "He needs hot water," she said to him as she sorted through her vials, "and bring clean linen towels if there are any to be found."

The soldier left, hurrying away to do her bidding. Her patient's breathing turned ragged. She glanced up. He stared at her, hostile, his muscled arms crossed over his chest. Suspicion filled his eyes. An aura of violence emanated from him. She fought for calm.

"You will need to remove your clothing and weapons, so you will be able to bathe," she said, gesturing at his ruined kilt.

"Not before you tell me who you are," he said, terse, his eyes hard. "No Egyptian surgeon dresses thus, wearing the royal color of purple and a king's ransom of gold." His hand dropped to the hilt of his dagger. "If your answer displeases me, by Horus, I swear I will send you to the gods."

She licked her lips, noting the fullness of his pupils. "You are burning with fever," she said, striving for calm, though her voice wavered, betraying her. "When the water comes, wash yourself as clean as you can. I will wait without."

The dagger came out of its scabbard, a sharp hiss. He lunged at her, his speed startling her. She cried out as he grabbed a fistful of her hair, rough, forcing her head back, baring her neck. The cold tip of his dagger pricked the soft spot underneath her jaw. She quaked, the movement making the dagger dig into her flesh. Tears came to her eyes, her vision blurred.

"Please . . ." she pled, soft.

He glared at her, filled with hate. "You are nothing but a whore of that coward Muwatallis, your words nothing but lies. Do you know how I have spent my day? Burying half my division in the ashes of the trees you burned—"

"I beg you," she implored, desperate, as the blade bit deeper into her throat. "I am not your enemy."

His eyes focused, just for a heartbeat. He looked down at her, uncertain, the pressure of the dagger eased just a little. "What is your name?" he asked, his breathing becoming labored. "I would know it before I send you to the gods."

She sobbed, exhausted. "Istara. Princess of Kadesh."

He snatched the dagger back, shocked into a brief heartbeat of lucidity. "Hatti's queen-in-waiting?"

"Once. No longer. I have betrayed Hatti." A tear slid down her cheek.

He shook his head, disoriented, confused, his eyes unfocusing once more. He brought dagger's point back against her throat. He pressed, slow. She felt her flesh opening, the burn of his blade as it tasted her blood. She looked up at him, despairing, reaching out to him, imploring. He cursed.

"Agh! I dream of you again. But where is the battle—"

Recognition flared in his eyes. The dagger slipped from his hand, hitting the rug with a thud.

"To think I almost killed you," he breathed. He gazed at her, reverent. Filled with wonder, he touched her face, his filthy fingers tracing the outline of her cheekbone. His eyes glazed over, turning blank, the fever's grip overcoming him. He staggered. His knees buckled. He landed on them with a grunt, his weight slamming into her, carrying her to the ground, trapping her.

She struggled to push him off, but it felt as though a granite pillar had fallen onto her. She couldn't move. Soon she couldn't breathe. Panicking, breathless, she called out for help. No one came. Her vision began to dim, black spots spiraled, swirling, faster. There, a sound. She scrabbled, clinging to the barest edge of consciousness. Someone was coming: the soldier she had sent for hot water. He ducked in carrying a basin of steaming water, another followed after, holding a bundle of linens.

With a cry of alarm, they rushed over, their sandaled feet sliding on the rug as they struggled to roll the unconscious soldier away. Darkness beckoned, soft, and warm. She sank down into it, wondering what it was she was supposed to be fighting for, when the weight left her and air flooded into her lungs. She shot up, heaving, her chest screaming in agony, burning with each new breath. After several heartbeats, her vision cleared. The soldiers had turned her patient over and had begun stripping him.

Her hands trembling, she sought to compose herself, straightening her things, scattered across the rug by their fall. He said he had dreamed of her, had looked at her as though he already knew her, yet they had never met. How could they? He was an Egyptian and she the Hittite queen-in-waiting, mortal enemies. The man was delirious. His words meant nothing. She stopped, setting aside one of the vials, noticing a detail in the rug. She had seen that detail before, could remember it, quite clearly. She looked around, astonished, realizing she had seen all of it before; the wounded, filthy man, the tent, the two soldiers assisting her—

She caught her breath. This was her vision. This was the man Baalat had shown her. She stared at him, the pieces falling together, shuddering as the second vision burst into her awareness, reminding her what he had once done for her, giving up his rations to her in Baalat's sanctuary. Her heart slowed, thudding, caught by the magnitude, the utter improbability of their paths crossing, not once, but twice, so many years apart. And yet, here he was, bleeding and fevered, in need of her healing abilities, just as she had once been in need of his rations.

She glanced at the soldiers, waiting for her, anxious. Trembling, she lifted a pair of stone vials. "This is a tincture to fight the blood fever, and this, for the pain," she explained as she dosed him. "Now, help me clean him, there is almost no time left."

It was a long while before the soldier's body lay cleansed of the thick layers of filth, revealing the extent of his injuries. Tying a clean linen cloth around his groin, Istara washed, stitched and bound his wounds, working long into the night, her fingers trembling from exhaustion and hunger. Turning his inert body from side to side, his men assisted her in silence, holding up an arm or leg while she bound it tight; pushing him upright for her to close the deep slashes across his back.

At irregular intervals, he returned to fevered consciousness, flailing, tearing his stitches; fighting against his men as they struggled to hold him down while she drugged him with the opiate, sending him shuddering back into oblivion.

Blinking back tears of frustration, she would unwrap his ruined bandages, and begin her work anew, repairing the damage he had wrought, until, in the dead of the night, the fires of his fever abated, and he calmed; his breathing slowing to the gentle cadence of one deep asleep. With soft movements, careful of his injuries, she wiped away the last of the sweat breaking from his body. Feeling the back of his neck for his temperature, she looked up at his men and nodded, exhausted. It was over. He would live.

The soldiers departed in weary silence, leaving her to her vigil. Tucking the blanket tight around him, she watched him as he breathed, quiet in the realm of dreams. Her gaze swept over him, curious. Despite his many bandages, his powerful body, thick with muscle, was defined, a warrior's body, bearing the scars of a lifetime spent in battle.

She gazed at his face, recognizing in its smooth planes the matured, hardened version of the young man who had fed her thirteen years before. His jaw had filled out, and his nose had been broken, leaving it sitting a little to the left, though it only seemed to enhance his commanding charisma. Lines creased away from the corners of his eyes, deeper ones furrowed his brow. There was something else too, less easy to place, an edge to him. His lips, thinned by the opium, curved down a little, making his expression harsh and forbidding. She remembered him smiling, his eyes warm.

He licked his lips. She wet a cloth and dribbled a little water into his mouth. He swallowed without waking, the lines of his jaw settling back into their fixed position, tense even in sleep. She sat back on her heels. She had seen these angles and edges before, in her surrogate mother's face, catching glimpses of it when Tanu-Hepa thought no one was looking. Loneliness.

Istara looked away, ashamed of her prying. Instead, she tried to remember how long it had been since she had eaten. She couldn't. She scoffed, it didn't matter, she wasn't hungry anymore anyway. Dizziness whispered through her. She lay down a little apart from his pallet, keeping her eyes on him, waiting for the reeling sensation to pass. It slid away, exhaustion following in its wake. She closed her eyes, shutting out the flickering patterns of the lamp's flames on the tent's ceiling.

A warm, shimmering light sparkled in the darkness of her mind, beckoning to her. She drifted toward it, letting its tendrils reach out and envelope her, soothing her. Then, there was nothing.

❋   ❋   ❋

In the coldest part of the night, Sethi's eyes opened, the darkness blinding him. He had been dreaming of her again. Movement beside him. He reached for his dagger, but his fingers only found empty space. More movement, the sound of shivering. A woman. Wary, he reached out. His fingers touched her arm, her skin as cold as stone. She moaned, a low bleat, huddling toward his touch.

Sethi searched his memory. When had he taken a woman to his pallet? Why had he not shared his blanket with her? He ran his hand over her, exploring. Her gown was in ruins, and everywhere, jewelry. Strange. She moaned again, her body quaking from the cold. Dragging the blanket out from under him, he drew her to him, tucking her head against his shoulder. Ignoring the twinges of pain deep in his body, he pulled her against him.

In the warmth of his embrace, she sighed. He could see nothing. Curious, he touched her face, making out its contours, her lips parting as his fingers drifted over them.

She breathed a word, filled with longing, tainted by grief. "Urhi . . ."

He snatched his fingers back. A Hittite name.

A gust of wind captured the tent's flap, and a blade of moonlight, blue-white, sliced over her. He stared, incredulous. It was her. The one he had seen so many times in his dreams. Relief cascaded through him. After years of waiting, wondering, searching, she had come to him, from out of nowhere. He held her fast against him, refusing to wonder how or why, simply reveling in the solidness of her. For the first time in his life, he felt whole, complete. Brushing his lips against her forehead, he closed his eyes and succumbed to the opiates, carrying her with him as he tumbled back into the realm of dreams, vowing never to let her go.

❋ ❋ ❋

Paser rubbed the back of his fist across his mouth as he looked over the sleeping pair, wrapped in each other's arms. Ramesses could not hear of this, no one could. He turned to Sethi's men waiting behind him, their eyes fixed on their feet.

"You were right to come to me. This, whatever *this* might be, never happened. Leave me."

He waited until they were gone and their footsteps had retreated to a safe distance before prodding Sethi with his foot. Sethi's eyes snapped opened.

"Lord Paser," he rumbled.

"Your men are good men," Paser said. "When they found you thus, they sent for me. No one else knows."

Sethi hauled himself up and leaned on his elbow, wincing. He rubbed his jaw and scalp, the rasp of his stubble loud in the confined space. He looked rough, tired.

"What do you mean . . . found me thus?"

A soft moan interrupted them. Istara rolled onto her back. Her face turned upward, her lips parted, soft, and inviting. Paser waited, watching Sethi as he gazed at her, his expression shifting in subtle turns from disbelief to deepening interest.

Paser cleared his throat. "Do you know who this woman is?"

Without taking his eyes from her, Sethi answered, low. "I do not."

Paser leaned back, his immediate fears alleviated, though new ones were springing up to replace them as Sethi lowered his hand to brush a stray tendril of hair from her cheek, the act tender, private, reverent. Alarmed, Paser cleared his throat, louder this time. Sethi met Paser's warning look.

"She tended your injuries," Paser said, sharp. "The pharaoh has had me searching for you—for her—all night."

Sethi's eyes darkened, unreadable. He gazed at her once more, his fingers still on her cheek. "I would know who she is."

"You would do better to concern yourself with preparing Pre for its departure," Paser snapped, reaching down to wake her.

Sethi caught Paser's wrist, stopping him, jerking him back. "Tell me."

Paser stared at Sethi's hand, stunned by the commander's breach of protocol. The Vizier of Upper Egypt was untouchable, by law. A heartbeat passed, tense. Sethi let go, murmuring an apology, saying he was not himself. Terse, Paser nodded. Sethi looked back at Istara, uncertainty flickering over his harsh features.

Unwilling to satisfy his curiosity after his gross behavior, Paser chose to give the commander an oblique answer. "She is the key to our survival, and our safe return home."

Sethi's brow furrowed. "She is a hostage?"

"Yes, and no," Paser replied as he pulled the blanket back. Their legs were tangled together, their hips touched, intimate. Jealousy, hot, sudden, and bitter welled up. Sethi had never loved any woman, he only took courtesans, and for years Paser had felt a quiet solidarity with Sethi, knowing he was not alone in his loveless existence. But this was different. He could sense Sethi's nascent territoriality, the change in him, leaving Paser alone to his fate. He turned on him, resentful.

"Do not make this mistake again," he said, sour. "Find another woman to satisfy your needs. This one cannot be touched. She is a gift from Re and belongs to Egypt—to Ramesses himself."

His expression taut, Sethi shifted on the pallet, pulling his legs free. Impatient, Paser pushed between them and shook Istara's shoulders, willing her to wake. Claustrophobia closed in on him. He needed to leave, to get away.

Istara stirred, sleepy. He hoisted her up and glanced down at Sethi, alone once more, as he always was, as he always would be. Satisfaction poured through him.

"This evening, you are to dine with us in the command tent. The pharaoh wishes to see you before he departs."

His gaze still on Istara, Sethi remained silent. Paser shifted her weight on his shoulder. "Then, until tonight, Commander."

※　※　※

Sethi watched them go, trying to remember what had passed since he left the pharaoh's tent, but there was nothing, only darkness. Anything could have happened. He looked down at the thin linen cloth covering his groin. He had done it before, taken courtesans while full of drink, without remembering; though they told him of it after, as they held their pretty hands out, waiting for his gold. He pulled his member free and examined it. It was smooth and dry. He tucked it back within its bindings, relieved. He had not touched her.

His hand brushed against something within the folds of the blanket. He pulled it out. A silver armband worked in great detail, the craftsmanship worthy of Nefertari herself. He stared at it, as a faint memory flickered, fading away before it coalesced. The woman had told him her name. He clutched the armband, as though to pull the memory from it. Nothing.

He cursed, frustrated. He had been dreaming of a woman he had believed he would never find, a woman he had begun to think was not even real. Yet here, in the midst of Egypt's ruins, he had wakened to find her beside him, as though he had brought her to life, just by wishing for it. He scoffed, his mouth twisting downward, sneering at his fanciful thoughts. She was real enough if she belonged to Ramesses, and Sethi knew he was no conjurer.

But—he turned the armband over in his hand, examining it, as though hoping for a clue—why would he dream of a woman, and search for her for all these years, only for her to be snatched away by the only man who could gainsay him? He slammed his fist against the pallet. How could he go to court and see her there, as out of reach as Nefertari? He caught himself. He could not think of this now. There was too much work to be done. He would think about it, later.

He rose, feeling the tugs of dozens of sutures. He looked himself over, assessing his injuries, impressed. The Hittites had done a fair work on him, but he had been well tended. He would heal. Ignoring the dull aches spreading across his body, he picked up a fresh kilt and wrapped it around his hips. Collecting his cleaned weapons, he inspected them before sliding them into their scabbards. As they settled into place, he grunted, appreciating their reassuring heft against his hips.

Pushing out into the cold, bright morning, he savored the welcome sight of Re-Atum's golden barque ascending the eastern horizon into a clear, blue sky. The smell of baking bread assailed his nostrils, and his stomach cried out, reminding him it had been two days since he had last eaten. He turned toward the cook tents, his thoughts prioritizing around food, his men, and the preparations for Pre's return.

He patted his pouch, feeling the shape of the woman's armband within. He would keep it safe until he could return it to the pharaoh. If he was fortunate, he would never see her again. The gods had played him a cruel game, but now, it was time to move on. Just like his injuries, one day his heart would heal. He thought of Edarru, waiting for him in Pi-Ramesses. She, at least, would be happy.

❋   ❋   ❋

Locked within the immortal realm, Baalat leaned over the vision pool, breathless. She had had to hurry, to buy herself what little time she could before Horus—fast becoming suspicious—would come looking for her. She stared at the pool, willing it to wake. Hurry. Hurry. She had watched as Istara faced Sethi's accusations, then his dagger. Baalat had not known about his dreams. She had asked the vision pool for the name of the god who had intervened. Its reply unnerved her. Silence. Sethi's destiny was being controlled from beyond even the realm of immortals. Baalat shivered. The Creator God.

The pool's silvered surface shimmered, tormenting her with its languid progress. The mortal realm coalesced, its blurred images firming, taking shape. There. Sethi walking across the camp, greeting his men, his hand drifting to the pouch on his belt, patting it.

A tug, hard, insistent. She followed it. Her view lifted, crossing the ruined plain, flying over the walls of Kadesh, toward the palace grounds. It stopped and spiraled down to the temple, piercing the roof of the sanctuary.

Surrounded by a thick haze of opium incense, Rhoha looked up and regarded Baalat's statue. She tilted her head in mocking deference, her lips twisting into an arrogant smile. She turned and flung the doors open. A draft of air rushed in. With a flourish of her gown, she descended the stairs into the temple.

Baalat gazed at her golden image, alone, and forgotten. Curls of incense drifted past her shimmering form, drawn toward the open door. From the distance, the cries of dozens, then hundreds of voices spread across the city, echoing down the empty corridors of the temple, tumbling, loud into her image's prison, *The King is dead! Long live Queen Rhoha!*

Horus's footsteps quick, determined, anxious, moved down the corridor. Baalat pulled away from the pool. The cries of Kadesh's people faded.

She turned, guilty, as Horus entered the Hall of Visions, his expression betraying his fear and uncertainty. She went to him, her hands held out, letting him draw her against him, his powerful arms enclosing her, fierce. He knew. He understood something bigger than them was happening and he couldn't stop it. He kissed her, his mouth possessive, unyielding. Sweeping her up, he carried her back to their bed, and made her his own, over and over, until she shuddered with ecstasy.

She woke, naked. Horus was still holding her, lost in the realm of dreams. She looked up at the gleaming white ceiling above their bed, watching the golden patterns change and shift. Fractals, a gift from Thoth. He had said they represented the mystery of their existence. She used to watch them for days, entranced. Now, she could only think of Istara, and Sethi, and of her own fate, fast approaching.

"Where are the others, why do they not come?" Muwatallis demanded as he paced back and forth, caged within the tight confines of the tent.

"Brother," Hattusilis said, watching him, uneasy, "there is no one left to lead them. All who remain are foot soldiers, farmers and conscripts who will wait for their orders. Without a leader, they will never come."

"You left them *leaderless*?" Muwatallis stopped, incredulous.

"That rock must have hit you hard," Urhi-Teshub scoffed, breaking the heavy silence. "Though your brother advised against it, you believed your ambush could not fail. It was *your* order that sent every king and noble from the camp, leaving the soldiers leaderless." He bowed, filled with reproach. "All hail the King."

"And where were you, you arrogant whelp?" Muwatallis shouted, lunging at Urhi-Teshub, grabbing hold of his son's tunic. "On your fool's errand, sacrificing my men to the royal enclosure. If you had done as you were commanded, we might have won."

Hattusilis pushed between them. "This is what they want, for us to fight, to lose our focus," he panted, grunting with the effort to hold Muwatallis back. "Brother, you must gain our freedom at any cost. Whatever Ramesses asks, concede to it. Once we are free, we can return to the camp, regroup, and attack once more. Between the three of us, we can still destroy Egypt."

"A fine plan," Muwatallis said, sour, letting go of Urhi-Teshub, "but how shall I even begin to accomplish such a thing? Ramesses does not send for me to discuss terms, and all my demands for an audience have been ignored. By now, he must know of our camp. He will not free us."

"Why could you not have faced Egypt in true battle?" Urhi-Teshub scowled as he jerked his tunic straight. "I have heard what the Egyptians are saying. Hatti fell because their king is a coward and a—"

"You dare speak thus to the King of Hatti? I am a god!" His face white with rage, Muwatallis shoved Hattusilis aside, sending him crashing into the stools. His hands went around Urhi-Teshub's neck, tightening, choking him. "I should have thrown you to the dogs when you were a babe for taking Asuru from me," he spat, ignoring his son's distress. "But you were all that remained to remind me of her, the woman who should have been Hatti's queen—not that slut Tanu-Hepa. And now you betray me by tearing my empire apart. If I have to kill you with my own hands to stop you, I will. You will never have my throne. Never."

Scrambling to his feet, Hattusilis struggled to prise his brother's hands free. "Do not send Urhi-Teshub to the gods," he cried, his fingers sliding, useless, over his brother's relentless grip. "Asuru died to give him life! Do not dishonor her sacrifice."

His eyes wild, Muwatallis roared, frustrated. He let go, rough, pushing Urhi-Teshub against the tent's wall. "For Asuru then," he panted, backing away, rigid with anger. "But only for her."

Silence, hostile and cold descended, the men retreating to the opposite corners of the tent. Urhi-Teshub rubbed his throat, eyeing his father's back with open hatred. Desperate to divert the tension, Hattusilis went to the tent's entrance and called out another request for an audience with the pharaoh. He waited. A brief creak of leather as a guard outside shifted his weight. Then, nothing.

Depressed, he returned to his stool and poked at the dying embers of the brazier. Footsteps approached. Low voices outside. The tent's flap opened. A gust of cold air. Two soldiers entered. Hattusilis rose and nodded at Muwatallis. His brother stepped forward. The soldiers ignored him. In complete silence, they took hold of Urhi-Teshub, bound his arms and dragged him away, struggling and protesting.

Hattusilis sank onto his stool, fear and uncertainty clawing into him. This was not how it was done. Ramesses should be discussing terms with Muwatallis—but his brother had changed the rules, and now Egypt had the upper hand. Anything could happen. The day stretched, agonizing, slow. Evening came. Food arrived, but he had no appetite. Across from him, his brother stared into the brazier, silent, uneasy, the platter beside him untouched.

Night fell. Hattusilis slipped in and out of fragmented dreams. Deep in the night, he woke to a furtive sound. Had someone come in? He peered through the shadows at Urhi-Teshub's pallet. Empty. The sound came again. Hattusilis sat up, his flesh prickling, dread circling him.

Huddled in a darkened corner, his brother shuddered, staring, unseeing at a sheet of papyrus he held in his hand. Hattusilis went to him. He took it. Horrified, he read the pronouncement, inked with Ramesses's cartouche. Tears blurred his eyes. No. His brave, strong nephew, full of ideals—gone to the gods. He sank onto his knees. Egypt had won.

✺   ✺   ✺

Flanked by his guards, Urhi-Teshub waited in the center of the command tent, his arms bound behind him. So this was how it was going to end. Ramesses was going to kill him, his life the price his father would pay for his arrogance. Urhi-Teshub scoffed. Ramesses would be doing the King of Hatti a favor.

Ramesses rose from his chair, his expression cold, hostile. He crossed his arms over his chest, taking his time looking over Urhi-Teshub, his gaze lingering on Urhi-Teshub's untended injuries, a look of gratification flickering in his eyes. "I understand you are the one who destroyed the queen's residence," he said, expressionless, "and are responsible for the death of four of her royal guards." He moved closer and lowered his voice. "We have your woman, Prince of Hatti."

Startled, Urhi-Teshub glanced at Ramesses, who watched him, sly, a cat with its mouse. Urhi-Teshub glared at him. "You have her body," he said, harsh, though his heart ached to say it.

Without taking his eyes from him, Ramesses called out. "Lord Paser, bring her in."

A rustle of material. Urhi-Teshub turned. The man he had confronted before the queen's tent ducked inside, two massive bruises purpling his face. A veiled woman stumbled after him, her head bowed. She wore a fine linen gown, and just one piece of jewelry, a silver filigreed armband. Urhi-Teshub recognized it. It had been one of his gifts to Istara. How dare they—

Paser pulled the veil from her face. She lifted her head and looked around, bewildered. Her eyes met his, then slid away, blank.

"Istara," he breathed, "by all the gods. You live." His guards held him back, restraining him. "For the love of Arinna," he spat, struggling against them, "let me go to my wife!"

"She is deep in the thrall of an opiate," Ramesses's voice continued from behind, flat, uncaring, bored. "We felt it necessary to take precautions. Lord Paser, that will do."

Unresponsive to his cries, Urhi-Teshub watched, powerless, as Paser led her, meek as a lamb, from the tent. He swiveled back to Ramesses, his heart pounding. "Whatever you ask, you shall have it. Name your price."

Ramesses returned to his seat. Resting his elbows on the chair's arms, he examined the rings on his fingers. He looked up at Urhi-Teshub, devious. "We will free you and the prisoners to return to your camp this afternoon. You will declare the battle lost and yourself the new King of Hatti. Tomorrow at first light, you will lead your father's army back to Tarhuntassa. If you fulfil these terms, Princess Istara will be sent back to you. However, if you do not do these things, or if your men attack our divisions as we march home, she will be executed."

Urhi-Teshub stared at Ramesses, disbelieving. Istara had warned him of the ambush, and this was how he intended to repay her? Ramesses met his look, expressionless.

"And what of my father and uncle?" Urhi-Teshub finally asked.

"They will be led to believe you have been executed." Ramesses replied, bland. "We will release them when we feel the time is appropriate."

"So you ask me to commit treason," Urhi-Teshub said.

"You said you would do whatever I asked," Ramesses answered, his attention drifting back down to his rings. "But perhaps it is too much for you. Since your wife will no longer be of any use, I will send her to the gods. Be grateful. The opiate will ensure she will not feel a thing."

Urhi-Teshub staggered, stunned by Ramesses's ruthlessness. The Pharaoh of Egypt was more than a match for the King of Hatti's machinations.

"So be it," he muttered after a long silence.

Ramesses picked up a sheet of papyrus. "You will be taken to the prisoners and escorted to the river," he said as he perused its contents. He glanced up. "We will be watching you, Prince of Hatti."

Urhi-Teshub choked back a bitter laugh. "Do so, for it will be the only way I can be certain Istara is safe from your dagger."

Ramesses met his look, enigmatic and uncompromising. He waved his hand, dismissing him. Shoving his guards aside, Urhi-Teshub pushed his way out of the tent, seething with anger. One day, Ramesses would pay, but for now, it was time to commit treason.

Sethi leaned back in his chair and wiped his napkin across his mouth, watching Henufkhet as he cleared the platters away; his movements fluid and graceful, a complex dance to which only the pharaoh's steward knew the patterns.

"Commander," Nefertari said into the post-dinner lull, leaning forward to see past her husband, "your valor in the battle against Hatti has not gone unnoticed by your queen. A little to the north of Waset there belongs to me a fine villa with rich fields surrounding it. You will accept it as my gift."

"Great Queen," Sethi bowed his head, his fist against his chest, "knowing Your Majesties are safe and unharmed is enough commensuration for me."

"Commander, the villa is yours, though your humility in accepting my gift pleases me well." She took a sip of wine. "And what of a wife to help you enjoy your new home? I do not believe the military life is so fulfilling it takes away one's desire for a home, wife, and children."

"Ah, beware, Commander," Paser said, patting the corner of his napkin against his mouth, "once our queen has decided you should be wed, you will be wed to a woman of her choosing before you even realize it has been done—" he raised his gilded cup to Nefertari, "—just as I was to Lady Imtes last summer."

Recalling the haste surrounding the vizier's marriage—in the wake of the delicious scandal of Imtes traveling alone one night to his estate—Sethi suppressed a smile at Paser's economy with the truth.

"If the queen were to find me a wife with Lady Imtes's qualities and beauty," Sethi answered, leaning in to collect a handful of almonds from an alabaster dish, "I would be delighted to oblige, although who could match a woman as fine as the queen's own sister? No, Lord Paser, when you wed, you took the last decent woman in Egypt. There is nothing for it. I shall have to remain alone."

"You propose for me a challenge, Commander?" Nefertari suggested, pleased. She took another sip of wine, warming to the subject. "Of course, I accept. I must wait until we return to be certain, but I have heard of a—"

Ramesses raised his hand, abrupt, cutting her off. She lowered her gaze, her lashes sweeping down against her cheeks. A faint smear of color crept up from her neck, staining her profile. Ignoring her, Ramesses drank the last of his wine, taking his time, letting the uncomfortable silence stretch, heavy and oppressive.

"Paser informs me he has advised you of your additional responsibility during the march home," he said as he pushed his cup to the side, watching Henufkhet refill it. He lifted the cup and swirled its contents. "You will protect the woman from Kadesh," he continued, his gaze on the ruby liquid, "to the death if necessary."

Paser met Sethi's look, the vizier's cold and unapologetic. Sethi suppressed a scoff. The vizier had done no such thing. "A great honor, Your Majesty," Sethi said, lowering his eyes to hide his irritation. "I will not fail you."

"Though she is a hostage of Egypt, she is not our enemy or a prisoner. You will treat her with all the respect due to one born of royal blood. Whatever she requests, if it is within your power to provide it, you will do so."

Sethi nodded. He reached for his cup, pleased by the steadiness of his hand, thinking of the woman in his tent; of her elaborate clothing and jewelry, Paser's veiled threats and the silver armband still tucked into his pouch, its slight weight suddenly heavy, filled with burden. Taking a sip, he asked, "And from whom are we holding her hostage?"

"The Crown Prince of Hatti, who is her husband," Ramesses said, expressionless. "It is our great fortune he values her life more than his own."

Sethi blinked, stunned. He had been dreaming all this time of Hatti's queen-in-waiting? He almost laughed. The gods were cruel indeed. He struggled to make the pieces fit. "But how is it even possible she is here?" he blurted, still reeling from the knowledge he had been searching for the only woman in the world he could never have. "Did Na'arn's division cross paths with her retinue in the mountain pass?"

"No," Ramesses answered, quiet. He took another sip of wine. "She came from Kadesh, alone, to warn me of the ambush. Though I left her protected within the enclosure, she fled. Last night, Henufkhet found her kneeling in the mud sewing my men back together. It was she who bound those injuries of yours, Commander. A skilled woman by the look of it." He turned, his gaze settling on Nefertari, hostile. "*These* are the actions of an honorable woman. A woman fit to be my queen. But you—what you tried to do. Your guards have admitted the truth. All of it."

Sethi lowered his cup, his own troubles falling to the side as the blood drained from Nefertari's face. She parted her lips, but no words came. Paser stood, abrupt, his seat toppling over. It hit the rug with a soft thud.

"My lord," he said, tight. "I advised the queen to use Princess Istara as a bargaining tool should the queen face grave danger. Her

Highness is not to blame for what happened. The responsibility is mine to bear."

"I admire your loyalty to your queen," Ramesses said, his eyes continuing to bore into Nefertari, wilting under his antipathy, "but I know the truth. You would never gainsay my command. But you, Nefertari, you are sick with your jealousies. Perhaps you thought yourself clever, using your family's wealth to pay the remaining costs of the campaign so you could stay by my side. Do you know what the council thought of your joining the march? A mockery. You should have stayed in Waset with your women, where you belong."

Paser stepped closer, his face ashen. "My lord, I beg you. This is a private matter." He tilted his head at Sethi, meaningful.

Sethi rose, grateful for Paser's meddling, for once.

"Lord Sethi stays," Ramesses snapped. Uneasy, Sethi sank back down onto his seat.

Returning his attention to Nefertari, Ramesses continued. "You willfully disobeyed my command to protect the Princess of Kadesh. Instead, you sent her out to die, thinking to rid yourself of her. But Re sent her to me to protect Egypt in its hour of need, not once, but twice. Be grateful she survived your little game because her life guarantees my men will live to see Egypt again, *you* will live to see your children again."

He stopped to take a deep drink of wine, swallowing it in short, hard gulps. Sethi caught the glint of tears in Nefertari's eyes, bright in the lamplight. Paser still stood, rigid, his eyes moving from Ramesses to the queen, back and forth, helpless. Never before had Sethi seen the vizier so undone.

Ramesses slammed his empty cup onto the table, making the golden platters rattle. "Across the river," he muttered, taut, "twenty thousand foot soldiers stand ready in Hatti's camp. Though I am loathe to say it, the Princess of Kadesh's life will prevent our enemy from launching a second attack. Her life will grant us the time we need to retreat. So, tell me," he demanded, harsh, his eyes cold,

"*Queen* of Egypt, who are you to dare to put yourself above the affairs of gods and kings?"

Stricken, Nefertari slid from her seat and sank onto her knees. "My lord," she pled, trembling, "forgive me, I beg you. I was afraid, so afraid. I forgot myself. Anything you ask of me, I shall remedy it. Please, Your Majesty. It is unbearable to displease you."

Ramesses scoffed. He shot a look at Paser and made an impatient gesture toward the camp. His expression taut, Paser bowed and left. Her breathing shallow, Nefertari huddled closer to her husband, her fingertips touching the arm of Ramesses's chair, plaintive. Using his elbow he shoved her away, rough. He turned in his seat and put his back to her. She cried out, distraught.

"Get out," he said. "I cannot bear your presence. I will not see you until Pi-Ramesses, perhaps not even then. I might send you away so I shall never have to look upon your face again."

Her body quivering, Nefertari took hold of the table's edge and pulled herself up. She looked at Ramesses, desperate, her chest rising and falling, caught by her ragged breaths. He ignored her. She whimpered and backed away, stumbling from the tent. From the vestibule, a shuddered sob. Then, she was gone.

Sethi turned his cup in his hands, studying the wine's swirl. He had witnessed a terrible thing. He wished he hadn't. A long silence passed.

"I have done a dishonorable thing," Ramesses said, abrupt, his words slicing into the oppressive quiet. "I have no intention of returning Istara to the Prince of Hatti, none at all. I have deceived him. Once we reach Pi-Ramesses, I plan to take her as one of my own queens, perhaps even as my first queen."

Sethi's fingers tightened on his cup. "My lord, if so, it is your decision, but why confide this to me?"

Ramesses fell silent. He poured himself more wine. Taking up his cup, he stared at it, then put it back down, its contents untouched. "Am I wrong to want to take her as compensation for the crimes Hatti has committed against Egypt?"

Sethi balked at the loaded question. Ramesses waved it away. "No. Don't answer. I know I am wrong. She has been bound in blood to Urhi-Teshub, yet I cannot bring myself to care. I must have her for myself. I want her by my side, in my bed . . . the woman's courage is undeniable. She is more than worthy to stand by my side."

Resigned, Sethi lifted his fist to his chest, regretting the years he had spent waiting for Istara. Hatti's queen-in-waiting. He scoffed. Even to him, the third most powerful man in Egypt, she was utterly untouchable. He bowed his head. "I will guard her with my life."

Quiet voices drifted from the vestibule. Paser entered, followed by a slim woman dressed in a beautiful white linen gown, her long, dark hair held in place by thin, golden band. Sethi came to his feet. Her dark eyes met his, glassy in the lamplight. A memory of her cradled in his arms exploded into his consciousness. His fingers had traced her lips. He had vowed never to let her go. His heart betrayed him, crying out for her, its longing visceral. His fingers tightened on his cup, his need to touch her overpowering. He stared at her, the one he had been waiting for, standing in front of him, only a few steps away. The one he could never have. It was too much. He emptied his cup. For thirty days, he would be forced to protect her on the long march home. No, it would be impossible. He couldn't—

He caught Paser watching him, narrow. Sethi wiped the back of his hand across his mouth and poured himself another drink. He tossed it back, seeking to numb his reaction to her, to regain his composure. As the wine did its work, he caught Ramesses gesturing to him.

"It has been decided it will be safest if you return with us to Pi-Ramesses," Ramesses said, gesturing for Sethi to move closer, "under the protection of Lord Commander Sethi."

"Princess Istara," Sethi bowed, though he kept his eyes on her.

Her eyes slid over him, vague, distracted. "Safest for whom?" she asked no one in particular.

Ramesses returned to the table and filled Nefertari's empty cup. He carried it back to Istara. "You will be well cared for. If there is anything you wish to have, you need only ask," he answered, avoiding her question. He held out the cup to her.

"Then I shall ask just one thing," she said as she took the cup, her words sliding together as though she had already imbibed more than enough wine for the evening. "I wish to know what you intend to do with me."

Ramesses waited until she took a sip. "I intend to take you Pi-Ramesses," he answered. "Kadesh has proven its loyalty to us with its blood. Though I cannot reward your father, your courage will not go uncompensated. You have my word as the Pharaoh of Egypt."

"You have news of my father?" she asked, faint, staggering a little, as though drunk. Paser caught her elbow, steadying her.

Ramesses lifted her chin, so her eyes met his. "During the battle, your father and his men turned against the Hittites to fight alongside the princes of Amurru," he explained, gentle. "He killed many of Muwatallis's men before he was overtaken. He died with honor, and my deepest respect."

A heartbeat of confused silence. "He is dead?"

Ramesses hesitated. "Beheaded."

She said nothing. Her eyes blank, she finished the wine. She held out her cup to Sethi. "I would have another."

He took it, careful not to let his fingers touch hers. Surrounded by silence, he refilled it and returned. She drank it all, handing the empty cup to Ramesses. Paser took it and set it aside. Her eyes glazed, she stood, swaying, staring at the table, unseeing. Ramesses glanced at Sethi and tilted his head toward the camp, the message clear. It was time to take her away.

Keeping his eyes averted, Sethi half-led, half-supported Istara as she stumbled, leaden, from the enclosure. Halfway to Pre's camp, she collapsed. He caught her, carrying her the rest of the way, tormented by the nearness of her, the familiarity of her body cradled against his chest. Haunted by the memory of the night before, he quickened his steps, thinking of the battle, of death, of anything but the forbidden woman in his arms.

Within his tent, he knelt and lay her on his pallet. Dropping a blanket over her, he checked the brazier's fuel, pausing to add more, his movements sloppy with haste, praying she wouldn't wake. Back out in the cold, clean air, the memory of her sleeping in his arms returned, vivid, visceral; an irrational, intense impulse to join her slammed into him. He bit back a curse, shoving his way through the tents, desperate to distance himself from her; her sudden, inexplicable, impossible presence in his life calling out to him like the beating of his own heart. He passed a group of soldiers sitting by a fire and sent one of them to put a pallet in the command tent. He watched the soldier hurry away to do his bidding, shouting after him to find a skin of wine as well. He half-turned, thinking to empty the wineskin, to blunt himself in drink. He stopped. No. It wouldn't be enough. He knew what he needed to do. Without looking back, he strode away into the night.

❋   ❋   ❋

Nefertari entered her residence, trapped inside the memory of her husband's brutal rejection, unable to escape his final, cold look of hatred. Tendrils of incense curled around her, the rich, earthy scent almost masking the accusing, metallic stink of blood—the lives of Egypt's men, sacrificed for her, soaked into the tent's walls; a constant reminder of the terrible cost she had forced others to pay so she could follow her husband to Kadesh.

A gust of wind lifted the blanket tacked over the rent made by Urhi-Teshub. Chill mountain air cut into her thin gown. She shivered. In the vestibule, movement. The material separating her residence from the vestibule lifted, quiet, discreet.

"My lady," Paser bowed, tight. He glanced over his shoulder, uneasy. "I vow I will do everything in my power to remedy this."

"There is nothing you can do," Nefertari answered, numb, her own words wounding her, cutting deep. "I am finished. Perhaps my husband will send me away—as Muwatallis did to his queen—stripping me of my wealth and titles. Banished. Forgotten."

"The gods would punish him," Paser muttered, though his expression betrayed tinges of uncertainty. "It is my fault for failing to defend you," he continued, dogged, miserable. "It is I who should be punished, not you. I will see to it. You shall not suffer for this."

"Lord Paser, you defended me well," Nefertari said, eyeing the blood-soaked walls of her residence. "Ramesses is right. My jealous, black heart has done this to me, my downfall is no one's fault but my own. An innocent woman came to aid us and I threw her out to die. While she was before me, I saw only his next conquest, whom my husband forced me to protect, to punish me for accompanying him on campaign. I could not bear it. I had to rid myself of her. I do not expect you to understand."

"If I were to love someone as you love him," Paser said, quiet, his eyes meeting hers, enigmatic, "I could not bear to see them with another, either."

His look unnerved her. She turned away. "How shall I go on without him?" she asked, ashamed of her weakness, the crack in her voice. "Who am I, if I am not his queen?"

"It shall be remedied. You must believe it," Paser insisted, firm. "The Princess of Kadesh did not die. We shall return to Egypt, and in time, other matters will arise to occupy the pharaoh. He will forget this. His anger will pass. Bear the return with grace. Do not let him see you in weakness. Remain strong."

She sank onto her chair. He knelt before her, worried, protective. His anguished look triggered a buried memory. It peeled open, layer by excruciating layer: The night of the battle, as her skin broiled in the heat of the encroaching fires, she had knelt in front of him, panting, the heated air almost impossible to breathe. He had pulled her head back to lay a dagger against her throat, his movements tender, gentle, at odds with the violence he was preparing to do to her. Through her terror, she glimpsed the tears in his eyes, his expression twisted by grief, his mouth opening to speak, just as the rain screamed out of the heavens, silencing him. *"If I were to love someone as you love him, I could not bear to see them with another, either."*

She caught her breath, suddenly seeing him with new eyes. Egypt's powerful vizier was a beautiful, elegant man, intelligent, honorable, courageous, an accomplished swordsman. Her heart stuttered, incredulous. *She* was the woman he loved.

Her thoughts skidded to a stop. Had he taken a woman he could never love as his wife and shackled himself to a lifetime of unhappiness just to please his queen? No. She wouldn't believe it. Unable to stop herself, she chanced the question.

"Why?"

Paser tilted his head, uncertain. "My lady?"

"Why support me as you do? You are Ramesses's vizier after all. You belong to him."

Shutters slammed closed over Paser's eyes. He looked away, saying nothing, the muscles in his jaw working, tense. Her suspicions sharpened.

"Lord Paser?" she demanded, tight, fearful.

"I must go." He rose, abrupt. "You should rest. We leave at first light."

He did not wait for her permission to depart. Avoiding her gaze, he backed three steps and turned away. In a heartbeat, he was gone.

Shaken, Nefertari looked down at her hands. Paser was in love with her. In the midst of her misery, a thought struck her hard. Her selfish stunt to meet Meresamun had sentenced her own sister to a lifetime of unrequited love. When she had last met Imtes, her sister's complexion had been pale, her eyes dull. Nefertari had teased her, assuming her sister's appearance was the result of sleepless nights spent in the act of love. Shame tore into her. How could she have been so blind to her sister's torment? Perhaps Paser had never touched Imtes. What if her sister spent her days walking through his villa, alone and unloved, enduring the mirror image of Nefertari's unhappy life—and she had done this to her, her own sister?

Nefertari cried out, guilt slamming into her, the enormity of her error overwhelming her. She clenched her fists, enduring her brutal awakening as other, lesser crimes revealed themselves, one by one. In everything her assumptions had been based on what she wanted to believe. For years, she had treated those around her like playthings, wielding her power without a thought, her blinkered vision causing lasting harm to others. Drifting within the memories of the countless acts she had perpetrated over the years, she wondered if she could ever overcome the damage she had done, not just to Imtes and Paser, but to everyone who had had the misfortune to cross her self-centered, oblivious path.

She gazed at the crown in her lap, unable to remember when she had taken it off; her fingers occupied with tracing the outline of the crown's golden feathers, one at a time. She had far to go, to repair the damage she had done, but she would try, until the end of her days, she would try.

She set aside her crown and went to her bed. Pulling the blankets back, she climbed in, still wearing her finery. Her thoughts drifted back to Ramesses. Her heart clenched, a fresh spear of grief impaling her. Broken, defeated, alone, she wept.

※　※　※

Sethi neared the campfires of Amun's whores, certain he was wasting his time. With so many women dead, whores were much harder to come by. There had been none left in either Pre's or Seth's camps. He shoved past a row of tents and looked around. Three women, all of them ugly, sat hunched in the mud, their hands stretched toward a low fire.

They looked up, one of them murmured his title to the others, a greedy look in her eye. They gathered around him, smiling, opening their gowns, letting him see their bodies, unwashed and rank with the stink of their recent fornications. He paused, repulsed by them, turning to make the long walk to the camp of Ptah, when he caught sight of another whore, sitting alone, half-hidden by the shadows, perched on a fallen tent pole. She looked cleaner than the others, her figure called to him, full, ripe, inviting. He felt his groin stir. He went to her and took her hand, ignoring the outraged protests of the others, pulling her into the deeper shadows between two tents. His need for release suddenly blinded him, urging him on, reckless.

Between his fingers, her gown's ties came apart. Her breasts spilled out, full, perfect, her nipples taut in the cold air. He groaned, and took one into his mouth, working with one hand to free himself from under his kilt. Grabbing hold of her buttocks, he pulled her closer to lift her up onto him. Pain slammed into his jaw.

He pulled back, catching her wrist before she could hit him again, squeezing tight. She cried out, furious, and kicked his shin. He grunted, ignoring the pain and yanked her closer, catching a glimpse of her face in the faint light. His hold loosened. The woman was far too beautiful to be a soldier's whore. She pulled free and stumbled away, clutching at the material of her gown, drawing it back over herself, her breathing ragged.

He eyed her as she worked. "You are no camp whore, are you?"

She shook her head, her fingers trembling as she fastened the ties of her gown.

He cursed, struggling to field his anger and escalating frustration, his member betraying him, still throbbing with need. "Yet you were with the whores," he said, sharper than he meant to.

She didn't answer. He rubbed his hand over his scalp, letting his gaze move over her. She was extraordinary, one of the most beautiful women he had ever seen. What was a woman like her doing in a war camp and amongst whores?

"What's your name?" he asked, tight, tucking his unwilling member back into the bindings of his loincloth.

"Meresamun," she answered, quiet, her eyes on the muddy ground.

He paused. Her name sounded familiar. He couldn't place it. He scoffed. What did it matter? It wasn't important. "Forgive me," he muttered. "I was mistaken. I will take you back to your fire." When she didn't move, he hesitated, realization striking him hard. "You have lost your man to the Hittites," he said, quiet, watching as she twisted her fingers together, confirming his suspicion. He cleared his throat, uncomfortable, guilt slicing through him. "Was I your first?"

She met his look, abrupt. Tears glistened in her eyes.

He turned away, her grief piercing him. His gaze moved to the whores, cold and miserable in their thin, stained gowns, huddling together, seeking warmth from each other around their meager fire. "A whore's life is a hard one," he said, looking back at her. "I can offer you a much better one as my concubine." He stepped closer. "Perhaps you have heard of me. I am the Commander of Pre."

"I know who you are," she said, low. Her stomach growled, loud. She looked up at him, the shadows accentuating the hollows in her cheeks. "Forgive me. I have not eaten since the day of the battle."

He nodded. "Wait here."

He roused several men, scrounging together two biscuits and a dried date wrapped in a scrap of linen cloth. He returned and handed her the parcel. Though her hunger was apparent, she took her time eating, conserving what little he had found. He watched her, curious. Her manners were elegant and refined. He wondered who her husband had been.

Tucking the remains of the food back into the linen, Meresamun dusted the biscuit crumbs from her gown. She met his eyes. "Thank you."

Sethi took her hand, gentle this time. "If you accept my offer, you will want for nothing."

Her gaze fell back to the shrunken parcel in her hands. "I accept, but only until the road to Damas when I must go my own way."

He blinked, taken aback by her strange request. She would not survive long, traveling alone and unprotected to Damas. "Then be with me until the road to Damas," he said, troubled by her broken expression. "Please. There is no need to tremble so. Though it may have appeared thus earlier, I am no brute. I will not hurt you."

He brought her to his command tent, warm and snug from the brazier's heat and gave her food and wine. He sat beside her, drinking, waiting, patient, giving her time. She ate in silence, defensive, her eyes averted. Her hand trembled as she finished her wine. He poured her another. She drank deep, her cheeks flushing, her body relaxing.

He took the cup from her hand and set it aside. He pulled her to her feet. Gently he traced the outline of her jaw. She closed her eyes. He let her, pitying her, sensing she was seeing her lost husband in his stead. Catching her chin, he lowered his mouth to hers, his fingers once more opening the ties of her gown. The material fell away. He drank in the sight of her full breasts and hips, running his hands over them, his thumbs circling her nipples until they hardened. He knelt and tasted her. Hunger, hot, and aching, tugged at his member.

He pulled his kilt and loincloth away and took hold of her, lifting her onto him, ignoring the sharp pain of his bound injuries, the fresh seep of blood. He wanted to be deep inside her, to lose himself in her, to purge himself of Istara's hold. He plunged, hard, into Meresamun. She gasped, her thighs clamping onto him. He drove into her again, his hands hard on her buttocks. Her arms came around his neck. She clung to him, whispering, pleading to the gods for forgiveness. He kissed her, murmuring she had nothing to regret, swearing to protect her. She shifted her weight, her breasts sliding against him, sending a thrill of pleasure shuddering through him. He rotated his hips, groaning. She felt so good, so tight. With her, he would forget, she was a gift from the gods. He sped toward the brink of his release. It was too soon. It would not be enough.

He would have to take her, again, and again. Anything to forget. To forget—

His member throbbed, and he staggered as he filled Meresamun with his seed. It wasn't enough. He lowered her to her feet and turned her around, to take her from behind. As he neared his release, an image seared through his mind, blinding him. Istara in his arms, asleep, her mouth turned up to his, inviting. He came, thinking only of her, emptiness filling him as he led Meresamun to his pallet and covered her with his blanket, granting her the respite of sleep. He lay awake, his heart betraying him, longing for Istara's warmth beside him.

Sleep evaded him. He stared, bleak, at the tent's ceiling, wondering what he must do to free himself of the woman in his dream, why the gods would torment him thus. Meresamun woke. Desperate, he took her again, this time as a lover would, patient, determined to bring her pleasure. She cried out, quaking from her release, sending him following soon after. Her pleasure soon turned to sorrow, and she wept, riven with guilt. He comforted her, though his own guilt rode him hard. When she slept again, he went naked to his chair to drink the rest of the wine, resolved to obliterate Istara from his thoughts, to drive her from his heart.

In the distance, a soldier called out the third hour. Sagging over the table, Sethi swallowed the last of the wine. He cursed the foulest oath he knew.

There could only be her. The golden cup crumpled in his fist.

Safe once more within Hatti's camp, Urhi-Teshub rubbed the back of his fist across his mouth, contemplating the woman standing before him. He considered killing her. His hand drifted to his dagger. No. He would not add regicide to his list of crimes this day. He pulled a chair over and took a seat. He didn't offer her one.

"You move fast," he said, taking in her glittering finery, the wealth of gold layered upon her arms and neck, "to take your brother's throne before his death has been confirmed."

"I am a diviner," Rhoha shrugged, returning Urhi-Teshub's look, untroubled. "The augurs have shown his fall. By taking the throne, I have done my duty, nothing more. However, there is one difficulty I now face. Kadesh has no king."

"And?" Urhi-Teshub snapped, goaded by her sudden silence.

She lowered her eyes, her lashes sweeping against her cheeks. "My lord prince," she said, soft, sly, "you already have an heir, all he needs now is his father and his inheritance."

Urhi-Teshub pushed from his seat, a wave of anger washing over him. "I have a wife."

She held up her hand. The lamplight flickered over the kinks and twists of her fingers, highlighting the distended knots of her knuckles, deformed and ugly. "I confess there is another matter which brings me to you—it is about Istara."

He glared at her. "Do not dirty her name with your mouth."

Rhoha turned, the material of her gown rustling as she took a seat. "As you wish," she smiled, smoothing out the folds of her gown. She glanced up, her smile fading. "Your *wife* is a traitor, she went to Ramesses before the battle, to warn him. Today the augurs were clear. Her life has been ended by the pharaoh's own hand."

Urhi-Teshub felt his mouth go dry. No. It couldn't be. "When?"

"When what?"

He grated the words out. "When did Ramesses . . . send her to the gods?"

She blinked, perplexed. "When she went to him." Misunderstanding his silence, she went to him, her fingertips moving up his arm to his shoulder, gentle, caressing. "You are overcome," she murmured. "It must be a terrible thing to learn your wife betrayed you. But you should be thankful, though the news is distressing, it is a good omen. The gods are protecting you. She was not fit to be your queen. She never was."

Urhi-Teshub scoffed at the parallel between her words and her twisted fingers. Jerking away from her touch, he bore down on her. "But, it seems, with divine convenience, you are."

"Of course," she said, her expression showing genuine surprise. "The gods have willed it. Together we will make a powerful alliance." Her gaze slid to his pallet. "We can seal our vows tonight."

"Do you ever stop?" he roared, flinging her aside, his long-suppressed rage for what she had done escalating, hot, virulent. "Istara is a hostage to Egypt, and very much alive."

Rhoha stumbled against a stool. She turned, a flash of anger flared in her eyes, sharp, dangerous. "Whether you accept it or not," she said, straightening her gown, "the augurs have shown the future. *I* will be your consort, ruling by your side. Why must you be such a stubborn fool and cling to the past? Istara is gone. Forever."

Her barbed words tore at him. Grabbing an empty pitcher, he hurled it across the tent. It smashed against a support pole, its jagged shards scattering, thudding against the skirts of her gown. "Enough!

Return to your throne, and may it be a lonely one. You will never have what you want from me. Istara will be returned to me, and she will be my queen, regardless of your black augurs and divinations."

Rhoha stood, unmoving, stubborn. He pulled his dagger free and lunged at her. "You will get out, you scheming, murderous whore, or it will be my blade on your throat and to the Under Realm with the consequences."

Her eyes dark, she backed away. Outside, the creak of chariot wheels and the soft thud of hooves against wet earth. Her escort departed. He turned away, trembling with anger, Rhoha's prophetic words burrowing into him, barbed and sinister. Tormented by his powerlessness, he cried out to the gods, offering them anything they wished if only they would protect Istara and keep her safe. A thin silence suffused the tent; his shallow, ragged breaths loud in his ears. Laying his blade across the back of his arm, he opened his flesh, grunting at the pain. He shoved the dagger up high, an offering, the blade's edge glistening black-red in the lamplight.

"My blood for hers," he whispered to the gods. The silence stretched, taut. He cut himself again, deeper this time. "My life for hers," he said louder, watching his blood slide down his raised arm. His skin prickled. He looked up at the tent's ceiling, sensing a presence, unseen, watching him. He held his breath, unwilling to break the spell. The gods were listening after all.

❋   ❋   ❋

Cocooned within the golden warmth of her apartment in Kadesh, Rhoha looked down at the babe in her arms, her heart soft and filled with love. She kissed her son's sleeping face and inhaled his sweet scent, milk and honey.

She looked up, catching Kadesh's commander, staring at her, hostile.

"I do not like repeating myself," she said. "The King of Hatti commands it."

Hasurna held her gaze. "Lord Urhi-Teshub has sent me no such command."

"Shall I arrest your wife and sons," she asked, soft, her gaze falling once more to her son, "and keep them below in the cold and dark until you have done as you are bid? Or would you prefer to join them in death, conspirators against Hatti?"

Hasurna looked away. A muscle in his jaw twitched.

She smiled. "I thought not."

Laying her son in his gilded cot, she tucked his little woolen blankets around him. His rosebud mouth moved as he slept. Her heart melted. She looked up, continuing, "There can be no mistakes, no chance for this to be traced back to Kadesh. The ambush must have all the appearances of a barbarian raid. You will find the traitor, and kill her."

A heartbeat passed, two. She waited. He lowered his chin a fraction. His eyes, cold, never left hers. "By your command," he said, tight, "and may Baalat forgive you."

His footsteps retreated. Rhoha scoffed at his words, turning to admire her reflection in the bronze mirror. She smiled at herself, reveling in her knowledge, discovered in the depths of her darkest, costliest incantations. The gods had no power over men anymore, which meant plenty for the taking, from the fools who still believed.

Paser ducked into the command tent and pressed his fist against his chest, eyeing the dim, deserted space, lit by the light of a single shuttered lamp. There was a creak of wood as Ramesses left his chair. He did not come forward. Instead, he lingered, silent, behind the table, his face hidden in shadow.

"Your Majesty," Paser approached him, wary, "I came as soon as I received your message." When Ramesses remained silent, Paser cleared his throat. "My lord, Amun is almost ready to depart."

Ramesses nodded, distracted, occupying himself with pushing a piece of papyrus back and forth across the table. "We will leave on time," he muttered. He lowered his voice. "I have need of your counsel. There is a matter troubling me."

"My lord?"

The papyrus shifted several times more before the pharaoh continued. "Last night, Sethi's reaction to Istara's arrival was unexpected." Ramesses eyed Paser. "I know you saw it too." He fell silent, brooding once more. He pushed the papyrus away and continued, his voice so low, Paser had to strain to hear him. "I dreamed something last night, something I cannot forget and am unable to explain. I walked in a city unlike any I have ever seen, more beautiful than I can describe. A great roar rent the sky and a flying barque with outstretched wings like a falcon swept down from the heavens, shining, golden. It came to rest on an enormous platform, hissing, black smoke pouring out from under its wings. A door opened and from within Sethi but not Sethi emerged, followed by Istara, but not Istara." He swallowed and pushed at the papyrus once more. He stopped. "I do not know what it means, but it has unnerved me, the likenesses they shared. You are the closest I have to a soothsayer. Tell me: My dream, is it a warning? Can I trust him—my own commander—with Istara?"

Paser felt the blood drain from his face. Fear clutched at him. He could not, would not, allow himself to be caught up in this, whatever it was. Ramesses lifted his head, waiting for an answer. Paser blinked, floundering for a beat, before hastening to the refuge of facts.

"My lord," he said, striving to keep his voice calm, "if your wish is to see Istara safe to Pi-Ramesses, then there is no other place for her but Pre, under Sethi's protection. Ptah's division is carrying the burden of the wounded, and Amun is dedicated to your protection. Unless—would you rather send her to Byblos with Bentesina?"

Ramesses shook his head, terse. "No. Not Byblos. I need her with our men." He moved back to his chair and crossed his arms over his chest. "May Horus forgive me, but I am not certain I can trust Sethi. That dream. It plagues me. He touched her face, as a lover would."

Paser shoved the memory of the previous morning away, of Sethi and Istara tangled together on Sethi's pallet, Sethi's fingers caressing her cheek. "Shall I arrange for someone to watch him?" he asked, taut, longing to distance himself from the matter.

Ramesses considered. "No," he finally answered. "I will not order one of my men to spy on Egypt's commander when the only evidence I have against him is a dream and his sudden need for wine when Istara arrived."

Paser searched his mind, desperate to escape the jaws of Ramesses's unwitting trap. A thought struck him. "You could send Lord Ahmen to Pre, with the command to carry Istara in his chariot. Give him no other orders. Once back in Pi-Ramesses, meet with him. From Ahmen, you will know the truth."

Ramesses rubbed his hand over his jaw, his troubled look deepening. "Lord Ahmen fought well and with honor. He deserves to drive my chariot on the return home." Ramesses sank back into his chair and reached out to pull the papyrus nearer. "To send him away, demoting him without explanation will only humiliate him." He pressed his palms against his eyes. "I am exhausted. Perhaps I am overreacting, seeing things which are not there."

He looked up, hopeful, waiting for Paser to reprieve him. But Paser knew he could not stop now. If he diverted the pharaoh, and Ramesses later found out what Paser knew, Paser would be sent to the gods. He must protect himself. Let Ahmen bring Ramesses the truth.

"Your Highness, when have your instincts ever been proven false?" he asked, using his most compelling voice. "You sensed Muwatallis's trap, and where he was hiding his men. You kept Istara alive and heeded her warning. If you sense your commander is untrustworthy, you must find out the truth, no matter what the cost. Egypt's security depends upon it."

Ramesses poked at the papyrus again, his unhappiness obvious. Finally, he nodded. "Yes, you are right. It shall be done. But with all my heart, I hope I am wrong."

❋   ❋   ❋

"Lord Ahmen, a message from Pharaoh, Blessed of Re."

Ahmen turned. A runner stood behind him, holding out a small scroll sealed with the impression of the pharaoh's cartouche. Taking it into the light of a burning torch, Ahmen broke the seal. He read the message and looked up, disbelieving.

"My lord," the runner broached, diffident, "the pharaoh commanded me to return with all haste. I was told to say your word would suffice."

Ahmen eyed the rows of chariots lined up, waiting to depart. He read the message a second time. There was no explanation, just the command. He would not join them.

"My lord?" the runner prodded, anxious, his dread of keeping the pharaoh waiting obvious.

Ahmen nodded, numb. "Tell Pharaoh I am his obedient servant."

The runner bolted away. Ahmen called for Dhet. The boy emerged from between the harnessed horses, his face shining with perspiration despite the chill in the pre-dawn air.

"All is ready for you, my lord," Dhet said, wiping the sweat from his brow with the back of his arm.

His heart heavy, Ahmen knelt beside the boy. "I will not leave today," he said. "The pharaoh has commanded me to travel with the Division of Pre tomorrow."

Dhet paled. "I will stay with you."

"No." Ahmen squeezed the boy's shoulder. "You will stay with the pharaoh's horses, no one else knows or cares for them as well as you."

"But," Dhet protested, loyal, "there will be no one to look after your horses and chariot."

"Then I shall have to do the work myself."

The sound of horns filled the plateau. It was time. Dhet looked away, then back at Ahmen, his eyes huge. "I am afraid to travel alone. If not you, to whom shall I answer?"

"You will answer to your heart," Ahmen answered, his own aching at the boy's wretched look. "Do your work with honor, worship Re, observe *Ma'at* and before you know it, we will be back in Pi-Ramesses."

Dhet pressed his fist to his chest. "I will not fail you."

"You are a good Egyptian," Ahmen said, finding a smile for the boy. "Now go. Re will watch over you."

He watched him go, worrying for him. Without his presence, he suspected the older grooms, jealous of Dhet's favored position, would make things hard for him.

Horns blared once more. Ahmen took up the reins of Ramesses's chariot and called to the horses. He knew there would be no further explanation. For the next thirty days, he would be left to wonder why Ramesses had chosen him instead of another to carry the Princess of Kadesh home.

He pulled up in front of the pharaoh's tent and left the chariot. His head bowed, he held up the reins, his heart pounding. Within his heart he prayed, begging the gods to intervene. Please, let Ramesses have changed his mind.

Ramesses pushed out from the tent, his battle regalia gleaming in the torchlight. Ignoring Ahmen, he took the reins and called to the horses. With a creak of wood and leather, he departed, his chariot obscured by the sudden surge of followers rushing past to pack the contents of the pharaoh's tent.

Ahmen backed away; devastated. He caught Henufkhet's look, filled with pity. It was too much, he had to get away, to where he could not be seen and judged by those who were less than him. He sprinted back to the deserted ground where the stables had been, finding Dhet, loyal to the end, standing alone, holding the bridles of Ahmen's horses, yoked to a chariot, waiting.

Tears burning his eyes, Ahmen took the reins and choked out his thanks. Dhet patted the horses, telling them to take care of Ahmen. He backed away, and with a forlorn wave, he turned and ran, hurrying to catch up to the others. Ahmen tightened his grip on the reins and looked across the ruined, windswept plateau, despair filling him. He was alone. Disgraced. Bleak, he wondered how far Ramesses intended him to fall.

Istara opened her eyes. She pushed herself up from the pallet, dis-oriented, her head swimming. A blanket slipped down to her waist. Close by, a brazier gave off a feeble amount of heat, its fuel almost extinguished. A bench. Rugs. Lamps. A linen hanging, unadorned, split the tent's interior in two. She leaned forward, reaching out to push aside the hanging. A wave of nausea rippled through her. She held still, waiting. Another wave, stronger this time—

She scrambled from the pallet, making it to the basin just in time. Shivering, she sank back onto her heels and wiped the tears from her eyes. Her fingers came away smeared with kohl. She stared at the black smudges, staining her fingertips, confused. When had she put on cosmetics? Her bloodstained gown was gone too, replaced by a white one, its edges embroidered in silver thread. She cleaned her fingers before touching the material, woven so fine, it must have come from the queen's wardrobe.

Her foot cramped. She shifted her position, noticing she still wore her sandals. Pulling them off, she rubbed her feet against the rug, letting its stiff weave massage them. Why would she have gone to sleep in her sandals? She gazed into the glowing embers of the brazier, trying to recall the last thing she could remember: the injured man in the tent, the one from her visions. She had spent hours tending him, had fallen asleep after, exhausted. Then . . . nothing, only darkness.

She eyed the basin, the vomit almost black, its sourness offset by a sickly-sweet tang. Opium. If she could smell it over the stink of her vomit, she had been given a very strong dose. She had learned during her studies when high enough doses were used on a patient, events during the drugging could be forgotten, sometimes permanently. Anything could have happened. A dark thought crossed her mind. She pulled up her gown. No blood. Relief shuddered through her. But if not to violate her, why had the Egyptians drugged her? For what purpose—

A draft of cold air. The lamps' flames danced. She turned. A soldier moved toward her. Alarmed, she rose to her feet. He pulled the linen hanging aside and stepped through.

It was him, the man she had spent the night sewing back together, but no longer was he the broken, fevered patient: he stood before her, charismatic, powerful, larger than even Urhi-Teshub, smelling of sex. He had removed most of his bandages, exposing his raw, sutured flesh to the open air, a soldier's trick to force his wounds to heal faster. His sudden presence filled the space, overwhelming her. He bowed, keeping his eyes averted from her, his gaze moving to the dirtied basin, then away from it, to the brazier.

"You are unwell," he said, his voice deep, commanding, strong. "Shall I send for a surgeon?"

Taken aback by his transformation, she looked over his injuries wondering how could he have recovered so fast. It had only been last night when she had tended to him. Unless . . .

"How long have I been drugged?" she asked, quiet.

Startled by her question, his eyes met hers. A spark, hot and intense flared between them. She caught her breath as a memory, visceral, poured into her. He had held her against his body, warming her, his lips had brushed her forehead, tender—

He blinked, turning his attention once more to the brazier. "I did not realize you had been drugged," he said, low, "although that *would* explain your odd behavior in Pharaoh's tent."

Istara's thoughts tumbled to a halt. "I was in Pharaoh's tent? When?"

The soldier's brow lifted. "It must have been a powerful sedation if you cannot remember last night."

"Last night? I don't understand—" she floundered, desperate to find solid ground. She tried a different approach. "When did I tend your injuries?"

His brow quirked, though whether it was from irritation or surprise, she couldn't tell. "The night before last," he answered, crossing his arms over his chest. "You were taken from my side early yesterday morning, while still half-asleep."

She stared at him, stunned. A day. Gone. Last night, she had been in the pharaoh's tent, drugged, wearing one of the queen's gowns. She couldn't stop herself. She had to know.

"Has Ramesses taken me to his bed?"

His gaze hardened on the brazier. "Not yet."

Frightened, she took a step toward him. "What do you mean, 'not yet'?"

He moved away from her, keeping his distance. "Last night the pharaoh gave you tidings of your father," he said, not answering her question. "Do you remember?"

"No," she whispered, a finger of dread touching her spine.

He remained silent a long while, the muscles in his jaw clenching. "In the midst of battle," he finally said, heavy, "the King of Kadesh joined our allies from Amurru. He took down a great many of Muwatallis's men before he was surrounded."

"And?" Istara breathed, her heart tight.

"The King of Kadesh has fallen," he said, his eyes locked on the dying flames of the brazier, "and with the greatest honor."

She sank to her knees, numb, disbelieving. She caught him watching her. He looked away.

"How—" She couldn't finish the question.

"May Horus forgive me," he said, his mouth twisting with distaste, "they took his head."

She choked. It was unthinkable. Beheading a king was forbidden. She looked up at the soldier, mute, seeking consolation. He turned away.

"I have brought a companion for you," he said, pushing aside the linen hanging, "I will send her in."

Istara rose, dismayed. "How can you walk away after bearing such news—are you heartless?"

"I have brought a woman to console you," he answered, taut, keeping his back to her. "Do not expect anything more from me." He reached out for the tent's flap.

She took hold of his arm, stopping him. Under her fingers, she felt his muscles tense. "I spent a long night by your side tending your injuries and fever," she said, grief making her words tight. "Now in my time of need, you refuse me the merest scrap of consolation. You have not even told me your name or title."

"Sethi," he replied, abrupt, "Commander of Egypt's Army, the King's Treasurer and Commander of Pre. And as to your attention during my hour of need, I wish to Horus it had not been your needle on my flesh. I wish it had been anyone but you."

Dismayed, she released him. "You are a cruel man, Commander, to wound me when I am already suffering. Am I so offensive to you?"

"My orders are to protect you," he said, harsh, "and I will do so, to my death. But do not ask more of me than this. I will only disappoint you."

Pushing back the flap, he ducked out into the morning air, leaving her alone. Numb, she returned to her pallet. Fragments of a murmured conversation, low and urgent drifted through the tent's thin walls. A woman entered and waited on the other side of the opaque linen. Istara ignored her.

"Princess Istara," the woman said, hesitant, "I am honored to have been chosen as your companion."

Istara lifted her head. That voice. No. It couldn't be. "Meresamun?" she called, her heart cracking, slivered with hope.

Meresamun pushed past the linen. "By Hathor's horns!" she exclaimed, incredulous. "*You* are the Princess of Kadesh?"

Istara reached out to her. "My father has fallen," she choked, realizing that by saying the words, she had made it real. Her father was gone. Forever.

Tears spilled free, hot and fat. Meresamun came to her, catching her in her embrace. She stroked her hair, hushing her. Istara clung to her, devastation sweeping through her as she grieved for her father, her for ruined marriage, and for Anash, who had never woken up. She had obeyed Baalat all her life, and in return, she had lost everything. Even if she had saved thousands, nothing had been left for her. Nothing. She was alone.

❊   ❊   ❊

Outside, Sethi stared at his feet as Istara's weeping and the soft sounds of Meresamun's reassurances carried out to him. Guilt sliced through him. Perhaps he had been too harsh with her. She had lost her father, after all. Meresamun offered Istara wine, to calm her. Istara drank and fell quiet. He left. She was best in Meresamun's care. He was a soldier, not a nurse, and yet, his heart ached to go to Istara, to hold her, to ease her pain—but he could not; he could never touch her again. He had to forget about her.

He ducked back into his command tent. It reeked of sex. He broke off a piece of sandalwood incense and crumbled it over the brazier's glowing fuel. Leaning against the table, he waited for it to ignite, trying to ignore the rumpled blankets on his pallet. He had slept little, taking Meresamun two times more, and each time, at his release, the memory of Istara sleeping in his arms returned.

He sank onto his chair, his attention drifting to a pile of reports. He sorted through them. An old order from Ramesses slipped free, regarding an increase in daily rations. He stared at the impression of the king's cartouche. Ramesses was omnipresent. Sooner or later, he knew everything.

He set it aside. He would not risk everything he had worked for just because he had been dreaming of a woman who could never be his. It was madness. The gods had been cruel to him, but the game they had played for the last thirteen years was over now—unless they wished for him to die.

Within the embers of the brazier, several flames flickered. The incense ignited. Long, languorous smoke trails curled away, cleansing the tent of the night's carnality. He watched the trails, thinking of nothing. The image of Istara, sleeping in his arms returned. He cursed and shoved the memory aside. Picking up his reed brush, he occupied himself with the work of preparing his division for the long march home. He paused, his gaze straying back to his unmade pallet. At least he had Meresamun. He hoped she would stay with him until Pi-Ramesses. He decided to offer her a fortune if she would.

✼ ✼ ✼

Meresamun brushed the hair from Istara's face, noting the dark shadows surrounding Istara's eyes, closed in fitful sleep. Once the initial shock had taken its toll, Istara had withdrawn into the privacy of her thoughts, suffering through long stages of weeping and silence. She had eaten nothing the whole day. All Meresamun could do was sit with her, and wait.

She added more fuel to the brazier, hoping a night's sleep would help. Tomorrow would be a better day. Once they began to march, Istara would have other things to think of. It was no good sitting in a tent, dwelling on the past.

Weary, Meresamun pushed aside the linen hanging and sank onto her pallet. As she untied her sandals, one of the guards called to her in a low voice, relaying Sethi's request to join him. She slumped, gazing at her pallet with longing.

"He requests my attendance, or he orders it?" she asked, quiet.

The guard shifted, the movement betrayed by the soft creak of leather. "My lady, he has requested it, but unless you are unwell, it would not be wise to refuse him. Do you wish me to say you are unwell?"

She closed her eyes. Even if she did not suffer at his hands, it would be another sleepless night when all she longed for was oblivion. She retied her sandals and got up.

"No, I shall go. Take me to him."

❃   ❃   ❃

Sethi set aside the last of his captain's reports just as Meresamun ducked into his tent. He rose and poured her some wine.

"How is she?" he asked as he held it out to her.

Meresamun took the wine and sipped. Her gaze roamed the tent, lingering on the untidy piles of papyri on his table, the unmade pallet, his half-finished dinner.

"She is grieving hard," she said. "She won't eat anything."

Sethi eyed Meresamun, noticing the droop of her shoulders. She looked as tired as he felt. He lifted his platter and held it out to her. "I saved you some roasted hare."

"Roasted meat?" Her brow lifted. "It is good to be the commander."

Pushing the maps and reports aside, he made space for her at the table. She sank down and pulled the meat apart, her fingers working, delicate, glistening with grease.

"It has been a long time since I have had roast meat," she said as she paused to take a sip of wine.

He leaned against the tent's support pole, crossing his arms over his chest. "How long?" he asked, hoping to ease open the closed door to her life.

She shrugged and carried on eating. He left her alone, resigned to her secrecy, occupying himself with poking at the brazier's fuel, stirring it back to life. She set aside the empty platter and wiped her fingers on his napkin.

"Stay the night with me?" he asked as he put more fuel on the brazier.

"You are the commander." Her fingers moved to the ties of her gown.

He reached over and stopped her. "You are tired, as am I. My heart is—just comfort me. Let me hold you while we sleep."

"You have also lost the one you love?" she asked, soft, her eyes meeting his, haunted.

"It would be better to say I am in the midst of losing her." Unthinking, he glanced toward Istara's tent. Meresamun's eyes widened. "I—" He stopped, at a loss how to remedy it. He turned away, cursing.

"Let us sleep," she murmured, touching his arm. "All will be forgotten in the morning."

His heart flooding with gratitude, he pulled off his belt. His kilt fell into a heap, he kicked it aside, watching as she untied her sandals and washed her feet, her gentle domesticity soothing him. She blew out the lamps, apart from one. He shuttered it as she shed her gown and came to him, seeking his warmth, pressing herself against him, shivering. Pulling the blanket over her, he chafed her arm, warming her. She settled against his shoulder. Within a heartbeat, she was asleep. He closed his eyes and followed her.

He dreamed again of Istara, only this time, it was different. They sailed high above the land, flying in a vast, strange barque, the floor of it clear, yet solid. Beneath them, a massive battle raged, and hundreds of large, flying birds made of metal, darted and swooped, fire coming from their wings. Their barque flew over a beautiful city, unlike anything he could have imagined, its towering white structures soaring up into the sky. The metal birds rained fire down on them; the city erupting into a firestorm, the parks and gardens incinerated, gone in a heartbeat. Istara cried out, anguished. His own heart ached, more than it ever had before. He took her to the bed, set upon the clear floor, and as the world burned beneath them, he made love to her, fierce and desperate, his final act, before he knew they too, would fall.

❋   ❋   ❋

Deep in the night, Istara woke, parched. She poured herself wine and peered through the hanging at Meresamun's pallet. It was empty. Alarmed, Istara plunged barefoot out of the tent into the cold night air, the wet earth soaking into the hem of her gown. She turned around, disoriented. Dozens of tents spread away into the darkness, all of them identical. Two soldiers, her guards, came after her. Forbidden to touch her, they flanked her, uneasy. One stepped nearer.

"My lady, are you ill?" he asked.

"Where is Meresamun?" Istara demanded, searching the shadows, her gaze moving down the silent rows of tents.

Her guards glanced at each other, nervous. A sound broke through night's quiet. She tilted her head, listening. It came again. The sound of a man in the act of love.

"You dare take her like a common whore?" she accused, outraged. "Meresamun is my companion and a free woman. Return her to me."

When they did not move, she pushed past them. "Then I shall liberate her myself. Your commander will know of this."

They ran in front of her, blocking her way. "You cannot!" one of the soldiers said, holding out his hands to stop her. "I beg you, cease. You have my oath she will be returned to you unharmed."

In the wake of his words, the sound came again, louder, clearer. She stared at the men, fear plain in their eyes. A memory burst free. Sethi had come to her the previous morning smelling of sex. No. It couldn't be. The man moaned again. She bolted toward the sound, her feelings, tangled and confused, goading her on, drawn to the sound of his lovemaking, a moth to a flame. Her guards followed, pleading for her to stop, their voices sharp with anxiety. She ignored them; she had to know the truth.

She ducked into the tent. The smell of sex overwhelmed her. Beside a shielded lamp, Sethi and Meresamun writhed in a passionate embrace, deep within the act of love, oblivious to her presence.

Mesmerized, she watched the commander's powerful body moving over Meresamun's supple one, her head cradled in his hands, his mouth on hers, hungry. Grinding his hips against hers, he pulled away from their kiss and stared at something only he could see. He held himself still, riding the brink of his release, groaning. Rocking his hips back, he whispered one word, dark with longing, tainted with need.

"Istara . . ."

She gaped at him, her knees weakening, as he plunged deep into Meresamun, sheltering her in his arms as she clung to him, riding out her own release.

Istara fled. Back on her pallet, her cushion clutched against her chest, she stared at the flames of the brazier. The one fleeting memory she had of Sethi returned. She was cold. He had held her and kissed her brow. In his arms, she had felt safe, secure, protected, cherished. She could remember nothing else, had convinced herself it had been a dream, but now, she was certain, something had passed between them. Something he hadn't forgotten.

It was a long time before she fell into a fitful sleep, dreaming disjointed dreams of Sethi mounting her, of his hands holding her head, his mouth on hers, of him saying her name. She woke, her body in an agony of need. Pushing aside the linen hanging, she eyed Meresamun's empty pallet. She lay back down, imagining Sethi holding Meresamun in his arms as he slept, just as he had once held her.

Fighting an irrational surge of jealousy, Istara stared at the tent's ceiling and searched her memories, picking through the events which had led her to this night. The siege against Kadesh. Sethi giving her his rations. Her life in Tarhuntassa. Tanu-Hepa's illness. Baalat's visit. Istara's promise to become a healer. The long years spent training. Her wedding. Urhi-Teshub's rejection. His betrayal. Her vision. Baalat's message. The journey to Egypt's camp. The battle—

She caught her breath as the individual events of her life coalesced. It was a path. All of it leading to Egypt's enigmatic commander.

Istara closed her eyes, her head beginning to ache. At every stage, through all those long years, Baalat had been there, guiding her to him. Yet now, when their paths had finally crossed, Sethi kept himself apart from her. Why? The night wore on. Istara tossed and turned, her heart crying out for answers. None came. The goddess was silent.

Quiet sounds broke into Istara's awareness. She sat up, her head aching. On the other side of the hanging, Meresamun sank onto her pallet, huddled into herself and wept, quiet.

"Meresamun?" Istara got up and pushed aside the linen hanging.

"Forgive me," Meresamun answered, brushing the tears from her eyes, "I have disturbed your sleep."

"Are you hurt?" Istara asked, moving closer.

"No." A tear escaped.

"Yet you come back from a night spent in the commander's tent grieving," Istara said, eyeing Meresamun, disbelieving. "I can end this. He has no right to take you. You are my companion, not his."

"He has the right," Meresamun whispered, looking at her feet. "I agreed to this arrangement before I became your companion. It is my own heart which causes my suffering, not the actions of the commander."

"Why?" Istara demanded. "You had the armbands. There is no reason for you to become his concubine, unless—" a stab of jealousy lanced into her, irrational, "—you wished to share his pallet?"

"The armbands were stolen while I slept," Meresamun pleaded. "I am not a paid follower. Telling stories is the only way I can eat. After the battle, no one wanted to hear them. I was starving. He gave me food."

Istara huffed. What was it with Sethi and food? "And what of Lord Ahmen?" she pressed, relentless, even as Meresamun flinched. "How could you lie with another when you claim your heart belongs to him?"

"I beg you," Meresamun cried out, anguished, "do not remind me of it. My burden of shame is great enough as it is."

Istara relented, silenced by Meresamun's stricken look. Her headache worsening, she sank onto the pallet. The noise of the breaking camp drew nearer: men shouted, horses whinnied, poles and ropes thudded onto the backs of carts. Each noise felt like a blow to her head. She rubbed her temples, seeking to ease the pain. It didn't help.

"When I am with the commander," Meresamun murmured, running her fingers along the faint pleats of her gown, seeking to bring them back together, "I cannot help but relive my time with Ahmen. It is why I grieve."

"And yet you left Ahmen before he woke," Istara pointed out, irritable, "when you could have remained."

Meresamun's gaze turned inward. "We like to believe we have some measure of control over who we love," she said soft, resigned. "But the heart goes where it will, and once it chooses we have no choice but to follow or stay away from the one it is crying out for."

Close by, a deafening crash, followed by a colorful string of oaths. Istara winced, pressing her fingers to her brow as Meresamun continued, "Should I have stayed with Ahmen, everything I have endured so far would have been for nothing. I must stay true to my path and return to Babylon, unless—"

Istara ceased massaging her temples. She waited. The silence stretched, taut. Even the camp fell quiet, as though it too waited for Meresamun to finish. Her companion shook her head. "I am selfish," she said, glancing at Istara, "speaking of this when you have much greater burdens to bear."

For a heartbeat, the pain in Istara's head subsided. Freed of its grip, her resentment and irritation melted away. She knew nothing of Meresamun's life; she should not judge. She squeezed her companion's hand, her thoughts drifting back to Meresamun's philosophy of the heart. A fresh onslaught of pain tore through her skull, sharp as a dagger's blade.

"Why does Sethi use you in my place?" she blurted, reckless, in its wake.

Meresamun's eyes widened. "I . . ."

The pain worsened. Istara stumbled back to her pallet. Memories overlapped and tangled: Sethi's dagger at her throat, his blade biting into her skin. His arms around her, warming her, his lips against her brow, tender. His back to her, telling her his orders are to protect her, nothing more. Another stab of pain. The images scattered. She lay down. Meresamun leaned over, her blue eyes filled with concern. Istara waved her away. It was only a headache.

Sleep called. Exhausted, Istara answered.

❋　❋　❋

Ahmen kicked out the remains of his campfire. Pre-dawn darkness closed in on him, claustrophobic. He could delay no longer. He stepped into his chariot and called to his horses, steering them across the plateau to Pre's breaking camp, the tension in his jaw increasing as he neared the fulfillment of his humiliation.

He turned the horses into the camp, ignoring the astonished stares of Pre's soldiers. Deep in the night, staring into the embers of his campfire, he had resigned himself to his demotion. In Pi-Ramesses, he would have his answers. Until then, whatever he had to face, he was determined to face with dignity.

He pulled up outside the command tent and approached the soldiers standing guard. Their eyes widening in recognition, they pressed their fists to their chests. He caught them exchanging a cautious look as one of them disappeared into the tent.

Resting his hands on his weapons' hilts, Ahmen waited, aloof, disregarding the curious looks of the nearby soldiers dismantling the camp. The guard reappeared and held the tent's flap open. Ahmen ducked in. Sethi stood at a table, alone, sorting through a pile of maps. He selected one and considered it. After several heartbeats, he set it aside and looked at Ahmen, his expression unreadable.

"Lord Ahmen-om-onet. Pre welcomes you."

"Lord Commander Sethi," Ahmen answered, reaching into his pouch, "I carry a command from the pharaoh. It affects both of us." He held it out.

Sethi took it and scanned the terse message. He blinked and read it a second time. After a brief, thick silence, he passed it back. "The Commander of Pre is honored to have the Lord Ahmen's assistance in this matter," he said, turning back to his map, brusque, efficient. "I will advise my men of the change in plans. You will drive on my right side, Naram will move to my left."

His fist to his chest, Ahmen acknowledged his orders, knowing nothing more would be said on the matter, not now, not ever.

In the distance, horns began to blow. Sethi gathered up the sheaves of papyri and stuffed them into a leather satchel. He slung it across his chest just as heavy raindrops began to slap against the tent's roof. He cast a dark look at the tent's ceiling.

"At least Pre will already be soaking wet before we must ford the river," he said with a bitter smile. "The Hittite gods are kind to us, are they not?"

He departed, leaving Ahmen, alone and unsmiling in the guttering light of a solitary lamp. He went to it and blew it out.

❊   ❊   ❊

Deafened by the roar of the pounding rain, Meresamun unlaced the ties of her cloak and lay it over Istara's shoulders. Pushing Istara's resisting hands down, she pointed at the tent's flap, mouthing the words: *Going out.* Istara nodded, her eyes dull, and huddled deeper into the cloaks.

Meresamun pulled back the flap and peered into the dense, gray light, barely able to make out the shape of several chariots lined up, their torches smoking, extinguished by the rain. Taking a deep breath, she pushed out into the downpour. Fat, cold drops splattered against her, soaking through her gown, plastering her hair against her skull, pounding down on her so hard she could barely see. Wrapping her arms around herself, she bolted across the center of the camp, shivering, her sandals slipping in the mud, and burst into the command tent. It lay dark and deserted. She cried out, frustrated, and plunged back into the rain, darting between the chariots, searching amongst the chaos, calling Sethi's name until her throat hurt. In a little clearing, she came to a halt and turned around, clamping her teeth together to keep them from chattering.

There. A little distance away, a lone chariot stood ready and waiting. She pushed the rain from her eyes and glimpsed the shape of a man standing with his back to her, holding the horses by their bridles. Perhaps he would know where Sethi was. She began picking her way over to him when someone caught hold of her arm. She turned. Sethi towered over her, rain sluicing off him.

"I heard you calling—where is your cloak?" He drew her against him. She huddled against his warmth, letting him shield her from the rain. "What brings you out here into this? Is Istara—"

"She needs a surgeon," Meresamun interrupted, the rain running down her face, blinding her. "She has fallen ill."

He glanced in the direction of Istara's tent, blinking the rain from his eyes. He nodded. "I will send my surgeon. Go back and wait for him." He turned and strode across the mud to the man standing with his horses. "Lord Ahmen," he bellowed into the roar of the rain, "come with me. There is a change of plans."

Meresamun staggered. It couldn't be. Ahmen was with the pharaoh, a day's march ahead. He couldn't be here. It was impossible, unthinkable—she turned, her heart clenching so tight she couldn't breathe. His head lifted. He turned the horses, his movements precise, meticulous, even in the pouring rain. Ahmen. Her heart jolted back to life. Hesitant, she stepped forward, hoping, fearing, willing him to turn, just enough to see her standing there.

He glanced back, his gaze moving toward her. Sethi passed him, gesturing him forward. Ahmen tugged on the horses' bridles and followed after Sethi, disappearing into the torrential rain. She cried out, devastated, and sank to her knees. Cold mud seeped into her gown and clung to her legs. Strong hands hauled her up. A soldier peered down at her; asked if she needed help.

She pulled free of his grip and ran, unseeing, back to Istara's tent, stumbling over stacks of wet supplies, her heart spiraling into darkness. Ahmen had looked at her, she was certain of it. Even through the pouring rain, she had felt his eyes on her. But he had turned away. Her thoughts tumbled, chaotic. What if he had learned she was with Pre and had come for her, only to discover her huddled together with Sethi in the rain? Riven with self-loathing, she heaped curses onto herself. No matter what she did, she always did wrong.

Outside Istara's tent, she let the cold rain pummel her, feeling nothing. Despite all she had done to reconcile herself to the goddess, enduring months of suffering, hunger, fear, and uncertainty—waiting, hoping and praying for her absolution—Sekhmet was determined to make her suffer to the very end. A vengeful goddess, impossible to appease, she had sent Ahmen to Pre, to torment Meresamun. Despair overwhelmed her. It was over. Ahmen had found her, but he no longer wanted her. Her heart closed over, tight, raw, aching. The last of her hope died, leaving her empty, lost, adrift in deafening silence.

A thin man approached, clutching a surgeon's satchel against his chest. "My lady," he said, blinking the rain from his eyes, taking in her disheveled state, "I am Ity, Chief Surgeon to the Division of Pre. I have been sent by the commander to attend Lady Istara."

Numb, Meresamun led him inside. Istara lay curled on the bench, dozing. He shook her shoulder. "Lady Istara, can you hear me?" She did not respond. He turned to Meresamun. "What ails her?"

"Head pain," Meresamun answered, vague. He tilted his head, waiting for her to elaborate. "She has not eaten for some time," she offered. He continued to wait. She searched her memory for anything else she could tell him. "Lord Sethi mentioned she had been drugged?"

He nodded, finally satisfied. "With opium?" he asked as he poked through his satchel. He looked up, impatient.

Meresamun shrugged, helpless. She did not know.

He huffed, not troubling to hide his annoyance as he rummaged through his things. Pulling out a stone vial, he measured out a dose of opium and rubbed the dense liquid onto Istara's gums. "I suspect the pain is an artifact of the drugging," he said over the steady thrum of the rain. "Tell the commander what she needs is rest. A blind man can see she is exhausted." He stood up, eyeing Istara as her breathing deepened. "At least she will be free of pain for a while. When she wakes, she should feel better. If not, send for me, and I will see what I can do."

Meresamun knelt as he left, watching Istara's features soften as the opium took effect. Her thoughts turned back to Ahmen. Fresh tears filled her eyes as the downpour subsided, easing to a gentle patter. Sethi pushed under the flap, abrupt, startling her. Damp, cold air followed in his wake. Expressionless, he looked over Istara, slumped on the bench, swaddled in cloaks.

"Is she ready to be taken to the chariot?" he asked, terse.

Meresamun came to her feet, hurrying to wipe her tears away. "The princess will not be carried on a litter?"

"Not this close to Kadesh," Sethi replied. "We have devised a harness for her within the box. She will ride seated on its floor, fastened to the box's side."

"You would tether her in like a goat?" Meresamun asked, sudden dread clawing at her. "My lord, she is Hatti's queen-in-waiting. What of the river crossing? Her gods—"

"I know well enough who she is," Sethi cut her off, sharp. "It pleases me no more than you, but I am oath-bound to keep her alive. I pray her gods will forgive me for the crime I am about to commit." He knelt and gathered Istara into his arms. Meresamun followed him, fretting, distressed by his sacrilege.

Using his bulk to shelter Istara from the soft rain, he carried her to his chariot and settled her inside it. From out of the heavy mist, the faint outline of another soldier materialized beside the pair. He knelt and held Istara in place while Sethi tied the harness's leather straps around her torso and shoulders. Finished their work, they rose and clasped forearms. Sethi departed. The soldier stepped into the chariot and wrapped the reins around his arms, quick and efficient.

Meresamun stepped out of the tent, confused. Sethi had said he would carry Istara, would not burden another with the responsibility. She moved closer, struggling to see through the murk, only able to make out the shape of the soldier as he called to the horses, turning them in a tight circle. A sharp gust of cold wind lanced through her wet gown. She shivered as he drove toward her. The fog thinned. The soldier looked at her. Her heart juddered. Ahmen.

The horses came to a standstill. He stood motionless, staring at her, shocked. Clarity poured into her. Ahmen had come to Pre for Istara. Out of all the men who could have been chosen to carry her to Pi-Ramesses, the pharaoh had sent Ahmen. Who else but the goddess could have moved the pharaoh's mind to make such a choice? Hope exploded in her breast, blossoming, spiraling outward, her dark, bleak world brightening, filling with color. Her heart pounding, she waited, not even daring to breathe.

Ahmen's lips moved. She read her name on them. He tore at his arms. The reins fell away, thudding against the chariot, startling the horses. Never taking his eyes from her, he crossed the rest of the distance between them, staggering to a halt just out of her reach. He gazed at her, drinking in the sight of her,

"Meresamun," he breathed, his voice cracking with disbelief. "You live."

She cried out, shuddering with relief, holding her hands out to him. It was over. Ahmen had found her. She had atoned. He took hold of her, his mouth falling onto hers, devouring her, reclaiming her as his own. Tearing his lips from hers, he gazed down at her, intense, possessive. Tears burned in his eyes.

"Come back to me," he said, tight, "and swear never to leave me again."

"I swear it," Meresamun breathed, her legs weakening as he groaned and pulled her against him, fierce; kissing her brow, her face, her eyes. She clung to him and wept, crying out his name, her heart bursting with joy, even as he kissed her tears away.

❉   ❉   ❉

Wrapping the reins around his arms, Sethi watched Ahmen and Meresamun, realizing far too late she was the woman Ramesses had been seeking the year before. Though he suspected neither Meresamun or his men would say anything of their arrangement, his instincts prickled. Ramesses had been searching for her. Blue eyes. He cursed. How could he have forgotten? There would be trouble ahead for him, he was certain.

Meresamun laughed, a clear, melodious sound, its perfection defying the dismal reality of their surroundings. A nearby knot of soldiers turned. In a heartbeat, they were cheering, clapping, and laughing too. Sethi felt his lips quirk, caught by the contagion, though he suppressed his smile. He belonged to no part of this.

He called to his horses and drove past Ahmen's chariot. Istara had woken. He tilted his head in greeting, but she did not see him. A distant look filled her eyes as she listened to Meresamun's laughter, a small smile playing at the corners of her lips. He drove on as she slipped back into the realm of dreams; her smile lingering on, a lodestone to his soul.

An hour into the march, just past the wretched slope where Sethi had lost half his division, heavy clouds rolled in from the west and gathered in thick layers above Pre. Rain began to fall once more, increasing in intensity until it fell in blinding, punishing sheets. Cold and sharp, it pounded down on him, sluicing out of his chariot, slapping against the mud. He glanced back at his men, trudging, stoic, ankle-deep in the black mire, using their spears to keep their footing.

Angling his head against the downpour, he called encouragement to his struggling horses, giving them their heads as they strained against the heavy drag of the mud. To either side of him, Ahmen and Naram kept pace, their jaws clenched, grim. Within Naram's chariot, Meresamun stood pale and shivering, gripping the top of the chariot's box as it lurched from side to side through the road's muddy furrows. Blinking the water out of his eyes, Sethi caught a glimpse of Istara, weighed down by her drenched cloaks; her hair plastered to her head, her slight frame hanging pale and limp in the harness. Cursing the rain, he pushed on, longing with all his heart to be free of Hatti's hostile, accursed land.

Four hours after leaving Kadesh, at the time of day when Egyptians at home would be sitting down to their mid-morning meal, the vanguard of Pre reached the river's ford at Shabtuna. Sethi pulled his horses to a halt, grateful the rain had finally ceased. A cool wind rose, and the clouds parted, offering tantalizing glimpses of blue sky. Sethi eyed the river crossing, wary, its swollen waters strung with two half-submerged sets of ropes stretching from the near bank to its opposite, marking out the boundaries of the ford's shallows. He glanced at the sky, watching the clouds as they parted and gathered anew, caught in the strengthening breeze. Muttering a prayer for the rain to hold off until Pre was through, he turned to Naram and gave the orders to begin.

❋　❋　❋

Istara dreamed. Fractured memories bled into each other, disjointed and chaotic. A new dream began, vivid. She walked beside the moat of Kadesh, plucking flowers from its edge. From within the moat, a water lily beckoned. She stretched out to retrieve it. A rough push from behind by someone unseen. With a frightened cry, she

tumbled into the moat, the weight of her gown and cloak dragging
her down into its cold, dark depths. She struggled, sinking deeper
into the inky darkness, helpless within the confines of her tangled
cloak. Terror seized her. She screamed. Water, cold and brackish,
poured into her mouth.

She woke, choking, submerged up to her neck in freezing water.
The cloaks, wrapped tight around her, confined her. Panicking, she
scrabbled within them, trying to tear them off. A man bellowed, but
she could not make out the words, the roar of the rushing water
deafening. A grip tightened on her, pinioning her legs and chest
against a solid mass, hurting her. The one who had pushed her into
the moat, her mind cried, the one who was trying to drown her. She
struggled to escape, throwing all her weight against her oppressor. He
stumbled, and she broke free, her cloaks billowing around her, tangling
in her arms and legs, pulling her under the water. She surfaced, seeing
the horrified faces of Pre's soldiers as she tumbled away from their
outstretched hands; realizing her grave mistake as her fingers slipped
free of the ford's slimy rope. She flailed within her cloaks, struggling
to stay afloat as the current caught her and swept her away.

She sped downstream, surges of brackish water plowing into
her, buffeting her. Along the banks, soldiers raced ahead, stumbling
over rocks, searching for a way to halt her progress. Caught in an
eddy, she spun around. Sethi swam toward her with sharp, powerful
strokes. He snatched at her cloak once, twice, the third time he
caught its hem, yanking her to him. She went under. Water poured
into her mouth. She surfaced, spluttering. Letting the current carry
him, he barrelled down the river behind her, hauling on her cloak,
closing the distance between them with agonizing slowness.

She kicked hard, pushing against the current, reaching out to
him, straining to make her arms longer. His fingers touched hers,
sliding over her hand, seeking her wrist. He clamped onto her and
heaved. She collided into him. His arm came around her ribcage,
pinning her against him.

He turned to the riverbank, where a crowd followed, waving their
arms, shouting encouragement. With slow, purposeful strokes—his

legs kicking hard—he towed her across the churning river. She prayed, wishing with all her heart she had learned how to swim. Her toes skimmed the silt bottom of the riverbed. She pushed against it, and little by little the river's depth lessened, the silt giving way to smooth pebbles.

He found his feet and stood, waist deep, swaying in the pull of the current. He hauled her up, his grip so tight she cried out. Soldiers pushed into the rushing water, staggering, holding their hands out to them. Panting, Sethi waded toward the soldiers. Hands grabbed hold of her, pulling her away from him. His crushing hold loosened, uncertain at first, then at his men's shouted reassurances, it slid away.

The soldiers slogged to the shore, hauling her between them, the current's grip lessening with each cumbersome step. They sloshed out of the waters and dragged her up onto the sodden bank.

Her legs gave out. She fell on all fours, coughing up river water, her fingers digging into the mud. Her chest aching and her throat burning, she clutched at the cold ground, reeling with gratitude. Meresamun burst through the knot of men, her face stricken, taut with fear. Whispering incoherent prayers of gratitude, she pulled at the tangled ties of Istara's cloaks and peeled them away. They slapped down against the mud, sharp, loud. Someone brought a dry blanket. Istara clutched at it, shivering, catching the glint of tears in Meresamun's eyes.

A skin of wine arrived. She sipped, enduring its burn against the rawness of her throat. As the wine warmed her, she became aware of the crowd surrounding her, the multitude of faces filled with concern. She searched for Sethi. A short distance away, he knelt on one knee, panting hard, his head hanging, naked but for a soaking loincloth.

He lifted his head, and his eyes locked on hers, dark and dangerous, silencing her gratitude. Pushing himself to his feet, he reached out to the soldier holding his kilt, belt, and weapons. He dressed, giving orders as he worked. Checking his blades, he dropped them into their scabbards and strode back to the distant crossing, rigid, furious. He didn't look back.

✳ ✳ ✳

The gods had heard his prayer. The rain held off until an hour after the rearguard crossed the river, then it arrived with sudden ferocity; pounding down onto Pre as though angry at having been forced to wait. Bending his head against the driving rain, Sethi led his division along the rocky, barren plateau between the mountains. The river surged alongside them, its raging waters snatching trees and boulders from its banks, carrying them away as though they were no more than twigs and pebbles.

He cut a look at Istara, drenched and huddling in her soaking blanket, standing beside Ahmen, her hands wrapped tight around the box's edge. She had refused the harness, insisting she could manage the last half of the march without it, rejecting even Meresamun's pleas to take what rest she could. He scoffed at Istara's foolishness, fueling his anger against her for what she had done at the ford, welcoming the heat of his indignation—anything to distance himself from her.

The downpour eased. In the distance, the blackened scars of a multitude of fire pits spread across the plateau, Amun's camp from the night before. Muttering a prayer of thanks to Horus, he shouted to Naram to prepare for the order to halt. The order went down the line. From the depths of Pre, ragged cheers rose. His men pressed on, their steps quickening, eager for the miserable day to end.

In the damp warmth of his command tent, Sethi set aside the day's reports from his captains. He yawned and pressed the heels of his palms against his eyes. An image flashed: Istara sinking under the river's waters. He ignored it and finished his wine. Wiping the back of his hand across his mouth, he began to tidy the reports. The image came again, visceral. His hands stopped their work. Once more he saw Istara disappearing under the dark, cold waters. He cursed and slammed his fist against the table. He had been irresponsible.

Distracted, he poured himself another brimming cup. His decision to go after her had been driven by his fear of losing her, of her sinking under the waters, never to return. But at what risk? He was already exhausted by the time he caught her; had brought her to the shore by will alone. He looked down. His cup was empty. He had tasted nothing.

Still holding the empty cup in his hands, he leaned forward, resting his elbows on his knees and stared into the glowing fuel of the brazier. If he had drowned, Egypt would have lost its commander. His grip tightened on the cup as shame coursed through him. He had let fear control him. He would not make the same mistake again. Others who had been willing to go after her, better swimmers than he, yet he had called them off, not trusting anyone but himself to save her. He left the table and shed his kilt and loincloth. Someone entered. He turned.

Her color deepening, Istara averted her eyes. He picked up his kilt, eyeing her as he tied it back around his hips, noting the dark shadows around her eyes, the sheen of perspiration on her face and neck, the faint tremble in her hands. Signs of fever.

"You are ill," he said, abrupt, willing her to leave. "Return to your tent. I will send for Ity."

"I will not keep you, Commander," she answered, her gaze flicking to his pallet, then away. "I came to thank you for what you did today, with all my heart."

He turned to add more fuel to the brazier, though it didn't need it. "I did what was required to protect you as commanded by the pharaoh," he said, tight. "There is no need to thank me."

He glanced at her. She looked down. Humiliation emanated from her. Shame sliced through him. He poured her some wine and held it out to her. Her eyes met his. He turned away.

"Commander. Please look at me."

"There is no need," he said, terse. "I have told you what you may expect of me. I beg you, leave me and allow me my pallet. Your gratitude is noted."

"I have heard the talk outside my tent," she persisted, stepping closer to him. "You could have sent another to save me. Instead, it was you who risked your life, Commander."

"And I regret it with all my heart," he snapped. "If Horus had not protected me, Egypt would be without its commander this night. It was a foolish mistake. One I will not make again."

"At least now you look at me." She placed her cup on the table and turned to leave.

"So it is your intention to torment me?" he bellowed, following after her, his temper igniting. "I wonder, is this how the future Queen of Hatti amuses herself at court, by toying with the men sworn to protect her?"

"Toying?" she repeated, outraged, her color turning hectic. "You are the one—" she stopped, fighting for composure. "Commander Sethi, the men who protected me are men of honor, able to accept my gratitude with grace. If you represent what sort of manners await me in Egypt, then I wish you had left me to those waters today, rather than force me to follow you to an empire of brutes."

He roared at her insult, snatching her to him. "You dare call the Pharaoh of Egypt a brute," he ground out, bearing down on her, "when you are the daughter-in-law of that pig Muwatallis?"

Her eyes cold, she glared at him. "Yes. I dare."

She pushed her palms against his chest, seeking to free herself. Furious, he pulled her closer, trapping her arms against his chest. She lifted her chin, defiant, bringing her mouth so near to his, he could taste the wine on her breath.

"I command you to release me," she said, stiff.

He barked a laugh and pulled her tighter against him. She cried out, indignant, writhing, struggling to free herself. He tightened his grip, forcing her against him. Her body slid over him, arousing him. His member betrayed him, awakening, springing to life under the material of his kilt, unrestrained by a loincloth.

She collided with him and staggered to a halt. Her breathing slowed, turning ragged, matching his own. He held still, willing himself to resist even as his anger fled, the banked fire within him igniting, dangerous, aching, forbidden. She met his look. His member hardened. Caught in his arms, she closed her eyes, her lips parting, inviting, just as they had done the morning he had found her sleeping on his pallet. His chest tightened. She was here, in his arms, willing, the woman from within his dream—

The last of his restraint fled. He drank in the sight of her, knowing, accepting he would die for what he was about to do. He lowered his mouth to hers and tasted her. A sudden, intense sensation of having kissed her thousands of times before cascaded through him. How was it possible? She staggered in his embrace, moaning, feeling it too. He kissed her hard, possessing her, his fingers tangling in her hair. She answered him, fierce, hungry, clinging to him.

He pulled back, fighting for reason, holding her at arms' length. What was he doing? She belonged to Ramesses. He could not take her. He had already gone too far. Unwilling to let her go, he drew her back into his arms, murmuring they could not go on; she was forbidden to him. She huddled against him, shivering, drawing the heat from him. He turned her to the warmth of the brazier. She swayed, sagging in his grip. He touched her temple. It was freezing.

"You need medicine," he said, lowering her onto a stool. "I will send for my surgeon."

She nodded, reaching out to pour herself more wine, her hands trembling. He went to the tent's flap—her shallow, uneven breathing filling his ears—and called to his guards to hurry and find Ity. Behind him, a clatter, followed by a thud.

Alarmed, Sethi turned. Istara lay sprawled on the ground. Wine poured from the toppled pitcher on the table, staining the rug the color of blood. He fell to his knees, taking her head in his hands. Her eyes opened, glassy and unseeing, her pupils dilated.

Cursing, he grabbed his blanket and wrapped it around her. She convulsed, hard. Pulling her onto his lap, he pushed the hair from her face, bracing her against the spasms wracking her body. He knew she should have rested after the crossing. Why had she insisted on standing the rest of the way in the pouring rain after such an ordeal? Stubborn, stubborn woman; she had brought this on herself. She spasmed again, her fingers digging into his arms. She was so cold. She cried out, frightened, begging him not to leave her alone.

His heart clenched. Catching her up against him, he whispered, harsh. "I could never—"

She sagged, her body heating up until it broiled. He tore the blanket from her and lay her on his pallet. The front of her gown lay soaked in wine. Keeping his eyes averted, he pulled apart the ties and washed her as best he could, her skin as hot and dry as desert sand.

His guards came in, followed by Ity, his kilt tied on crooked. Ity knelt and examined Istara, muttering to himself over the severity of her fever and the need to break it. Pulling out several vials from his satchel, he mixed their tinctures together in a little silver dish. Holding up her head, he poured the foul-smelling concoction down her throat. He waited. Nothing happened. He sent for more blankets and swaddled her in them, drawing them tight. Within her bindings, she lay silent and still, her flesh burning. Unable to do anything more, Ity lay a dozen scarabs and ankhs over her torso, and began the long incantations for healing and protection.

The night passed, slow. Alone in the shadows, Sethi watched, waited, and prayed.

For the next three days, Sethi led his division through the relentless rain toward the Great Wood of Amka, his thoughts dwelling on Istara, unconscious within Ahmen's chariot. Without the warmth and rest she needed, the fever continued to ravage her body, leaving her gaunt and wasted. The rain pummeled down, ferocious, cold and brutal. Though still half a long iter from their destination, Sethi called an early halt, ignoring the astonished looks of Ahmen and Naram. Pre could make up the distance later. He had to get her out of the rain.

In the humid warmth of his tent, Sethi went over his reports, waiting, uneasy, as Ity examined Istara. The surgeon muttered to himself, bleak, as he poured more of the foul-smelling tincture down her throat, staining the corners of her mouth an inky black. He packed his satchel and came to his feet, shaking his head. There was nothing more he could do. He left, murmuring unless the gods intervened, he did not expect her to survive the night.

Sethi looked down into his cup. He turned it, slow, watching the wine swirl. His mother—once a serving girl to the high priest at Iunu—had told Sethi a tale the priest had told her while deep in his wine. During the Golden Age of gods and men, mortals could bargain with the gods. The priest had said it could still be done, by saying the right secret word, which could carry a mortal to a place between worlds where the gods would claim their price, but only one man knew that word: Iunu's Keeper of Ancient Knowledge, himself descended from the first Keeper. It was said his ancestor had written down the words uttered by Sekhmet herself.

Once he had gained enough wealth, Sethi traveled to Iunu to satisfy his curiosity, longing to know the truth. Bribed with enough gold, the Keeper emerged from the depths of Iunu's library, squinting in the light. He led Sethi to the eroded obelisk raised by the first men and women and pointed to an inscription, faded with age and written in unrecognizable symbols. He read out in a strange, incomprehensible language, Sekhmet's instructions given to the first men and women to honor her father, Re-Atum, above all else. A fortune of gold had to be offered—the price of two villas—but finally, unwilling, the Keeper wrote out the sounds of the secret word in the sand, erasing it right after, fearful. But Sethi had been quick enough and remembered. It was a beautiful word.

Istara thrashed, moaning, and threw off her blankets. Sethi set aside his cup, and cradled her against him, hushing her. Despite her burning heat, he sensed the chill presence of death. He looked over his shoulder. The shadows within the tent coalesced, forming into a man with the head of a jackal. Anubis stepped closer, his fangs glistening, hungry.

Sethi cried out. Anubis would not have her. Clutching Istara against him, he shielded her from the god. He closed his eyes, praying the Keeper had not lied, and said the secret word.

Pain, brutal, excruciating, spiraled from his extremities to his head in rotating waves. His feet, then his legs, torso, and arms disintegrated, shattering into small solid squares, all of them the exact same shape and size. Horrified, he screamed, but no sound came. The pieces of him flew back together, and the pain ended, abrupt. He staggered, whole once more.

He looked up, wary. A bleak, empty hall surrounded him, its walls, floor, and ceiling constructed of massive ashlars of stone, the smallest of them at least twice his height. Ahead, torches flickered alight; their flames, a cold, pale blue, guided him to a corridor. Led by the light of the cerulean flames, he came to a wooden door. He pushed it open and found another silent room, cast in the same cold blue light, empty save for a massive stone plinth rising out of the ashlar beneath.

A crude wooden cage perched on its top, a key beside it. He went to it, curious. Pain tore into his chest, a deep wrench. He staggered, breathless. A sudden sensation of emptiness, fleeting. Something warm moved in his hand. A heart, beating. His heart. He watched it, marveling at its continued existence outside of him. A shudder within. A dull ache, a tightness, heaviness. He clutched at his chest, as the nascent beats of his replacement heart commenced, its chambers empty, lacking a soul. He searched the room for the one who would take his payment. In the deepest shadows, the outline of a man with a falcon's head moved. Sethi blinked, uncertain, wondering if he had imagined the creature. When he looked again, it was gone.

He lifted his heart up to the cage, watching it beat once, twice, three times. His heart—the key to his eternal life, the price demanded by the gods—sacrificed so Istara might live. Setting it atop the rough wooden slats, he closed the door. He placed the key in the lock, hesitating, considering what he was about to do, preparing himself for the annihilation of his eternal soul. Courage.

Istara's faint cry pierced the epochal silence, filled with terror. The walls shimmered, sliding toward transparency. The cage wavered, fading, ephemeral. A tentacle of deep cold touched Sethi's spine—the chill of Anubis, ravenous, preparing to snatch its prey. Sethi grabbed hold of the waning cage and turned the key. The room imploded. Massive ashlars tumbled around him, chaotic. Only the wooden cage remained intact, his beating heart falling away, receding into the endless distance. An explosion of virulent pain as his existence shattered anew, the pieces of him skittering across a vast, dark, silent expanse. A murky light in the distance, the flicker of lamplight. His fragments plummeted toward it, coalescing, spiraling back into his world, back to Istara.

Anubis looked up startled, and met Sethi's eyes. He snarled, furious, deprived of his quarry. He faded, the shadows around him sliding apart, returning to their places within the tent, innocuous. Warmth returned.

In Sethi's arms, Istara cooled. He lay her back onto her pallet, savoring the sound of her soft, gentle breathing. He stroked the hair from her face, refusing to think of his sacrifice. She lived. Nothing else mattered. Nothing.

❋　❋　❋

Istara woke to the thumps and shouts of Pre breaking camp. Thirst overwhelmed her. It took a long time to struggle out of her blankets. Leaning against the bench, she rose to her feet, trembling. Weakness saturated her limbs. The jug of wine on the table taunted her from what felt like an impossible distance. She lunged for the central support pole and clung to it, her heart pounding.

"My lady!" Footsteps hurried across the tent. A thin man appeared, catching her by her shoulders, muttering at her foolishness as he settled her on the bench. He brought her wine, his gaze moving over her, scrutinizing her. "We have not been properly introduced." He bowed. "I am Ity, Chief Surgeon of Pre. If I may, I would like to examine you."

He checked her palms, joints, and soles of her feet for heat and discoloration. Pulling out a small instrument, he tested her glands for pain and swelling. His lips pursed, he felt the back of her neck for fever, making quiet sounds of approval. "Re has heard our prayers," he said as he sat back on his haunches. "How do you feel?"

"Weak. Hungry. Tired," Istara answered, breathless from the effort of speaking.

"This is normal for the recovery period," Ity said, retrieving a stylus and wax tablet from his satchel, murmuring to himself as he made several notations. "Extra rations will be placed in Lord Ahmen-om-onet's chariot. You must eat, and often, to regain your lost strength. Had you been at rest in a villa, I would expect you to find strength within a week, but the march will slow your recovery. For the next few days at least, I must insist that you sit."

"No harness," Istara protested, faint.

He gave her an indulgent look. "Of course not. A ledge is being made for you to sit upon within Lord Ahmen's chariot." He packed his things back into the satchel. "Your morning meal is on its way, eat well and do your best to conserve your strength. These next few days will be crucial to your recovery. I march with the vanguard, should you have need of me."

He left just as Meresamun entered with a tray of food, followed by a woman carrying a pitcher of steaming water, towels and a clean gown. Meresamun knelt beside Istara, her eyes warm.

"Praise the gods," she breathed, "you have returned to us. I have been praying for you night and day."

"I am—" Istara swayed, breathless.

"Save your strength," Meresamun smiled, gentle. She uncovered a bowl and held it up, its contents steaming and smelling of cinnamon. "Lentil soup has been made just for you. Eat as much as you are able for today we must march straight through the woods of Amka without any stops."

The soup was good. Istara ate almost all of it. When she finished, Meresamun removed Istara's stained gown and helped her kneel in a shallow basin to be bathed. Naked and shivering, Istara eyed herself, noting the ridges and points of her bones, protruding, painful; the chafes and blisters the harness's straps had left against her skin. Three days Meresamun said, that's how long she had burned with fever, but the gods had answered their prayers. Toweled dry, and dressed in a fresh gown, Meresamun had just finished tying a cloak around Istara's shoulders when Ahmen's chariot arrived.

Istara settled on the ledge. With a quiet call to the horses, Ahmen released the brake. They departed with a lurch, passing pockets of frantic activity as the last of the camp's tents were dismantled and soldiers coalesced into their marching formations.

At the head of the torchlit column. Sethi stood beside his chariot conferring with his captains. He glanced at Ahmen, and lifted his chin in acknowledgment. One of the captains addressed him. He turned back, his gaze sliding over Istara, bland, as he continued his conference. Istara's chest tightened as she perceived his silent message. What had happened between them was over. He had returned to the role of her protector, distant and cold. She could expect nothing more.

Horns blasted. The men around Sethi lifted their fists to their chests and dispersed down the lines to their companies. Stepping into his chariot, Sethi wrapped the reins around his arms, brusque, and gave the order to move out. He pulled ahead, keeping his gaze fixed in front of him as he passed Ahmen's chariot, ignoring her. Istara looked down at her hands, clenched in her lap, enduring the humiliation of his sudden, brutal rejection. Blinking back her tears, she caught Ahmen watching them, curious. She looked away, but it was too late. He drove on, though his eyes remained fixed on Sethi's back, suspicious and sharp.

Deep within the Great Wood of Amka, Hasurna crouched, itching at the bug bites covering his legs and arms, cursing the filthy, bug-ridden animal hides he had been forced to wear over his kilt and tunic. To either side of him, forty of his men—also miserable in their stinking skins—waited, their numbers bolstered by an additional fifty barbarians from the Andarah Tribe, their dubious support paid for with a fortune of temple gold.

Yesterday, as the evening shadows deepened, Egypt's first division had passed through the gorge below them. Istara had not been with them, but he had seen Muwatallis and Hattusilis, bound and riding in the vanguard, surrounded by a contingent of chariots from Amurru. He had been stunned to see them alive when Urhi-Teshub had announced them dead.

Everywhere, lies and deceptions. And now, this. Forced to murder Istara so his wife and sons would live. For the hundredth time, Hasurna checked the sharpness of his dagger, fretting the forest's damp had dulled its edge. With his vile act, he might protect his family's lives, but he could never return. Tonight, he would welcome his death, the payment for his terrible crime. He spat, sickened. Rhoha was lying. The only traitor to Kadesh was its new, dangerous queen.

In the quiet of the forest's gloom, he heard someone grunt. He glanced behind him. Takde, Andarah's savage chieftain crouched, his jaw slack, handling himself under his skins. Disgusted, Hasurna moved away. Takde carried on, his breathing ragged. He finished and wiped his hand across the front of his skins, his eyes fixed on the track below, hungry, intent.

Hasurna watched him, wary. No matter what happened, he had to get to Istara first.

❋   ❋   ❋

Istara longed to see a sliver of sky. Crowding up along either side of Amka's narrow, muddy track, massive cedar trees soared upward, their thick boughs blocking out the light, a solid roof of deep green. For hours, Pre had marched through the forest's dripping gloom, pushing its way through the dank, claustrophobic wood. Again, she looked up, desperate to see sky, fighting the feeling of being buried alive, longing to breathe clean, open air again.

Ahmen's chariot lurched past a wall of rock, water trickling down its face. He shifted his weight, guiding the horses with gentle commands across the muddy rivulet at its base, his eyes flicking back and forth, searching the dense undergrowth for movement.

More hours passed. Daylight faded. Istara's buttocks ached, and her back hurt. She longed to stand, to ease the cramps in her legs. The forest's gloom deepened. Fatigue crept over her, her tiny reserves abandoning her. She eyed the leather satchel tied to the side of the chariot, containing her food. No. She couldn't bear to eat in front of the others, not when everyone else was hungry. Ahmen had said no halts could be made in this forsaken place. Her stomach growled, loud. She pressed her fingers against it, ashamed. Ahmen glanced at her.

"Eat," he said, curt. "The surgeon ordered it."

"I can wait. We must be close by now."

"We are not," he muttered. "The mud has slowed our progress and sapped the men's strength. We have at least another two hours to go, and darkness is coming fast. Your prayers for our protection would not go amiss."

"Protection?" she repeated, struggling to comprehend what a division of five thousand could possibly fear. "From what?"

"On our way to Kadesh, Amun lost twelve men and seven horses," Ahmen answered, grunting as he steered the horses around a fallen log. "We learned the hard way the barbarian tribes infesting this forest are not afraid of our numbers. They wait until dusk, when the shadows are thickest, then they come, taking armor, weapons, horses." He scoffed. "Cowards."

Her hunger deserted her. She prayed, watching the deepening shadows, vigilant. At the thirteenth stanza of her prayer, ululations, fierce, chilling, pierced the forest's heavy quiet. Sounds of fighting broke out further down the vanguard. Fear, visceral, raw, clawed at her.

Ahmen yanked the horses to a halt. Shedding the reins, he pulled his bow from its holder. "On the floor," he ordered. "Do not make a sound."

Scrambling from her perch, she wedged herself into the space under the narrow bench, pressing her face to her knees, making herself as small as possible. The sound of running feet neared. Sethi shouted to Ahmen, a question. Ahmen answered, abrupt. Sethi ran on, his commands carrying over the ululations of the barbarians. Quaking with terror, she prayed. The ululations drew closer. The pounding of running feet, coming out of the darkness from the front of the line, straight at them. She dug her fingers into her knees, the prayer forgotten. They were alone.

Ahmen's bow creaked as he took aim. He released, the bowstring smacked, loud, against the leather of his bracer. He fired, again and again. Still, they came. Her heart pounded, erratic, her chest so tight she couldn't breathe. She shrank against the box's side, hoping, praying the shadows would hide her.

A clatter. Ahmen's bow slid across the floor, no longer useful. A soft hiss, as his *khopesh* left its scabbard. The grunt and thrust of close combat. The barbarians were right behind her, the stink of their untanned skins making her gag. Ahmen cut his way through them, his blade thudding against their bodies, their anguished cries loud in her ears. Their blood splattered over her, hot, sharp, metallic.

The fighting stopped, abrupt, ending as quick as it began. She glanced up, desperate with hope. Ahmen's eyes darted back and forth. His chest lay slick with blood, and he panted, hard. He nodded at her. It was over. A flurry of untanned skins erupted from the undergrowth. A sickening thud. The chariot juddered. Ahmen crashed down beside her, unconscious. She stared at the blood pouring from his scalp, pooling underneath his head. No. Please. No.

Rough fingers tangled into her hair, hauling her out from under the bench. She struggled, crying out as her captor yanked her head back and inspected her, his breath hot and rank, stinking of rotten teeth. She retched, bile, burning hot, splattered down her front. He laughed, malicious, and wrenched her out of the chariot. Frantic, she screamed for help, stumbling after him into the darkness, her hair caught in his merciless grip. An explosion of pain mushroomed out from her jaw in sickening waves, blinding her. She screamed, agonized. He hit her again. Her legs gave out. Silence.

She came to hanging upside down over her captor's shoulder. Blood trickled from her mouth into her eyes. Apart from his heavy tread on the forest floor, silence surrounded her. So, this was how she would end: in the mud of Amka, at the hands of a savage. She wept, despairing. He stopped and tossed her face-first onto the ground. She slammed into the mud, her palm impaling on the jagged point of a fallen branch. She bellowed, howling in agony, pain ripping through her as she pulled her hand free, the sudden heat of her blood spreading over her cold fingers, startling.

Ignoring her cries for mercy, he flipped her over, shoving her gown up to her waist, his eyes dark, expectant. His filthy fingers closed around her throat, holding her down as he fumbled under his skins and pulled his member free. She felt it probing against her, the ripe stink of it bringing fresh tears to her eyes. He bent over and licked her mouth, his tongue furred and foul. She retched again. Caught in his vicious grip she gagged on her bile, choking, fighting to breathe.

Maddened by pain and fear, she groped in the mud. Her fingers closed on a rock. She yanked it free and smashed it against the side of his head. He reeled back, roaring, furious, swinging his fist into the air.

"You are Takde's slave now," he spat, a gobbet of saliva trailing from his mouth. "Mine."

Her heart folded. The slave of a barbarian. A fate worse than death. Praying his blow would kill her, she closed her eyes, waiting. A dull thud. Takde juddered. Warmth spread across her torso.

The bloody point of a spear protruded from his chest. His jaw slack, he toppled forward, carrying the spear straight to her heart. Panicking, she pushed against him, struggling to resist his enormous weight. She had no strength left. The spear pressed against her ribs, the pain exquisite. Sobbing, she cried out to Baalat. The pressure eased. Takde's weight slid away. He slumped over onto the ground beside her. She scrambled to her knees and stared at the dead man. Baalat had saved her. She gibbered, scrabbling in the mud to escape. Strong hands took hold of her. She screamed, kicking her legs, thrashing, frantic. A voice, familiar, rough, pierced her terror.

"Istara, are you aware?"

"Sethi?" she cried, ragged, incredulous, relief shuddering through her. "How—"

"Your screams carried well, thank Horus," he answered, terse, as he sawed off a length of his kilt. He tied it around her injured hand, so tight, it hurt. Kicking Takde onto his belly, he pulled the spear out with a grunt. Shaking off the gore, he looked around, wary, his eyes cold in the pale moonlight. "It is dangerous out here. We need to get back."

He offered her his hand. She took it, and crept down the slope after him, shivering, trembling, weak. Sethi had come after her, alone, just like in the river, once again risking his life for hers. He tightened his grip, possessive, protective, and led her into the darkness.

✳   ✳   ✳

Halfway back, Istara succumbed to shock. Sethi caught her as she fell. Cradling her against him, he shoved his way through the undergrowth toward the flickering light of Pre's torches. Shouting for Ity, he pushed his way to his chariot. The surgeon came running, a flaming torch held aloft in his hand. He stumbled to halt, blanching at Istara's ravaged state. He turned her hand over, eyeing the blood-soaked linen, his expression grim.

"She has lost much blood," he said, reproachful. "There is only so much I can do. I fear she will not survive after all she has suffered."

"Not all of the blood is hers," Sethi retorted. "She will survive. You will see to it. Do what you can now, and the rest when we make camp. She rides the rest of the way with me, in the harness. What of Lord Ahmen-om-onet?"

"A blow to the head," Ity replied, peering, bleak, at the blood leaking from the gouge in her chest. "He has returned with his senses, thank Hathor."

"Good. Ride with him. I would have you close by, should the princess's condition change."

Sethi set Istara down inside his chariot, watching Ity as he knelt in the mud and emptied his satchel onto its floor. The surgeon took up a stone vial and poured a large dose of tincture into his palm. Dabbing his finger into it, he rubbed the inky liquid against her gums. He looked up at Sethi.

"She could wake at any time," he said, brusque. "This will numb her pain as I work."

Sethi nodded, though a wave of fear rippled through him. Istara lay like one already dead, pale and still. Meresamun appeared from the shadows, her face tight with worry. With a cry, she dropped to her knees beside Ity, murmuring her willingness to assist. Ahmen arrived a heartbeat later, a bloody gash across his scalp. He took in Istara's pitiable state, his expression grim.

"Commander," he said, pressing his fist to his bloodied chest, "The pharaoh will know of my failure to protect her."

Sethi swatted away Ahmen's words. "I should not have left you alone. The fault is mine."

Further down the line, someone called Ahmen's name, urgent. He turned. "I must go back," he said, "they are searching the dead." He looked back at Istara. "She refused to eat any of her rations. I suspect she did not for the sake of the rest of us."

Sethi folded his arms across his chest. Stubborn woman. Without nourishment, her meager reserves would have been exhausted just from riding in the chariot. Ity peeled back the soaking linens around her hand. Fresh blood slid out from the gaping hole in her palm. He turned her hand over; the jagged exit wound still contained sharp splinters of wood. Ity muttered a particularly foul oath. Her color blanching, Meresamun handed him a waterskin. He sloshed its contents over Istara's wound, rinsing away the worst of the mud and blood, complaining about the lack of light. Meresamun brought the torch nearer. Under its flickering light, he began the painstaking work of sewing up Istara's hand.

Sethi left Ity to his work. He turned to Naram, waiting to give him the vanguard's report. Thirty men injured. Twelve dead. Sethi cursed, sending messages down the line, telling his captains to take a defensive stance, praying there would be no more attacks. Ahmen approached.

"You might want to see this." He held out a dagger.

Sethi took it, turning it over in his hand, curious. He stopped and lifted it to the torchlight. The pommel bore the sigil of the House of Kadesh. He glanced at Ahmen, perplexed.

"The man who carried it," said Ahmen. "I know him."

Sethi waited. Below, Ity worked on, complaining, irritable. The horses shifted, and the chariot moved. Ity slapped his hand against the chariot's floor, bellowing with frustration.

"He was the Commander of Kadesh's army," Ahmen continued. "Hasurna. I brought him up from the plateau before the hyenas took him."

Sethi blinked. He handed the dagger back. "So it was a rescue attempt, using barbarians against the vanguard to draw us away from her. It seems the Prince of Hatti intends to attack us after all."

"I am not so certain," Ahmen answered, "if they were meant to rescue her, why did she end up like this? And, as one of them fell, I heard the cry, 'Protect Istara'. There was also this, in Hasurna's belt, if you can read Akkadian."

"Just."

Ahmen handed a folded piece of papyrus to him. Sethi opened it and looked it over. It was an order to provide Hasurna with temple gold, in the name of Rhoha, Queen of Kadesh.

"Rhoha?" he asked, puzzled. "Who is she in all of this?"

Ahmen shrugged, taking back the note. "I have no idea."

"A question for Lord Paser then. Search all of the dead. Save anything which might interest him."

Ahmen pressed his fist to his chest and left. Sethi turned his attention back to Istara, lying limp within the box, her ruined gown and awkward posture reminding him of a filthy, broken doll he had once found in the gutters of Pi-Ramesses. Ity tied off the linen bandage. Despite the sutures, blood continued to seep through the linens. He felt for her pulse. It took him a long time. He looked up, his mouth curving downward.

"Pray."

The disk of Re-Atum's barque had just lifted from the horizon as the last of Pre's rearguard filed out of the forest onto the plain. From his position atop a low hillock, Sethi breathed a prayer of thanks. The worst of the march was behind them. On this side of Amka, they were in lands loyal to Egypt. There would be no more forests, just rolling grasslands, giving way to the desert. He breathed in, savoring the clear, clean air. Calling to his horses, he drove them down the hill and made his way through the camp, his thoughts returning to the woman in his tent, praying his sacrifice might protect her, for just a little longer.

The heat hit Sethi like a wall. Beside Istara's pallet, the brazier burned red hot. He knelt beside her, astonished by how small and frail she looked. She lay very still, her skin almost transparent, her breathing so faint, he wasn't sure she still lived. He touched her cheek. Her skin felt as cold as stone. Ity began to pack away his things. Sethi turned to him.

"You are giving up?"

Ity looked up at him. Dark circles shadowed his eyes. "My lord, I am no sorcerer. There is nothing more I can do. She is nearing her end."

Blinking hard, Sethi took hold of her face and pressed his forehead against hers, the act of a lover. "Fight this," he whispered, willing her to hear him. "Come back."

Ity cleared his throat, uneasy. "Commander . . . ?"

Sethi pulled back, resentful, leaving Istara alone and vulnerable on her pallet. Ignoring Ity's disapproving look, Sethi tucked her hand into his.

She shuddered. Ity darted to her, listening for her heartbeat. He sat up, shaking his head. resigned. Her body flattened, her *ka* slipping free. Sethi choked, disbelieving. The gods were taking her after all.

Istara woke inside a bleak, empty hall, the walls, floor, and ceiling constructed of massive ashlars of stone, the smallest of them at least twice her height. Ahead, torches flickered alight, their flames—a cold, pale blue—guided her to a corridor. Led by the light of the cerulean flames, she came to a door. She pushed it open and found another silent room, cast in the same cold blue light, empty save for a massive stone plinth rising out of the ashlar beneath. Atop it sat a crude wooden cage, its door closed.

She peered inside. A heart lay on the rough slats, beating still. Curious, she tugged on the cage's door, but it was locked. In the shadows, she sensed movement. She looked up, dread tingling through her. A man stepped toward her, taller than Sethi, his body lean and powerful, every muscle defined. On his chest, beautiful golden markings rotated and reformed into new patterns, endlessly. Around his hips, a resplendent kilt, and on his upper and lower arms, thick golden bands. He took another step and left the shadows. Istara gasped, stifling a cry. His was not the head of a human, but a falcon's. She gaped at him, horrified.

Tilting his head, he fixed an unblinking eye on her, expressionless. His hand came to rest on the top of the cage. He spoke, his voice beautiful, deep, resonating. She stared at him. His beak did not move. Instead, his words filled her mind.

Istara, daughter of Amunira, I am Horus. You have arrived at the threshold of the immortal realm. Though your heart has traveled this far, your body still lingers in the mortal realm, and until it expires, you may not pass. As we wait for your body to give up its last breath, I shall tell you of a great and noble sacrifice.

The heart locked within this cage belongs to me, it was left here by a mortal man, in return for saving the life of a woman he loved. This was no small surrendering, but a terrible one, for without this heart, he cannot make the journey to his judgment or experience the immortal realm. No, when this man dies, he will cease to exist, returning to nothingness, becoming void. It is the rarest of sacrifices, one the gods have not seen in an eon. Istara, when you lay dying of fever four nights ago, Sethi gave up his eternal soul in return for your life.

Stunned, she gazed at the heart, beating in its cold, bare cage. Sethi's heart. She longed to touch it, to hold it against her own. His secret, hidden sacrifice. He loved her more than any man ever could. She trailed her fingers against the bars.

"And now," she whispered, stricken, "I am dying again."

Horus tilted his head to look at the heart, his movement aloof, detached.

He knew the risk he took, making such a sacrifice. There is no certainty in the mortal realm, though it is unfortunate for him to have yielded so little from such a great loss. Those of us in the immortal realm are not beyond feeling pity for him. It is why I have joined you here, while you wait. You should know what this man gave up for you; he deserves at least this much. Come, your last breath draws near. It is time for you to enter the immortal realm. Your goddess, my consort, awaits.

The air split, as though sliced by a blade. The rent shimmered, pulling apart, opening, stretching until the space was the height and width of a large door. On the other side, in a place of glittering radiance, stood Baalat, just as Istara remembered her from her dream as a child. Baalat stepped through the impossible doorway and joined them in the cold, blue chamber, stars of light cascading down the length of her gown in an endless stream. Her lips curved into a gentle smile. She lifted her hand to Istara.

Daughter of my heart, you are welcome to join me in the immortal realm, where your loved ones await.

Drawn by the goddess's enigmatic presence, Istara moved out from behind the plinth and walked toward the flattened, sundered space. She leaned forward, hesitant, and peered into it. Strange creatures progressed past the doorway, men with eagle's wings and heads; a creature with the body of a lion, the head of an ox and the tail of a scorpion. There were others too, even stranger beings, diminishing in size with distance.

Her father stepped into view, whole and strong, he smiled and beckoned to her to join him. Anash came and sat at his feet. Istara cried out, tears springing into her eyes. She stepped closer. Her mother arrived, her eyes warm and full of joy, holding out her hands to her daughter. Longing to join her family, Istara moved closer.

At the doorway's threshold, a cutting sensation flowed through her. She felt the weight of unseen bonds falling away, liberating her from a prison she had never realized caged her. The connection to her mortal life diminished. The solidness of her previous existence dissipated, sliding into nothingness. She looked down; the edges of her body smeared, lengthening, stretching, drawn to the glittering light of the immortal realm.

A tug, sudden and sharp pulled on her, so strong her body slid back into its shape, quivering, unstable, its edges blurring. Something clung to her, refusing to be cut away. She searched. There, a tendril. She grasped onto it and followed it. Behind her.

The pull from the doorway increased, insistent. She heard Baalat murmuring, pleading. What was she saying? Istara couldn't make out the words. Horus's voice rose, angry, sharp. Were they arguing? Hurry. Turn around.

Straining against the doorway's drag, Istara turned with agonizing slowness. Blood pumped from Sethi's heart and slid, blue-black, down the plinth toward her. She reached out to touch it. Horus shouted. Baalat cried out, begging him to stop. Horus's hands pressed against Istara's shoulders, shoving her toward the doorway. Istara closed her eyes, straining against his weight, her fingertips sweeping downward. She touched the blood. Sethi. A thousand memories washed over her, memories they had shared, and ones yet to come, going on through eternity. Her bonds returned, clamping over her, locking her back into the prison of mortality. The doorway wavered, its pull ceased.

She fell to her knees. Baalat came to her. Istara lifted up her fingers, stained with Sethi's blood.

"Take my heart," she breathed. "I must go back."

Baalat's fingers touched her forehead.

Darkness.

❋   ❋   ❋

Baalat stepped around Istara's inert body, and ran her hands along the edges of the opening, avoiding the concerned looks of Istara's parents. She closed the portal and turned to face her consort just as he transformed into his true self: a man, entire, not the fantastical, hybrid creation of the imaginings of mortals.

He came after her, his grip on her shoulders hurting her. "Whatever you are doing," he said, harsh, "it stops now."

"You cannot stop this," Baalat said, meeting his gaze, steady. "None of us can."

His hold on her lessened. "What do you mean?"

She hesitated, uncertain how to begin. Comprehension flickered in his eyes. "The vision pool," he said, quiet. He let her go. "What have you kept from me?"

Moving to the cage with its imprisoned heart, she asked, "Have you never wondered what it must be like to live with uncertainty, to have limited time?" When he remained silent, she reached up, tracing the outline of his jaw, its contours as familiar to her as her own heartbeat. "Do you not wonder what it would be like to savor the sweetness of each passing, fleeting moment. To live."

He pushed her hand away. "I have not."

"We are relics," she continued, quiet. "Our era is long gone. Our existence is purposeless, meaningless. It is an eternity of nothing."

His jaw tightened, though a glimmer of agreement flickered in his eyes.

Trailing her fingers over the shifting outline of one of the golden tattoos on his chest—the image of a fractal—she continued, "I know you think of it. We all have."

"Perhaps I have," he said, dismissive, "but nothing can be done about it."

"You know that is not true."

He stared at her, taken aback. "The alternative is unthinkable."

"To me, it is not."

Taking her chin in his hand, he lifted her face up to his, his eyes dark. "To live is to die. I will not lose you. It would be unbearable to face immortality without you."

She sighed. "It seems I do not have a choice."

"I do," Horus answered, severe. "If Istara will not enter the portal, I will seal her in here until Sethi dies."

Uneasy, Baalat looked at Sethi's heart, bleeding still, beyond the barriers of reality. Horus followed her gaze. He cursed, causing the illusion of the walls to waver.

"Who is this mortal," he demanded, his hands clenching into fists, "that he is able to transcend our boundaries?"

"One chosen by a power greater than us," Baalat whispered.

Horus paused. "The Creator?"

Baalat lifted her shoulders. "Who can say? The Creator abandoned us when we warred against men. Perhaps he has returned." She looked at the cage, its slats slick with blood. "This much I know: Sethi's sacrifice gave her the strength to overcome the pull of the portal, to overcome *you*. I have sensed another controlling his path, a power outside of us, but for what purpose I do not know. As for myself, the vision pool showed me a prophecy: Since the beginning of time, Istara's destiny and mine have been bound together. She is meant to return, and it is I who must send her back." She turned back to Horus. "My love, I do not have a choice."

Horus stared at the beating heart. Baalat waited, letting him work it out. He turned to her, wary. "If you . . ."

Baalat looked away. "I have had eons to prepare myself for this."

He came to her, his breathing shallow. "When she dies, you will die."

She reached out to him. "We will still have time. Imagine the love we will make never knowing when I shall breathe my last."

Horus took her hand and ran his thumb over the back of her fingers. "I have loved you since before time existed, and will love you after it ends. It is our purpose to be together. You cannot break our bond."

She pressed his hand against her heart. "I must. It is my destiny. My love, let me go."

❋   ❋   ❋

The darkness diminished to a single point. Istara shuddered and opened her eyes. She sat up, disoriented. Illuminated by its blue flames, the stone chamber still surrounded her. Beside her, the opening to the immortal realm glimmered, faint, vaporous, her family gone. Baalat moved out from the shadows, Horus close behind her, his muscled arms crossed over his chest. Baalat's eyes caught hers.

Istara, you face a choice. To continue on to the immortal realm, or to return to the mortal one. But, before you decide, know the risk you will take.

If you decide to return, you will go back to a world fraught with pain and suffering. Without our presence, men have become fickle creatures, drawn to baubles and power, their hearts craven, changing upon a whim.

What you go back to today could change tomorrow, and you might find yourself regretting your choice to return, wishing you had remained here. So I ask you: Do you still wish to return to a place where you may be forced to endure a life you will not be able to escape, except through death?

Istara looked at Sethi's heart, fresh blood pumping out with each beat. Her heart clenched anew at his sacrifice. She moved to her knees. "My lady, I am willing to take the risk. My heart is yours to take. I beg you, let me go back to him."

You may only make such an offer while in the mortal realm, Baalat replied, *and only when it is done to save another. There is now only one way for you to return: a god must pay the cost.*

A finger of dread touched Istara. "And . . . what is the cost?"

Baalat's gaze flicked to Horus. They shared a look, then his diurnal gaze tilted onto Istara, hard, cold and unblinking. *Let that be my concern,* Baalat answered, soft. *Do you still wish to return?*

"Only if I am certain no harm will come to you if I do," Istara countered, feeling Horus's stare boring into her, unnerving her.

Baalat smiled, a quiet, secret thing. *No harm will come to me.*

Istara hesitated. Baalat waited, patient. Sethi's heart bled, calling to her, drawing her back to him, irresistible. "Then I accept," she breathed.

Her eyes gentle, Baalat brought her fingers to Istara's brow and stroked it, her touch soothing, reassuring. Tendrils of light ignited inside the goddess's body, darting and swirling, surging toward her hand, alive. They slipped free and wove outward, wrapping around Istara's head, snaking around her body, binding her tight, a cocoon of light.

Horus cried out, falling to his knees, no longer a falcon-headed being, but a man, perfect, beautiful, strong. He begged Baalat to cease even as she wrapped her arms around Istara and drew her into her embrace, shuddering, her light leaving her, her immortal power draining away, returning Istara to the world of men.

Too late, Istara understood what was happening. She cried out, begging Baalat to stop. The chamber dimmed and faded away. A rushing sound filled her ears. Then: Nothing. Darkness. And in the silence, the sound of a beating heart.

Istara returned, still pleading for Baalat to cease. Trapped inside a tight wrapping of blankets, she panicked, claustrophobia snapping at her. A pair of hands came to aid her. Strong and steady, they freed her, helped her to sit. A voice, low and reassuring, sought to soothe her. She opened her eyes. Painful white light blinded her. She cried out, retreating to the safety of darkness; the horrifying truth of what she had done closing in on her, shearing her in two, accusing, brutal. She shuddered, her mind splintering under the colossal weight of her debt. No. It was far too great a burden to bear. Riven by helpless and regret, she succumbed to her grief and wept.

❅ ❅ ❅

Sethi gaped, incredulous, at Istara alive and grieving before him, her anguish tangible. He touched her shoulder. She flinched and pulled away, defensive. He sat back on his haunches, wary, a tremor of fear sliding through him. How could she be alive? Ity had declared her dead, had noted the time of her death in his journal.

He waited, watchful and silent, trying to find an explanation for what he should not be seeing. Perhaps *he* had died. He felt for his pulse. It beat steady and strong. Confounded, he stared at her, trying to make sense of her sudden to return to existence. Perhaps Ity had been wrong. He had just begun to consider sending for the surgeon when she quieted. She lifted her head, opened her eyes, and looked right at him. He leaned toward her, slow, and waved his hand before her face. She did not respond. He blinked. She had returned blind. Cautious, he touched the back of her hand.

"Istara?"

She looked down, unseeing, at his fingers on her hand and hiccupped, soft. The innocent, ordinary sound of it reassuring. The tightness in his chest eased by a margin. Ity must have been mistaken.

"A terrible thing has happened, I have—" she fell silent, stricken.

"What has happened?" he coaxed, gentle. "Tell me."

She shook her head, her tears glimmering in the lamplight.

He looked down and inhaled, sharp. Her bandages were spotless. He pulled them away, dread circling him. Turning her hand over in his own, he ran his thumb over where she had been impaled, finding only healthy, unmarked skin.

"Your hand—" he breathed, stunned, disbelieving, "—there is not even a scar. You are whole again. How—?"

She raised her face to his, her dilated eyes unnerving him, and nodded at the bandages around her calves. He unwrapped them, cautious, apprehensive. The linens fell away. Istara touched her legs, searching for the puckered lines where the sewn flesh should have been. Her fingers stilled.

"She has renewed me, with her own living light."

Fresh tears slipped free. He tried again to touch her. This time, she succumbed. He kissed her brow, hushing her, fearful, uneasy, her words haunting him. An hour earlier, Ity had left to find his pallet. Alone, vanquished, Sethi had cradled Istara's broken body against his. She had died. And now she lived, whole again. *She has renewed me.* Hope kindled. Perhaps his sacrifice had been enough to save her. Not once, but twice.

❋ ❋ ❋

A cold, blue chamber. Sethi's heart, bleeding. An impossible portal. Her father, beckoning her to join him. Horus and Baalat, arguing. The light, burning her, blinding her.

Istara stirred. The crackle of burning fuel, the rich scent of frankincense. Sethi beside her, snoring, soft. She opened her eyes, cautious. The light did not hurt as much. She peered into the murk. Was that the outline of the table? And there, Sethi's chair?

Sethi turned onto his side. His hand went to her waist, pulling her to him, his grip strong, even in sleep. He settled her in his embrace. She let him. In his arms, she listened to his breathing, deep and even, and to the beating of his heart, steady and strong, somehow existing in two places at once: within him, and locked within a wooden cage, possessed by Horus. She pressed her palm against his chest, savoring the heavy thud of his heart, thinking of his sacrifice, made without her knowing. Without asking for anything in return.

Sethi's breathing changed, he stirred, waking. He touched her cheek, gentle, a caress. "Can you see me?"

Against his shoulder, Istara shook her head.

"Perhaps your sight will return in time," he murmured. "You have suffered much."

"I died," she said. "I should not be here at all."

Silence. She sensed he was waiting for her to continue, to explain. She couldn't, not yet. Pushing herself away from him, she sat up. The quiet stretched, thick, uncertain.

He cleared his throat. "It is going to be difficult to explain how you are alive and whole again. Ity declared you dead."

"Clearly, he was mistaken," she said, wry. When he said nothing, she continued, "In my eleventh year, my surrogate mother, the Queen of Hatti, fell into a deep sleep. Her heartbeats and breaths came so far apart, it seemed certain she was dead, but she was not. She returned, as I have. Tell him that."

Sethi made a sound of approval. "I will. However, your vanished injuries will be less easy to explain. Give me your hand. Not that one. The other one."

He wrapped the linens back around it, pulling them tight. A soft hiss, as he drew his dagger from its sheath. A quiet grunt. He took her hand again, and the warmth of his blood spread onto the linens. He moved to her legs and bound them with neat, precise movements.

"Will you tell me what happened while you were gone?" he asked, quiet, as he cleaned his dagger and slid it back into its sheath.

She drew her knees up to her chest. He deserved to know, after all he had done for her. "There was a chamber," she began, hesitant, "lit by blue flames. A man with a falcon's head met me—"

"Horus." Sethi breathed the name, reverent.

"Yes. An intimidating god," she remarked, thinking of Horus's powerful bearing, his baleful gaze. When Sethi remained silent, she continued, "A doorway opened in the air, an impossible thing, leading to another realm. Lady Baalat stepped through and invited me to join her there. Within were strange creatures, some I could recognize, parts of at least, the others . . . no, I don't know what they were."

He touched her hand. "And then?"

"I saw my father," she whispered, her heart clenching at the memory, "whole and strong. He beckoned to me. I longed to go to him. As I drew nearer to the door, I felt as though invisible bonds were coming free, releasing me from my body. It was a wonderful feeling. I became blurry, luminous, I was—"

"A doorway?" Sethi interrupted, perplexed. "Where was the Hall of Truth, the scales for weighing the feather against the heart?"

Istara shrugged. "Perhaps it is different for Egyptians. Although it was not what I expected either."

"But you did not pass through the doorway?"

"No."

A heartbeat of quiet. "Why not?" he asked, soft.

"Your heart bled," she said, blunt. "It called to me. It brought me back."

He said nothing.

"Why did you do it?" she demanded, harsh, suddenly angry and resentful. "Why would you do such a thing?"

Silence. Then, the rasp of his hand moving against his unshaven scalp. "I could not bear to lose you," he finally said, low. "It is something I am unable to explain—but there it is, it is what I have done. I regret nothing." His hand closed over hers. "I can no longer pretend I do not have deep feelings for you, not after this, when you know all. But you must understand we can never be. You are forbidden to me."

"You gave up your heart so I could belong to another man?" she asked, incredulous.

He scoffed, bitter. "When you say it like that—" he fell silent for a beat. "No. I gave up my heart for you, and only for you. You were dying. I needed you to live."

She pulled her hand out from under his. "War might have thrown us together, and I will not deny our attraction, but we know almost nothing of each other. Anyone looking from without would think your act insane."

He laughed, hollow. "Perhaps I am."

She sensed his hesitation. There was more. She held herself still, waiting.

"I have been dreaming of you," he continued, wary. "The same dream for thirteen years. All this time I have been waiting for you, searching for you. And now I have found you—"

She closed her eyes, the crushing weight of his confession, and their complex, entwined destinies oppressive, suffocating her. "What . . . kind of dream?"

He took her hand again and kissed her palm, slow. She shivered.

"A vision, of a terrible battle, of fire, and you in the middle of it, in a ruined gown, wearing jewels, searching for me. To close the distance between us I must fight, hard, more than I have ever done, and just as I am about to reach you—" He kissed her palm again. "At least now, I know how I will die."

She shivered again, feeling the sudden burden of eternity pressing down on her. Her skin prickled, prescience enveloping her as she sensed distant destinies—glimpsing impossible cities, flying barques, wars, devastation, retreat, silence, renewal—the goddess's memories stirring within her. The significance of it incomprehensible, enormous, terrifying—

"You gave me your food once," she said, desperate to divert herself from her frightening thoughts. "I was starving. You gave me all of your rations."

"I doubt that," he murmured. "You were a princess in Kadesh. How could I ever—"

He fell silent. She could almost hear his thoughts organizing, the pieces falling together. "The sanctuary. *You* were that waif?"

She smiled, despite herself. "I was."

"I had my first dream that night." He shuddered. "But you were only a child. What madness is this?"

Istara reached out to still his hand, rubbing against his scalp again, agitated. "You are not alone in this. I had a vision too, of the night I spent sewing you back together after the battle. I now realize I spent most of my life learning to be a surgeon just so I could tend your injuries. A promise I made to Baalat, to save someone I loved."

She could feel him staring at her. "Who?" he asked.

"My surrogate mother, Tanu-Hepa, when she fell into the deep sleep," Istara admitted, quiet. "Baalat came to me in a dream and offered to save the queen if I learned to be a healer. I was desperate, so I agreed. Tanu-Hepa lived."

"So Baalat planned this—" he paused. Unease seeped from him. "How did you get back?" he asked, suspicious.

"Baalat returned me," Istara replied, her throat tightening as a fresh wave of guilt slammed into her "She gave up her immortal light. All of it."

Sethi remained silent, brooding. "Horus tried to stop her," Istara blundered on, speaking without thinking, "I can sense her within me, her memories, her fears. When I die, she will die."

Sethi cried out, anguished, and lunged to his feet. He stumbled to the table. Items scattered, rolling away, thudding onto the rug.

The sound of wine pouring, him drinking, noisy, gulping. He came back and put a cup in her hands. She sipped, grateful.

"I know our destinies are decided by the gods," he said, ragged, "but to be aware of them moving us toward a place of their choosing, it is oppressive." He shuddered. "I would do anything to feel as though my choices are my own again."

She looked up at him, though she could see nothing but shadows against the light. "For women," she said, unable to keep the reproach from her voice, "most of our choices are never our own."

"And that is a wrong I have long believed should be remedied," he said, terse. He took the empty cup from her and set it aside. "I came from nothing. No blood, no family, no wealth. I made my way as a street fighter, believing my abilities, determination, and decisions were my own. But now I wonder if my rise to power, my successes, even my sacrifice to save you—were they my choices at all? What if I am merely following a fixed path, already decided?"

"They *were* your choices," Istara insisted, troubled by the sudden uncertainty in his voice. "The gods may guide our way, but we choose our path. I could have decided not to learn the art of healing, could have refused to warn Ramesses. I chose those paths. Because I chose to return to you, Baalat will die. Despite knowing the cost, she still offered me the choice."

"I am just a soldier," Sethi finally said after a long, heavy silence, "a man of the present. I only know this—" he pulled her against him, embracing her, "—you are here, alive, the woman of my dreams." He let her go, abrupt. "A woman I can never have."

She thought she understood. "Because of Urhi-Teshub?"

He scoffed. "I would it was only that. No," he continued, his voice dark, "Ramesses intends to take you for himself."

"He cannot," she protested, rising to her feet, panicking, fear lancing into her, sharp, "Even if I have run away from him, I am still Urhi-Teshub's wife. Unless . . . has he—?" She couldn't finish the question. Perhaps Nefertari had killed him, after all.

"Your husband has not fallen," Sethi said, terse. "He has agreed to ensure Egypt's safe retreat, with your life cast as the bargaining chip. But even if he holds to his end, you will not be returned to him. Ramesses intends to claim you as compensation for Muwatallis's crimes. You will be the next Queen of Egypt, Ramesses's third wife. I will only be able to see you from a distance, if at all."

She staggered. Sethi caught her and pulled her back down beside him. She closed her eyes, Baalat's voice filling her mind. *So I ask you— do you still wish to return, risking such uncertainty? Where you might be forced to endure a life you will not be able to escape, except through death?* Baalat knew. Everything. Why did she let her return? Why would she give up her immortality if Istara's life was to be spent as Ramesses's unwilling queen? None of it made sense. Sethi stroked her hair, gentle.

"Istara?"

She lay on her back and stared into nothingness. A piece, moved once more. When would it end?

"How long until we arrive?" she asked, tight.

He lay down on his side, facing her. She could just make out his eyes, dark black with kohl.

"Twenty-five days," he answered, quiet.

"Then grant me those days," she whispered, angry, resentful, reckless. "Do not let me have returned for nothing."

He moved over her and touched his brow to hers, the caress of a lover. "I cannot know you. The risk is too great."

She reached up and touched his jaw. "Then love me without knowing me. Let us at least have this. Sethi—"

He didn't let her finish. His mouth covered hers, silencing her, his fingers tangled in her hair, holding her head, just as she had dreamed he would. She clung to him. He whispered her name, and she sighed. It was worth it, all of it. In his arms, she was complete.

PART IV

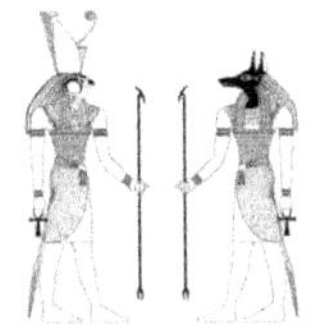

PI-RAMESSES

Summer 1274 BCE

ONE

Summer. Reign of Ramesses II, Year 6

Istara woke, savoring the luxury of a bed after weeks spent sleeping on a pallet. She rubbed her palm against the crisp linen sheets, watching the painted hieroglyphs along the cornice waver, coming to life in the flickering light of the lamp's flame. From the river delta, the cry of a black-crowned heron pierced the deep quiet of the night. She listened to it, grateful. At least one familiar thing from her past remained in this strange, exotic, white and gold world.

Beside her, Sethi shifted in his sleep. She turned and gazed at his battle-hardened features, long memorized and locked within her heart during their stolen nights together over the last month. He stirred, and woke. His eyes met hers, dark, enigmatic. Despite the heat, she shivered.

He pulled her to him, his arms surrounding her, possessive, his kiss desperate, aching. She shared his anguish. This was their last night. Tomorrow, Ramesses would take her away from him, forever.

Sethi's kiss deepened, his passion burning hotter than the blistering desert heat of The Horus Way, ravishing her until her body throbbed with need. He grasped her buttocks, dragging her onto him, pressing her groin against his. She caught her breath. He was rock hard. Despite the heat, her nipples hardened. He caught her breast in his hand, his lips moving against her taut nipple through the thin material of her gown, tracing the outline of her breast's peak, slow, tantalizing. She moaned as rivers of pleasure washed over her, the scent of her sex rising up, betraying her need. During the long, chaste nights of the march, this was what she had longed for. To be alone and naked with him. To be taken by him, to feel him inside of her. To be his.

His mouth went to her neck, his teeth dragging against its hollow, hungry; his hands sliding up her back, tangling in her hair. Groaning, she moved against him, aroused by his member pressing against her. Her fingers went to his kilt, urgent, searching for its ties, tugging them apart. Pushing aside the material, she pulled on his loincloth, longing to touch him, to taste him. His member sprang free, straining, eager. He groaned. Tightening his hold on her, he rolled over, positioning himself on top of her, his member brushing against her.

She clung to him, willing him to go on, to finish what they had never before dared to start. He reached down, his hand catching at her gown, shoving it up to her waist. He sat up, kneeling between her legs, naked, poised to take her, the silver scars slicing across his muscled torso catching in the lamplight. His eyes raked over her, pausing on her secret place; slick, ready, waiting. With a quiet groan, he pulled her up to him, his mouth hovering over hers as he held her face in his hands, his eyes on hers, his filled with longing, desire, love. She whispered his name and he relented, kissing her, crushing her against him, his grip fierce. Caught in his hold, her crotch slid along the length of his member, sending a spasm of pleasure arcing through her. His member came to rest at her threshold; a subtle kiss, filled with promise. She held still. Waiting. Hoping. Aching. He cried out, anguished, and released her.

"We cannot," he panted, ragged, his voice betraying him, filled with yearning. "I must leave." He lowered her onto the bed, and reached for his belt, fastening it over his rumpled kilt, his movements jagged, rough.

"Please." She caught his forearm, her body crying out for him. "Stay."

His hands clenched into fists, his muscles flexing under her fingers. He stood, his eyes black, still burning with desire. She tightened her hold, a silent plea. He cut her a look, filled with warning, and eased back, her fingers slipping away. At the door, he paused, his gaze lingering on her, his hand tightening on the handle; his struggle to stay away from her, visceral.

"There is only so much a man can withstand," he said, low. "I know what more there can be—" his chest rose and fell, agitated, watching as she knelt on the bed, her gown slipping down, exposing her shoulder, the curve of her breast, "—the things I want to do with you, the pleasure I long to give you." His eyes hardened, his jaw clenched. "But I am your protector, and if it means I must protect you from myself, then by Horus, I will do so."

He hesitated. Istara waited, her heart crying out to him, pleading, willing him to return. He yanked on the door's handle and strode out into the torchlit corridor. The door slammed behind him, heavy, final. Emptiness surrounded her. Her heart pounded, erratic. She stared at the closed door. Come back. Please.

Her fingers brushed against his cushion. She pressed it against her face, surrounding herself with the lingering notes of his scent, rich tones of myrrh and cinnamon. Sethi. Clutching his cushion to her chest, she stared at the wavering flame of the lamp, numb. Never again would he lay beside her, cradling her body against his. Never again would he caress her face, his secret, private tenderness disguised by his brutality, strength, and power. Never again would she feel the touch of his lips against hers, his love for her searing into her soul, binding her to him beyond the boundaries of their lives. It couldn't be over. He knew her secrets. He knew Urhi-Teshub had broken her heart, had never known her, had almost killed her.

She huddled over the cushion, bereft. Once more, she was alone, a piece on a game board, waiting to be moved. She crept to the door and sank to her knees. Pressing her palm against the thick wood, she whispered a prayer, willing him to come back to her. A taut silence seeped from the corridor. She caught her breath. He was right there. She called his name, tentative, hopeful.

She heard him shift his weight. Silence fell in its wake, thick with resistance. She blinked, tears filling her eyes. He would not come back. It was over. She whispered his name, a farewell, before her grief overcame her, and she succumbed once more to the anguish of a broken heart.

✳ ✳ ✳

Sethi heard her call his name. He pressed his palm against the door, willing himself to stay away. Her weeping came to him now, soft and low, her suffering tangible.

He sank to his knees and leaned his forehead against the door, his chest constricting as he thought of Ramesses taking her, a bauble he would parade in front of Hatti's diplomats, then set aside in one of his harems when he moved on to his next interest. And on that day, when he condemned her to her sequestration, Sethi knew he would never see Istara again. He choked; the thought was unbearable.

A tear slid down his cheek. He touched it and stared at the glistening drop. Never in his life had he wept; not when he found his mother, lying in a pool of blood; not even when he believed Istara was dead, his shock numbing him beyond the walls of grief. More slipped free, silent. He let them fall.

It was a long while before Istara quieted. Her breathing slowed, then softened into the cadence of sleep. He closed his eyes and followed her. In the realm of dreams, he found her waiting for him in his tent, a smile on her lips. She came to him, her lips touching his. He took her to his pallet, her naked body soft and warm against his as he made love to her—she cried out, looking over his shoulder, her eyes wide and frightened. He turned. Ramesses stood over them, holding his *khopesh* high. Istara vanished. Ramesses's eyes glittered. The blade fell.

Sethi came awake with a start. Gray light filtered between the pillars of the corridor. He pushed away from Istara's door and climbed the villa's outer stairs to the roof. He faced the east and waited. Pink and orange light spread away from the horizon as Re-Atum's barque approached. Sethi watched, patient, as the golden disk made its stately ascent, grateful he had woken in time to relish its triumphant return from the Under Realm.

Movement at Istara's door drew his attention away from the eastern sky. Her door eased open, cautious. She looked down, then slipped back into her room. The door closed, slow, quiet, Istara's disappointment palpable. He closed his eyes, shutting out the warm light of a new day, reliving the memory of her stricken look as he left her. It seemed his prophetic dream of dying on a battlefield fighting his way to her was wrong after all.

Ramesses was going to kill him, and soon.

It was good to be back. Ramesses sank onto a divan, naked. Atet, Imi, and Kiya, his companions for the night, slid down beside him, sinuous, their skin gleaming with rose oil. It had been a long night, but he wasn't finished yet. He had saved the best for last.

He closed his eyes. Kiya knelt between his thighs and took him in her mouth. He shifted his hips, letting her take him deeper. As she pleasured him, he thought of Istara, imagining her under him. Tonight, he would take her, again and again. His wife, his queen. His member hardened. Kiya lifted her mouth away, and Imi leaned over, her tongue sliding over his shaft, teasing him. He groaned as Atet, his favorite, took her turn, pulling him deep into her throat, her lips tight around him. Hot, he thrust into her. He heard her gagging. He hated that sound. He pulled out.

"Get on your knees," he commanded. "Now."

Triumphant, Atet knelt on the rug, arching her hips to him. Kiya, and Imi surrounded her, drizzling almond oil over her buttocks, letting it run down her cleft. They stroked her, teasing her, circling her anus, sliding their fingers into her, opening her for him. Atet gyrated, panting, hot with need. Idle, Ramesses stroked himself, enjoying the show. She loved to be taken there. A rare flower.

He entered her, slow. He dared not damage her; her tight offering gave him too far much pleasure. She groaned, bucking under him, impatient to have all of him. Kiya slid behind him. He could feel her breasts pressing against his back, slippery with oil. Her fingers slipped up his thigh, and stroked his testicles, tugging on them. He moaned. He loved that. Atet was so tight, so insatiable, he wanted—

He lurched, shuddering, his member throbbed, sending waves of pleasure cascading through him. Around his member, Atet writhed, as Imi licked her, bringing Atet, crying out to her release.

He waited for her to return. She pushed against him, hungry for more. He laughed and slapped her ample buttock. It was time for them to go. She pulled away from him and rolled over, coy.

He pinched her nipple, amused. "I could almost fall in love with you, you filthy creature."

She squealed, delighted. Imi brought him wine, and he watched as they dressed, helping each other with the ties of their gowns, flirting with him, still. They left, giggling, thrilled, their excited chatter drifting back to him from the corridor. A whole night with him. They were lucky; he was not known to keep his women for more than a few hours. But it had been a long, dry campaign, and he had not had a woman for more than sixty days. He leaned back on the divan, satisfied. Tonight, he would be able to be gentle with Istara. His companions had done their work well; his pent-up lust had been thoroughly slaked.

A quiet knock at the door. Henufkhet entered, his head bowed. "Your Majesty, if it pleases you, Lord Paser is waiting to see you."

Ramesses rolled his eyes. His vizier was the last person he wanted to see. Hauling himself to his feet, he went to the basin and washed his member. "It does not please me," he said, picking up a linen towel and drying himself. He glanced at Henufkhet's reflection in the bronze mirror. "Can it not wait?"

"He said it concerns Princess Istara."

A flicker of apprehension ignited. He suppressed it. "Send him in."

Setting aside the towel, he took up a fresh kilt as Paser entered, bowing, his fist against his chest. Tying his kilt around his hips, Ramesses eyed his vizier. Paser looked tired, drawn, tense.

"Whatever it is," Ramesses said, terse, "come straight to it."

"Your Majesty," Paser said, inclining his head, "last night, soon after Pre arrived, Lord Ahmen came to me with grave news. Pre suffered an ambush in the Wood of Amka. Men from Kadesh, disguised as barbarians attacked the vanguard at dusk. Istara was taken by one of the barbarians. Sethi was able to rescue her, but he was too late. She later died from her injuries."

Stunned, Ramesses sank onto a divan. "Istara is gone? It is my fault. I brought this onto—"

Paser cleared his throat. Ramesses looked up.

"She," Paser made the sign against evil, discreet, "—may Horus forgive me—Istara came back from the dead."

Ramesses stared at Paser. Had his vizier lost his mind? "I cannot believe someone like you could even say such a thing," he scoffed, disbelieving. "All know none come back from the dead. It is against *Ma'at.*"

Paser had the decency to look ashamed. "I also doubted Ahmen's account," he admitted. "I sent for the surgeon who attended her: Ity, Pre's Chief Surgeon, a renowned healer from Iunu. He showed me the record, the time of her death, and his notes. Her heart stopped for the full count of seventy. He swears upon the light of Re-Atum she was dead when he departed."

"He can swear all he likes," Ramesses said, pouring himself a cup of wine. "If she is alive, he made an error. You are jumping at shadows."

"Am I?" Paser asked, sharp. "The day after he declared her dead, she refused his care, even though one of her injuries was serious." Ramesses sipped his wine, waiting as Paser hesitated. "He claims she avoided him by staying each night in the command tent with Sethi, who would not let him in."

"And how much gold did our good surgeon ask of you for this slanderous story?"

"None," Paser answered, terse, "and I offered him nothing in return."

Ramesses finished his wine, resentful. It had been such a good night. He stood up. "I will not be diverted by camp gossip. Nothing has changed. I will make Istara my wife tonight as planned."

"My lord, forgive me," Paser stepped closer, paling. "You cannot. It is too dangerous. The rumor she has returned from the dead has already circulated throughout Pre, soon the whole city will know. There were others present when the surgeon told Ahmen and Meresamun—"

"Meresamun?" Ramesses interrupted, abrupt.

"Ah," Paser blinked, caught off balance by the sudden change of direction. "Yes. She was with Pre. It seems she was trying to make her way back to her family in Babylon."

"To think after all the places we searched," Ramesses mused as he picked up a dried fig from the fruit platter, "and after all the couriers I sent," he scoffed, biting into the fig, "Ahmen finds her in the mud of Pre."

Paser frowned and said nothing.

"What now?" Ramesses demanded, annoyed.

"It concerns Sethi," Paser lowered his voice, though they were alone. "Ity only mentioned it since he recognized Meresamun from the message you sent to Iunu with her description. A whore told him of a blue-eyed woman called Meresamun who shared their fire for one night soon after the battle. She was taken away by Pre's commander. She never came back."

Ramesses pressed the heels of his palms against his eyes, tired of Paser. "It was someone else. Meresamun would never be among whores."

"My lord, the woman described her precisely," Paser persisted, dogged. "An opportunity to service the Commander of Pre is not a memory a whore soon forgets."

Ramesses turned on Paser, irritable. "Why do you carry these tales to me? Why should I care?"

"Sethi knew you were looking for a woman called Meresamun," Paser answered, cautious, "and yet, he took her for himself. Then, instead of accommodating Princess Istara in a tent of her own, he kept her with him in his command tent, alone. He has a devoted military at his fingertips and would make a dangerous enemy should he decide to challenge you. By taking these women, he has already challenged you. You must remove him before it is too late."

"Do not presume to tell me what I must do," Ramesses snapped. "I will do as I see fit."

His back rigid, Paser bowed his head.

"Send for Ahmen. I will see him in the Audience Chamber once the petitions are finished. From him, I will have the truth." Ramesses paused. He had thought of what he was about to do often enough during the long march home, though now it was time, a deep spasm of guilt slammed into him. Stifling it, he pressed on, ruthless. "By my command, Nefertari is to quit her residence in the palace and move to the royal harem in Waset. Order the first queen's apartment to be made ready for Egypt's new queen. Change everything. I want no trace of Nefertari left behind."

Paser blanched. "Your Majesty," he sank to his knee, "I beg you, Nefertari is your first queen. She is sacred. It would upset the order of things. Think of the misfortune you could bring upon Egypt if Istara *has* returned from the dead, your—"

"Silence!" Ramesses shouted, glaring at Paser. "Istara will be my first queen. Your superstitious nonsense has no place in my presence. Nefertari is disgraced and no longer fit to sit by my side. If you cannot obey my command, then you may be relieved of your position as vizier."

Paser's eyes glittered, dark. He was furious, Ramesses could tell, but Paser had the sense to bow and back away.

✳   ✳   ✳

Alone on her terrace, Nefertari watched Re-Atum's barque rise. No one attended her. She had returned to an empty apartment, her ladies gone. Servants still cleaned and brought her food, but she had to prepare the platters herself. All those times she had yearned for privacy—she scoffed, rueful.

She lifted her golden cup to the east, and took a sip of the mead offering, honoring Re-Atum's return. As she intoned the prayer of thanks for the god's gift of a new day, her gaze strayed to her husband's deserted terrace. She had heard him last night, as she lay awake in her bed, listening, her heart aching, as he fornicated with his women, their cries breaching the quiet of the night.

No longer did she resent his women, or him. In her pride, she had tried to have it all. He was the Pharaoh of Egypt. No queen had ever commanded a pharaoh's fidelity. Who had she been to believe herself any different? It could have been her there with him, but instead of accepting her fate, she had fought it and driven him away.

She pushed her aside platter, untouched, thoughts of the march home returning to torment her. Before they left Kadesh, Ramesses had ordered her chariot to be driven further back in the vanguard, eliminating any chance of him seeing her. And every night, he had timed his arrival to the enclosure to occur after she was within her tent. He had suffocated her, for thirty days, a prisoner to his hate. Her appetite had fled, and never returned.

Without eating, the rigors of the march had taken their toll. Her weight dropped, leaving her bony and emaciated. Cut off from her husband, she felt as though she was nothing, no one. At least she still had her children, had even been allowed to see them, though her eldest, Khepeshef, had been cold and distant. She had been thorough in her work if Egypt's heir had turned against her as well.

A knock at her door. No one was announced, there was no one to do so. She rose, hopeful, hastening to straighten the folds of her gown against her thin frame. Please, let it be Ramesses sending for her. Please, just let her have one chance to prove to him how much she had changed.

Paser came onto the terrace. He did not bow, nor would he meet her eyes. He gripped the hilts of his daggers, his knuckles white. She had never seen Egypt's vizier so undone. He glanced at the pharaoh's terrace, his jaw clenched. A look of despair sliced across his face. She quailed. Don't say it. Please don't say it. Paser . . .

"Your Highness," he said, low. "The end has come. May Horus forgive me, you are to leave the palace this afternoon for your new residence in Waset's royal harem."

Nefertari staggered, her world shattering, the pieces of her life plummeting away. Numb, she sank onto the divan. Paser knelt before her. Against all protocol, his hands took hers. She clung to him.

He bent his head over their clasped hands. "I am sorry. I am so sorry. It is unbearable to carry this news to you. My lady—"

She choked. "There is more?"

Paser nodded, anguished. "I would not have you hear of it in the harem, with no friends around you. Ramesses intends to make Princess Istara his first queen. Tonight."

Nefertari's heart shattered. She cried out, uncaring of who heard, or saw. Startled, Paser moved away, distancing himself from her. Vanquished, she slid from the divan. Nothing mattered anymore. She was ruined. There was nothing left for her but loneliness and regret.

❋　❋　❋

From the back of the crowded, pillared hall, Ahmen heard his name called out by the Master of the Audience Chamber. Men and women moved aside, making space for him as he worked his way to the pharaoh's throne. His heart pounded. Soon he would know the truth, why he had been sent away, and what his fate was going to be. He reached the base of the royal platform and sank to his knee.

"Rise, Lord Ahmen-om-onet," the Master of the Audience Chamber intoned, "Pharaoh Ramesses welcomes your return to Pi-Ramesses."

Ahmen moved to his feet, catching Ramesses's look, the discreet nod of approval. Hope ignited. Perhaps it had been a test, one he had passed. Gesturing to the Master of the Audience Chamber, Ramesses murmured to him. The Master stepped forward and clapped his hands three times. Quiet fell.

"His Majesty wishes a private audience with Lord Ahmen-om-onet."

The hall erupted into activity, its pillars echoing with chatter as it emptied of courtiers, attendants, petitioners, officials, and guardsmen. The doors closed. A dull boom echoed through the vast, empty space. Silence fell. Ramesses rose from his gilded throne, his kilt rustling as he descended the steps.

"It is good to see you," he said, taking hold of Ahmen's shoulder. "By all the gods, when I heard the news you found Meresamun, all I could think was: What if I had not sent you to Pre?"

Ahmen felt his confidence soar. Ramesses was not angry with him. "We were bound together this morning," he said, recalling how beautiful Meresamun had looked, her hand clasped in his, "at the Temple of Isis, just as Re-Atum's barque rose."

"May you have many years of happiness together," Ramesses smiled, thin. He moved to a pillar and leaned against it, crossing his arms over his chest. "And, why did she leave?"

"Guilt," Ahmen answered, fighting the upwelling of shame he endured every time he thought of what his actions had put her through. "The need to atone."

"So," Ramesses looked down at the flail in his hand, toying with it, "a slave has shamed us."

Ahmen stiffened at the veiled insult. "She suffered much."

"Perhaps not that much." Ramesses looked at him, oblique.

"What are you suggesting?" Ahmen asked, low.

Ramesses pushed away from the pillar and paced before the steps of the royal platform. "How did she leave Waset without being found?" he asked instead.

Ahmen blinked, sensing a trap being laid. Why hadn't Ramesses answered his question? "A fishing boat," he replied, cautious.

Ramesses stopped pacing. "So that is how she slipped through our fingers." He scoffed. "A fishing boat, of all things."

He returned to his throne and stood in front of it, deep in thought, tapping his flail against his thigh. Ahmen waited, uneasy. He knew Ramesses well enough to know what he was doing; he was playing cat and mouse. Ahmen was the mouse. He fought for calm. Soon Ramesses would show his claws. Perhaps he was going to take Meresamun from him, after all.

Ramesses seated himself on his throne. "Lord Ahmen-om-onet," he said, formal, "you will tell me what you know of the relationship between Commander Sethi and Princess Istara."

Ahmen stared at Ramesses, astounded. He had sent Ahmen to Pre, to spy? All his suffering, his humiliation, all of it, to commit a dishonorable act? He bridled, angry, and looked away, refusing to answer.

Ramesses lowered his voice. "I have heard dark rumors. He is my commander. I would know the truth from someone I trust before I decide what to do with him. Let me ask you this way: Has Sethi made Istara his woman?"

Ahmen folded his arms over his chest. "How would I know? I did not share his pallet."

"I have heard she slept in his command tent, that they made no secret of it."

It was true. Ahmen had often seen them emerge together in the morning, smiling, affectionate. But to betray Sethi, a friend, just to satisfy Ramesses's morbid curiosity over the sleeping habits of the Prince of Hatti's wife? It was a small, petty thing. Not worth Ahmen's sudden, brutal demotion. He would not give Ramesses anything. He shook his head, terse.

"I had other things to occupy me."

"Like keeping an eye on Meresamun?"

The question was soft, menacing. He caught Ramesses watching him, his eyes narrow. "Meaning?" Ahmen demanded, his voice hardening.

"Perhaps you should ask her."

"I am asking you."

"Ah, it seems Meresamun is a secret keeper, just like her new husband."

Ahmen's hands clenched. Ramesses was only a few steps away. After everything he had suffered for Ramesses, this was how Ahmen would be repaid, with slurs against his wife? Ramesses looked at him, dark.

"Until you arrived, it seems Sethi's pallet was not quite as cold as it should have been."

Ahmen roared, furious, and lunged up the steps. Springing from his throne, Ramesses caught Ahmen's wrists, twisting his arms behind his back. He leaned close and whispered, "Sethi bought and fucked Meresamun, over and over. It is him you should hate, not me. We are on the same side."

Ahmen jerked free, panting, searching his memories from the last thirty days. Sethi had been friendly to him, had spent several evenings sitting by the fire with him, drinking wine and talking of mundane things. He had never seen the commander look at Meresamun once. His gut tightened as he realized not only had Sethi not looked at Meresamun, the commander had gone out of his way to avoid her, leaving whenever she arrived, neither of them ever looking the other in the eye.

Desperate, he raked over his memories, seeking for anything that would prove Ramesses wrong. Meresamun had told Ahmen of the night of the battle, of the harrowing experience she had endured. But she had been with Amun, should have marched back with Amun, yet she ended up in Pre as Istara's companion. His spine tingled. He hadn't asked why, and she hadn't offered an explanation. Another fragment unfolded. He had learned after he had found her, it had been arranged for her to ride with Naram, far too high an honor for a mere lady's companion. He hadn't dwelled on it, though it had troubled him, why Sethi would grant her such a privilege.

No longer blinded by his happiness at having found her, he reconsidered all the evidence he had cast aside over the last month, each singular piece innocuous enough, but connected together, damning, ugly. The truth reared up, slow; horrifying, brutal, monstrous. His wife had been Sethi's concubine. Rage juddered through him. Everyone would have known, everyone but him. And to hear it from Ramesses. It was unbearable.

"We were never on the same side," he spat, backing away, shaking. Everyone had betrayed him. Meresamun, Sethi, Ramesses—even Istara. Blind with fury and riven with humiliation, he stumbled away, lurching down the stairs to the doors. Halfway across the hall, he stopped. He turned and glared at Ramesses, standing rigid, before his throne.

"It is true. All of it. Kill him, before I do."

⁂ ⁂ ⁂

The door closed behind Ahmen. Ramesses stared at it, trembling with rage. He had held his anger in, waiting to be certain, hoping Paser's information had been wrong. Now there was no doubt. From the heartbeat he had asked the question, he knew Ahmen knew the truth. For the first time in his life, Ramesses was the last to know. Humiliated, furious, he ground his teeth. How dare Sethi keep Istara in his tent for all those nights. He knew Ramesses intended her for his queen. Did he think Ramesses was a fool? Did he believe his power as Egypt's commander would protect him?

An image, unwanted, flashed, vivid into Ramesses's mind. During their many visits to the courtesan houses, he had seen Sethi mounting women often enough. It was a small step to imagine Istara beneath his commander, writhing in ecstasy, instead of one of the courtesans.

A sharp snap. Ramesses looked down. Within his hand, the royal flail sagged within its bindings of gold, broken in two. He cast it onto the throne's seat. It was only a symbol. A new one could be made. He strode away, seeing nothing. He would tear his commander to pieces. Ramesses was Pharaoh. He was Egypt. Sethi was no one. Nothing.

THREE

A pounding at the courtyard door. From her secluded bench amongst the palms, Istara rose, fearful. Perhaps it was the pharaoh, sending for her already. A shout from outside, imperious, impatient. The blood draining from their faces, Sethi's guards hastened to open the door. A pair of palace guards pushed in, announcing they were escorting the pharaoh's courier, who carried a message for the commander. A servant bolted away to fetch Sethi, while another hurried to escort the small party into Sethi's elegant reception room.

Keeping to the shadows at the edge of the courtyard, Istara slipped to the open doorway. Sethi approached. He caught her eye and shook his head, tight, his expression filled with warning.

Within, the men spoke, low. She couldn't make out the words. She waited, anxious. Were they taking her now? Was it over already, without even a chance to say goodbye? She looked around frantic, what if she hid? If she ran away? They couldn't take her if they couldn't find her. Footsteps. The soldiers and courier were coming. She shrank back against the wall, holding her breath, hoping the shadows would hide her. They strode past, murmuring to themselves. The door to the courtyard opened and closed again. The lock slid back into place. Calm descended, tenuous. She went to the doorway. Sethi stood beside a table, his jaw clenched, staring at a missive in his hand. Apprehensive, she took a step closer.

He looked up. The papyrus crumpled in his fist. "Ramesses knows the truth," he said. "This afternoon I must face him to the death in the palace training ground. You are to attend as well."

Irrational, desperate hope flared in her heart. "You have the chance to defeat him?"

"The pharaoh is a god," he said. "You know he cannot be killed."

"No. Horus is a god," she answered, taut. "Ramesses is a man, pretending to be a god. You could kill him if you wanted to."

"But I will not."

She stepped over the threshold, closing the space between them. "Do you not love me? Or want to be with me?"

He looked pained. "You were educated to be a queen. I do not believe you cannot see what would happen to Egypt if I did such a thing."

"I do not see," she said, bitter. "Explain it to me, so I understand. You are its commander, after all."

He tossed the ruined papyrus onto the table. "Very well," he muttered. "Killing him would bring chaos into Egypt. Within the day I would be executed and Ramesses's eldest son, an untried youth of fourteen would be forced to take the throne, with Paser ruling as regent in his stead. However, without a commander to support him, the vizier would not be strong enough to manage the nobles who would intrigue and maneuver for power, seeking to take Nefertari as their wife, whose lineage is the strongest link to the pharaohs of the past. Through her, her new husband could usurp the throne. Soon, Ramesses's sons would fall to one misfortune after another, until nothing remained of his legacy.

"The annihilation of an entire bloodline has happened before, after Akhenaten died, just fifty years ago. Egypt nearly fell apart. It is also the reason why Hatti became our bitterest enemy. Suppiluliuma's son was murdered when he came to Egypt to marry the only remaining daughter of Akhenaten, who followed him in death soon after, said to have been poisoned. No. I will not be the author of such instability, of such bloodshed."

Istara swallowed, chastened by the severity of his reply. "Then what of me? Am I to sit and watch, while the man I love is murdered by the one who intends to take me, unwilling, to his bed? What a brief memory Ramesses has. If not for me, he would be dead, with Egypt's mighty divisions in ruins. He is less honorable than Muwatallis. Even he would not go so far as this."

Sethi said nothing. She turned her back to him. Her gaze fell to the floor, and within its polished surface she imagined Sethi falling to Ramesses's blade, Sethi's eternal life obliterated because of her. A tear slipped free. Furious, she brushed it away. She drew a shuddering breath. "So long as you live, there exists hope for us, however small. But after this, I will not even be able to see you in my dreams."

His fingertips touched her arm. "You must accept it," he said, low. "We are finished. I go to my death willing. To have loved you, and know you love me in return is enough. I am complete."

She brushed another tear away. He tugged, beseeching. She relented, and turned.

He caught her chin. "Look at me."

She lifted her eyes to his and read in them the depth of his love, of his sacrifice. They could not let it end this way. Her heart clenched. Ramesses could not be the first man to have her. "Do not leave me like this," she whispered. "Please."

He gazed at her, his longing for her plain. He cupped her face. "I will die this day. The act you speak of is a bond, sealed with love. Your innocence protects you from a worse torment, the knowledge of love given, then taken away far too soon. To leave you yearning for one who is gone is a cruel legacy."

Her gaze moved to the discarded papyrus, lying beside a fresh arrangement of white roses. She looked back at him, suspicious. "In Tarhuntassa, white roses represent death."

His gaze remained on her, steady. "They do here, too. I had them put out this morning."

The last of her barriers crumbled. He had known all along what his fate would be, had willingly sacrificed everything for her. She pulled free of him, and touched a rose petal, catching its enticing scent, still warm from the sun. She envied its obliviousness of their unhappiness. Returning to him, she tried again. "I would rather yearn for you than never—"

"I beg you," he interrupted, his chest rising and falling, agitated. "Do not ask me again."

Silenced, she thought of his eternal heart, locked within its cage, existing outside the mortal realm, waiting to be extinguished on his death. She closed her eyes, willing him to understand. "Claim me," she whispered, "and your every movement, every breath, every word will be written upon my heart, for eternity. You will be immortal yet."

He groaned, agonized. She could feel the heat of him. Though she longed to touch him, she held herself still, waiting.

For a time, there was only the ragged sound of his breathing as he fought to reconcile himself to her request. He quieted. Outside: The mundane sound of a servant sweeping the courtyard. In the distance, chatter. Someone laughed.

He moved behind her, his speed startling her. He took hold of her waist, his other hand sliding up her spine to her neck, gathering her hair in his fist, baring her neck to him. For several agonizing heartbeats, nothing happened. She shivered with anticipation, a prisoner to his will. He had never treated her this way before.

His grip around her waist tightened, possessive. "Though I die today," he murmured against her ear, "I will never leave you."

Time stopped. She memorized everything. His strong hands, roughened by war, gripping her; the coolness of the room; the heat of his body behind hers; the earthy scent of him, almond oil, myrrh, cinnamon. Soon her memories would be all she would have left. She pulled each fragment to her, cherishing them, sealing them deep within her heart.

His lips brushed the back of her neck, light as a butterfly's touch. She shivered. Delicious sensations rolled through her as he moved toward her ear. He caught her lobe between his teeth, holding her captive while his tongue traced its outline, slow. She moaned, willing him to continue. He did.

She pulled free and pressed herself against him. His arms came around her, his strength surrounding her, sheltering her. She clung to him as his fingers curved around her skull, drawing her to him. He hesitated, his lips almost touching hers. She held her breath, her heart thundering, threatening to burst. Please. Don't stop.

His mouth descended onto hers, possessive. Held fast against him, she succumbed, answering him, ascending to heights she had never known possible. He stopped, holding her face in his hands, his breathing uneven. His eyes caught hers, the question clear. Her body cried out for him. She glanced at the door, then back at him, urgent.

He kissed her, tender, letting her feel the depth of his love, his sacrifice, his willingness to do it all again. Her knees weakened. He caught her. Cradling her against him, he strode across the blistering white heat of the pillared courtyard, through the shade of the jasmine-scented pleasure garden, past the lotus pools into the inner courtyard. He didn't look at her, he just walked on, carrying her, determined, protective. She watched him, savoring his firm grip on her, sensing somehow, impossibly, she had always been his.

He pushed the door of his apartment open. His bed lay bathed in light. Istara shivered, pleased. She would see him. All of him. He knelt and lowered her onto the bed's soft linen cover, his eyes moving over her. Worshiping her. Memorizing her. His fingers traced the outline of her lips. She closed her eyes. His lips touched hers, confessing his love for her, claiming her as his own, forever.

She reached out, drawing him to her. He pulled off his belt and moved over her, still clothed in his kilt, the bed's wooden frame creaking as it took his weight. He kissed her eyelids, the base of her ears, her throat. She clung to him, savoring the warmth of him, the solidness of his body over hers, watching the beat of his pulse, steady and strong. Imagined it silenced.

"I understand now," she whispered, "why you didn't want me to have this."

"Would you have me cease?" he murmured as he kissed her eyes, catching her tears as they escaped.

He waited, patient, gazing at her, stroking her face, his tenderness undoing her. She sobbed, fresh tears spilling onto the pristine linens.

"No," she breathed, her heart aching. "Please. Make me yours."

✳ ✳ ✳

Horus didn't have to search long to find his consort. He found her, where she always was, leaning over the vision pool. She glanced back at him, her eyes bright with unshed tears. He hastened to her, his gaze drawn to the clear, bright surface.

Below, the sun-drenched gardens of a sumptuous villa, filled with color and verdant with life, filled the scene. Beside a shallow pool, dotted with blue lotuses, a group of servants huddled together, fearful, whispering. Several of them looked, furtive, at a closed door.

Horus waited, wondering what had upset Baalat, who grieved, quiet, against his chest. He held her, kissing her brow, whispering words of reassurance. Shadows moved, following the sun as it transited the sky. Still, he waited. Then, over the soft susurration of the palms rustling in the breeze, he heard something. Muted cries, neither the sound of ecstasy nor grief, but the two mingled as one. The sound of two hearts breaking.

Baalat leaned closer. The view slid through the roof of one of the buildings. She wept, silent, as she watched Sethi make love to Istara, cradling her against him, his face wet with tears.

Horus delved and read Sethi's mind. He looked at Baalat, her eyes still fixed on the pair. "Ramesses is going to kill Sethi. Today."

She choked, nodding, and backed away, unable to watch any longer. Without her there, the view began to fade. He watched the condemned pair, mourning even as they coupled, knowing the full extent of their love, and suffering for it. The pool silvered, and they vanished.

He turned away. With Sethi gone, Istara would not live much longer, and when Istara died—he swallowed. No, it was too soon. He looked back at the silent vision pool, his heart clenching, coming to terms with what he must do, what he must sacrifice to keep Baalat alive.

He strode from the hall, and crossed the vastness of the immortal realm, to the emptiness of its furthest reaches. At the edge of the realm, he looked down, into an endless, shifting abyss. Into eternity. He gritted his teeth, how had it come to this? He turned and counted a hundred paces back from the edge. He hesitated. Was that fear he felt? He crushed the unfamiliar feeling. There was no time to waste. He had to protect Baalat.

He lunged forward, bursting into a run, his feet pounding across the smooth surface. He reached the edge and threw himself over it, still running, crying out Baalat's name, soaring into infinity. He looked back at the immortal realm, suspended within formless space. Baalat came to a staggering halt at its edge. Anguished, she fell to her knees, her gown billowing around her. She reached after him, screaming his name.

He closed his eyes and sped away, plunging through the fabric of space and time, tumbling past an infinite number of worlds, toward his final destination. From where, he knew, there could be no return.

FOUR

Istara's hand held in his, Sethi made his way through Waset's palace, leading her past subdued courtiers, servants, and guardsmen. The pharaoh must not have made any secret of his intention to execute Egypt's commander. Guards raised their fists to their chests as Sethi passed, bowing their heads, stricken, murmuring his name. Alongside him, Istara proceeded, pale, silent, and withdrawn, a lamb for the slaughter.

He left the shadows of the colonnade and entered the courtyard outside the pharaoh's training ground, the heat hitting him like the blast of a bread oven. Guardsmen snapped to attention, tilting their spears toward him—an honor reserved for the pharaoh—their fists pressed tight against their chests. Several blinked hard, their eyes glittering in the brilliant light.

Tightening his grip on Istara's hand, Sethi crossed the blazing courtyard into the coolness of the training ground's shadowed vestibule. He nodded at the nearest guards to close the doors. They hesitated, unwilling to be the ones to seal the Commander of Egypt's fate. The captain of the guard came forward. He bowed low.

"My lord," he said, his words taut with grief. "All of Egypt mourns this day. May the gods protect you on your journey."

"Close the doors," Sethi said, quiet, looking over his stricken men, his heart clenching, "as Pharaoh has commanded."

He waited as the captain and his guards heaved on the enormous doors, struggling to dislodge them, their sandals sliding on the stone flags. More guards joined them, their muscles straining, until first one door, then the other shifted, closing with an ominous, low boom. Without, a wooden beam slid into place, sealing them inside. Silence descended.

Sethi turned. In the blistering white heat of the training ground, Ramesses waited, alone, a *khopesh* in each hand, his muscled body gleaming with oil. On his right forearm, he wore a narrow wooden armguard, protecting his arm from elbow to fingertips, another lay on the glittering sand, waiting for Sethi.

Moving to the vestibule's deepest shadows, Sethi pulled Istara into his arms and kissed her for the last time, brief, tender. He drew away, his eyes moving over her, drinking his fill of her. "Do not weep until I have gone," he said, ragged, "I would not see you grieving while I still live."

Her eyes glistening, she clung to him as he stepped back, her fingers slipping through his. She said his name, her voice cracking as he let her go, a plea.

His heart tight, he backed away and walked out into the drenching light. He stopped before Ramesses and dropped to his knee. A *khopesh* landed on the ground beside him, sending up a spray of sand.

"Commander Sethi," Ramesses said, cold, "are you prepared to go to the gods?"

Sethi met the pharaoh's gaze, calm. "I am."

Ramesses narrowed his eyes, dissatisfied. Under his hostile glare, Sethi picked up the armguard and fastened its leather straps onto his left arm. Pulling the *khopesh* to him, he rose and retreated several steps. He brought his sword up into the opening stance and waited.

"Despite the evidence damning you," Ramesses said, taut, "I must demand your answer. Have you known my future queen?"

"I have," Sethi answered, looking at Istara, watching them, stricken.

"And for how long have you been taking what is mine?" Ramesses asked, low, dangerous.

"This afternoon was the first and only time," Sethi replied, his eyes still on Istara.

"So you took her to spite my judgment," Ramesses breathed, his face darkening. "You truly are a whore's son."

Bristling at the slur against his mother, Sethi pushed into Ramesses's space, forcing him to take a step back. "By Osiris's blood," he said, "you go too far. I could not even contemplate such a foul thing, to use Istara in such a way. Despite your wealth and power, even you, a god, cannot overcome the bond between a man and a woman. If I had to do it all again, knowing how it will end, I would. I am honored to die for her. She is worth this and more. Much more."

"Fine words," Ramesses spat after a brief, stunned silence, "but two facts remain: you have broken my trust, and taken what belongs to me. I will not be merciful."

"I welcome your blade," Sethi said, dark, as he lifted his sword. "The more I suffer, the better."

Ramesses swung his *khopesh* toward the vestibule, where Istara stood, pale and trembling. "You wish to suffer?" he scoffed, incensed. "So be it. I will send you to the gods to face an eternity tormented by your noble thoughts of love, while *my* wife and *my* queen sleeps in my bed and forgets about you, you pretentious piece of gutter trash." His expression twisted by vengeance, he lunged at Sethi, swinging his *khopesh* high. The blade hissed down, hard, fast.

Spinning his own blade around, Sethi caught Ramesses's *khopesh* against the inner curve of his own before it met with his shoulder. Straining against Ramesses's strength, he felt his own blade biting into his skin, opening his flesh. He pushed it away with a grunt, staggering, his sword held up before him, ready. He glanced at his shoulder. The blade had gone deep. He ignored the pain. "Far better for you to do what you will to me now," he returned, harsh, "I already gave up my soul to Horus to save Istara. Once I fall, there is nothing more for me. I will be annihilated. These last breaths are all I have."

Ramesses glared at him, incredulous, incandescent. "You blaspheming, lying son of a back-alley whore, you dare speak of such things?" He raised his sword once more, bearing down on him, "All know none may return from the realm of the gods. You have convinced her of these lies to make her heart your own, may Ammit devour you!"

He fell upon Sethi, delivering a relentless onslaught of strikes and slashes. Sethi parried, his blade connecting with Ramesses's flesh more than once; the pharaoh's blood splattering over him, hot, angry. Ramesses threw his shoulder back, as though to make a sweeping strike, leaving his chest exposed, inviting Sethi's attack. Sethi slashed, his blade biting into nothing more than air as Ramesses slipped to the side and completed the feint. Caught off balance, Sethi stumbled. Ramesses's blade slammed down, carving deep into his leg, opening Sethi's thigh from his groin to his knee.

Grunting hard, Sethi staggered, suppressing his pain. Retreating a step, Ramesses lowered his *khopesh*, waiting, his eyes glittering. Sethi cut a look at his thigh. The slash was deep, and bleeding hard. Lifting his eyes back to Ramesses's, he raised his sword in readiness for the next attack. Ramesses rushed at him, pushing him back across the grounds, ignoring opportunities to deliver fatal strikes, choosing instead to cut Sethi where he would experience the greatest agony.

Two more rapid circuits passed under Sethi's feet, the white sand turning red in his wake. Caught in the glare of Re-Atum's barque, Sethi's instincts told him he had fallen to another feint. Ramesses's blade sliced deep into his bicep, biting into bone. Sethi stared at the sword's blade buried in his arm, feeling nothing. Calm descended. From outside himself he watched Ramesses struggle to dislodge the *khopesh*. The pharaoh heaved at the hilt with both hands, once, twice, three times. It yanked free. Pain exploded, exquisite, blinding.

Sethi's vision sparkled brilliant white, then dulled to dark shadows. Reeling backward, he slammed into one of the vestibule's pillars.

Lowering his bloodied *khopesh*, Ramesses followed him, panting. "It is over," he said, his blood-spattered chest rising and falling with exertion. "Give up your weapon. I will leave you my dagger. If you have not already succumbed to your injuries by the time Re-Atum's barque descends, you may use it to end your life."

Staggering to find his feet, Sethi leaned against the pillar, drowning in pain. Turning to the shadowed entrance, he searched for Istara. She stepped out onto the blood-soaked sand, her eyes found his, then fell to his injuries. Lifting her hand to him, she took several tentative steps across the grounds. He shook his head, once. She halted, her hand lowering to her side, her anguish palpable.

His throat burning, he spat, tasting the metallic scent of his blood. He pushed away from the pillar, hearing himself speak as though from a distance. "No," he rasped, "I die as the Commander of Egypt's Army, defending to my last breath. You will grant me my death, after all I have done for you, and for Egypt."

"I will not," Ramesses retorted, merciless. "You will die from your injuries or by your own hand. I refuse to grant you a quick and honorable death. It is my wish that you suffer in torment until your last breath." His blade swept up, then down, aiming for Sethi's sword arm.

Sethi lunged sideways, his guarded arm hanging torn and useless, and brought up his sword, catching Ramesses's curved blade in his own. Leaning all his weight against it, grunting with the strain, he pressed Ramesses's blade down, forcing the pharaoh's arm to twist backward, holding him immobile. Ramesses screamed, furious, and slammed his guard against Sethi's jaw. Pain exploded. He recoiled, stumbling sideways, and spat out a molar.

Ramesses followed him, relentless. Struggling to find his feet, Sethi saw the guard coming down once more. Its edge slammed deep into his torn arm. Ramesses grinned, savage as he ground it against the exposed cavity of Sethi's bone. Bellowing, Sethi broke free and staggered away, demented with pain, his sword flailing in front of him, useless.

Lifting his *khopesh* with both hands, Ramesses smashed the flat of his blade against Sethi's. Both blades shattered. Tossing aside his broken sword, Ramesses pulled his dagger free and threw it onto the ground. A spray of bloody sand splattered against Sethi's shins.

"You will not be interred," Ramesses spat as he stalked before him, "your name will be stricken from the records, your villas destroyed, and your servants and horses sent to Nubia's mines for the rest of their days. Your body will be thrown into the desert to be torn apart by hyenas. You never existed. You are no one. By my command, your name will never be uttered again."

Sethi dropped to his knee, fighting to overcome the jagged waves of pain tearing his body apart. Blinking the sweat and blood from his eyes, he found Istara, her chest heaving, despair stalking her. Spitting the blood from his mouth, he summoned the last of his strength and pulled himself to his feet one final time.

"Istara," he cried, his voice bloody, defiant, "I regret nothing."

Ramesses roared, furious. His armguard swung high. It hurtled down; violent, deadly. Sethi held Istara's eyes. The blow came, sending stars exploding across his skull. He slammed onto the wet sand. Darkness. Silence.

✳ ✳ ✳

Ramesses stared at Sethi's ruined body, sprawled sideways, his blood leaching into the sand. He drew a shaking breath, seeking to calm himself before facing Istara. He could hear her running, closing the distance between them, her breathing ragged in the stillness of the hot air. Pulling apart the guard's ties, he shook off the bloodied thing and tossed it aside. He swiveled and caught her. She struggled, frantic, trying to escape. He shook her, hard.

"Sethi lied to you. It is impossible to sacrifice one's eternal life for another to live. He lied to you, so he could bed you."

She stilled. Her eyes, filled with hate, met his. "You may be the Pharaoh of Egypt, used to having what you want," she spat, "but you shall never have me. I will never be your queen."

She jabbed her fingers, hard, into a deep gash in his arm. An explosion of jagged pain shot through him, hot and sharp. He recoiled, grunting. Slipping free, she fell to her knees beside Sethi, and pressed the dagger against her breast, gasping as its tip bit into her flesh.

Ramesses scrambled after her, reaching for the dagger. She pushed on it, stifling a cry of pain as it eased in. A bright red patch of blood blossomed out, spreading across her breast.

"I beg you, cease!" he erupted, panicking.

Cradling the dagger's hilt in her hands, she regarded Sethi's butchered body in silence. A solitary tear slipped down her face. "I will be a token in a game no more," she whispered. "It is enough. I die here today, beside the one I love. Baalat, forgive me. Horus, I beg you, forgive me."

She pushed against the hilt, shuddering as the blade entered her breast, driving toward her heart.

Falling onto her with a cry, Ramesses grabbed her hands. Grunting, fighting her resistance, he freed the blade. Blood gushed out. Frantic, he sawed a strip of linen from his kilt and pressed the wadded material against her breast. Oblivious to him, her eyes remained on Sethi.

"I command you to live!" he shouted, unthinking, desperate. She did not respond. He placed her hand over the compress and bolted across the blood-soaked grounds, fearful. The blade had gone deep. She might not live, even with a surgeon's attention. He entered the vestibule, grateful for having had the foresight to have his surgeon wait outside. As he reached the door, an explosion of brilliant white light surged past him in complete silence, engulfing him, blinding him.

He stumbled, surrounded by a dense cocoon of blinding white. Shielding his eyes, he called out to Istara, his voice deadened by the thick atmosphere. Dread crept up his spine. He could not see past his outstretched hand. By increments, the glare subsided, from burning white, to a bright glow, to faint shadows, to the vague outline of forms and shapes. Squinting, his eyes watering, he made out the contour of Sethi's body. Stumbling, he pushed his way back through the shifting, viscous light, cursing with frustration. Nothing felt real; even the ground felt unnatural.

He stopped beside Sethi. His chest taut, he turned full circle, his eyes narrowed, searching. He called out Istara's name, once, twice, three times. Nothing. Fear crept up his spine. Footsteps approached. He spun around, defensive.

A beautiful, powerfully built man, wearing an elegant kilt, stepped in front of him, his bearing regal. Across his chest, strange, golden tattoos shifted and rotated. From behind the man, Istara appeared.

"No," Ramesses breathed, stunned, staring at Istara. Through the rent of her bloody gown, her breast lay whole again. "It cannot be. This is not real. I am dreaming, or dead."

"You are not dead, nor are you dreaming," the man said, his voice edged with disdain. "At great cost to myself, I have come to undo the damage you have wrought before it is too late." He knelt beside Sethi and touched his brow. "He still lives, though not for long." He looked up at Istara. "Know this, daughter of Kadesh, what I am about to do is not for you, or for him, it is for my consort."

Ramesses stared at the man, his strange words washing over him, what did he mean 'his consort'? He scrutinized the man, who wore thick golden armbands, reeking of age and more finely wrought than anything Ramesses possessed. Of course. He almost laughed at the audacity of his commander. Though Sethi thought he had kept it a secret, Ramesses knew he nurtured a quiet obsession for the arcane—Paser's spies had informed him of Sethi's continual search for ancient knowledge and reclusive sorcerers—seeking what should be long forgotten. Ramesses scoffed. So his commander had prepared, had sent for a sorcerer to aid him, who clearly had not wanted to do so. A quiver of admiration shot through Ramesses, Sethi had always been a dark one, but to try to escape death? Ramesses hadn't expected that.

"Whoever you are," Ramesses said, shoving his way between the man and Sethi, "I grant you, your sorcery is powerful," he glanced at Istara, "and you will be greatly rewarded for saving Princess Istara, but you will go no further. I forbid you to interfere with the justice of Pharaoh, a god."

The man glared at him. The air around him shimmered. He changed shape, his form sliding, seamless, into that of a man with a falcon head, wearing the double *sekhemti* crown of Upper and Lower Egypt. Ramesses staggered, astonished, fear pounding into him. He sank to his knees, breathless, his mind skidding around the edges of the creature kneeling before Sethi, unwilling to accept what his eyes were seeing. Horus, the god he had worshiped his entire life, was *real*, he lived and breathed—

His thoughts juddered to a halt. Why would Horus aid Sethi? Fearful, his gaze moved to the butchered body of his commander. What had he done?

Horus shifted, becoming a man once more. "It is not I who has interfered," he said, "but you, Ramesses, Pharaoh of Egypt. Enough. Even here, in this temporary space between realms, we are running out of time. He breathes his last."

Moving Sethi onto his back, Horus placed one hand against Sethi's chest, the other on his brow. He closed his eyes. Ramesses watched, his heart tight, as tendrils of light gathered in Horus's torso, spiraling together, growing, coalescing, pulsing, building into a shining, living thing. Horus lowered his head, shuddering as the light surged down his powerful arms to his fingertips. Threads of light wove outward, wrapping around Sethi, covering him in layers of golden, shimmering light, concealing him within a glowing cocoon. Breaking the connection with a groan, Horus fell back on his haunches. Only a single tendril of light remained within him. Lost, it searched the darkness for its brothers.

He rose and inspected Sethi, wrapped in his light, waiting while it saturated Sethi's broken body. Ramesses remained on his knees, his heart pounding, willing Horus to speak to him, to acknowledge him as his servant, the Pharaoh of Egypt. But Horus ignored him, he walked past him, toward the dense wall of white light encircling them. He stopped, abrupt, and tilted his head, listening, turning in a slow circle, his eyes raking the hidden sky, searching. With a startled cry, he ran and leaped into the air, transforming into an enormous falcon, his wings pounding, the sweep of them deafening as he tore away, surging up to the invisible heights. Another brilliant explosion of white light eclipsed the space. Ramesses tumbled to the ground, blinded once more.

The white light diminished, and by degrees, the natural light of day returned. Rising to his feet, Ramesses staggered, struggling to gain his bearings, to align his mind back to the dull, flawed ordinariness of the palace. Istara knelt beside Sethi, running her hands over his clean, uncut flesh, weeping, overcome, oblivious of Sethi's blood—his old blood—seeping into her gown.

Sethi stirred and sat up, slow, disbelieving. He looked down at his body, stunned, marveling at himself, whole again. Istara cried out, taking his head in her hands, sobbing, telling him of Horus, using his light to heal him, to return him to life, just as his consort Baalat had done for her. With a cry, Sethi took her in his arms, holding her tight against him, possessive. Over her shoulder, he met Ramesses's eyes, fierce, triumphant: no longer just a man, but something more, a man with the light of a god in him. Untouchable.

Ramesses backed away, horrified by Istara's words. He fled to the doors, stumbling over the broken pieces of the *khopeshes*, Horus's words replaying in his mind: *I do this for my consort.* Hathor. Istara called her Baalat—the goddess from whom he had stolen the gold all those years ago in Kadesh.

He pounded against the door, desperate to leave, to put space between himself and the two kneeling the bloody sand, bathed in the approving light of Re-Atum; their connection to the gods more real than his own.

His flesh crawling, humiliation ground into him, threatening to crush him. Compared to them, he was nothing, just a man with a golden crown, born of no one; his tenuous right to the throne gained by his grandfather, a commander in Horemheb's army, fulfilled through a quirk of timing and circumstance. Ramesses had bolstered his own nebulous claim to the throne through his marriage to Nefertari, shamelessly usurping her royal blood as his own.

The bar against the door scraped free, followed by the muted grunts of his guards as they pushed their weight against the heavy doors. By increments, the doors loosened and crept open.

Ramesses looked back at Sethi, still cradling Istara against him, kissing her tears away. Had his commander spoken true? Had he found a way to give up his eternal life to save a woman he believed would soon belong to another? Shame cascaded through him. He would never have done the same.

The doors swung open and thudded against the walls. Light from the outer courtyard flooded into the vestibule. His guards knelt before him, silent, subdued, their eyes darting to the bloodied training ground, several wiped away tears, not troubling to hide them. Realization, burning hot, seared through Ramesses. Egypt's commander was more loved than its pharaoh. He felt the silent condemnation of his subjects, crowding around him, closing in on him, suffocating him.

He stumbled into the outer courtyard, Horus's brutal rejection tearing the blinders away, exposing Ramesses for what he was: a vain, arrogant, selfish, grasping man, using his power as a weapon against his own people, a tyrant. In his arrogance, he had turned both his vizier and Ahmen—his oldest and only friend—against him. He was alone.

At the opposite side of the courtyard, Nefertari, flanked by two guards, entered, stripped of her crown. Barefoot, her head bowed, she made her way to the palace gate—reduced to nothing more than skin and bones, a shadow of her former self, a simple gown hanging loose on her frame. She lifted her head. Her eyes, large in her gaunt face, met his, her love for him plain despite all he had done to her.

He staggered to his knees as the truth slashed into him, brutal, glaring. *He* had done this to her, his choices, his actions. He had made her what she became, and then he had punished her for it. He clenched his fists. No more.

She slowed, coming to a stop, a flicker of hope glimmering in her eyes, faint, uncertain. He held her gaze, thinking of the thousands of wrongs he had committed against her, at times inflicted upon her for nothing more than his amusement. Shame enveloped him. Nefertari. His first queen, the mother of Egypt's heir; her only crime her love for him. Paser was right. She was sacred, and Ramesses had treated her as though she was nothing—disposable—his power blinding him until her life became meaningless, worth nothing more to him than his scorn. What would have happened to him, and to Egypt if he had replaced her with Istara? He stilled, the thought chilling him despite the stifling heat. Another thought struck him, sending a tendril of hope shooting through him: Horus had let him live. Ramesses had been granted a second chance; one he would not waste.

Silence saturated the courtyard. No one moved. Heat poured down on him, baking hot, a furnace. He lifted his hand to her— bloody from his crime committed against the gods—and called her name, his voice ragged. She stepped forward, hesitant, fearful. He called to her again, a plea, tears cutting into his eyes, blurring as she moved toward him, her fingers catching at her skirts, lifting them up as her steps quickened, her breathing jagged and desperate in the heavy air. She sank to her knees before him. Her lips trembled, his name slipped from them, filled with longing; an oasis to the desert of his soul.

"Never again will you suffer because of me," he said, his chest aching, dragging her to him, the faintness of her existence against his blood-splattered chest breaking him in two. She shuddered in his arms, clinging to him, sobbing, quaking, weak, whispering her regrets, her sorrow for all she had done. He tightened his hold on her and looked up into the sky toward the blinding disk of Re-Atum's barque, thinking of Horus, somewhere out there, flying free, once more in their world, watching over them, just as he had done in the days of gods and men. He shivered, despite the heat. With the return of the gods, the world would change; his power would change.

He collected Nefertari into his arms and strode away, carrying her, as fragile as a wounded songbird, back to the royal apartments. As he left the courtyard, the astonished cries of his men burst forth, exultant, shouting Sethi's name, hailing Egypt's commander, their sandaled feet pounding against the flagged stones, a roar of joy rising up, spreading through the palace, a thundering.

Tightening his hold on Nefertari, Ramesses pressed on, and did not look back.

Horus heard her falling. With the last of his diminishing immortal power, he surged across the blinding blue skies toward the sound of her beating heart. An explosion of white light, brighter than the sun, pierced the sky's arc. It plunged from the heavens, a star, trailing the pure white light of the immortal realm. It slammed against the top of a dusty cliff in total silence, its brightness eclipsing the sun. The light melted away, revealing Baalat, lying on her side, silent and still, her gown fluttering in the wind.

He plummeted to her, transforming into his true form, hitting the ground running. The last of his immortal light trickled away, absorbed by the crushing pressures of the mortal realm. He staggered, shrieking with agony as he endured his final transformation into a mortal man.

It ended, after what felt an eternity. Panting, he stumbled over to Baalat and carried her out of the blistering sun into the meager shade of a stunted tree. Pillowing her head on his lap, he stroked her hair, waiting. Night fell. Stars blossomed one by one in the sky's canopy. Still, he waited.

Her eyes opened. She sat up and looked around, disoriented. She saw him, Horus, but not Horus. She touched his face, just as she had done hundreds of thousands of years before, when they had lived and loved in the world of gods and men. He caught her hand in his and pulled her against him, overwhelmed. Being mortal was remarkable, intense, terrifying.

"You followed me," he said, his heart tight.

"Yes," she whispered. "Always."

He made love to her, bathed in the light of the moon. Then, it came, abrupt, harsh, merciless. He held her as she endured her transformation, her perfect body shuddering as it succumbed to the pressures of the mortal realm, turning her into a flawed, fragile being. She rose, seeing the world anew.

"There is so much. Of everything," she breathed, rapt, her expressions shifting and changing, betraying the emotions cascading through her. "It is almost too much to bear, to feel so many different things all at once."

He caught the glimmer of the sun cresting the horizon and nodded at the sky. "Look what we have been missing."

They walked to the cliff's edge, reverent. She gazed, breathless, at the magnificent vista, awakening in the clean light of a newborn day. A vast river cut its way through an endless golden desert; its lush, green banks dotted with irrigated fields, low-roofed towns, white palaces, golden obelisks and airy temples.

She pointed, delighted, at a flotilla of skiffs racing along the river's waters, the sunlight playing across her diminished, yet still beautiful features. Catching a tendril of her hair drifting in the breeze, Horus reveled in the feel of its silken texture between his fingers, thrilled anew by the wonder of being alive.

Her fingertips touched his. "What shall we do now?"

He pressed his lips against her brow, savoring the feel of her skin, warmed by the sun. All around him, possibilities unfolded, endless, a thousand paths waiting to be explored, reminding him of the tattoos that had once rotated and shifted on his chest, never the same pattern twice.

"Nothing." He smiled, relishing the sudden uncertainty of his existence. "Everything."

❋   ❋   ❋

Confined within his apartment in the royal palace of Tarhuntassa, Urhi-Teshub stood by a burning brazier and stared at the pharaoh's unopened message in his hand. He pressed down on the seal. It split in half. The pieces fell away and shattered against the stone floor. He pulled the papyrus open and read its contents, the words brief, final: *Prince of Hatti, find another queen.*

Urhi-Teshub held the papyrus over the brazier. He let go. The words of Ramesses II, Pharaoh of Egypt fluttered down into the flames and ignited, burning bright for the merest heartbeat before crumbling into ash. Urhi-Teshub stared at the ashes, numb. He had committed treason to save Istara, would have gone to the gods if not for the intervention of his uncle, Hattusilis, the usurper.

His confinement had been bearable knowing Istara would be returned to him, but now, despite all he had done to keep her safe—

Enraged, he strode to the door and pounded against it, desperate to ride out, to find her and bring her home, where she belonged. Ramesses would not keep her. She was his, bound to him before the gods. He pounded harder, punching the door, venting his rage, bloodying his knuckles. He would burn Ramesses's cities, tear his vassal's kingdoms apart—

Urhi-Teshub lifted his head, quieting, sensing an opportunity presenting itself. He let it coalesce, waiting as it took shape. He smiled, cold. At last, a way out of his long imprisonment.

He called to the guards, demanding an audience with his uncle. He waited, his hands, warm and sticky with blood, resting on the hilts of his daggers. He would succeed. Whatever the cost, however long it would take. First, his freedom, then, his throne, and then— his queen.

Istara.

THE CALL OF ETERNITY

BOOK II

The Immortal Realm

Teshub, the once-powerful and mighty storm god, woke to the sensation of flames burning across his arms. He cracked an eye open. Symbols, glowing red-orange, crackled to life along the backs of his forearms. Rubbing his eyes, he sat up wondering how long he had slept this time. The last time he woke, Horus had said more than one hundred thousand years had passed in the mortal realm, though, he had added with a wry smile, Teshub had missed nothing. Teshub pushed his long dark hair, tousled from sleep, back from his eyes, hoping this time he had slept even longer; it was a good way to pass the meaningless, useless, endless time.

The symbols brightened, glowing, demanding his attention. He lifted an eyebrow, savoring the long-forgotten sensation of cold fire spreading along his arms. It had been an eon since he had followed the actions of mortals on his flesh, when he last lived in their realm, a god. But those days, once filled with opulence and glory, had come to their brutal end when the savage wars of gods and men reached its fatal impasse. Thoth, infinitely wise and rational—standing in the place of the Creator God who had abandoned his creations once the first blood had been shed—had called for their evacuation, sealing them into the immortal realm, the new home of the gods, sentencing them to an eternity of silence.

And yet, after an epoch of dormancy, the fiery symbols which had once ignited and extinguished endlessly on Teshub's arms, flamed again. Strange. He leaned forward, intrigued, tingling with anticipation.

A long time passed before he sat back, troubled. A man—a prince—had sacrificed twelve bulls to Teshub, begging him to spare the life of the woman he loved, a woman he had almost killed with his own hands. She lived, but the prince had then lost her to another, a pharaoh. The prince wanted her back, but first, as dozens of bulls fell to his blade, he pled for success in his campaigns against the pharaoh's vassals so he might win back his right to the throne. Then, with the armies of the empire behind him, he would bring war to the very gates of Egypt until the woman bound to him in blood was returned.

The flames subsided, though the glow remained; the connection between Teshub and the prince remaining, tenuous. Teshub got up and moved across his sumptuous apartments, undisturbed for millennia, wondering if Baalat still used her vision pool. After enduring the crushing weight of the endless epochs of wasted time, an upwelling of purpose ignited in him, raw, visceral. Hope bloomed in his chest—to be useful again, to have a reason to exist. He hurried through his rooms, eager. As he reached the outer vestibule, a gilt card lying on the threshold of his apartment lit up, glowing pure white. Curious, he bent and collected it, recognizing the elegant handwriting of Baalat.

Turning the card over, he read her words. He blinked, and read them again. No. It couldn't be. Waving his hand over the panel bearing his sigil, the door to his residence slid open. He left, striding through the realm toward the apartment of Baalat and Horus.

Preoccupied with Baalat's disturbing message, he was halfway to his destination before he realized the vast realm's wide avenues lay quiet, shrouded in silence. None processed. Doors stood sealed, the sigil of the ones within hovering without, glowing white. Teshub walked on, alone, trepidation bearing down on him. A tremor, deep within the foundation of the realm vibrated against his feet, faint. Slowing his steps, he halted, waiting, his skin prickling. There. Another tremor, so faint it almost felt like he might be imagining it.

He quickened his pace, uneasy, disturbed by the realm's ominous silence. Within the courtyard of their home, the entrance to Baalat and Horus's apartment stood open. He entered, calling their names, hoping Baalat's message had been an elaborate diversion, nothing more. On the table, a glass of wine, half-finished. In the bedroom, an unmade bed, its silken covers trailing onto the floor, a cushion halfway between the door and the bed. On the room's ceiling, the fractals of which Horus had been so proud were gone, vanished as though they had never existed. Teshub turned, searching for something, anything, to help him understand why two of the highest gods among the pantheon would throw away their immortality for two mere mortals. He looked down at the card again, turning it over, hoping to find more, but there was nothing, only her brief words. They were gone. One day they would die so two mortals could live. It made no sense.

The symbols on his arms lit up again. Another tremor shot through the realm's foundation. The floor trembled. The wine in the glass shivered. Golden symbols flared to life on his arms, so bright the walls reflected its light. He staggered, staring at the arcane lettering as it coalesced, its movements stately, regal, inexorable, the symbols older than time itself. After an eon, the Creator God— the father of his existence—had broken his punishing silence. The symbols solidified; the glare faded. Teshub read the message, burned, indelible on his arm. He sank down onto the bed, stunned, and read it again.

You are next.

ACKNOWLEDGMENTS

My most heartfelt thanks go to Kath Stansfield whose editorial reviews, emails, support, and little kindnesses over the past year helped to bring this book to its fulfilment. When I stopped believing in myself, she told me not to give up, sending encouragement and giving me the courage to push this story to publication. To have such incredible support from an author I admire so deeply has been a wonderful, precious gift. My gratitude is enormous.

To my husband, Anders, who has been terribly, awfully, heinously neglected as I agonized over every. single. word. Who bought me more screens, (at three now), and keyboards when the letters wore away, and then a laptop so I could keep writing while in the hospital. Who fed the cats and watered the garden, who spent evenings letting me work out complexities of the plot while he listened, saying nothing, drinking his wine, waiting, patient, a knowing smile on his face.

To Chris O'Byrne, print designer and copy editor, who patiently worked through all the fine details of layout and grammar. There were a lot of emails. A lot. Sometimes at 4:00 a.m., which he answered right away. My hero.

To Debbie O'Byrne, graphic designer, for making the maps exactly like I imagined them to be and for creating a cover I will cherish for the rest of my life. I was lucky to meet you. One day, I hope we'll get to have a Starbucks together for real.

To Linda Pohl, thank you for your beta reads and feedback in 2014; your support and thoughtful ideas helped to make this story into what it finally became.

To my moral supporters, for cheering me on every step of the way: Lisa Buchanan, Antonia Bezinović, Cecilia Peltola, Alison Wright, and Ronny Morris. You didn't have to, but you did. It meant a lot. A whole lot.

To my wattpad readers who wrote to me to tell me how much they loved the book, who couldn't wait for updates, and even sacrificed sleep to read through the night. You sent the book to number one where it remained for four days straight. If I ever needed proof of concept, you granted me that. I love you guys.

And finally, to Marcelle, my best friend, who read the very first draft all the way back in 2006 and in 2013 said, "Just self-publish; it's going to be fine." And then she smiled, as though she knew a secret.

Over five years of academic research and several trips to Egypt were undertaken to write this book. In addition, trips to the various museums (The Louvre, Copenhagen's Glyptoteket, The British Museum, The Egyptian Museum, Cairo) that house the only statues of several of the Egyptian characters in this book were also visited—some of them many times. Last, but not least, with the help of an Egyptian archaeologist friend, I was able to gain an even deeper understanding of life in ancient Egypt by exploring long-lost ruins and temples forgotten by time.

Despite the wealth of historical records and evidence of ancient Egypt's phenomenal existence, there is, by stark contrast, almost nothing left of its greatest enemy, Hatti. Less than one hundred years after the events of this book, the Hittite civilization completely collapsed, leaving behind almost no trace of its existence; for a long time we only knew of Hatti through the records of Egypt. Since then, fragments have been found, though the physical evidence is still scant. Under the punishing weight of three millennia, its once great cities crumbled away, their foundations lost in the waving grasses clothing the northern mountains of Turkey.

The once formidable city of Kadesh is now nothing more than a hill in the middle of fields, situated roughly twelve miles southwest of present-day Homs, Syria. It has not failed to occur to me that this part of the world has suffered far too much violence and tragedy; the parallels between what happened at Kadesh and what is happening in our present world much too close for comfort.

To this day, archaeologists are still searching for the Hittite version of what happened at the Battle of Kadesh. Historians have suggested that if Egypt had been defeated at Kadesh, the world's history would have turned out substantially different. Egypt's supremacy would have ended prematurely, changing the balance of power in the remaining empires and affecting the rise of later ones, making it not unlikely the world we live in today could have turned out quite different to the one we know.

Until the Hittite record is found, we only have Ramesses II's version, which strains credulity—he claims the gods came down and fought alongside him as he faced the hordes of the Hittites alone, all his men having fled in terror. This story has been an attempt to retell the historic events of that time with life breathed back into the people who lived and loved in that opulent, glamorous, dangerous world.

Apart from the characters of Istara, Rhoha, Edarru and the immortal gods, the characters in this book are based on real historical figures, places, and events. Every effort has been made to follow the history of the 13th century BCE with the greatest possible integrity.

E A Carter

GLOSSARY

Distances

Long iter = 6.5 miles (10.5 km)
Short iter = 1.64 miles (2.65 km)
Half a short iter = 0.82 miles (1.3 km)

Hatti

Mesedi - Hittite King's personal bodyguard
Gal Gestin - 'Chief of the Wine Stewards', the highest position in the Hittite Court, second in power to the king
Under Realm - The place of the dead, where one's soul journeys through the seven gates of the realm, overcoming great hardship between each one, before reaching the Immortal Realm

Hittite Gods & Goddesses

Teshub - Hittite storm god, highest god in Hittite pantheon
Sharruma - Hittite god, son of Teshub and Arinna, god of the mountains
Ba'al - Amurrite god, son of El, god of fertility, storm, thunder, lightning, war, vanquisher of the god of death

Baalat - goddess of love, beauty and healing
Arinna - Hittite sun goddess, consort of Teshub

Egypt

arghul pipe - a double pipe, single reed woodwind instrument

barque - a boat, used to traverse the waters of the Nile, also represented as the boat carrying Re-Atum across the sky, as the sun

ka - the ancient Egyptian concept of one's vital spark, similar to the soul, which survived death

khopesh - a sickle-sword

Ma'at - the concept of truth, order, harmony, law, morality, and justice, upon which the ancient Egyptian society functioned

palanquin - a covered litter for one passenger, consisting of a large box carried on two horizontal poles by bearers

Under Realm - the place where Re-Atum's barque travels during the night

Regalia

Atef crown - white headdress decorated with ostrich feathers, also worn by Osiris

Khepresh (Blue) crown - a blue leather headdress with gold disks, worn during battle

Nemes headdress - a blue and gold striped head cloth

Sekhemti crown - a double crown, combining the white and red crowns of the kingdoms of Upper and Lower Egypt, also worn by Horus.

Uraeus - a representation of a sacred serpent and an emblem of supreme power

Egyptian Gods & Goddesses

Re-Atum - A primordial god, the creator, believed to be the sun itself
Re - the sun god, an aspect of Atum
Horus - god of the sky, war and hunting
Osiris - god of the afterlife, resurrection and regeneration
Ammit - a soul eater, who waits at the scales of justice to consume
     the hearts of the evil
Sekhmet - goddess of war and healing
Hathor - goddess of love, beauty, joy, and fertility
Isis - goddess of marriage and wisdom

Divisions of Egyptian Army

First Division of Amun - the pharaoh's division, led by Ramesses
Second Division of Pre - led by Sethi
Third Division of Seth
Fourth Division of Ptah
Fifth Division of Na'arn - comprised of soldiers from the vassal
     kingdoms of Amurru, led by Bentesina, High King of Amurru

Ancient Egyptian Calendar

The ancient Egyptian calendar is comprised of three seasons, plus a celebration week at the end of the year. They are: Akhet - Inundation of Nile (Aug 29-Dec 26), Peret - Planting (Dec 27-Apr 25), Shemu - Harvest (Apr 26- Aug 28) and the Celebration Week (Aug 24-Aug 28). There are four months in each season, each month lasting thirty days, divided into three ten-day weeks.

A Note on the Counting of King Years

Years were not counted the same in the Bronze Age as we count them today. During those days, years were counted separately within each empire and kingdom against the years of their king's reign.

King Muwatallis of Hatti was crowned in 1295 BCE, which means in the summer of 1274 BCE when the Battle of Kadesh occurred, the year in Hatti was Year 21 of his reign. In Egypt, Pharaoh Ramesses II was crowned in 1279 BCE. At the Battle of Kadesh, the year in Egypt was Year 5 of his reign.

According to modern chronology, the Battle of Kadesh took place on July 3, 1274 BCE.

ABOUT THE AUTHOR

E A Carter is a Swedish-British-Canadian. She's a drinker of tea, rescuer of cats, fighter of lupus, taker of photographs, and writer of books.

Her debut novel *The Lost Valor of Love* is the first book in the Transcendence series and is the Gold Winner of Adult Fiction in the 2019 Wishing Shelf Book Awards, and a finalist winner in the First Novel and Historical Fiction categories in the 2019 Indie Author Network's Book of the Year Awards.

The Call of Eternity is the second book in the Transcendence series and was shortlisted in the 2020 Page Turner Awards.

The Rise of the Goddess is the third book in the Transcendence series and was a finalist in the 2021 Page Turner Book Award.

The Lost Letters: The Dark World of Narcissistic Abuse was shortlisted in the 2021 Page Turner Book Award, won Highly Commended Non-Fiction Author and a PR campaign from Palamedes PR in London.

In 2021, *I, Cassandra* won Honorable Mention in the 9th Annual Writer's Digest Self-Published eBook Awards.

Find her @ authoreacarter.com